OUT OF SEASON

Tom Gilroy
Out of Season

Published by BooxAI
ISBN: 978-965-578-682-8

OUT OF SEASON

TOM GILROY

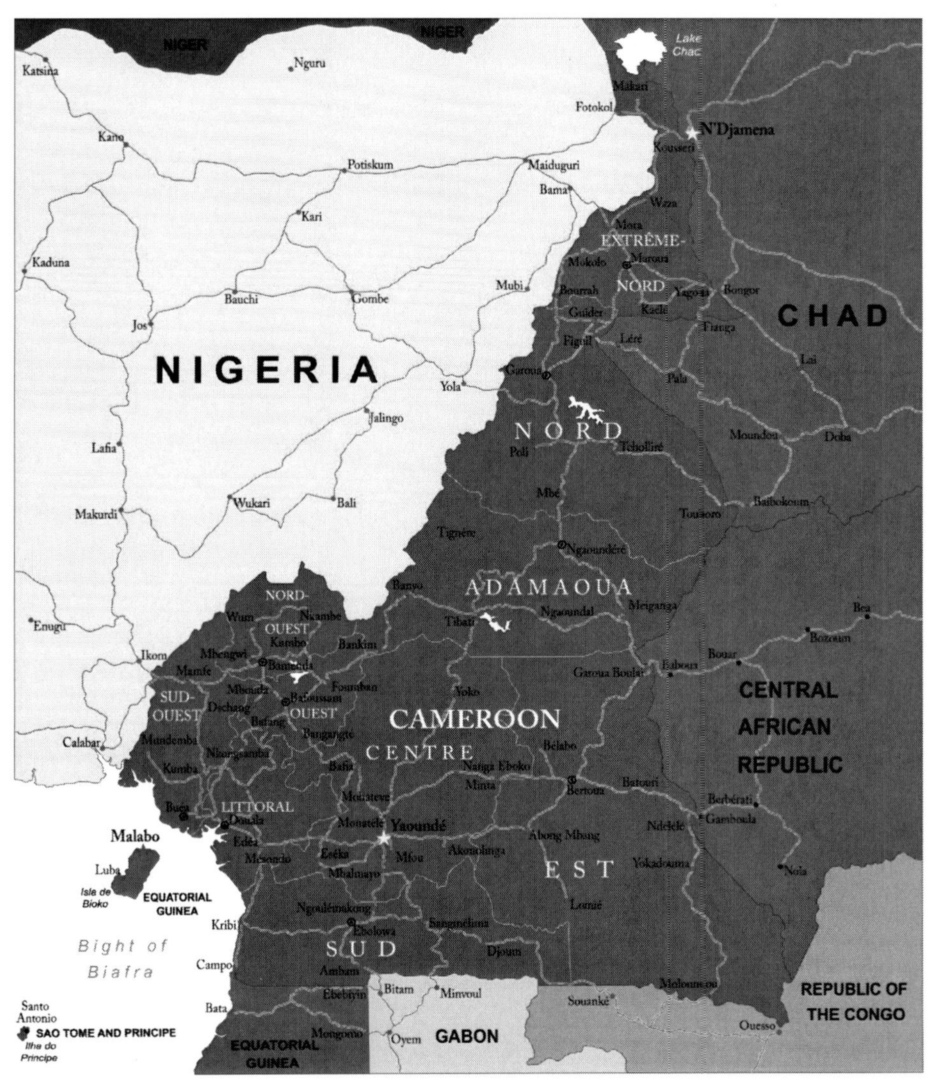
NIGER
NIGER
Lake Chad
Katsina
Nguru
Makari
Fotokol
N'Djamena
Kousseri
Kano
Potiskum
Maiduguri
Bama
Kari
Mora
EXTRÊME-
NORD
Kaduna
Mokolo
Maroua
Mubi
Bauchi
Gombe
Yagoua
Bongor
Guider
Kaélé
CHAD
Jos
Figuil
Léré
NIGERIA
Garoua
Lai
Yola
Pala
Jalingo
NORD
Poli
Tcholliré
Moundou
Doba
Lafia
Mbé
Wukari
Bali
Makurdi
Touboro
Tignère
Ngaoundéré
Banyo
ADAMAOUA
NORD-
OUEST
Wum
Nkambe
Ngaoundal
Meiganga
Tibati
Enugu
Kumbo
Bankim
Bozoum
Ikom
Mbengwi
Bamenda
Bouar
Mamfe
Foumban
Garoua Boulaï
SUD-
OUEST
Dschang
Bafoussam
OUEST
Yoko
CENTRAL
AFRICAN
REPUBLIC
CAMEROON
Bafang
Bangangté
Calabar
CENTRE
Bélabo
Kumba
Bafia
Nanga Eboko
Bertoua
Batouri
Buea
LITTORAL
Douala
Berbérati
Gamboula
Malabo
Yaoundé
Edéa
Abong Mbang
Luba
Eséka
Mfou
Akonolinga
Isla de Bioko
EQUATORIAL
GUINEA
EST
Yokadouma
Nola
Lomié
Kribi
Ebolowa
Sangmélima
Bight of
Biafra
SUD
Djoum
Campo
Ambam
Bitam
Minvoul
Moloundou
REPUBLIC OF
THE CONGO
Santo
Antonio
Bata
Souanké
Ouesso
SAO TOME AND PRINCIPE
Ilha do
Principe
EQUATORIAL
GUINEA
Oyem
GABON

PART I

N'DJAMENA
1980

CHAPTER 1

Even at that distance, the automatic weapons fire woke him. Mark Reilly leaned up on one elbow, disoriented for an instant in the dark, while the sensation, as familiar now as it was damning, spread like a wave from his stomach downward and settled somewhere in his groin. It took only a second to remember he was in his usual room at the *Relais du Logone*. The war, or what was left of it, was safely contained in N'djamena, across the river.

Of course, he'd have to cross over in a few hours; it was, after all, why he'd come. But that was later. His heart, which had been pounding hard enough for him to feel it in his ears, slowed. Mark looked over toward where he knew the window was located. He'd shuttered it the night before when he arrived. Partly, that was to block out the noise—African towns, even dusty backwaters like Kousseri, never slept completely. Mostly, though, it was for the darkness. For some time, he'd had trouble sleeping in anything less than total blackness. The room was still dark, but he could see slashes of pale gray light bleeding into the room through the slats in the shutter.

The gunfire picked up slightly. It was coming from almost

directly across the river, though on the far side of the Chadian capital, which made sense. Since the Libyans had shed all pretenses four months earlier and brought in tanks and troops to support the coalition led by Goukouni Oueddei, the "rebels" of Hissene Habre had been driven out of their last stronghold, a poorer *quartier* along the Chari river, at the southern end of N'djamena. Most of Habre's troops had straggled across the desert toward Abeche, on the Sudan border, or slipped across the river into the refugee camps in Kousseri. But there were still a few of his loyalists hiding on the outskirts of the capital.

Either that or the factions that made up Goukouni's coalition were already at each other's throats. Well, that would come, too, though probably not yet.

Mark groped for his watch on the floor next to the bed. It was a cheap Timex he'd bought from some thief at the airport bar in Lagos, and the luminous dial was shot. Tilting it toward the shutters, he was just able to read the hands. It was 6:15. The Chadians were right on time. To get a jump on the heat, everything in Africa started early, and war-making was no exception. Even at its heaviest, the fighting almost always stopped around noon, when the combatants fell into a fly-swatting torpor.

They started killing one another again around four when the sun began its descent, and a light, steady breeze picked up, signaling that the worst of the heat was over, at least for another day. Sometimes, on the hottest days, the resumption of shelling was almost a relief.

There were, of course, periods of intensive, bloody fighting. Thousands of Chadians had died in the past year, and another hundred thousand had run for their lives and were now packed into refugee camps in Kousseri. Overall, though, the war had about it a laconic, almost lazy pace, as if the Africans, so often criticized for what Westerners considered a lack of sustained effort, weren't quite up to it in the war-making department, either. There were even stories about the Chadians stopping pitched battles to let trucks carrying Gala, the excellent locally brewed beer, pass. Not that Mark blamed them for that: Gala was about the only thing Chad had going for it.

He had never found anyone who actually witnessed such a "beer truce," but that was often a problem with African reporting. Anyway, it sounded right, and he'd used it once in a feature about the lighter side of the war.

Mark got out of bed and walked to the window. Christ, they were pimps, every last fucking one of them. At least most of the others made a decent living out of it. He threw open the louvered shutters so they bounced noisily off the relais' masonry walls.

The sun wasn't up yet, but it wouldn't be long. The fighting sounded louder now, but it was still a long way off.

The room had once had a reasonably pleasant view across the confluence of the Logone and Chari Rivers to the sprawling, dust-streaked Chadian capital. That was gone now, another victim of the war. The Cameroonian Army had thrown up a two-meter earthen levee along the river bank to catch stray bullets and the occasional errant mortar round that had killed more than a few Kousseri residents since the start of the latest round of fighting.

"Shit," he muttered to himself. He was starting to sound like one of his stories. The latest round of fighting. They all used terms like that just to make it sound a little newsier. The truth was that the Chadians had been killing one another for most of the 20 years since independence. The reasons were as numerous as the factions doing the fighting. They all had ridiculously arcane French acronyms, like FAN and FAP, and Mark's favorite, FAT, and they all, at one time or another, had fought with or against most of the other factions.

The only thing approaching certainty in Chad was that today's ally was tomorrow's sworn enemy. This made covering the war correctly impossible since most U.S. editors insisted on clearly defined good and bad guys. That is when they were interested in Africa at all.

And now the Libyans had muddied things further. At least they'd generated some interest; Qadaffi was good copy, if nothing else.

Two African women, their wrap-around skirts tight across their hips, walked tranquilly along the crest of the levee, with wide, enamel bowls balanced on their heads. If they ever thought about it, the women no doubt appreciated the protection afforded by the levee, but the river bank was Kousseri's main road. They wouldn't give it up, not even for a war.

Behind him, away from the river, Mark picked up the muffled, rhythmic sound of women pounding millet. It had, no doubt, been going on for hours already, but it wasn't something he "heard" anymore.

Since his earliest days as a Peace Corps volunteer, so many years before, it was a constant of village life: the dull, regular thumping of the giant pestle against the wooden bowl, over and over for hours, like a heartbeat that everyone heard but never really listened to anymore. It was backbreaking work, too, pounding the tiny kernels into powder. Mark had tried it just to make the village women laugh when he'd first arrived in Diarrere. After five minutes, his arms ached, and he was sucking for air. The women did it for hours every morning of their lives from the age of about seven or eight.

They started early, around four o'clock, to have the millet ready for breakfast. Early on, the pounding woke Mark, but he got used to it and even came to enjoy the sound since it meant he had two more hours to sleep. Mark had always loved to sleep late, but Africa changed that. The whole continent rose before dawn, and over the years, he had picked up the habit, albeit grudgingly.

It seemed to him that half his adult life had been spent in the back seat of a broken-down taxi, careening through some shantytown in the pre-dawn darkness on the way to an airport to fly somewhere he didn't really want to be. The huts, with their mud-stained walls and rusting metal rooves blotchy and diseased-looking in the dark, always depressed him, and the sun, smoldering below the horizon, exhausted him before the day had even begun.

Mark looked at his watch again. It was almost 6:30. He hadn't eaten much the day before on the trip up from Douala, and he was hungry. But he knew Emil wouldn't open the *relais'* restaurant for another half hour. The bastard had gotten pretty goddamn comfortable off the war.

With the shutters open, there was enough light in the room for Mark to find his leather carrying bag. It was by the door on one of the two wooden chairs which, along with the bed, made up the room's furnishings.

The *relais* had electricity, but Mark left the light off. It was better than a lot of places he'd stayed over the years, and Emil did his best to keep the rooms reasonably clean. Still, it was the kind of place that looked better at night than it did in the day. He pulled out a change of clothes and threw them on the bed. Then he grabbed his shaving kit and went into the bathroom.

Like the rest of the *relais*, it was clean enough, though the toilet, a chain-flush type with the water tank above it, smelled strongly of shit and some harsh disinfectant. It had a cheap plastic seat with a crack in it that pinched like a son of a bitch if you weren't careful. A quarter roll of harsh, brown toilet paper sat on the floor next to the toilet.

The shower was in the far corner, just a cold-water pipe with a spray head on the end of it. The tile floor sloped slightly toward a rusty drain in the center of the room. There was no shower curtain.

Mark pried a sliver of green Palmolive soap from where it

was stuck on the sink and turned on the shower. He felt the water with his hand and exhaled heavily. It would be hot, damn hot, in another few hours, but at 6:30 in the morning, the desert has a chill that is difficult to describe to someone who's never been.

Mark wet a forearm, then slowly inched the rest of his arm under the spray until the shoulder was wet. Breathing in sharply, he backed in all the way. The water felt like ice, but there was no telling when he'd have a chance to get clean again.

CHAPTER 2

Mark climbed the levee and looked out across the Chari toward N'Djamena.

He counted six *pirogues* on the river, all downstream from the *relais*. The canoes' occupants were fishing, casting the big nets in a circular arc, then pulling them slowly back toward the boats. Six wasn't many compared to the dozens of idle *pirogues* that lined both banks of the river, but it was six more than the last time Mark had been to Kousseri.

The brave ones, probably, taking a chance that the worst was over, for now anyway. Or maybe just hungry. There had been little to eat in N'djamena the last time. What little food was still being grown in the countryside couldn't be transported into the city because of the heavy fighting.

No one fished back then, either. Both sides were using the river to move supplies from Kousseri to their *combatants,* and that made anything that moved on the river, day or night, fair game for one side or the other.

Mark walked down the levee to the water's edge. The river was down noticeably from his previous visit. But that had been in November, right after the rainy season; it was March now, the dead center of the dry period.

About 100 meters upstream from where Mark stood, an old man and a young boy, both naked, were standing in knee-deep water, washing themselves. There was a steady stream of human traffic on the levee now, women mostly headed to or from the market further up the Logone, but neither the man nor the boy appeared to notice them.

It was on the bank there, exactly where the boy and old man stood, that Mark had waited a year earlier for a *pirogue* to take him across to the Habre stronghold.

It was late, after midnight. Habre's partisans were loading a dozen canoes with supplies: drums of cooking oil and gasoline, sacks of rice and dried fish, and boxes Mark could not identify.

He was to wait for them to cross over, and the lead *piroguier* would see if Habre agreed to the interview. If the answer was yes, Mark would cross in the second wave.

There was no other way to get to Habre; the larger and better-armed Goukouni forces had control of the rest of the city and of the ferry that linked Chad to Cameroon and the outside world.

The *pirogues* floated low and heavy in the water as they slid away from the bank. There were two men to a boat, but even so, loaded down like that, the pirogues were difficult to control in the strong current.

From that spot just upstream from the *Relais du Logone,* the Habre supply boats had to float downriver for about 300 meters until they reached a tapered spit of land called the *Bec du Canard*. It was there that the Logone emptied into the Chari River at a 45-degree angle.

The problem for the Habre people was that after the *pirogues* reached the *Bec du Canard,* they had to fight their way out of the Logone current in order to catch the Chari's, which flowed south to the Habre camp. But even with experienced *piroguiers* paddling furiously, there was a short, deadly period when the Logone eddy brought the boats within firing range of the Goukouni positions.

The *pirogues* moved after midnight, but darkness didn't help much that night. It was exceptionally clear, the way African nights near the desert can be, with so many stars that the sky seemed more milky-white than black. The full moon, though, was the real problem. It lit up the river like some oversized floodlight. From his place on the riverbank, Mark had no trouble following the *pirogues,* strung out on the water like the crooked links of some giant chain, as one by one, they neared the *Bec du Canard.*

The lead *piroguiers,* leaning forward, dug their paddles frantically into the Logone, pulling to get out of its current and over into the Chari's. From where Mark sat, their progress seemed agonizingly slow, as if the currents conspired to hold the boats in place so that no matter how hard the boatmen worked, they were condemned to going nowhere.

And then Goukouni's forces opened fire. Mark had never seen tracer bullets before and was surprised to be able to follow their trajectory. They seemed deceptively slow and benign like fireflies moving slightly faster than normal over the water.

By the time the middle *pirogue* in the flotilla reached the confluence, the night was filled with red-orange lights. Some disappeared into the black water, short of the *pirogues,* but many more streaked over or between them.

The first scream, short and guttural, with a hint of surprise, came from somewhere on the other side of the *Bec du Canard,* but it carried well across the water, and Mark heard it clearly. Two more screams came in quick succession; they echoed just a little, the way noise does over water so that the first had not quite disappeared before the second one sounded.

And then it was over. The last of the canoes surged into the Chari's current and floated quickly south. The tracers continued for another few minutes, but the boats were clearly out of range now, and the bullets disappeared into the river, well short of their target.

The whole drama had taken no more than a few minutes, but watching from the bank, it seemed much longer, as if the intensity of the event had somehow altered its physical reference. The Chadians who had helped to load the boats started to leave; there was nothing more to see, really, and the empty *pirogues* would not return for an hour or more.

But Mark didn't move, not even after the others had disappeared over the bank. It was cold by then, and he wore only a short-sleeved shirt, but it didn't matter. He wasn't sure when he'd started to pray, whether it was when the tracers began flying or afterward, but he didn't stop. He hadn't done it in years; he couldn't even say for sure he believed in a God, at least that kind, but that didn't matter either.

It was a simple prayer, like the first ones the nuns taught him. He mouthed the words to himself, over and over, asking, begging, really, that the answer might be no: that Habre didn't have time for a journalist, or was ill, or wounded or busy torturing a prisoner, anything at all so long as he didn't have to go.

At some point, Mark realized that he had only to get up and walk back to his room at the *relais.* No one would come looking for him. The interview was his idea, after all, and the *piroguiers* who would have to take him over couldn't have been too crazy about making a second trip.

But options weren't always what they seemed; they weren't always real choices at all, but only mocking reminders of past weakness. Mark didn't move.

When he spotted the lead *pirogue* cross in front of the *Bec du Canard,* it was after three a.m. The moon had slipped lower in the night sky and was nowhere near as bright; there were even a few clouds that blotted it out for minutes at a time. A dozen or so tracers arced out over the river from Goukouni's forward positions, but the currents were kinder coming back, and none of the boats drifted into range. There wasn't much point, anyway; the *pirogues* were empty now, and Goukouni's men knew it.

One by one, the boats crunched up onto the bank near where Mark sat. A handful of Chadians appeared out of the darkness behind the bank and quickly unloaded three long, thin bundles, all wrapped in rough cloth, from three of the boats. The porters struggled to carry the clumsy forms back up the bank while the *piroguiers,* all glistening with sweat in the meager light, quickly hauled their boats all the way onto the bank.

The lead *piroguier* spotted Mark and hurried over to him. His name was Ahmat, Mark remembered. He was short for a Chadian, but extremely muscular, almost like a weightlifter, which was rare for a northerner.

He wore a wool ski cap, ripped cut-off shorts, and an oil-stained vest. He was barefoot. Though it was very cool by that time of night, Mark could see he was soaked with sweat.

"Ce n'est pas possible ce soir, monsieur," Ahmat said, still trying to catch his breath. His French had the guttural, sing-song accent that French expatriates found so amusing to mimic.

"C'est dommage," Mark lied, his heart pounding.

"Le President dit que peut-etre demain ou apres demain," Ahmat added. Habre was barely hanging onto the poorest neighborhood of the city, but his people still referred to him as President.

Ahmat didn't say why the interview wasn't possible, and Mark didn't ask.

"Tu passes demain soir, d'accord?" Ahmat asked, then hurried back to his boat without waiting for a reply.

Mark didn't go by the next night or any other. The day after, he took the ferry across, which then was a kilometer upriver from its normal location, safely out of range of Habre's mortars.

Goukouni's headquarters were north of the city then, also well-removed from the fighting. But it gave Mark a N'djamena dateline, and that was what counted. He wrote an "on the frontlines" type piece, which was close to the truth, and said that repeated requests to visit the Habre headquarters had been turned down.

He did collar a Habre political official in Kousseri for balance and described in detail the nighttime supply convoy. All in all, it worked out well. The papers he wrote for loved it; some of them even paid him on time.

But the memory of those few hours on the river bank bothered him, even for a while after he'd returned to Douala. He tried to talk about it with Deborah once, but she either didn't understand or didn't care. Probably the latter. Hell, she almost certainly was involved with the French prick by then; she may already have decided to leave with him.

Mark glanced at his watch and then over at the *relais.* It was five after seven, and the restaurant's back door, which opened onto a terrace facing the river, was still shut tight.

"Goddamn it, Emil," he said out loud. He turned and walked back down the levee and around the building to the front door.

The *Relais du Logone* was a U-shaped complex, with the restaurant bar set back away from the road and closest to the river; the rooms ran from the restaurant to close to the road, on either side of a potholed, dirt parking area.

Mark zipped up his sweatshirt a little higher. The sun was just peaking over the levee in the east; it wouldn't warm up for another two hours. And in another four hours, it would be so hot that it would seem impossible.

As Mark came around the side of the *relais,* a gust of wind caught him in the face. He instinctively closed his eyes, but it was too late. He took off his glasses and wiped a sleeve hard across both eyes, which were already watering from the swirling sand.

Heat and dust: They were the two constants there on the edge of the greatest stretch of sand in the world. There were villages in the area that dated back thousands of years, but somehow, man's hold on the place seemed remarkably tenuous, like some fragile loophole in the laws of nature, that the heat and dust would get around to closing sooner or later.

The front door of the restaurant was open, and Mark could hear the clank of cheap dishes.

"Shit," he muttered and walked inside.

The *relais'* main building, like all the old masonry structures built by the French, was dark inside. The French had realized early into their African occupation that the sun was their most redoubtable foe. The architecture reflected that understanding. The walls were thick, and all the windows and doors had heavy, louvered shutters that were opened only at night or in the very early morning.

The dark, wooden floor of the building was warped in places and dull from years of harsh soap and no wax. Two overhead fans hung from the high ceiling, one over the bar area and the other toward the back, which Emil had partitioned off as a restaurant.

He hadn't turned on either fan yet.

As Mark entered, Emil, dressed in white with an apron on, came toward him from behind the bar, carrying a tray filled with coffee, French bread, and jam.

"Bonjour, Mark," he said, his wide grin already in place. *"Tu as bien dormi?"*

"Oui, merci, Emil," Mark said. "But why the hell didn't you open the terrace door? I've been standing out there for a half hour, starving to death."

Emil's grin widened to show surprisingly straight, white teeth. *"Trop de poussiere,"* he replied, laughing. It didn't take much to make Emil laugh.

Mark laughed, too, though he was still annoyed.

"There's always too much goddamn dust, Emil," he argued, then followed Emil into the "restaurant."

In fact, it was just the back half of the building, set off from the bar by several yards of a cheap, green cloth—the kind found in any African market on the continent—thrown over a rope that ran the full width of the room.

For whatever reason, all of the *relais'* windows were in the bar area upfront. With the curtain cutting off the light from the open front door, the "restaurant" was quite dark. There were a couple of light bulbs that hung on wires from the ceiling, but Emil hadn't turned them on either.

Only two of the dozen or so tables in the area were occupied: an enormously fat African sat alone at the one closest to the door; in the back, three whites, almost certainly French *militaire,* were eating breakfast.

Emil took the tray to the African's table, and Mark sat down at one as far from both parties as he could get.

The African was well-dressed, in one of the locally made *"complets,"* a kind of African leisure suit. He was probably a *functionaire,* since they were about the only Africans that could afford Emil's prices.

Mark didn't know him, but that didn't mean anything; since the refugee camp population had swelled to 100,000—some aid workers insisted it was higher—the Cameroonian government in Yaounde had dispatched a small army of officials to feed and house the Chadians, and more importantly, to keep them under control.

Emil headed back to the kitchen, which was in a small shack behind the bar.

"Cafe complet, mon ami?" He asked Mark.

"Oui, s'il te plait, Emil," Mark answered.

Emil showed his teeth again. *"Pas de Gala?"* He asked.

"Peut-etre apres," Mark said, smiling back.

It was their standard joke, and Emil chuckled on cue. It

wasn't even that funny; Mark probably would have a beer before he headed across the river. Up there, drinking before the sun was up didn't raise too many eyebrows, and it sure as hell made looking down the barrel of a Kalashnikov a little easier.

Emil disappeared through the curtain. He was a funny one, Emil. It was hard to imagine how he'd made a living before the war came along, but he'd cleaned up ever since. Mark liked him, though, and he knew the feeling was mutual. He had been one of the first Western reporters to the border when the latest round of fighting broke out, and Emil tended to view him as an old and honored client.

Even at the height of the war, when the hotshot correspondents from Paris and the American boys from Nairobi were sleeping four to a room, Emil saved a bed for him. And in all the times he'd stayed at the relais, Mark had seen Emil's smile waver only once, when a Cameroonian *gendarme,* who'd had too much to drink, accused him of being a Chadian.

Once, when they were alone at the bar, Mark had asked him where he was from, but Emil just smiled and said, *"D'ici."* So, Mark dropped it.

Emil came back through the curtain with a full tray. He unloaded the bread, jam, coffee, sugar, and condensed milk onto Mark's table.

"Merci, Emil," Mark said, reaching for the coffee pot. He was damn hungry; even the Nescafe, which Emil made so strong that milk barely changed its color, smelled good. He glanced up at Emil, who hadn't moved. Mark put the coffee down and reached into his pocket. The other times, he'd just paid for everything when he checked out, but hell, maybe Emil had had some trouble with reporters not paying their bills.

"Non, non, Mark," Emil said quickly. He glanced over at the African *functionaire,* who was busy with his breakfast, then slid into the chair opposite Mark's.

His smile widened again, but this time from embarrassment.

Mark was surprised. They kidded each other pretty regularly and had talked seriously once or twice; Emil had even once bought Mark a beer when there was no one else in the place. But this was a first.

"Mark, tu es americain, n'est-ce pas?" Emil asked.

"Oui."

Emil glanced quickly over at the *functionaire* again, who was still working his way through the breadbasket, then leaned forward across the table and lowered his voice.

"Would you like to buy some dollars?" He asked in a whisper.

Mark noticed for the first time that there were several strands of gray in Emil's short, spongy hair. He was older than he looked, probably, but that wasn't that unusual in African men.

Mark exhaled, disgusted. One of his honorable colleagues had no doubt run short of CFA, the African *franc* used in most of the old French possessions, and had somehow convinced Emil to accept dollars instead.

And now the poor bastard couldn't get rid of them. If he took them to a bank, they'd be confiscated since it was illegal in Cameroon to hold foreign currency. Emil could always smuggle them across the border to Nigeria; illegal black market operations flourished in most of the larger cities. But he'd lose plenty in the exchange and probably have to pay off border guards on both sides.

That was a lot of trouble for a few dollars.

"Combien, Emil?" Mark asked. He didn't need dollars and was short of CFA as it was. But Emil had done him a few favors in the past.

"Cinq mille," Emil said, leaning forward and lowering his voice even more.

Mark stared at Emil over the top of his coffee cup. Emil's French was pretty basic, but he wouldn't have made a simple mistake like that.

"Emil, where the hell did you get five thousand dollars?" He hissed.

Emil grinned. *"Je les achete,"* he said, conspiratorially.

"From who?" Mark demanded.

Emil shrugged. "The big merchants, mostly," he replied.

"Where do they get them?" Mark asked, interested now.

"The Chadians pay for everything in dollars now," Emil explained.

"The Chadians?" Mark exclaimed, trying to keep his voice under control. "Where are they getting dollars from?"

"C'est les Libyens qui les leur donnent," Emil said.

"Since when?" Mark demanded. It'd been only four months since his last visit, and he sure as hell hadn't seen any dollars in Chad. There had been little money of any denomination then, though there was some talk that the Libyans were trying to pay Chadian soldiers with *dinars,* the worthless Libyan currency.

Emil shrugged again. *"Depuis deux, trois mois,"* he said.

Mark thought a moment. It didn't make sense. "Emil, are you sure they're real dollars?" He asked.

That made it twice he'd seen Emil's smile waver. Emil glanced over at the African again, then reached cautiously inside his apron. He slid his closed fist across the table to Mark, who took the bill.

Mark quickly held up the dollar close to his face, angling it toward what little light reached them from the door. It was a $50 note, not brand new, but not filthy and tattered, either, like so many of the CFA bills that circulated in a place like Kousseri.

He strained his eyes, looking for the red and blue threads that he'd read somewhere that proved a dollar was real. They were visible.

Mark passed the bill back to Emil along the side of the table farthest from the African *functionaire.* Emil, who was clearly very worried, stared at him.

Mark spread his hands and shrugged. "It looks real to me, Emil." The smile returned.

"Alors, tu veut les acheter, mon ami?" Emil asked.

Mark emitted a short, humorless laugh. He didn't have five thousand dollars to his name, anywhere, in any currency. Shit, he didn't have five hundred.

"Desole, Emil," he said, shaking his head.

"Ce n'est pas grave," Emil said, smiling and getting up from the table. "I can sell them in Nigeria, but I thought it might interest you."

Mark laughed, for real, this time. Emil was offering him a deal.

"Merci, Emil," he said, meaning it. "It interests me plenty, but unfortunately, I'm just a poor journalist."

Emil laughed and nodded. To Africans, there was no such thing as a poor American. Mark was just being polite. But Emil could appreciate that: in Africa, a tactful lie was always better manners than a flat rejection.

Two of the Frenchmen left while Mark was on his second cup of coffee. He didn't know either of them, but both nodded curtly at him as they passed, and he did the same, just whites acknowledging their common predicament.

The African *functionaire,* who, Mark saw, had polished off the entire basket of bread, staggered up from the table shortly after that. He slipped on a pair of cheap, plastic sunglasses and lumbered toward the door. A moment later, the sound of a badly tuned car motor starting up floated in from the parking lot.

The third Frenchman waited until the *functionaire's* car turned around and whined toward the *relais'* exit, out by the main road, before he rose from his table and came over to Mark's. He was young, like the other two, and short, even for a Frenchman, with reddish-blond hair cut very close to his round head.

He looked slightly overweight, soft, really, though that might have been an impression caused by his skin; it was extremely fair and heavily freckled, especially on his arms. It was hard to imagine he needed to shave more than once a week.

"Bonjour, monsieur," he said, too friendly for a Frenchman.

"Bonjour," Mark replied politely. He was used to the routine by now.

"Je peux?" The Frenchman asked, gesturing at the chair Emil had vacated.

"Je vous en prie," Mark said.

The Frenchman sat down quickly. He was carrying a pipe that had apparently gone out; he poked it into the side of his mouth, pulled a Bic lighter from his shirt pocket, and expertly re-lit the tobacco.

"Ca vous gene?" He asked suddenly, withdrawing the pipe and clearly prepared to extinguish it if Mark so wished.

"Non, non," Mark assured him.

The Frenchman slipped the pipe back in the corner of his mouth and smiled around it.

"I forgot that most Americans were anti-tobacco these days," he said. "You are American, no?"

Mark shook his head. "Russian," he said, straight-faced.

The Frenchman's laugh was a bit late and a little too hard, but it was a nice try. He'd done this before, too.

"Are you crossing over today?" He asked, nodding sideways in the direction of the river.

"Oui," Mark said. No sense dragging it out.

"Your first time?" The Frenchman wanted to know.

"Non." The Frenchman waited to see if Mark would elaborate, then smiled when he didn't.

"You know, we are all on the same side," he said, still smiling.

Mark smiled, too, hoping it would keep him from laughing, but it didn't. The Frenchman joined in, but again, his heart wasn't in it.

"Look, I'm a journalist, that's all," Mark said earnestly. The Frenchman nodded emphatically. He wasn't there to contradict an ally.

"Et votre consul la, monsieur Feraldi, vous le connaissez?" He asked.

Mark exhaled sharply, his hands spread wide. "I know he's here, but I wouldn't say I know him."

"Il est un peu special, n'est-ce pas?" The Frenchman asked carefully, not sure that was the way to go.

Mark laughed. The French used the word to mean weird or eccentric, and that fit Martin Feraldi just fine. But then, he wasn't really a consul, and Feraldi probably wasn't his name.

"We paid him a visit, *juste pour dire bonjour, quoi, mais. ...*" the Frenchman explained, shaking his head to finish the thought. "Then we invited him over to our place for dinner or just a drink. He said he was too busy."

The Frenchman gave his teeth a rest and pointed with the pipe stem in the general direction of Kousseri.

"No one is too busy in a place like this," he said.

You ought to know, pal, if you're sitting here with me, Mark thought.

"And his friend is worse," the Frenchman complained. "I have never even seen him."

Mark had, just for a second, the one and only time he'd bothered to go by the "American Consulate" in Kousseri. He'd talked to Feraldi, too, but the Frenchman was wasting his time if he thought Mark could help him.

"Whaddaya want?" Feraldi asked, stepping out onto the small veranda and holding the door closed behind him.

The "consulate," which, for diplomatic purposes at least, was billed as a temporary replacement for the bombed-out embassy across the river, was housed in a run-down "villa" on the northern edge of Kousseri.

It was set back from the same laterite road that ran by the *relais* and had a kind of thorn-bush hedge that surrounded a vegetationless "yard" and afforded some privacy from the passing traffic. Not that there was any secret about the place. Everyone in town referred to it as "the American house," and any doubts were dispelled by the Jeep Ranger and the white Ford station wagon parked under an acacia tree on the shade side of the villa.

It had been some time since Mark had seen an American car. The two vehicles looked enormous and about as inconspicuous as a yacht on the Chari.

It was almost noon, and Mark was sweating freely from the walk over from the *relais.* Feraldi, if that was indeed his name, was still in his bathrobe, a heavy flannel job that hadn't been cleaned in a while. He had a pair of Dr. Scholl clogs on his feet. He was about 45, medium-height, and not so much overweight as out of shape. Even if Feraldi wasn't his name, he was probably Italian; he was dark, with lots of thick black hair on the part of his legs that showed below where the bathrobe stopped.

He hadn't shaved that morning, maybe not even the day before, and it looked like he combed his oily hair with his fingers, straight back, as if to emphasize the receding hairline. There was a stale odor of cigarettes and whiskey that drifted out the door with him, though he wasn't drunk.

Mark had seen him before, not Feraldi, but others just like him, so similar in style and attitude that any distinction was merely cosmetic. They all had the slight tremor in their hands and the aggressive insecurity, like aging punks who had suddenly discovered they weren't very tough after all.

Africa had been crawling with them since Saigon fell.

"I just thought I'd drop by and say hello," Mark said.

Feraldi scowled and shook his head. "I don't talk to reporters," he said.

"Who do you talk to?" Mark asked, smiling. But Feraldi wasn't a kidder.

There was a muffled yell from inside the house, and Feraldi opened the door just enough to stick his head inside.

Mark caught a glimpse of another man, thin, bald, and surprisingly old, sitting in front of a sophisticated two-way radio. The man, who was dressed only in shorts and a droopy sleeveless T-shirt, did not turn toward the door when Feraldi opened it, so Mark saw only a fleeting profile.

Feraldi hissed something that Mark could not make out, then turned and closed the door behind him again. Mark couldn't see the generator, but he heard its hum now; it had to be a big one to run the radio and the air conditioner sticking out of one of the side windows.

"Do me a favor, and don't come back here," Feraldi said, finished with the conversation.

"What if I lose my passport?" Mark asked, still smiling, but feeling the blood flowing to his cheeks. It didn't matter now.

Feraldi stared hard at him, his eyes closed halfway, his mouth open just a little. It was a look that must have scared somebody sometime. After a moment, Feraldi turned and walked back into the house.

"Asshole!" Mark hissed, angrier and louder than he'd intended, as the "consulate" door clicked shut.

No, he couldn't help the Frenchman.

"Et vous, vous rentrez ce soir?" The Frenchman wanted to know.

"That depends," Mark said.

"On what?" The Frenchman pressed, not quite so friendly now, and his face a shade pinker.

Mark stared at him for a second. That skin and a short fuse: it was a bad combination in this heat, he thought.

"Whether I get the story I came for," Mark said firmly. Emil walked by with the *functionaire's* dishes. Mark caught his eye and put his thumb to his mouth. Emil laughed and nodded.

The Frenchman smiled indulgently at the interruption.

"You don't want to stay the night in N'djamena," he said confidently.

Mark smiled. Goukouni was so furious at what he viewed as French betrayal that any *militaire* who ventured across the river would have been shot on sight. This was why they were reduced to debriefing aid workers, doctors from Medcins sans Frontieres, and journalists in the *relais.*

"Still pretty bad?" Mark asked, smiling harder, trying not to laugh.

"Awful," the Frenchman assured him.

Emil brought Mark his beer.

"Monsieur?" He asked the Frenchman.

"Rien pour moi," the Frenchman said, in that unique way the French had of denying an African's existence, or his humanity at least, even while addressing him.

"Perhaps you'd care to stop by our place and have a drink when you get back tonight," he said to Mark as Emil disappeared back through the curtain.

"Perhaps," Mark lied. "As I said, it depends."

The Frenchman's smile seemed to be frozen on his face. "You know the house?"

"Oui," Mark replied, glad it was ending.

The Frenchman pushed back his chair and got up.

"Au revoir, monsieur," he said, bowing slightly.

"Au revoir," Mark said to the small, round back as the Frenchman brushed aside the curtain and disappeared out the door.

CHAPTER 3

Mark paid Emil for the room and the meal, and slid his suddenly much thinner wad of CFA notes into a shirt pocket, and started for the ferry landing.

He was going to have to watch his money. Closely.

Most of his reporting trips were financed in advance by the newspapers or magazines he wrote for; they either asked him to go or he proposed a trip, and they accepted. Either way, they paid his expenses. But not this time.

"Thks yr offer but suggest wait till Qadaffi makes another move." "Thks yr idea, but unless have major new Q development, 'fraid must decline." And so on.

Mark wired back testily that Qadaffi was not the only story in Chad; predictably, that got him nowhere. So, without too much thought or money, he'd flown to Maroua, Cameroon's northernmost city, and the last stop on the Cameroon Airlines shuttle. In the past, he'd rented a car in Maroua and driven the last 250 kilometers to the border. But that was expensive and thus out of the question. So, he'd waited most of the afternoon at the Maroua taxi gare, then sat in the middle seat of a violently shimmying Peugeot station wagon, squeezed between an enormous market woman, whose robes smelled overpoweringly of dried fish and a hung-over Cameroon Army sergeant, for the three-hour ride to Kousseri.

And the truth was that Mark had no burning reason to make the trip then, not from a news standpoint, anyway. But since the night he'd spent on the riverbank, waiting for word from Habre, he'd felt a dreadful kind of urge to come back whenever he could, even sometimes, like now, when there was no news and he couldn't afford it. It was so strong at times that he stopped doing the routine news items and commodity reports that paid the bulk of his pathetic salary and instead spent hours devising telexes that he hoped would convince one of his "strings" to finance a trip to the border.

But when they did, it changed nothing. He'd been back four times, and each trip simply confirmed what he already knew so well. And still, he came, like some helpless cripple making the same bogus pilgrimage, year after year, though he knew beforehand there would be no miracle. Mark didn't know if he even wanted one, or if he did, exactly what he'd want it to change. The past, maybe, but even miracles had limits.

And now he'd need a damn good feature, maybe two, just to break even. Perhaps the dollar thing would do it. It would depend on how many they were talking about. The more, the better.

But he'd have to find out why dollars, instead of francs or CFA, and how the Libyans were working it.

That wouldn't be easy. The Libyans weren't big on interviews, certainly not on something like that. In fact, they did their best to maintain the pretense that Goukouni was running the show. Most of them stayed out of sight, on bases outside of N'djamena that were heavily guarded and off-limits, even to Chadians.

The few that Mark, or any of the other hacks, had been able to corner spouted the usual rubbish about friendship and solidarity between Third World brothers oppressed by the twin evils of Western imperialism and Zionism.

Mark shifted his leather carryall to the other shoulder. It wasn't nine o'clock yet, and the air still had a coolness to it, but that wouldn't last long. The sun had crept up over N'djamena and was rising fast. Mark's shirt was wet across his back, and he could feel the sweat beads forming at his temple.

The Cameroon landing site was surrounded by an open, dusty expanse, devoid of any vegetation, that sloped gently from the road down to the riverbank. During the war, refugees loyal to the Goukouni side sometimes gathered there to talk or to stare across the river at the plumes of black smoke that curled up from their city.

The end of the fighting changed all that. A line of trucks waiting to cross over now stretched from the river's edge back almost to the road. A constant flow of Africans, most of them carrying enamel basins or tightly roped bundles on their heads, moved toward the river, where dozens of *pirogues* lined the bank. A smaller, but still steady flow of Chadians passed Mark on the road, heading into Kousseri.

Mark was surprised at the number of trucks. There were several tankers, their Shell and BP logos barely visible beneath the grit and oil stains, and a dozen or more Berliet and Mercedes rigs overloaded with what looked like food and maybe cement.

All of them were filthy, covered with a thick coat of reddish-brown dust from the week-long trip up from Douala or one of the Nigerian ports. The ferry was a small, dual-pontoon model, straight out of French Army surplus, and could only carry one of the big trucks at a time. This meant that even running flat-out from dawn till dark (when a strictly enforced curfew on the river was still in effect), some of the trucks wouldn't cross over until the following day.

Well, Africans could wait with the best of them, especially

truck drivers. They were fair game for every idiot army private or bored *gendarme* drawing road check duty, and if they couldn't afford it or didn't feel like paying the requisite "dash," they could sit a long time while the bastards "checked" their papers.

Compared to that, waiting for the ferry was a piece of cake.

Mark saluted the lone Cameroonian policeman at the loading area, then walked down the line of trucks toward the water. The waiting truck drivers stood near their rigs, alone or in small groups, talking. In another hour, most of them would be sitting on the shaded side of the trucks or lying on mats underneath them, arms thrown over their faces to keep the flies off.

Mark could see the ferry coming back from the N'djamena "port," a smaller landing area almost directly across the river. Two figures clad in the camouflage gear and sky-blue berets of Goukouni's presidential guard, each with a short-stock Kalachinikov cradled in front of him, stood on either pontoon. Another one would be riding in the rear.

The sensation, not at all unpleasant physically, started in Mark's stomach and spread downward. He became aware of his heart because he could feel it, hear it almost, pounding in his chest. Pretty soon, his mouth would dry up, too. But that was all right; he was used to it, even welcomed it almost, since the anticipation was, in so many ways, worse than the fear itself.

Mark walked around the first truck in line, a BP gasoline tanker, to get a better view of the ferry as it approached.

On either side of the ferry landing, *piroques* lined the bank. Most of the canoe owners sat along the bank in groups, talking and watching the ferry return. A few were doing repairs on their boats, for the most part, "stitching" up cracks in the wood caused by the alternating wetness of the river and intensive dryness of the desert sun. They used what looked like crochet needles to bore holes on either side of the cracks, then laced cord, or if they could afford it, wire through the holes and pulled it tight, like a doctor stitching up a deep cut.

The stitching was never watertight, but it was only a short trip across the Chari, and the veteran *piroguiers* got used to baling water during the inevitable wait for passengers or supplies to carry the other way. It added years to a dugout's life, and most of the *pirogues* on the Chari had at least one such "scar."

Mark glanced up the riverbank. There were a half dozen *pirogues* loading what looked like sacks of millet or flour; two or three others were taking on passengers.

He shielded his eyes and looked out at the river. The sun was rising almost directly across from where he stood, and even wearing sunglasses, the glare of the water was intense. He counted another seven *pirogues* crossing over, five riding low in the water, obviously carrying supplies, and the other two loaded with refugees.

Some of them were headed home, anyway; not many compared to the number still in the camps, but given the durability of past "coalitions" in N'djamena, it was hard to blame the cautious ones.

The ferry neared the Cameroonian bank. It carried an aging Berliet ten-tonner, no doubt empty—there wasn't anything to take out of Chad—and a handful of passengers, most of them older men dressed in the simple, long tunic worn by peasants throughout the Sahel.

The two *combattants* on the near side of the ferry stood with their legs slightly apart, scanning the landing area through ink-black aviator sunglasses. Their heads rotated slowly from one side to the other so that from a distance, they looked almost like battery-operated toys.

Mark backed up a step instinctively as the ferry slid up the bank and stopped. Several civilians on the shore hurried to lower the ramp.

One of the *combattants* hopped off the ferry. He ignored the workers entirely and stood, tense and alert, watching the crowd nearby. The other one stayed onboard and, from his perch on the pontoon, looked out over the whole landing area.

The Berliet coughed to life as soon as the ramp was in place and then rattled slowly down off the ferry and up the riverbank toward the road. The BP tanker started up and inched slowly up the ramp onto the ferry as several of the workers yelled and waved contradictory directions simultaneously to the driver.

Mark waited until the truck was on the ferry before he approached the *combattant* standing guard on the shore. He was a young one, no more than 16 or 17, but that probably made him a battle-weary veteran in Chad. Both sides had suffered such heavy losses that by the end, the only recruits left were young boys.

Mark smiled and nodded a greeting, but the Chadian only stared straight ahead, the black sunglasses revealing no hint of his mood.

"Bonjour, monsieur," Mark said earnestly. *"Uh, je suis journaliste americain. Est-ce que vous permetez que je mont a bord?"* He asked, gesturing at the ferry.

The *combattant* took one hand off the Kalichinikov and flicked it at Mark dismissively.

There was better than a 50-50 chance that he spoke no French; the northerners had never liked their colonial masters and had resisted learning the language.

"Ecoutez," Mark began, pointing across at N'djamena. *"Je voudrais..."*

But the Chadian cut him off brutally, jerking the Kalichinikov around in front of him and yelling something harshly in Arabic.

Mark instinctively took a step backward and held up both hands.

"It's no use; he won't let you on," a voice in French said from behind Mark. Mark turned his head carefully. Alain Resnais, the current AFP correspondent, smiled at him.

"Salut mon general," Alain said heartily, mocking a salute in the direction of the Chadian soldier. The *combattant* glanced at Alain then resumed his watch and ignored the two white men.

"C'mon," Alain said to Mark, waving a hand toward the bank downriver. Mark followed him.

"None of them speak French, and anyway, they've got orders not to let anyone on the ferry," Alain explained as they walked. "We can take a *pirogue*." Alain obviously had a particular boat in mind as he ignored the entreaties from the idle piroguiers they passed. Near the end of the line of boats, he climbed into one where a short, wiry African sat, baling out the shallow puddle in the bottom with a rusted tin can.

"Alors chef, on est deux aujourd'hui," Alain said cheerfully as he settled into the bow of the canoe.

The Chadian put down his can. *"Deux cent francs,"* he said firmly.

Alain feigned shock. *"Mais t'es un voleur!"* He shouted, loud enough that several of the *piroquiers* nearby stopped their conversations and glanced over.

"Deux cent francs," the owner insisted.

"Si on est un ou deux, c'est le meme trajet," Alain protested.

The Chadian made no move to push off. *"Deux personnes, deux cent francs,"* he said.

Mark stepped around the African and sat down. *"Allons-y,"* he said, motioning to the Chadian.

"Deux cent francs," the *piroguier* repeated, still not moving.

"D'acord, mais allons-y," Mark said, irritated. They were arguing over 50 cents.

The Chadian pushed off and hopped nimbly into the boat. He pulled a long stout pole from the bottom of the pirogue and, standing up, shoved it hard into the water until it bit into the sandy bottom. That late in the dry season, he'd be able to pole most of the way, except in the middle of the Chari, where he'd have to paddle.

"T'es un voleur," Alain yelled. The Chadian's mouth tightened, but he said nothing.

"Alors, ca va?" Alain asked Mark, smiling again.

"Ca va," Mark shrugged. He was facing the *piroguier* and squatting to avoid sitting in the puddle that covered the bottom of the canoe. Carefully, he turned to face Alain.

"I had an interesting talk with one of your roommates this morning," he said.

Alain grinned. "Which one?" He asked.

Mark shrugged. "Short, reddish-blond hair, skin like a baby's ass," he said.

Alain laughed. "Ah, *Maitre le Paquet,*" he said.

"That's not his real name?" Mark asked, smiling.

Alain shook his head. "No, but every time France has a problem somewhere in the world, his solution is to *'mettre le paquet,'"* he explained.

Mark laughed hard, and Alain joined him.

"I don't even know his real name," Alain said. "But be careful Mark," he added, serious again; "he's a real bastard."

Mark shook his head. "I doubt I'll be talking to him again. I couldn't help him, and I don't think he liked me much," he said.

Alain nodded but didn't look like he agreed.

"Hey, I don't have to live with him," Mark said. He was trying for a laugh, but Alain barely managed a smile.

It was a sore point, not only for Alain but all the AFP correspondents shuttled in at regular intervals to cover what was, for the French, a pretty big story. They already had the onus of being owned by the French government, which didn't help much with the Chadians, not then, anyway. Worse, they stayed in a room in the compound in Kousseri housing the dozen or so French *militaires.*

To be fair, the only other habitable place in Kousseri was

the *Relais du Logone*, and the AFP, which ran a chronic deficit, couldn't afford Emil's prices. Certainly not when there was free lodging just down the road. Not that it was really free; it was common knowledge among the other reporters and, no doubt, the Chadians that the AFP correspondent was expected to keep his roommates abreast of what was going on across the river.

Neither Alain nor any of the others Mark had met liked it, but they all did it.

"How's things with you?" Mark asked, changing the subject.

"Bof," Alain exhaled disgustedly, the way only the French can. "Six months in paradise; I can't complain."

Mark smiled. It was more like four months, but he didn't blame Alain for thinking it was longer. The rest of them came up for a few days, or a week or two outside, if something major was happening. Doing it every day for months, and AFP demanded at least a story a day, no matter what, must have been murder.

It had certainly taken its toll on Alain. He'd never be thin, but he'd lost a lot of weight since the last time Mark had seen him. The khaki shirt that had seemed a size too small the last time flapped loosely in the light wind on the river. Even the droopy, black mustache that made him look like some Corsican pirate seemed leaner now.

He'd calmed down some, too, adopted the kind of breezy confidence laced with cynicism that reporters in places like that had a patent on, more as a defense mechanism, really, than a true reflection of their feelings.

Mark was eating breakfast at the *relais* the day Alain arrived. It was his first crack at an overseas story, and he'd come by looking for someone to cross over with.

Chad, and especially the Libyans, were still big news back then, and the *relais* was jammed, mostly with French reporters from the major Paris papers and magazines. Reuters and AP had their Abidjan-based people there, and two of the three French television stations had even sent in crews.

Most of them had paired off by then, anyway; those that hadn't made up excuses for why they couldn't cross with Alain. It was nothing personal; just that right then, no one wanted too close an association with AFP. It was France, and vice versa, at least as far as Goukouni's people were concerned, and that made life miserable for the agency's correspondent assigned to cover the story—and anyone else that got too close.

For once in the post-colonial era, the French had sat one out. They got tired of seeing their carefully arranged coalitions and fragile truces disintegrate and decided to retire to the sidelines and simply re-establish ties to whichever side won.

They no doubt preferred Goukouni since his coalition included the malleable and historically pro-French southern troops of the corrupt Abdel Wadal Kamougue.

And Habre, a tough, shrewd leader who never liked the French, had the celebrated abduction of Madame Claustre—and some reports claimed, the personal, cold-blooded assassination of a French officer sent to rescue her—on his record.

But none of that was enough to induce Paris to heed Goukouni's increasingly urgent pleas for help. Nor did the French really believe that Goukouni and his Christian allies from the south would ally themselves with the Libyans.

Qadaffi had already annexed the Aouzou strip in northern Chad to a general outcry from all the Chadian factions, and his radical Muslim pronouncements terrified the southerners. It was even widely reported that he had Goukouni detained against his will while on a visit to Tripoli.

But the French failed to reckon with the almost Nazi-like hatred that Habre provoked in his enemies, particularly the southerners. Faced with imminent defeat at his hands, the Libyans were easily the lesser of two evils. Goukouni was well aware that once invited in, Qadaffi might not be so easy to get out, but that simply exacerbated his bitterness over what he viewed as the French betrayal.

Mark preferred to work alone. He'd gotten used to it over the years, and in a place like Chad, a lone reporter was less visible than pairs or groups of them. In N'djamena, which was then still on a war footing, with heavily armed, often nervous, Chadian and Libyan troops manning roadblocks everywhere, that was no small consideration.

But Alain was clearly desperate by the time he got to Mark's table, so Mark soaked him for two Galas and agreed to share a *pirogue* across to N'djamena.

The reception was worse than Mark expected.

"C'est vous l'Agence France Presse?" An angry young *combattant* in green fatigues and aviator sunglasses asked Mark after he and Alain filled out the required immigration forms at a small guard post the Chadians had erected just up from the "port." The *combattant's* tone left no doubt about his feelings toward AFP and probably anything French.

"C'est moi, monsieur," Alain said before Mark could answer. Alain's mouth was open, and he appeared to be short of breath.

The *combattant* picked up his gun. *"Venez avec moi,"* he ordered and walked quickly up the hill toward the road. It wasn't clear if he meant both of them or just Alain, and for a second, Mark thought about denying he even knew the French reporter. Hell, he didn't know him; all he'd agreed was to share a *pirogue,* not the interrogation, or worse, that the Chadian had in mind.

Alain turned to look at Mark before following the *combattant* up the hill. His eyes were wide, and his mouth hung open as if he weren't getting enough air. Christ, his predecessor, must have warned him, but then that wasn't the same thing. It wasn't even close.

Mark managed a smile. *"Ca fait partie de la routine,"* he lied. Then he led the way up the hill.

The *combattant* waited impatiently as they struggled in the heavy sand at the top of the bank. He then led them to a parked Peugeot 404, an early 70's model with square fins, and gestured at the rear door.

"Montez," he barked, then circled around and climbed quickly into the front passenger seat, cradling his Kalichikov so that the barrel pointed out the open window. The driver could have been his younger brother, though he wore civilian clothes: a badly torn western-style knit shirt and a pair of cheap, locally-made pants. He wasn't armed, at least not as far as Mark could make out.

It was a short ride. About a kilometer north of the port, the driver pulled into the *Gendarmerie Nationale*. It was a long, one-story structure with thick masonry walls and heavy louvered shutters on the windows. The outside had once been painted pale yellow, but it was reddish-brown from the dust now. Like most of the buildings in the city, it was pock-marked with thousands of bullet holes. A large metal sign arched across the entrance identified the building, though several letters in *"Gendarmerie"* were missing.

The driver skidded to a stop in the sand, and the *combattant* jumped out. He yanked open the back door and waved impatiently for Mark and Alain to follow him. A few soldiers milling about in the parking area stopped their conversations to stare at the two reporters. Alain looked over at Mark as they hurried to keep up with the combattant, but Mark didn't return the glance.

It was going to be bad, and he was having trouble breathing now himself. He didn't have a lot left to offer somebody he didn't even know, and he sure as hell didn't feel like smiling. They followed the *combattant* inside the building. It was surprisingly crowded, mostly with soldiers, in an assortment of uniforms and half-uniforms: full-dress fatigues, khaki and the darker green, the light camouflage outfits of Goukouni's guard, and some in military tunics and blue jeans.

The entry hall was lined with weapons leaning against the wall. Most were AK-47s, but there were a few older-looking French carbines and even a portable grenade launcher.

The *combattant* led them through the large, open main room to a desk at the back. The other soldiers, mostly teenagers, glared at Mark and Alain as they passed. At the desk, an older man, obviously an officer, sat writing something in a notebook. He either didn't realize they were standing in front of him or didn't care because he kept writing for some time.

He was one of the biggest Chadians Mark had seen, with broad shoulders and a thick chest that stretched the khaki uniform tight across his biceps.

Finally, he glanced up, stern and maybe a little angry. The *combattant* stiffened and saluted sharply, but the officer stared straight and hard at Mark and Alain.

Mark, who had instinctively removed his sunglasses when he entered the building, noticed the officer still had his on. In fact, so did many of the *combattants* standing around, and Mark wondered how they could see. N'djamena had been without electricity—and running water—for more than a year so that whatever light there was came from outside. But the *Gendarmerie's* shutters, the kind that opened out from the bottom, were firmly closed, though it was still early and not hot yet.

The result was an eerie kind of twilight, with only a few threads of sunlight sneaking in, where the shutters were loose or cracked. What made it even stranger was that no one seemed to notice the darkness. It was as if it made no difference or even was preferable that way. Mark had a wild, momentary image of the lights blinking back on miraculously and the assembled troops rising as one to blast them out again.

"Alors?" The officer asked his tone a long way from friendly.

The *combattant* from the port said something quickly in Arabic. The officer's face tightened noticeably.

"Qu'est-ce que vous faites ici?" He asked, almost shouting now.

Because of the sunglasses, it was impossible to tell whether he had directed the question to Mark or Alain. Mark left it for Alain to answer. Hell, it was his language, and he'd gotten them into this in the first place. But Alain didn't speak. Out of the corner of his eye, Mark could see him, staring wild-eyed now, not at the African, but somewhere behind and above him. His breathing was so short and fast that he probably couldn't have spoken, even if he'd wanted to.

"Mon capitaine," Mark said, praying that wasn't an insult, *"on est tous les deux journaliste. On est venu pour temoigner votre victoire, et le retour au normale de la vie au Chad."*

It was bullshit, and they both knew it, but the Chadians were touchy about the Libyan presence, and it didn't seem like the time to bring it up.

The Chadian officer snorted his disgust. *"Vous etes qui?"* He demanded of Mark. Mark gave him his name, which, in any case, he had on the immigration forms in front of him.

"Americain?"

"Oui, mon capitaine," Mark replied respectfully.

The African snorted again.

"Quel journal?" He demanded.

Mark gave him the name of a paper in Boston. The Chadian had obviously never heard of it, and probably not Boston, either.

"Et vous?" He asked, his voice louder, the tone angry, addressing Alain for the first time.

Mark heard Alain try to slow down his breathing enough to answer.

"Je suis correspondant de l'Agence France Presse, mon capitaine," Alain managed, though he had to stop once in mid-sentence in order to catch his breath.

The officer stared at Alain for a second, then suddenly slammed his huge forearm onto the desktop and came halfway out of his chair.

"Les francais sont tous les laches et les menteurs," he yelled, his face not far from Alain's now. Mark had instinctively backed up a half step at the African's explosion, but Alain didn't move.

It was too late for Mark to remind the Chadian that he wasn't French, that he didn't even know Alain; it wouldn't work now. But he cursed himself for not trying it at the port. The noise elsewhere in the room stopped entirely, so Mark didn't need to turn around to know that everyone else was watching them. His heart, already pounding unhealthily in his chest and ears, kicked into a higher gear.

"Mon capitaine," Alain pleaded after what seemed like hours. His voice sounded like someone else's.

"Tais-toi!" The Chadian screamed, his face thrust forward, almost touching Alain's.

For a moment, Mark thought the African would hit him, but he didn't. They stood like that, stone still, like actors in some drama, with the room hushed around them, so quiet that Mark could hear the *combattant* from the port breathing next to him.

Finally, the officer eased slowly back into his chair. A few of the *combattants* behind them began moving again and talking. Soon, the noise was back to what it had been. The Chadian stared up at Alain for a while longer, then waved the back of his hand in the general direction of the door. He said something in Arabic to the *combattant,* who motioned with his head for Mark and Alain to follow him.

In all, the interrogation had taken five minutes. But following the combattant back to the Peugeot, now parked in the shade of an acacia tree, it was the sunlight that Mark found hard to adjust to as if the light had gained in intensity during their short time in the dark.

Alain opened the back door of the car, but the *combattant,* surprised, waved an arm at him and barked something in Arabic. Alain didn't understand, but Mark pulled him firmly by the shoulder and closed the car door.

"It's OK. We can go," he said quietly in French.

"Sorry," Mark said, a little embarrassed.

"I asked what the hell you're doing up here," Alain said. "There's nothing going on."

"Uh, one of the papers I work for wanted an update; you know, are the Libyans settling in for a long stay, and that sort of thing," Mark lied.

Alain laughed a little and shook his head. "Did they think Qadaffi was just going to pack up and go home after he had helped his good friend Goukouni?" He asked.

Like Frenchmen everywhere, Alain found Americans' views on world affairs hopelessly naive.

Mark shrugged and smiled.

The *piroguier* poled the boat expertly between two other dugouts at the "port." It was reasonably crowded, mostly with *pirogues* unloading sacks of millet or flour and even a few bags of rice, which was something of a luxury in that part of Africa.

Mark handed the Chadian two hundred CFA pieces, then hopped out of the *pirogue* and struggled in the deep sand to catch up to Alain. The immigration shack was empty now, so Mark and Alain trudged up the sandy bank to where the taxis waited for fares. They passed a half-dozen young boys struggling in the sand with *pousse-pousses,* a kind of local wheelbarrow, that were loaded with the food sacks brought over in the *pirogues.* The boys took them up the hill, then unloaded the sacks into a waiting taxi and hurried back down the slope for another load.

"Is there much food in town?" Mark asked Alain.

Alain shrugged. "More than before, but no one's getting fat," he replied. "The market is open most days now, though."

“What do people pay with?” He asked, trying to sound simply curious.

Alain shook his head. “You know the Africans; they’ve always got something stashed away.”

Mark didn’t know anything of the kind, but he grunted his agreement. Either Alain was holding out, or he didn’t know about the dollars. Or else Emil was full of shit. The taxi drivers, who had been standing quietly in a group talking, ran at Mark and Alain as they approached, elbowing each other and hissing *“messieurs, messieurs.”*

Mark and Alain ignored them and walked to the first taxi in line, a battered white Peugeot, and climbed in the back seat. The driver, a thin young man dressed in a full, sky-blue boubou and cheap black sunglasses, climbed quickly behind the wheel and started the motor.

He glanced in the rear-view mirror.

“L’Hotel Tchadien,” Alain ordered.

CHAPTER 4

The taxi headed north on Avenue Charles de Gaulle, which ran the length of N'djamena, more or less parallel to the river.

A handful of workers were plastering over the bullet holes that marred the facade of the Chad-Libyan Bank like some architectural acne. Mark turned for another look as they passed the building and saw that the north wall had already been patched and whitewashed.

That was the exception, though. Just up the road, the once neat, two-story U.S. Embassy lay in rubble, with half the upper level blown open by a direct mortar hit. On the ground floor, windows and doors had been blown or kicked out, and Mark caught a glimpse of papers strewn everywhere.

The evacuation had been chaotic, by most accounts, with hushed-up stories of panic and forgotten procedures in high places. There were also unconfirmed reports that the Americans had left sensitive documents behind in the embassy's safe and were more than a little worried they would fall into Libyan, and thus Soviet, hands.

Mark had a hard time picturing Martin Feraldi, face

blackened, swimming the Chari in the dead of night to retrieve them, but maybe they had special teams for that sort of thing.

Or else it was all bullshit; that kind of rumor was always floating around Africa.

There were a few more cars on the street now, mostly taxis and the Toyota Land Cruisers the *combattants* favored. More people, too, not just the soldiers any more, but civilians, even some women carrying bowls or baskets on their heads.

But N'djamena still had a long way to go. *Combattants,* alone or in small groups, and all heavily armed, were everywhere, walking in the dust on the side of the road or just standing in the shade of the now mortar-blackened trees that, along with the river setting, had once given the city a surprising grace and charm.

Clean-up hadn't even begun. The streets were littered with a mixture of rubble from the blasted buildings and garbage and goods from households and stores that had either been destroyed in the fighting or ransacked later.

Except for the Libyan Bank, there was no sign of reconstruction anywhere. Mark didn't know much about architecture, but it was clear that many of the capital's buildings would have to be razed and rebuilt from scratch.

More than anything visible, though, N'djamena had a hollow feeling to it, a kind of numbness, like some trauma victim whose pain had been mercifully postponed by shock. At the same time, there was a constant tension in the air, as if those who had returned, knowing that it was only for a short time, kept nervously checking to see that the river and relative safety were never too far away.

The Hotel Tchadien was on the north side of the city, about a half kilometer back from the river, not far from the airport. The building itself was a flat, graceless structure with two symmetrical wings jutting out in opposite directions from a central lobby, like an oversized, vaguely abstract copy of a 1950s-era American motel. It hadn't had electricity or running water for well over a year, and the bathrooms just off the lobby stunk overpoweringly of the shit that overflowed the dry toilet bowls.

What little glass the French architects designed into the hotel had long since been shot out by one faction or the other. But given its location (for a while, the war had raged virtually on its doorstep), the Tchadien had held up relatively well, certainly better than many other buildings in town.

There were measles-like pock marks from automatic weapons fire on most of the exterior walls, but no gaping mortar holes anywhere, and most of the hotel's furniture had survived the fighting intact.

It was also the best place in N'djamena to pick up news. The few diplomats and aid workers who had returned to Chad stayed there, and it wasn't unusual to run into one of Goukouni's top aides, or even an occasional Libyan officer, in the dining room or at the outdoor bar in the back.

The taxi skidded to a stop in the sand driveway that curved around the front of the lobby. Mark yanked on the inside lever, but nothing happened. The driver, remembering it didn't work, jumped out and, with a quick, firm tug, opened it from the outside.

"A toute a l'heure, Mark," Alain said, not moving. *"Je dois voir quelqu'un."*

"D'accord," Mark said, relieved. He didn't want any company chasing the dollar story, and now he wouldn't have to make up an excuse.

"I'll meet you here at one for lunch?" Alain asked.

"Or we can have a Gala later," Mark hedged. Money was tight, and he was never that hungry in Chad anyway. He took his time digging in his pocket for change to pay the driver.

"Ca va, Mark," Alain said, shaking his head.

"I'll get you later," Mark said, hoping that wouldn't be necessary.

The taxi roared back onto the street, with the driver changing gears only when the whine became unbearable.

Mark walked up the steps of the hotel and into the lobby. It was a large room whose ceiling seemed even higher than it was because of the twilight-like darkness. Curtains, made of thick green velour fabric, covered the windows at the back, near the door to the terrace. The reception desk was up front, just inside the door, which was a lucky break for the young African behind it; anywhere else would have made it difficult to see the forms that even the Tchadien made its guests fill out.

"Bonjour," Mark said, giving a short, lazy salute.

"Bonjour, monsieur," the African said, polite but not returning the smile. *"Vous voulez une chambre?"*

Mark hoped not. *"Peut-etre,"* he said. *"Le bar est-il ouvert?"*

"Oui, monsieur," the African said.

Mark walked across the dark lobby and out onto the terrace. It had probably once been, if not beautiful, a pleasant place to eat or have a drink. But the war and years of neglect had taken a toll. The empty pool, with wide, unseemly cracks in the cement and a puddle of black water in the shallow end, gave the terrace the feel of a vacant lot. What little shrubbery had survived the war, and the water cutoff was leafless and dying.

Mark crossed over to the bar, a large open area with a cement floor and canvas canopy to keep out the sun. There were a dozen battered wooden tables with chairs. Three young *combattants* in the dark green uniform of Kamougue's southern forces sat at the table nearest the counter, drinking beer.

They glanced up briefly at Mark with the same sullen defiance that had become something of a trend, like the aviator sunglasses they all wore, even in the shade. Mark ignored them and sat down at a table where he could see the rest of the terrace and the lobby door. A waiter appeared, and Mark ordered a Gala.

Four months earlier, beer had been in short supply, as had just about everything, but apparently, that was no longer the case.

Mark thought about asking if there was anything to eat when the waiter returned with the beer, but then decided against it. He could make it until dinner, and he hoped to eat across the river at the *relais.*

The beer was lukewarm, but it tasted fine anyway. Among expatriates who had been around, Gala has generally been considered the best beer in Africa; better than Star in Nigeria and even the Harp lager the Guiness brewery in Douala turned out. It was the one thing anyone coming to Chad could look forward to.

A murmur of voices came to Mark from the other side of the pool. He hadn't seen them when he walked out onto the terrace, but now he noticed two men talking animatedly at a table near where the diving board had once been. Mark recognized one of them, a short, heavy-set Frenchman with dark hair and the olive skin of a Mediterranean, but he had never seen the other one before.

He wasn't an African, or at least not a Chadian. He was probably about Mark's age, with curly, very black hair and a full, dark mustache. His complexion wasn't much different from the Frenchman's; he might even have been French, from Marseilles or Corsica.

Probably, though, he was Libyan.

Mark sipped his beer and watched them. They were too far away for him to eavesdrop, and in any case, from the sounds that drifted across the terrace, they were speaking Arabic, which Mark did not understand.

Calvady, the Frenchman, spoke a lot more than the Libyan—if that's what he was—and gestured repeatedly with his hands.

Neither of them appeared angry, but Calvady was obviously making a case for something.

The last time Mark had been up, the one phone at the Kousseri Post Office had gone down, so he and a reporter from Le Monde left at midday, racing to file stories from Maroua before their deadlines. Twenty kilometers from Kousseri, their rental car broke down.

Neither of them knew anything about motors, but Calvady, who passed them on his way back to the border, stopped and, after a quick look, unhooked the fuel line and sucked on it until gasoline started to flow again. He re-attached the line, and the car started immediately.

Mark and the French reporter had thanked him profusely. It was the middle of the day, and they were a long way even from the nearest village. But Calvady waved aside their thanks.

Thirty years earlier, he explained, he'd been a trucker running goods from N'djamena to Abeche. Once, his truck had broken down on an isolated stretch of road in the desert. He spent a day under the truck, out of the sun, before another vehicle passed. It was an African, alone, in a beat-up Berliet. He managed to get Calvady's truck going again, then followed him for two days, fixing it several more times, until they reached Abeche.

"He saved my life, no question about it," Calvady explained. "I offered to pay him, but the only payment he wanted was my promise never to pass anyone stranded on the road. I've wanted to, many times, but then I remember what it was like lying under that truck, and I always stop."

Mark drained his glass, disappointed, a little surprised, really, that he had already finished his beer. He glanced over at Calvady and the Libyan. Mark didn't want to interrupt their discussion, but he wanted to talk to Calvady, and he couldn't wait all day. If he left and came back, the Frenchman might be gone, and there was no guarantee Mark would be able to find him.

And Mark had to talk to him. Calvady had lived most of his life in Chad, even stayed through a lot of the fighting; if anyone knew something about the dollars, he would. Mark fought the urge to have another Gala and got up. He dropped 200 CFA on the table and walked toward the pool.

"Monsieur Calvady?"

The Frenchman looked up sharply, stopping in mid-sentence.

"Oui?" His eyes widened in question. He was friendly enough, but wary, too, like someone who'd been asked for too many favors in his life and gotten used to turning them down.

He obviously didn't remember Mark.

"Uh, you helped me a couple of months ago when my car broke down," Mark said, struggling a little and feeling the blood rush into his cheeks.

"Ah bon," Calvady said. He was still polite, but there was a hint of impatience in his voice.

"Over in Cameroon," Mark tried. Shit, it had only been a couple of months. "I was with another journalist; we had a clogged fuel line, and uh, you..."

"Ah oui," Calvady nodded, remembering. *"Vous etes anglais."*

"Americain," Mark said, nodding as if they were the same thing.

Calvady's companion, who had put up with the interruption calmly, maybe even a little bored, now turned slightly in his seat to get a better look at Mark.

Mark met his dark, expressionless gaze for just a second. The bastard was Libyan, no doubt about it. He had the tan skin and European features of a Berber. His clothes, a pair of plain, formless cotton pants and a short-sleeve button-down shirt were identical to the Chinese and North Korean imports Mark had seen in places like Conakry and Malabo.

"Alors, ca va?" Calvady asked. He wasn't pushing, really, but he clearly wanted to get back to what he'd been discussing with the Libyan.

"Oui, merci," Mark said quickly. "I'm very sorry to disturb you, but I wanted to say thanks again."

"It was nothing," Calvady smiled, meaning it.

"I was hoping I could buy you a beer at least," Mark said. He was running out of things to say, and the son of a bitch Libyan hadn't taken his eyes off him.

"Ah, merci, but I must leave shortly," Calvady said.

"Dommage," Mark shrugged. It wasn't going to work. "Maybe another time." He started to back away.

"Yes, of course; maybe tonight at the Hotel Chari," Calvady said politely, not caring one way or the other.

"Tres bien," Mark said. *"A ce soir."*

He nodded at the Libyan, who didn't acknowledge the gesture, then turned and walked toward the lobby. He'd have to stay the night now; there was no way around it. The curfew was still in effect, and the Chadians didn't kid around about things like that.

But Mark had stayed in worse places than the Tchadien and for longer than one night. He'd just cross over at dawn and, with a little luck, still get to Maroua in time for the last flight to Douala.

The African at the desk pulled out a registration form, and Mark filled in the information quickly. They were always the same: name, address, nationality, passport number, and date and place of birth. Has anyone in Chad ever even heard of Buffalo, New York?

Mark slid the card back across the counter, and the clerk handed him a key.

As it turned out, he didn't need it: the locks on both sides of the room's door had been pulled out, leaving a sizeable hole. The room itself was dark, like the lobby, with the same green curtains covering a narrow window that faced the hotel's front "garden."

Mark felt a thin, almost invisible layer of sand on the linoleum floor as he walked over and deposited his bag on the bed, a single, metal frame model. A rough gray blanket was folded neatly near the foot of the foam mattress, but there was no sheet or pillow. He walked over and pulled back the curtain to let in some light. The window had been shot out, and a pile of broken glass covered the floor near the curtain.

Mark stood for a moment, looking out at the "garden," which might once have been pretty but now was a barren, parched patch of sand between the hotel and the road. He could feel the heat wafting through the hole where the window had been. He looked at his watch. Not even 10:30 yet. It was one of Africa's curious distortions: the combination of an early start and the crushing heat made the daylight hours seem so much longer that mid-morning felt like three in the afternoon.

And three in the afternoon felt like hell on earth.

Mark closed the curtains and, after a second's hesitation, picked up his bag and left.

CHAPTER 5

The sergeant said he'd been a teacher at a lycee in Moundou until he joined the southern forces near the end of the fighting. Probably after it was clear that Habre was finished, Mark figured, but saw no reason to bring it up. Mark had picked him up at the Presidential Villa, where he'd gone on the off chance he could wangle an interview with Goukouni or one of his top aides.

But Goukouni was "out of the country," which meant Tripoli, and all his aides were tied up, as they usually were unless Le Monde or French TV were in town. The sergeant was a kind of consolation prize, ordered to show Mark around Habre's old stronghold, which until recently had been off limits to reporters.

Mark had read Alain's piece on it in Le Monde, so it wasn't exactly fresh news, but it hadn't gotten much play in the U.S., so he could probably sell it to someone.

They didn't find a cab until they'd walked halfway back to the Avenue Charles de Gaulle. Mark was sweating freely when one finally stopped. The driver turned out to be a Southerner, so Mark's guide spoke to him firmly in Sara. The driver wasn't impressed. He turned in his seat, held out a hand, and said something back.

"He wants to know if you are paying," the soldier explained, turning a little toward Mark in the back seat, but not enough that he had to look him in the eye.

"Oui, oui," Mark said impatiently, waving at the driver to get going.

It was hot in the car, even with all the windows open and the car moving, but it was a damn sight better than walking.

They turned onto de Gaulle at the Hotel Chari—N'djamena's other resting place and by almost any measure a nicer place than the Tchadien—then headed south along the river.

Mark's guide was talkative and friendly, eager to please, really, like a lot of the Southerners. It was no wonder the French liked them. The sergeant's smile disappeared, though, at the mention of pay, and Mark thought for a moment he'd blown it. It wasn't the question, though, but the government's extremely slow payments that prompted the change in mood.

He brightened noticeably when Mark explained that he was American. Did Mark want to buy some dollars? Mark said that he didn't have too many CFA with him, but maybe on his next visit. How many dollars were they talking about?

The Chadian reached into his shirt pocket and withdrew two fifty-dollar bills. That was a lot of money for a sergeant anywhere in Africa—in Chad, it was a small fortune.

Mark inspected the two bills closely. Like Emil's, they weren't brand new, but they were not falling apart either. As far as he could tell, they were real.

"Where did you get them?" Mark asked as casually as he could manage, handing the bills back to the African.

"Les Libyans," the sergeant replied, surprised Mark had to ask. "But you can't buy anything with them," he added disgustedly; "you have to change them into CFA."

"Is the Central Bank open again?" Mark asked, knowing it wasn't.

The Chadian shook his head. "You have to take them to one of the big *commercants,* but they say there are too many dollars now, and they can't change them all."

He stuffed the bills back in his shirt pocket like so much scrap paper.

"What do you do if the *commercants* won't change them?" Mark asked, trying to keep it conversational.

The Chadian shrugged. "Take them to the Frenchman, but he pays less than the *commercants,"* he explained.

Mark didn't see how else to word it. "Which Frenchman is that?" He asked.

The sergeant, who had been talking freely, glanced over at Mark, who was afraid he'd pushed too hard. But the African shrugged and looked back at the road.

"I don't know his name," he said. "He's old and fat and always wearing little shorts." Mark almost laughed. Africans were amazed and revolted at the idea of grown men, especially older ones like Calvady, running around in little more than their underwear. And it was Calvady they were talking about. Mark hesitated, trying to decide if it was worth the risk.

"How much does he give you for one of those?" He asked, gesturing at the sergeant's shirt pocket.

"Deux mille cinq cents," the Chadian replied. *"C'est bon?"* He asked, suddenly remembering Mark was an expert.

Mark had to clear his throat. *"Uh, oui, c'est pas mal,"* he said, nodding his assurance.

It was damn good—for Calvady. Five thousand CFA, about $25, for two fifty-dollar bills. Holy shit. Anybody with some CFA and a way to change the dollars, even if it was at a discount on the Nigerian black market, could make a fortune.

Mark stared out the window, thinking hard. They passed the *lycee,* its sprawling sand playing field empty. The school hadn't reopened yet, and it was hard to imagine the teenagers Mark had met, with their Kalashinikovs and their sunglasses, meekly returning to class.

Something didn't add up: Emil was African, so the chances of his getting picked up in Nigeria were pretty slim. But a Frenchman, running around Maiduguri in his short pants with a sack full of dollars, was another story. Maybe Calvady had an African partner.

The taxi jolted off the paved road. Mark had forgotten for a moment where they were headed. The dirt roads in the African *quartier*, Habre's old stronghold, were rutted and uneven, and the driver slowed a little to spare the car's already worn suspension.

The three of them automatically rolled up the windows against the swirling cloud of dust kicked up by the car. It made the inside of the car stiflingly hot, but that was preferable to the dust. There were no villas in the African *quartier*, only mud-brick huts or an occasional, crudely built cement house, all with corrugated metal rooves that had long since lost their shine and now glinted, dull, and gray in the hot sun.

The driver veered right and fishtailed toward the river. Near one of the *quartier's* larger compounds, Mark's guide said something in Sara, and the taxi skidded to a halt.

"C'est ici," the sergeant said to Mark as he opened the door.

Mark slid down the short incline to the riverbank, which stretched a good 25 meters to the water now that the Chari had receded to its dry season configuration.

Alain's article was detailed and graphic, so Mark had a pretty good idea of what to expect. The first pile of bones, close to the high-water mark, were bleached neat and white and could have been the remnants of any kind of animal—except for the handful of skulls, surprisingly small, that sat upright in the sand a short distance away.

"Regardez," the Chadian commanded, bending over and

pointing at the backs of the skulls. Each had a small, neatly circular hole in roughly the same place.

The sergeant, who had obviously done the tour before, straightened up and strode toward the water. *"Venez,"* he called impatiently to Mark, who lingered over the skulls. Closer to the water, there were better-preserved skeletons, dozens of them, just in the short stretch of beach that was visible from where Mark stood.

One lay on its side, a pair of green running shorts hanging limply to the pelvic bones. There was a pair of western-style sneakers, still laced, on its feet. Most of the skeletons had been picked clean, either during their time underwater or, more recently, by the enormous vultures that roamed from the Waza Game Park, south of Kousseri, up into Chad.

A few of the bodies still had some flesh on them, just scraps really, parched, dry and white and stiff, that fluttered like paper in the light breeze. Many of the skeletons had their wrist bones bound together, with wire or cheap cord mostly, though one was tied with a length of bright green nylon rope, the expensive kind that was hard to find in Africa.

"Venez," the sergeant called, walking quickly downriver. He was getting into his work. "There are many more."

"Merci, ca suffit," Mark said, more sharply than he'd intended. He got the idea. The Chadian stopped abruptly, slightly confused, maybe even disappointed. Mark turned and headed back to the taxi. He could hear the sergeant's footsteps crunching in the sand as he followed.

Mark did not meet Alain for lunch. He wasn't in the mood, for one thing, and now he couldn't afford it. He'd have to pay for the room at the Tchadien and whatever Calvady drank, assuming he showed up at the Hotel Chari.

Maybe the old bastard would offer to pay. God knew he could afford it.

Mark's guide, who was clearly in no hurry to get back to his post, suggested a tour of the southern part of the city, and Mark agreed. The dollars were his big story; if he could get the details —hell, even if he couldn't, he'd do something on it, but a fast and easy color piece on life returning to normal in war-torn N'djamena might sell too.

After a short, animated argument in Sara between the driver and the sergeant, Mark assumed over money, they headed east, away from the river. Habre's old stronghold was emptier than other parts of the city, which was no surprise. In spite of an amnesty offer, most of Habre's supporters were still holed up in the refugee camps in Kousseri.

The central market, however, was crowded. The small, square stalls did not have much in them, not even compared to a backwater like Kousseri, and luxuries like meat and vegetables just weren't available. But there was food, millet mostly, and some rice, which the *commercants* scooped out of 50-kilo sacks and weighed on ancient, blackened scales.

Mark didn't see any dollars, but he didn't really expect to. The smaller merchants wouldn't take them; most of them probably had no idea what they were.

The driver headed back toward the center of the city through *quartiers* Mark didn't recognize.

The taxi was stopped several times at checkpoints around the city, but the gut-twisting tension of four months earlier was gone. The *combattants* manning the posts were calmer, at times even bored, and most simply accepted the explanation given by Mark's guide and let them pass.

Mark decided to push their luck and ordered the taxi driver to head east on the road to the airport, where the Libyan troops were said to be bivouacked.

They didn't get far. Three heavily armed soldiers, all in the light gray uniforms of the Libyan army, pulled the taxi over just east of the airport turnoff. Another man, whom Mark hadn't seen at first, emerged from the shade of a tree near the side of the road and walked over to the taxi.

He was older than the other three and shorter, with broad shoulders and a full, very black mustache. He wore a slightly different cap than the other three, but the uniform was the same. There was no doubt he was in charge. He glanced quickly at the driver, then much longer at Mark in the back seat. Finally, he said something quietly in Arabic. The driver and Mark's guide, who had been nervous about the detour to begin with, and was now scared shitless, got out of the car with all the enthusiasm of condemned men taking their last walk.

Mark opened his door to follow, but one of the younger soldiers said something sharply in Arabic and shoved the door closed again. He wasn't invited.

The driver and the southerner followed the officer—Mark had decided that's what he was—back into the shade on the side of the road. The three younger soldiers drifted back enough to get out of the sun, but two of them kept an eye on Mark in the taxi.

Mark couldn't hear what the Libyan said to the driver and the sergeant, but he didn't need to; it was a reprimand, polite but firm. The two Chadians didn't open their mouths, but nodded repeatedly.

They didn't actually run back to the car, but almost. The driver made a wide, skidding turn on the laterite road and whined quickly through the gears, heading back the way they'd come. Mark's guide muttered something about forgetting he was on duty shortly, then stared out the window. No one spoke again until the taxi stopped in front of the Tchadien.

Mark paid the driver and thanked the sergeant. He lied and said he hoped the Chadian would have a beer with him next time Mark was in town. The sergeant quickly hopped out of the taxi. He had enough time for one now if they hurried, he said stiffly, his pride still a little dented.

Shit, Mark thought. *"Tres bien,"* he said.

It was 2:30 and very hot, even under the shade on the terrace. Mark was glad not to run into Alain, who either hadn't waited for him or, like Mark, hadn't bothered to show up. The sergeant soaked Mark for two Galas and even then made no move to go, his duty apparently forgotten. So, Mark lied and said he had to go to his room and write a story.

CHAPTER 6

Mark left for the Chari Hotel shortly before sundown. He couldn't find a taxi, so he ended up walking. It wasn't that far, no more than a 20-minute walk, but the sun dropped quickly that close to the Equator, and it was getting dark when he entered the lobby.

The Chari was the older of N'djamena's two hotels, a still elegant three-story structure with an open terrace garden in the back that sloped gently down to the river bank. Apart from a splattering of bullet marks on the outside walls, the Chari had survived the war better than many of the capital's other buildings.

Mark passed through the lobby, dark except for two lit candles on the reception desk, and out onto the terrace. Reasonably intact garden chairs and low tables were spaced discreetly around the terrace. A lighted candle on each table almost managed to lend the place an air of quiet, easy charm.

Mark was surprised to see most of the tables occupied, almost half with expatriates. He waved to a group of Catholic Relief Service workers he had met in Kousseri the last time he'd been up. So it was safe enough for them to come back. He'd stick that in his feature; it was a nice detail. He didn't see Calvady right away, then spotted him at a table halfway down the garden toward the river.

The old Frenchman was sitting alone but leaning back in his chair, talking to a group of younger whites at the next table. Mark walked over. As he got closer, he recognized the three bearded men and a heavy-set woman with short hair as members of a Medcins sans Frontieres team. Mark had seen them work once on a teenage combattant with a bullet in his side.

It was at a makeshift hospital outside Kousseri that smelled of blood and too many people. The fighting was heavy at the time, and the hospital tent was jammed with wounded men on filthy cots and their families who squatted around them, feeding them or swatting futilely at the swarms of flies that buzzed everywhere.

The doctors performed the surgery, with only local anesthetic, on an operating table in the middle of the crowded tent.

Mark nodded at the doctors and the nurse, and they did the same. They didn't look as exhausted this time, but their faces all had the drained, pale intensity that chronic overwork and commitment seemed to produce.

"Bon soir, Monsieur Calvady," Mark said as soon as there was a pause in the Frenchman's conversation.

Calvady turned, the wariness there again, then a smile when he recognized Mark.

"Bon soir; assez-vous," he said, gesturing at a chair. Calvady leaned back just to finish his conversation with the medical team, then turned and smiled at Mark.

"Vous prennez une biere?" He asked, then laughed. "There isn't anything else."

"Yes, thanks," Mark said, "but I wanted to buy you one."

Calvady pursed his lips and waved his hand; he was buying.

"Non, mais j'insiste," Mark protested, hoping he didn't sound too insistent.

"You buy another time, my friend," Calvady said. He raised a hand, and an African in a clean white jacket appeared out of the darkness. Calvady drained the last of a Gala into his glass, handed the waiter the empty bottle, and ordered two more.

"So, what did you see today?" Calvday asked, smiling. "The beach?"

"Yes, I saw the beach," Mark replied, not sure how to bring up the dollars.

"Impressive, isn't it?" Calvady asked. "Of course, the others executed people too; that's war. But Habre...," he said, shaking his head slowly. *"C'est un vrai sauvage."*

Calvady sipped his beer, then leaned forward slightly and lowered his voice.

"Unfortunately, he is probably the only one who could end this shit, once and for all," he said.

"So, you don't think it's over?" Mark asked, keeping his voice low, too.

Calvady exhaled sharply in disgust, shaking his head.

The waiter brought their beers. He filled Mark's glass halfway, then left the bottle on the table. Calvady dug in the pocket of his shorts and pulled out a large wad of CFA. From their table in the middle of the terrace, Mark could see the water, shining black in the moonlight, and beyond it, the dim outline of the far bank on the Cameroon side.

Downstream, in the distance, the cooking fires in the refugee camps flickered like candles in the wind.

"A votre sante," Calvady said, raising his glass for a moment before taking a long drink.

"Merci; et a la votre," Mark said, doing the same. "And thanks again for helping us on the road."

Calvady pursed his lips and waved a hand again. "It was nothing," he said, and meant it.

Mark had felt heavy and a little drunk from the two beers with the Chadian soldier in the midday heat; now, though, with a breeze blowing up from the river, drying the sweat inside his shirt and on the back of his neck, the Gala tasted good, and Mark felt his body relax into the garden chair.

They both drank for a moment in silence; then Mark leaned forward slightly and poured himself some more beer to break the mood. Is there any possibility of doing business in Chad yet? He asked. Calvady shrugged. Perhaps, he said, though it would be very difficult. Mark nodded.

How would the Chadians pay? The Central Bank was closed, and as far as anyone knew, the Treasury was empty. Calvady shrugged again; it wasn't the Chadians who would pay, he said.

That left the Libyans, Mark said quietly. Calvady inclined his head a notch, bowing to the obvious, without actually confirming anything. Mark could feel the Frenchman's wariness, even a vague unhappiness at the turn the conversation had taken; he'd forgotten for a moment that Mark was a reporter.

What kind of business was there to be had? Mark asked, backing off a little.

Calvady spread his arms, smiling at the question. There was enough rebuilding in N'djamena to keep every French construction company in Africa busy for years.

But wouldn't it be risky to bring back equipment and personnel? It was calm for the moment, but that meant little in Chad.

Calvady shrugged.

"You have to take risks to make money," he said.

"Whom do you negotiate with?" Mark asked, not caring. He was trying to get them close to money again.

"Ah!" Calvady said, throwing his hands up just a little. *"Voila le probleme."* He raised a hand at a waiter serving a group two tables over.

"Une autre biere," Calvady said when the African hurried over.

"Monsieur?" The waiter asked Mark as he removed the empty Gala bottle in front of Calvady. Mark realized he had been talking and thinking more than drinking. He filled his glass and guzzled what was left in the bottle.

"Oui, merci," he said, handing the empty to the waiter.

"Who do you write for?" Calvday asked as the waiter headed off.

Mark named a paper he wrote for more or less regularly. Calvady nodded, feigning interest. He'd never heard of it, and he was getting bored.

"There seem to be a lot of U.S. dollars floating around N'djamena these days," Mark said quietly. Calvady had his glass to his lips. He stared at Mark over the top of the glass, not bored anymore.

"Ah, oui?" He asked.

"People say the Libyans are using them to pay the Chadian soldiers," Mark said.

Calvady shrugged and shook his head.

"Je n'en sais rien," he lied.

The waiter brought the beers, poured them, and left. The French medical team got up to go. They exchanged goodbyes with Calvady and nodded to Mark. They were probably going into the hotel restaurant to eat. Even the Chari wouldn't have much; maybe an omelette and *frites* or rice and fish, the small fresh-water kind they pulled from the Chari that had a thousand tiny bones.

Mark hadn't eaten since breakfast, and that had only been bread and coffee, but he wasn't hungry, just a little light-headed from the beer. It felt good to be sitting outside in the night air, cool at last, drinking a good beer. The thought of moving to the restaurant, which would still be hot from the trapped heat, didn't appeal to him at all.

Even the dollar story right then didn't matter, not really.

He'd drop it, and Calvady could relax again, and they could drink some more and talk about what it was like 30-some years ago when the Frenchman first came out.

But when Calvady turned back to look at Mark, it was to excuse himself, maybe even to go join the doctors. It was in his face and the way he pressed down on the arms of his chair.

"Ecoutez, mon ami... ""

The *combattants* say you change dollars for them sometimes," Mark said, slurring his words just a little.

Calvady's arms came back to the table. He stared at Mark for a moment, then down at his nearly full glass of beer.

"Do you intend to write a story about this?" He asked.

"That depends," Mark lied.

Calvady leaned back, sipping his beer. He glanced calmly back at the tables behind them, but they were empty, except for one up near the hotel lobby, where two Africans sat talking quietly.

It was dinnertime, and most of the people who had been drinking on the terrace were in the restaurant.

Calvady looked across the candle at Mark. He didn't look angry or even particularly concerned, but he wasn't thinking about leaving anymore.

"Listen, my friend," he said finally; "you said I did you a favor on the road over in Cameroon. Now, I would ask one in return."

"I assure you I won't use your name—if you give me the details," Mark said, trying to limit Calvady's appeal.

The Frenchman sipped his beer, thinking.

"Or that I'm French," he insisted.

"I'll just say a West European source," Mark hedged.

"No, everyone will still know. A well-informed source," Calvady suggested.

That didn't mean shit, and most editors wouldn't buy it, not from a stringer, anyway.

"A long-time business source," Mark countered.

Calvady shook his head emphatically.

"That could be an African or anybody," Mark said, trying to keep his impatience from showing.

Calvady exhaled noisily. "What do you want to know?" He asked.

"First, how many dollars are we talking about?"

Calvady shook his head impatiently. "Impossible to say. Ouf, maybe the Libyans know, but they aren't telling me," he said.

"What's your guess? Are we talking thousands, or tens of thousands, or what?" Mark pressed. Calvady stared hard at Mark across the table. The son of a bitch didn't like this at all.

"Over a million, probably; possibly more," he said.

It was Mark's turn to stare. *"Nom de Dieu."*

"Ah oui, c'est beaucoup d'argent dans un pays comme le Tchad," Calvady agreed. *"Mais ce n'est rien pour la Libye."*

"Why dollars?" Mark asked. "Why not CFA or French francs?"

"Dollars are easier for Libya; all their oil is paid for with dollars," Calvady replied.

"But why don't they just use the dollars to buy CFA or francs and then bring them in? It'd make more sense."

"Ecoutez, mon ami, demandez ca aux Libyens," Calvady said, not trying anymore to hide his exasperation.

"But it doesn't make sense," Mark insisted. He wanted the story now. It was a big one if he could explain it all, and no one else had it or was probably even close. It had been a long time since he'd been first with a major story. A long goddamn time.

Calvady sat staring at Mark, wanting to stop there, to get up and walk away because there was nothing in it for him except trouble. But he needed to know what was going to be written, to control it if he could. He rubbed a hand back and forth across his forehead, then exhaled deeply.

"There is not much of a market for CFA or even francs for that matter," he said, lowering his voice further. "And both currencies are tightly controlled. Anyone trying to buy large quantities of either would almost certainly draw attention to themselves," Calvady explained.

He hesitated, then went on. "There was a rumor some months ago that the Libyans tried to buy a large amount of CFA through a Swiss company they control, but they were blocked at the last minute by French intelligence."

"Do you know anyone who might be able to confirm that?" Mark asked.

Calvady made a face. "The Libyans," he suggested.

Mark ignored the sarcasm. He didn't give a damn what Calvady thought of him; besides, he wanted to keep the bastard talking.

"So, the Libyans didn't really have a choice," he prompted.

"The dollar is an international currency," Calvady said as if explaining a simple idea to a particularly slow student.

"Whose exchange rate can vary enormously depending on the circumstances?" Mark asked.

Calvady shrugged. "Supply and demand, like everything else," he replied.

Mark poured what was left of his beer into his glass. He looked back toward the hotel, hoping to spot the waiter. He wanted another beer, and he needed a little time to work out his next question.

The two Africans got up to go, and almost immediately, a waiter appeared out of the darkness to snuff out the candle on their table. Without electricity, candles were a valuable commodity in Chad and probably damned expensive. Supply and demand.

Mark had to yell to the waiter to get his attention; when he came over to their table, Mark ordered a Gala.

"Monsieur?" The African asked Calvady.

"Non, merci," the Frenchman said, not looking up.

Maybe he'd had a few before Mark arrived, or maybe he thought Mark was trying to get him drunk.

The waiter left. It was quite dark now on the terrace, with all but their candle extinguished. Mark could still make out the river, though only because it was a slightly different shade of black than the banks on either side. There were fewer fires flickering in the refugee camps, and they seemed smaller and farther away.

"I know the *commercants* and some Cameroonians are taking their dollars across to Nigeria to change them," he said, looking back at Calvady and leaving the question unspoken.

The Frenchman emitted a hiss, full of disgust and frustration.

"La, vous commencez a m'emmerder, monsieur," he said, anger creeping into his voice for the first time.

Mark didn't blame him, but he didn't care either. It had been a long time since he'd wanted a story, gotten excited about it so that, for a little while anyway, it was all that mattered. It was partly the beer, of course, but that didn't change anything.

Calvady stared across the table at him, his mouth set tightly as if he never intended to open it again. They were a strange breed, the old colonialists and a dying one, but it was hard to drum up much sympathy for them. In some ways, they knew Africa and the Africans better than anyone, but for all their years there, and in most cases, an inability to survive anywhere else, including France, they clung to the memories of empire and the us-versus-them mentality that forbade any assimilation.

Calvady probably kept in touch with the African trucker who saved his life and may even have shared a beer from time to time with him, but he would no more have invited the African and his family over for dinner than he would have let a wild beast into his home.

The waiter emerged silently from the blackness behind

Calvady as if a piece of darkness had taken on outline, then substance.

It came to Mark as the waiter poured his beer. Just like that, clear and certain, the way things sometimes did when he was younger, when his ambition was still intact, and before the line between his instincts and the rationalizations had blurred.

It was the beer, mostly, and Mark had enough practice with alcohol to avoid putting much faith in that kind of epiphany. But this time was different.

Of course, Calvady didn't sell the dollars in Nigeria. Emil and the others would be satisfied buying them at twenty-five cents on the dollar and selling them in Maiduguri for 50 cents, which is probably all they'd get from the black marketeers there.

But that wasn't enough for Calvady, especially factoring in the risks of a white man crossing over frequently and subtracting whatever bribes he had to pay.

The waiter left. Mark watched him dissolve into the darkness back toward the lobby.

No, a $5,000 or $10,000 profit was a fortune for Emil or most of the *commercants,* but it wasn't nearly enough for a European to risk a Nigerian jail. Calvady could have used an African accomplice, but that would have reduced the take even more and put him at the mercy of a black man, an unacceptable combination.

So, he was taking them out. Paying 25 cents on the dollar, then taking them to Europe, Switzerland maybe, or Lichtenstein, where bankers didn't ask questions, and exchanging them for their full value.

Calvady drank what was left of his glass of beer. He glanced quickly at his watch in the candlelight and pushed his chair back. He was leaving. Limited to where it was, the story couldn't do him too much harm.

"Je vous prie de m'excuser, mon ami," he said, getting to his feet. There was a formality to his words, but the anger was gone.

Calvady reached in his pocket for the wad of CFA.

"The only thing I'm not clear on, *Monsieur* Calvady, is whether you take the dollars out through Cameroon and catch the SwissAir flight on Friday to Geneva or whether you've got a deal with the Libyans and go out through Tripoli," Mark said.

He was breathing harder now and had trouble getting it all out without a pause for air.

Calvady stopped counting CFA notes and stared down at Mark. After a moment, he slid the money back into his pocket and sat down again.

It was the second one, through Libya; Mark hadn't been certain, but now he was. Calvady could get all the way to Douala with a small bribe at the Chad border; there was no regular customs search on the flight down from Maroua.

Then, he could simply check the dollars at the SwissAir counter and walk out through immigration and customs clean.

But the problem was that even on local flights, Cameroon airport police sometimes checked bags, as did *gendarmes* at the country's numerous roadblocks. And the Cameroonians could be tough as hell, especially on a Frenchman with a suitcase full of illegal currency.

"I don't understand what you are asking," Calvady said, settling back into the chair.

The hell you don't, pal. But Mark admired the Frenchman's poise. He was nervous, maybe even a little scared now, but he didn't show it. His hands were steady on the table in front of him, and his words came quietly, unhurried.

Mark repeated what he'd said, but just for form; they both knew what the question was.

It was the Libyans, he knew; it made more sense. There hadn't been a commercial flight into N'djamena in over a year, but Libyan planes flew in every day, carrying troops or supplies, then returned home.

There were regular flights from Tripoli to cities throughout Europe.

"I suppose Swiss customs might look pretty closely at a businessman who came through often with a passport full of Libyan immigration stamps," Mark continued. "But with a little help from your friends, you could get around that."

"You should be a novelist instead of a journalist, my friend," Calvady said.

"If the Libyans didn't stamp your passport, you could fly someplace else first, say Greece or Malta, where customs are a lot looser," Mark said, trying to keep the excitement out of his voice.

Calvady was shaking his head, not so much in disagreement as unhappiness with the conversation.

"You overnight there or catch a connecting flight, and then you're just another European businessman arriving from another European city," Mark said. "But eventually, you have to go through customs with the dollars. Do you just walk out the "Nothing to Declare" door?"

Calvady stared across the table at Mark, but said nothing.

"What if they stop you?" Mark asked, genuinely curious.

Calvady snorted in disgust. "What do you think, that there is no risk?" He asked, almost shouting. He shook his head and, with difficulty, lowered his voice again. "Oh, excuse me; I forgot you were American," he added bitterly.

He stared across at Mark, the anger apparent now, but he was thinking too, thinking damn hard.

So, it was as simple as walking out of the airport. Well, why the hell not? Mark had never been stopped in Switzerland or anywhere else in Europe. He'd never tried to sneak anything in, but hell, all it took was nerve.

He didn't even know if Switzerland, or any of the other easy banking countries, had laws against bringing money in. If they did, it probably wasn't a hanging offense.

"You said before that I did you a favor over in Cameroon," Calvady said again.

You're dreaming, pal, Mark thought. "That's true," he said, "but..."

Neither of them saw the Libyan approach. Suddenly, he was there, just to the side of Calvady's chair. He said something quietly in Arabic.

Calvady was clearly startled for a second; there might even have been a trace of fear on his face as he jerked his head around at the sound of the Libyan's voice. But he recovered nicely, and his voice was steady and quiet when he replied in French.

"Bon soir, Monsieur Haloud; vous etes en retard." Calvady did not get up, and the two men didn't shake hands. The Frenchman waved an arm in Mark's direction. "Do you know *Monsieur...?*" Calvady had forgotten his name and looked to Mark to introduce himself.

"Monsieur Mark Reilly," Haloud said quietly before Mark could reply. The Libyan spoke carefully, pronouncing his name correctly.

"Bon soir, Monsieur," Mark said, lifting himself halfway out of the seat, only to lose his balance and fall back heavily into the chair.

Haloud stared hard at Mark for a moment. Calvady said something in Arabic, and the Libyan sat down in the chair next to the Frenchman's.

He was older than Mark had first thought, in his late 40s probably, though there were few lines in his face, and his thick black hair and mustache showed no hint of gray. He wore the same shapeless khaki pants and short-sleeved shirt he'd had on at the Tchadien that morning. As he sat down, Mark caught a whiff of Palmolive soap.

"You were stopped on the road past the airport this

afternoon," Haloud said, not taking his eyes off Mark. It wasn't a question.

"I didn't know that was off-limits," Mark replied.

"Your memory is a short one, then," Haloud said. "You were stopped at the same place four months ago."

Mark felt the blood rush into his face. He was glad the light was bad. He smiled and shrugged at the Libyan, whose expression didn't change.

"A third time, and we would be forced to assume it was not just forgetfulness," Haloud said. His French was slow and guttural, like most Arabic speakers, but he knew the grammar.

"Who's we?" Mark asked quickly. He was aware of his heart starting to pound in his chest; it was pointless, really, maybe even dangerous, but right then, with three beers in him, Mark didn't care.

Calvady didn't look well. He was leaning forward, his elbows pressing down on either arm of the chair and his hands clasped in front of his mouth.

"The government of Chad and its friends," Haloud replied in the same slow, even tone.

"I was with one of President Goukouni's personal guards," Mark said. "Are the Libyans now in command of Chadian troops?"

"He is new. He made a mistake. He has been reprimanded," Haloud said.

"Monsieur Reilly, vous nous excuserez," Calvady said, trying to snap Mark out of it.

Mark ignored him. "Still, he was a Chadian sergeant, being dragged out of a taxi and threatened by Libyans," Mark said, leaning forward and jabbing a finger at Haloud for emphasis.

Calvady wiped a hand down the length of his face.

"They were not Libyans," Haloud said. "They were Acyl Ahmat's men."

Mark smiled to keep from laughing. Acyl was a pro-Libyan

northerner who belonged to Goukouni's coalition. Some of his followers were light-skinned, and it had become something of a euphemism in Chad to ascribe Libyan personnel to Acyl any time it was convenient.

"Oh, well, then excuse me," Mark said, still smiling. "I made a mistake." The Libyan glared at him over the candle.

"Monsieur Reilly," Calvady tried again, almost begging now.

"Oui, oui, je vous quitte," Mark said, struggling out of the chair. He looked down at Haloud.

"So, you must be Chadian, too," he said. "You and Monsieur Calvady must go way back?"

Haloud said nothing but continued to meet Mark's gaze. It might have been the candlelight, but the bastard didn't seem to have to blink.

Mark had trouble pulling his small pile of CFA from his pocket.

"Ca va, ca va," Calvady said impatiently.

"Ah vous etes tres gentil, Monsieur Calvady," Mark said, slurring his words badly.

"De rien," Calvady managed without looking up. *"Bon soir, Monsieur Reilly,"* he said, bearing down on the "good night."

"Bon soir, Monsieur Calvady," Mark said, then bowed stupidly in Haloud's direction. *"Monsieur."* The Libyan said nothing.

Mark turned and, with the slow, exaggeratedly erect gait of drunks everywhere, walked toward the darkened hotel.

CHAPTER 7

Breakfast service at the *Tchadien* started early, but Mark was waiting when the waiter, a frail, aging African in a white serving jacket that had collected and saved coffee stains for years, opened the door.

The waiter motioned vaguely at a table near the door, but Mark ignored him and walked over to one closer to the back of the room. The restaurant was surprisingly large, with about 30 tables in all, with a raised area in the middle of the floor, perhaps where a band used to play.

The sun wasn't up yet, and no one had pulled back the curtains—the same green velour ones that hung in the lobby and in his room.

Mark thought about opening them himself, at least the ones nearest his table, but his head ached, and his legs felt too heavy for the effort the short walk across the room would require. So, he sat down. Closed up like that, the dining room smelled strongly of mildew and last night's beer. Like most things not tailored to the climate in Africa, the heavy curtains, once denied the protective shroud of air conditioning, had started to rot.

The waiter, who had disappeared into the kitchen for a moment, reappeared and came over.

"Bonjour," Mark said.

The African raised his chin at Mark.

"C'est combien, le cafe complet?" Mark asked.

"450 francs," the waiter replied.

"Et le cafe simple?"

"Deux cents."

"Bon, je prends un cafe," Mark said. The waiter, who either had other things on his mind or nothing at all, turned and shuffled back to the kitchen. Mark tugged what was left of his cash out of his pocket and laid it on the table. He counted it again. His stomach was making noises he could hear, but there was just no way.

He had to get back across the river, and even bargaining hard, the bush taxi down to Maroua and a taxi from the Douala airport to his apartment would take most of what was left. At some point, he'd need a beer, too.

Calvady picking up the tab had helped, but Mark had blown whatever he saved at the roadblock on the walk back from the Hotel Chari.

The combattant had been a young one, no more than 17. He was one of Acyl's men, and he was nervous. Mark had shown his press card and passport, and that was usually enough. But the soldier had never dealt with anything but French reporters before, so he told Mark to wait until his commander showed up on one of his sporadic checks.

By then, the walk had cleared Mark's head a little, and the aura of angry righteousness had given way to what was approaching panic. Only a few cars passed him, but Mark was certain that each one was Haloud's men coming to pick him up. They could do anything they wanted to him. An interrogation in some tent at the Libyan camp east of N'djamena; hell, even put him on a plane back to Libya.

Someone might wonder what had happened, friends in Douala, or maybe Alain, but Calvady was the only one who'd know, and he sure as hell wasn't going to say anything. So, Mark "dashed" the Chadian a thousand CFA. He could have gotten away with half that, but he didn't have any 500-franc notes.

Back in his room, Mark packed his carryall, then stretched out on the bed to think, his shoes still on. The river wasn't that far, no more than half a kilometer, and at that point in the dry season, he could wade most of the way across.

Once, he'd sat up and grabbed the bag, intending to go. He could make it; there wasn't any question. But he'd have to get by the roadblocks without being seen. The villas along the road, too. They were occupied now, mostly by officers whose guards slept outside.

He lay back down again to think about it. At least get out of the room; maybe just hide in the bushes behind the hotel, then walk to the port at first light and cross over like nothing had happened.

Mark fell asleep like that, or not exactly sleep but something in between, so that his dreams were more recollections than fantasy. Back to when he'd first arrived in Diarrere, after the Peace Corps had taught him *Wolof* and then sent him to a *Serrer* village, and the language seemed as unfathomable as ancient Greek.

And he sat, like the village idiot, with the men under the Baobab tree grabbing their balls, howling with laughter as he repeated the bad words over and over. *Jool* was a prick, and *Derrh* was cunt, and *Jahm* was fuck, though they used it only as a verb, never a noun.

"Boogirou Derrh, Modou?" The women would ask, laughing when he passed by where they sat in the shade, sifting millet or shelling peanuts, the babies and small children clinging to them or playing in the dirt.

Didn't he want any pussy? The Serrers always formed their questions in the negative, as if "no" were a more natural response in life than "yes." Mark finally learned enough to laugh with them, then to tease back, even occasionally inviting one of the laughing women back to his hut.

By his second year, there were times, not always, or even often, but times nevertheless, sitting with the *Serrers* he knew best, drinking warm beer outside his hut after dinner, talking about the prettiest girls in the village, or the rains that didn't come often enough, or even God, when they all forgot there was any difference between them.

The peace never lasted long, an hour at most, and then someone would show up to ask a favor: a loan, help with a well, or medicine from his medical kit.

They all thought he knew something about sickness because he was white and had the kit.

They all had their *gris-gris,* the amulets, and necklaces, sometimes just a piece of leather cord, that they bought from the *marabouts* and *gris-gris* men to ward off a myriad of evils, physical and spiritual.

But the villagers also had great respect for more conventional medicine, which was rarer than protein in Diarrere. Having a white man with lots of it come live with them was an unexpected bonus to the wells and latrines Mark was supposed to bring them.

Mark became reasonably proficient at disinfecting and bandaging the cuts and burns, and a Peace Corps ointment worked wonders on conjunctivitis, even in advanced cases, when the pale yellow mucus ran like syrup from the patient's eyes, attracting swarms of flies.

He also dispensed more aspirin than was prudent for aches and pains, real and imagined.

But he could do nothing for the babies that vomited up

every bit of food they consumed and whose bones protruded from their skin like so many sticks under a thin cloth.

Or for *Omar*, Mark's 10-year-old neighbor, who always had a smile but never much energy and who one day lay down on the dirt floor of his hut, whispered goodbye to his mother, and died.

Mark couldn't even help himself the first time he came down with malaria. Unsure what it was, he lay for days in his hut, unable to get up, burning with a fever so strong that his eyes felt as though they would explode from their sockets.

At times, he was close to delirium, unable to recall a word of *Serrer* with which to reassure the anxious villagers who came to see him. Once, in the middle of the night, he woke covered with sweat. In the blackness of the windowless hut, he forgot where he was, not just the name of the village, but that he was in Africa at all.

The darkness and the fever were to blame, of course, and it passed quickly. But for those few seconds, he had no idea, none at all, and it terrified him more than anything in his life before or since, even more than the thought of dying.

Twice, Mark bolted upright in bed, his mouth foul and dust-dry and his heart pounding so hard it seemed to be trying to break free of its place in his chest.

Someone had knocked at the door.

He could make it to the open window, just beyond the curtain. And then to the river. It wasn't that far, and the Chadians would all be asleep by then. But he didn't move, only sat on the edge of the bed, staring at the darkness by the door, trying and failing to slow his breathing. The door wasn't locked; it was only a matter of time before they realized it.

The second time, he forced himself to walk to the door and open it. There was no one. He stepped out into the hallway and peered in the direction of the lobby, but if possible, that was even darker than his room.

He closed the door behind him, then groped his way back to the bed. He felt around for his bag, then sat down on the edge of the bed, holding the bag across his legs, listening for footsteps that didn't come and waiting for dawn.

The waiter brought his coffee and then walked back to the kitchen.

Mark poured himself a cup, frowning at the ink-black color. Even in his dump of an apartment in Douala, morning coffee was something he looked forward to. There was something hopeful in the ritual, with its aroma and routine, a notion, however brief and ultimately false, that things might work out.

But that was in Cameroon, which grew and roasted some of the best coffee in the world. For reasons that Mark had never examined, Chad, even northern Cameroon, never saw the real thing; instead, they imported Nescafe crystals, arguably the worst drink in the world, from three thousand kilometers away.

The Tchadien compounded the sin by making it impossibly strong so that even with careful pouring, a layer of black sludge clung to the bottom of the cup and made finishing a cup of coffee a health hazard. The hotel had no cream or sugar but only a can of French long-life milk, the sweetened variety. It had an unsettling pinkish hue and the viscosity of motor oil on a cold day. The coffee turned from black to murky brown. He took a sip and shuddered instinctively at the sweet-bitter combination. The caffeine went to work immediately; before he finished the first cup, his hands were trembling.

It was the last thing he needed, really; his nerves were shot as it was.

But hell, Haloud had probably forgotten him before he got out of the *Chari* garden. The Libyan had more to worry about than a drunk reporter unless Calvady told him. Or worse, if he'd heard them talking. Christ, who the hell knew how long the son of a bitch had been standing in the dark.

There was something else, too: what if it wasn't the Libyans, but only Haloud, and maybe a couple of others, helping Calvady and getting paid off? Mark didn't know if that was possible; he doubted it, really. But if it was, and that's what was going on, it would be Haloud's head if Mark wrote the article.

Mark put the coffee cup down. It was time to get out of there. There was a soft, dim light around the edge of the curtains now; by the time he got to the port, he'd be able to cross over.

"Vous permettez?" Calvady asked, suddenly standing there, holding the back of the chair across from Mark. Mark had been staring across at the windows and hadn't seen him enter the dining room. He glanced quickly at the door, but there was no one, only the Frenchman, dressed as always, though his shorts and shirt were clean ones.

"Oui, oui," Mark said, extending a hand at the chair. "But I've only got a minute; got to get back to Douala."

"A long voyage," Calvady sympathized. "Have you a car on the other side?"

"Yes," Mark replied, not sure why he was lying.

The waiter appeared, and Calvady ordered coffee and bread. When the African withdrew, Calvady pulled his chair in slightly and rested both arms on the table.

"Ecoute, Mark," he said, an elder advising a young protege. This was going to be good. Mark had dealt for years with Frenchmen in Douala, even eaten at their homes, and never been addressed as anything but Monsieur Reilly.

Calvady was tu-toi-ing him after three beers.

"You were very foolish last night, my friend," he said. "Libyans don't share our sense of humor."

Mark shrugged, conceding nothing. Calvady lowered his head, looking down at the table as if trying to control himself.

The waiter brought a tray with coffee, bread, and jam. Calvady handed him a 1,000 CFA note and told him to keep the change. The African, who had barely opened his mouth since

Mark entered the dining room, suddenly smiled, revealing large gaps between the half dozen or so teeth he still possessed.

"Merci, monsieur, merci," he said, backing away from the table and bowing, almost like a Muslim at prayer.

Calvady looked back at Mark; he wasn't smiling anymore.

"I did not think you were a stupid man, Mark, but perhaps I was wrong," he said. Mark said nothing. It was bad enough that he had to listen to the bastard; he sure as hell wasn't going to help him.

Calvady poured himself some coffee, then heaped jam onto a large piece of French bread. *"Oh, pardon,"* he said, with the bread halfway to his mouth. He held out the basket of bread to Mark.

He hesitated for a second—God, he was hungry—then shook his head. *"Merci,"* he said. Calvady nodded and put the bread down, but on the other side of the table, near where Mark had left his pile of CFA.

Calvady glanced at the money, then back at Mark.

"Haloud is not a man to fool with, my friend," Calvady continued between bites. The bread was old and rubbery, and chewing it was clearly an effort. "He was very angry last night; he thought you had insulted him, and you did."

That was Haloud's problem. Mark slipped the money back into his pocket. The pre-dawn light filtering in around the edges of the curtains made him feel better. He'd be across the river in 20 minutes.

"He wanted to have you picked up as an American spy," Calvady said.

Bullshit, Mark thought, though he felt his heartbeat accelerate.

"I convinced him you were only drunk and that you were kidding," Calvady said. "I told him Americans were great kidders."

Mark smiled. "Yes, a nation of comedians," he said.

Calvady frowned again. "Don't mock me, my friend," he

warned, an edge to his voice now; "you're not across the river yet."

Mark stared across at the old Frenchman, who carefully layered jam onto another piece of bread, then tore off an enormous bite with his back teeth like a dog ripping meat from a bone.

The fat little pimp was threatening him!

"If I believed you, and I'm sorry, but I don't, Monsieur Calvady, I'd walk over to the *Presidence* and ask for an escort to the port," Mark said with more confidence than he felt.

"Ah, you don't understand, my friend," Calvady said, disappointed. He glanced over toward the dining room entrance, and Mark followed his gaze.

There was no one.

Mark was about to turn back to Calvady and excuse himself when three Libyans entered. Two could have been Haloud's brothers, with the dark, thick hair and full mustaches, and last year's Peking fashions.

The third, in the light-khaki uniform of the Libyan troops, was the officer from the roadblock where Mark had been stopped the day before.

Calvady nodded a greeting, which the three Libyans returned. The officer glanced briefly at Mark. They walked to a table toward the back of the room, not far from the terrace door.

Calvady smiled across at Mark. "I'm afraid the Chadians will do what their Libyan friends...advise," he said, enjoying his choice of words.

Mark felt his pulse quicken. He looked over Calvady's shoulder at the Libyans. The officer had taken the chair facing Mark; in the dim light, that far away, it was hard to tell whether he was watching him or not.

"I told Haloud that as an American, you were in a position to do him, us really, a service," Calvady said, again choosing his words carefully.

"You're right, I don't understand," Mark said, waiting for the tingling in his bowels to stop spreading.

"C'est tres simple, mon ami," Calvady said quickly, leaning forward, "You are a free-lancer, no?" Mark nodded and stared past Calvady at the Libyan. The son of a bitch hadn't moved.

"Well, I would like you to do a free-lance...job for me," Calvady was saying. Mark looked back at the Frenchman but didn't say anything. Calvady smiled; he enjoyed this.

"I don't know what they will pay you for your article, but I will pay you more, a lot more, not to write it," he said.

"How much?" Mark asked. The offer would look good in the story; a figure, if it was big enough, would be even better.

"Ah, that depends on whether you are also willing to do the job I mentioned," Calvady explained.

Mark tilted his head a notch and spread his palms. It was good stuff, really. He wouldn't be able to come back to N'djamena, of course, at least not while the Libyans were there, but just then, coming back wasn't on the top of his list.

"You have some Cameroonian friends?" He asked, smiling at the word as if he didn't quite mean it.

Mark nodded. They were about the only friends he had left in Douala.

"Tres bien," Calvady said as if congratulating him on the feat. "I, rather we, would like you to set up a small company; it will be easier if you have a local partner."

"What kind of company?" Mark asked. He didn't really give a damn, but he was curious; it wasn't what he'd expected.

"A very small, simple company ...to import American products," Calvady said. Mark said nothing, waiting for the Frenchman to go on.

"It would not take much of your time; you could probably even continue to write," he added. *"Ca vous interresse?"*

"Oui," Mark lied. "What kind of equipment?"

Calvady shrugged as if that wasn't important.

"Different kinds," he said. "Mostly for oil exploration and production."

Mark nodded slowly, thinking. The Cameroon government didn't make a lot of noise about it, but since oil was discovered offshore, near the Nigerian border in 1979, production had risen fast.

Oil companies, French and American, had flooded into Douala, and the best estimates Mark could get had Cameroon pumping as much as 200,000 barrels a day within a few years. Not much on a world scale, but it was plenty to either improve the lives of Cameroon's eight million people or make a handful of them very rich.

Douala, which had become something of a boom town because of the oil, already had its share of oil service companies, and more were coming in every month.

How did Calvady expect to compete with them?

"So, what do you say, my friend?" Calvady asked.

"I'm still listening," Mark replied. The Frenchman smiled and reached down for his *portefeuille,* which he had set on the floor next to the chair.

"You are American, so I assume you want to be rich someday," Calvady said, still smiling. "Or maybe you already are," he added, glancing over at where Mark had laid out his money.

Fuck you, pal, Mark thought. "Not yet," he said, smiling back.

Calvady opened the sack, and Mark could see that it was stuffed so tightly with notes that the Frenchman had trouble extracting an envelope. A couple of $50 bills came part way out, but Calvady nonchalantly tapped them back in and zipped the portefeuille closed.

He slid the envelope across the table with his fingertips.

"Voila deux milles dollars, mon ami," he said.

Mark left the envelope where it was and kept his eyes on Calvady.

"It's for your...expenses and as a sign of good faith," Calvady explained.

Mark glanced over at the Libyans. They were eating and talking, not paying any attention to him.

Shit, Libyans ate in there every day; they were just having their breakfast. Mark slid his chair back to get up. As he did so, the Libyan officer stopped whatever he was saying to the other two and stared across at Mark. The two civilians also turned to look over at him.

Mark felt his heart start to pound again, and his breathing accelerated so that he had to open his mouth a little to get enough air. His hand trembled noticeably when he picked up the envelope.

Calvady stuffed a last piece of bread in his mouth and sprang to his feet. He slipped the *portefeuille* over his wrist and smiled, holding out an arm to let Mark lead the way to the door.

"I'll drive you to the port, my friend," he said.

CHAPTER 8

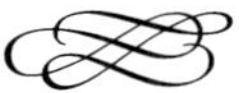

Emil was glad to see him. He pushed a Gala in front of Mark even before he sat down on one of the bar stools. *"Merci, patron,"* Mark said, which set off an explosion of laughter from Emil.

The beer tasted good, and after the lukewarm Galas in N'djamena, it was nice to have a cold one again, even at 7:30 in the morning.

"Tu prends du cafe, Mark?" Emil asked.

"Merci, Emil, mais ca suffit," Mark said, pointing at the sweating green bottle in front of him. That set Emil off again; it really didn't take much. He kept working, even while he was laughing, his head bobbing up and down behind the bar, filling a tray with a pitcher of coffee, cups, and a basket of bread.

Mark finished the Gala quickly and thought about having another beer, almost calling out to Emil, but then demurred. He drained the dregs from the bottom of the bottle. He really had to get back to Douala, and the airport was hours away, assuming he could find a taxi. He dropped some CFA on the table and grabbed his bag.

It was warm when he stepped out of the *relais*; not uncomfortable yet, but even so, he'd be dripping wet by the time he got to the taxi *gare*. The passenger door of a white Peugeot parked near the relais' entrance swung open as Mark descended the steps.

"Montez mon ami," a voice called from inside the car. *"Je vous depose a la gare."*

Mark recognized the voice even before he bent down to look inside the Peugeot. The Frenchman smiled out at him, the pipe clenched firmly between his teeth, and a hand extended toward the door. Mark couldn't think of an excuse fast enough: the beer, no doubt, and nothing to eat. He climbed in next to the Frenchman, shifted the bag to his lap, and closed the door.

"Merci," Mark said.

"De rien," the Frenchman said, shaking his head as if driving foreign journalists around Kousseri was a favorite part of his job.

After the taxis in Chad, the Peugeot seemed remarkably clean and well-maintained. There was no sand anywhere, not even on the floor; the seats still had springs and padding. Drops of water from a recent washing quivered on the windshield as the Frenchman spun the car in a quick turn, then headed it out of the *relais* parking area and onto the laterite road.

He drove too fast, like Frenchmen everywhere, and didn't seem to notice the car shudder whenever it bounced too hard through a deep pothole. He had the air conditioning on very high, which felt nice, though it would make getting out again that much worse, especially if it was to squeeze into a packed bush taxi for a three-hour ride in the heat of the day.

"Alors, c'etait interressant?" The Frenchman asked, smiling briefly over at Mark, then back at the road.

"Comme toujours," Mark replied. This was pointless. They had already grilled Alain, no doubt; in any case, the taxi *gare* was less than a kilometer away.

"So, are our Libyan friends making themselves at home?" The Frenchman tried, keeping his eyes on the road this time.

Mark glanced over at him. He had the pipe firmly in place, though it did not appear to be lit. His skin still looked dangerously fair, but that would never change, no matter how long he stayed, how careful he was about the sun, or how high he turned the air conditioning.

Some people just weren't made for Africa.

The Frenchman looked across at Mark, waiting for an answer. Mark smiled at him.

"Libyans?" He asked, feigning surprise. "They left."

The Frenchman was getting used to Mark's sense of laughing on cue. He wasn't going to lose his temper this time, not if it killed him. But what the hell was the point? Mark couldn't tell them a thing they didn't already know from Alain.

Except for the dollars, maybe, if Alain hadn't caught on. Mark didn't think it was likely, not that fast, anyway. Even if he got part of it, it would take some luck for Alain, or any other reporter, to figure out the whole damn thing.

Mark glanced out the window. They were almost to the *gare.* He felt tired from the night before and too many beers without anything to eat. And he was already dreading the three-hour ride in a sweltering taxi. He and eight Africans, sweating on each other, with some *Fulbe* kamikaze at the wheel, hurtling them through the tiny villages that punctuated but didn't really break the monotony of the parched savannah.

Once, Mark had liked, no loved, trips like that; he didn't mind or even notice the discomfort and was sorry when they ended. But some things that seemed admirable at the age of 22 were, for whatever reason, pathetic at 35.

The Frenchman had asked him something, but Mark hadn't caught it. Something about the airport, but he wasn't sure which one.

They pulled into the *gare*. Immediately, the small boys and the women who sold lottery tickets, peanuts, baby clothes made in China, and biscuits that tasted like sand ran alongside the car, yelling and pressing their wares against the windows until the Frenchman stopped the car. They crowded around both doors, elbowing for space and hissing *"monsieur, monsieur"* over and over again.

The Frenchman ignored the Africans and turned halfway in his seat. Mark hadn't answered his question. Was the airport still off-limits? And were the Libyans still guarding it? He was polite, but he wasn't smiling anymore. This was the price of the ride.

The airport. The bastard probably knew more about it than Mark did. Except that there were dollars, hundreds of thousands of them at least, flying out under his nose.

Maybe he didn't know that. But Mark wasn't going to tell him.

God, he was tired. And he appreciated the ride, even if it was for a reason. The Frenchman was just doing a job and was probably under pressure, maybe a lot of pressure, even if what he came up with didn't change a thing. He still worked for the government, after all.

But relationships, even the most random and superficial, sometimes take on a momentum, or direction anyway, that minus the will to alter it, dictate how they are to proceed.

"The airport's gone too," Mark said, pulling the door latch. "The Libyans just rolled it up, stuffed it into one of those big Anatovs of theirs, and took off."

The Frenchman's smile returned, a little tighter perhaps, but there nonetheless, so that an optimist might have believed he was mildly amused.

"Alain didn't tell you?" Mark asked, shaking his head at the negligence. "The place is all yours again."

The Frenchman's face flushed dark pink, though to his credit, the smile stayed in place like a frozen rope. Mark realized he'd been trying for that, which didn't make him feel too good. But hell, the guy had no sense of humor.

“Thanks for the ride,” he said, meaning it.

“De rien,” the Frenchman said evenly.

Mark hopped out into the crowd of hissing vendors. He flung the car door shut with his bag, keeping the other- hand casually but firmly over the envelope in his back pocket. He heard the Peugeot pull away fast as he strode through the crowd toward the taxi loading for Maroua, occasionally shouting *“non, merci”* at the more aggressive vendors, who trailed behind him like avid disciples.

PART II

DOUALA

CHAPTER 9

Anyone who has ever been to Douala, even just passing through, to catch the Ethiopian Airlines connecting flight across to Nairobi or on an Air Afrique shuttle on its way up the coast, remembers the heat.

Day or night, it hit first-time arrivals like a hot, damp blanket wrapping itself tightly around them so that breathing always seemed to require an additional effort. Even for the few weeks in November, just after the rainy season, and again in March, during the "small" or mango rains, when the sky was blue and relatively clear, the city simmered under an oppressive humidity that never broke.

"Like Houston in August, only hotter," was the way U.S. oilmen described it, but even that didn't do it justice. There was a claustrophobic, vaguely menacing feel to the heat as if it were more than just the random result of atmospheric conditions that close to the Equator.

The only relief was the rain. Douala averaged about 12 feet of it a year, with three-quarters of that falling from July through September when it could pour non-stop for a week or more.

Expatriate wives could take the children and flee for most of the rainy season, leaving the men to carry on alone.

Business activity slowed to a crawl during the period, in part because the spending population dropped off but also because the rains and the more or less permanent flooding made even getting to work an ordeal.

The only exceptions were Douala's many bars and its sizeable army of prostitutes, who did a brisk business in the rainy season, especially from the seasonal "bachelors."

A lot of new arrivals were also dismayed to find that Douala, which on most maps looked to be on the coast, was, in fact, 20 kilometers inland. Instead of tropical beaches, they found themselves on the banks of the Wouri, a muddy estuary in the middle of a mangrove swamp that was so prone to silting up that it had to be dredged year-round to allow container ships to reach the city's surprisingly modern port.

Until the oil started flowing in 1979, Douala had only a handful of buildings of more than five stories. That had changed, of course; there was a construction boom underway, with the huge, perpendicular cranes poking up everywhere, providing a skeletal preview of the future skyline.

Even so, the city's preponderant look was still that of a colonial river town: sprawling, dilapidated warehouses lined the port road, and the main government buildings were crumbling masonry structures that hadn't seen a paintbrush since the French pulled out. Like African cities everywhere, most of Douala's residents lived in the *"quartiers,"* the filthy, overcrowded slums that spread out from the city center, like an uncontrolled infection, to any patch of unoccupied space.

Some of the *quartiers,* like Akwa and Daido and Bonaberi across the Wouri Bridge, had achieved a kind of middle-class status and boasted modest apartment houses and even small villas with electricity and running water.

But others, like Nylon and Congo and Bassa, were squalid,

crime-ridden *"bidonvilles"* where *ju-ju* feuds flourished and where even Cameroon's tough, sometimes brutal, *gendarmes* entered only with caution and lots of back-ups.

In the middle of it all, Paul Soppo Priso, Cameroon's wealthiest man, had carved out a privileged "ghetto" of paved streets and large, white villas with tile rooves and elaborate gardens. Some had swimming pools; all had high cement walls with metal spikes or glass shards on top or impenetrable hedges running all the way around and were guarded day and night by watchmen.

Demand for Soppo Priso's villas, steady since independence in 1960, soared with the white tide of oil and service company personnel. The sudden scarcity pushed rents up quickly. Prices for the villas doubled or even tripled literally overnight as Soppo Priso and a small but growing band of lesser real estate barons, many of them *Bamileke* merchants, cashed in on the shortage.

By 1980, some of the larger villas in Bonapriso were fetching a million CFA, or about $5,000, a month in rent. The inflation and the resulting scramble for expatriate housing provoked, or at least exacerbated, tensions between the longtime French business interests and the newcomers, who were, for the most part, Americans.

After decades of serenity, the French suddenly found themselves outbid, sometimes for the houses in which they'd lived for years. U.S. oil companies snapped up offshore leases the French oil giants Total and Elf wanted, then farmed out work to the newly arrived U.S. service firms instead of to established French ones.

American banks like Chase Manhattan and Bank of Boston followed, as did International Accounting Associates, Deborah's company; all of them aggressively selling better service and undercutting the unofficial but longstanding price agreements of the established French firms.

For the Cameroonians, the problem was also money — who would get it?

Since independence, the country had been an uneasy mosaic of conflicting and mutually distrustful tribes, regions, and religions, all elbowing for what they considered was their right to a larger share of the pie. Oil and its attendant benefits just made it worse.

Mark and Deborah arrived in 1978 before the economy heated up. International Accountants had an office in Nigeria, and when its president flew in for a visit in late 1977, he heard about promising seismic data next door in Cameroon. Back in New York, he checked with bankers and was stunned to hear that even without oil, Cameroon had the highest credit rating in black Africa.

It had a thriving economy fueled by cocoa and coffee exports and none of the disastrous debts that were starting to take their toll on the Ivory Coast and Nigeria. Cameroon was also one of the only countries on the continent that fed itself.

He decided to send someone in for six months.

Deborah wasn't the company's first choice. Some of the directors had misgivings about sending a woman, but the president, a young, aggressive Yale graduate, liked Deborah and wasn't afraid to take a chance. And Deborah, unlike most of the associate accountants at the firm, was willing to go.

She had never been to Africa and only knew what Mark had told her. But the challenge intrigued her, and she knew Mark was desperate to get back. He had gone to journalism school at Columbia and naively thought that after two years in the Peace Corps and three more crisscrossing the Sahel as a food aid "checker" for USAID, newspapers would be lining up to hire him as an African correspondent.

No one was even vaguely interested, so he spent the first two years after graduation in New York writing for a newsletter that covered the specialty steel industry.

When International Accounting's board finally approved Deborah's assignment, Phillip McKenzie, the president, took Mark and her to dinner to celebrate. He was too classy a guy to say so, but they knew he had gone out on a limb for her.

She didn't disappoint him. She was paying her way after three months; within a year, the office was solidly in the black. International Accounting formed a Cameroon subsidiary in 1979 and, within six months, had a virtual lock on all the major U.S. firms and was making inroads into the entrenched French market.

Deborah did it by herself, first out of a room in their apartment, then managing an office of six locally trained accountants and an office staff of 12. Partly, it was luck, coming in just as the need for accounting services soared; mostly, though, it was Deborah.

She was a damn good accountant, miles ahead of what the French could offer, and she was a tireless saleswoman for International Accounting. Her French was only fair, but she worked at that, too, until she could get through lunch alone with the chief financial officer of a French firm. She worked too hard and too many hours and worried constantly that she wasn't doing enough. But she loved it.

Maybe because of the work or because she had never been anywhere else in Africa, Douala never got to her. She found the heat a nice change from winter in New York, and the city itself, she said, looked pretty much like what she'd expected and so fascinated her.

Mark, who had counted the days until they got there, hated Douala from the start.

He wasn't prepared for the humidity, with its cloying, exhausting wetness, or the way he sweats just walking from their air-conditioned apartment to his air-conditioned car so that his shirts developed a permanent, brownish stain where they stuck to his back like wet stamps. He hated the look of the city, too: the rundown, aging buildings, mildew climbing the walls like some infectious disease, and the rusting metal rooves that had long ago lost their luster and turned a sooty gray-black.

His reference was Dakar, of course, which wasn't fair. The Senegalese capital, with its white sand beaches and moderate climate, was more Mediterranean than African. It was no accident that the French made Dakar the capital of their African empire, and it was no surprise that tourism was a major part of the city's economy.

No one came to Douala on vacation.

It was a business town, and no one ever made a pretense of being there for anything else. Even the arcane, and some said volatile, manoeuvering within the government, which the embassy crowd in Yaounde never tired of parsing, got little attention in Douala. Business was what people talked about, even after-hours, at poolside lunches on the weekends, or the overly formal dinners that went on every night of the week in Bonapriso; meals that always tasted the same because everyone shopped at *Monoprix* or *Sudanaise,* the two supermarkets in Douala, and always looked and felt the same because they were served by the same Africans in white uniforms, to the same people who talked about the same things, because nothing in Douala changed much, certainly not since the night before.

The women sometimes got in a complaint or two about the help, the cooks and houseboys, and nannies that made life miserable for them. But that usually got covered in their morning coffees, which allowed the men and Deborah to use the dinners to talk about business. That was important to her because within the small, tightly knit expatriate community in Douala, friendships, or relationships anyway, were as important to a company as the service it offered or the price it charged.

Deborah handled her unique status well. She was friendly with the wives and never condescending, though she avoided their coffees like the plague, using work as her excuse. If they hated her, it wasn't obvious.

The men, most of them from Texas, Oklahoma, or Louisiana, had no trouble with her sex or her Wisconsin accent. It didn't hurt that she was attractive, but she never used it. Deborah was as naturally gregarious as most of them were; she also knew her business and made a point of knowing theirs in a place where inefficiency was endemic, that counted for a lot.

She was as good at the dinners as she was at accounting; her only problem was Mark.

Most of Deborah's business came from oil or oil-related companies, all of which were under constant pressure from the Cameroon government to keep quiet about the country's exploration and production.

President Amadou Ahidjo had seen the discovery of oil destroy much of neighboring Nigeria's traditional economy, especially its agriculture, and he wanted to avoid that happening in Cameroon.

Most of the oil men didn't like reporters at the best of times. But in Douala, there was nothing to be gained from talking to one, nothing at all, so none of them did. A lot of the oil company personnel, themselves struggling with an unfamiliar situation, clearly didn't even like to be around Mark.

They had no choice but to include him in the invitations to Deborah, but conversations tended to dry up when he approached. Discussions at the sit-down meals were often uncomfortable as the oil men tried to make a point without giving anything away. They sometimes joked, lamely, about not talking with a reporter around, and Mark would laugh and protest that he wasn't working, but that didn't help much.

So, he stayed as far away from Deborah and her clients as gatherings like that allowed. And he drank, usually too much, though in fairness, that was not something that started in Cameroon. Deborah wouldn't hear of his not coming along; it wasn't as bad as Mark made it sound, and anyway, he was her husband, and they'd just have to get used to it.

But then came his first reporting trip, to Gabon for a week, to write about the country's declining oil reserves and the *Transgabonais*, an economically questionable but technically magnificent railroad cut straight through the heart of the rain forest.

When Mark got back, he begged out of several dinners, claiming he had deadlines to meet. Deborah protested, but not overly. Thereafter, he accompanied her less and less, at first finding excuses but finally just insisting he didn't want to go. They had a fight about it once, a big one, with tears and bitter words, and then lovemaking right there on the couch in the living room, but even then, Deborah was arguing a principle more than any heartfelt desire to have him along, and Mark knew it.

The truth was that it was easier for both of them if he didn't come.

The invitations kept coming and always included him, and sometimes, if Deborah begged hard or long enough, Mark went along. But within a year, it was understood in the community that Deborah came alone, and that was fine with everybody.

It took a few months, but Mark eventually found people who would talk about what was happening in the oil sector. A few were Cameroonians whom the government forced the oil companies to hire and who resented the secrecy surrounding the industry. Others were expatriates who worked for the service companies that flooded into Douala once production began. They had to know exploration and production details in order to bid on work for the big oil companies, and a lot of them didn't mind talking as long as they weren't identified.

Though no one came right out and accused her, some of the oil men thought Deborah was feeding Mark the information. A few made pointed references to his articles, which were getting good play in the U.S.; at one dinner, a Texan who had had too much to drink pressed her hard for Mark's source of information.

Mark, who was slightly drunk when she got home that night, wanted to drive over and punch the bastard's face for him. Deborah talked him out of it, but from then on, he went after the oil story as hard as he could. Once, during an argument about something else, Deborah accused him of going out of his way to embarrass her. He denied it, but when she persisted, Mark told her to go to hell. He'd never spoken to her like that before, and he apologized, at length, when he cooled down. But after that, if the oil companies complained about his stories, he never heard about it.

At some point, Mark stopped hating Douala. He didn't love it—Douala wasn't that kind of place—but getting off the plane from Maroua, he realized he was glad to be back. Even the humidity felt good, like a wet kiss after the lip-cracking dryness of the North.

The Douala airport terminal was a modern, efficient structure, all marble and glass, that would not have been out of place in Miami. Like so many of Douala's newer buildings, the air conditioning was cranked all the way up so that walking in from the sizzling tarmac sometimes provoked a sharp, painful headache.

It was as if the airport officials didn't want anyone to forget that the building was a quantum leap from the old terminal, a modest, colonial-era relic that sat at the far end of an abandoned runway.

A customs inspector at the door eyed Mark closely, but when he held his bag up, ready to open it, the African waved him through. Mark fought off the urchins who grabbed at his bag, wanting to carry it for a small *dash,* then haggled with three taxi drivers until he found one that would take him into town for 300 CFA. That was the official price fixed by the government, which meant that it was largely ignored.

The two chauffeurs who had turned him down cursed the third one angrily; a group of drivers loitering in front of the terminal joined in the denunciation. Mark's driver shouted angrily at them out the window, gesticulating at his detractors with one hand and turning the key with the other. He slammed the rickety *Renault 12* into gear and pulled away fast, flailing with his free arm at one of the drivers who had run over to pound on his roof.

"What language is that, *Douala?*" Mark asked as they skidded around the big curve that led to the airport exit.

"Non chef, Bassa," his driver said, now grinning widely.

No wonder they didn't like the bastard; nobody liked the *Bassa. Bassa* didn't even like other *Bassa.* At least, that was the rap among the other tribes. The *Bassa* were from the rainforest near Edea, an industrial city southeast of Douala. Other Cameroonians claimed they were a brooding, surly lot, even dangerous sometimes, given their strong devotion to *ju-ju.*

"Did it rain?" Mark asked. There were puddles on the side of the road and water in the potholes they rattled over.

"Oui, chef, hier," the driver said, proud to be of service.

That was good news on two counts. It meant an early end to the Harmattan, the desert wind that blew a brown cloud of sand down from the Sahara and hung it over the city like a shroud. In the bad years, it lasted for months at a time and coated everything: cars, humans, and even closed-up apartments with thin, gritty dust that even constant sweeping failed to eliminate.

The rain was also good for business: Mark wrote for a couple of commodity services, and all of them would take at least a few paragraphs on the first rain. It made a difference in the coffee and cocoa harvests. That was the good side of free-lancing: selling the same news to two or three different outlets.

More than that for big news. It's like Libya buying Chad with U.S. petrodollars. Yes, that would sell nicely.

The taxi squeezed through the crowds, walking the streets of New Bell, Douala's largest *quartier*. It was the only way to and from the airport, and it was always slow going, but worse after a rain. The brown, stagnant puddles forced pedestrians onto the road; few of them, certainly not the market women, with baskets of *cocoyams* or *plantains* perched on their heads, their wide behinds swinging slowly as they walked, or the workmen straining to keep their overloaded *pousse-pousses* from tipping over in the potholes, paid any attention to the driver's angry horn blasts.

A gang of small children, most in rags and all barefoot, smiled and yelled insults at Mark and the *Bassa* and banged the side of the slow-moving taxi with their fists. Mark didn't even look at them. But the driver yelled back, holding his arm threateningly out the window; he swung occasionally, but the children were too fast. That prompted louder insults and jeers and a kind of competition among the boys to see who could get closest to the driver without getting swatted.

The crowds finally thinned out at the traffic circle near the far end of *New Bell*. The *Bassa,* muttering to himself, whined quickly through the *Renault's* gears as the car picked up speed on the *Avenue des Palmiers,* named for the enormous palm trees that lined both sides of the street.

The *Avenue Charles de Gaulle* wasn't crowded—it was not quite rush hour yet—and Mark was glad for the air rushing in the windows.

The driver cut through *Bonapriso* to avoid the bottlenecks in *Joss*, near the Central Bank. The streets were empty except for a handful of day guardians; some were playing cards together under a tree from where they could watch several villas at once. A few others were asleep in front of their respective gates, on the hard wooden benches that local artisans made in an Anglophone *quartier* out near the new soccer stadium.

Mark and Deborah had never lived in *Bonapriso.* They could have, and in truth, Deborah would have preferred it. But since his Peace Corps days, Mark had hated the army of servants that went with the villas and so had held out for an apartment in the *Tour de Wouri,* across the street from the Central Bank.

It was a light, spacious two-bedroom place with air conditioning that worked and a backup generator that kicked in automatically when the power went out. It had tile floors throughout, not carpets like in the newer buildings, which mildewed after six months, even with air conditioning, and left a musty, rotting odor that no amount of cleaning ever removed.

As the taxi left *Bonapriso,* at the intersection near the *Brasserie du Cameroun,* they hit traffic again. The two *gendarmes* that manned the control post there eyed the taxi but let it pass when they saw Mark in the back. He heard the whistle sound from the car behind them. The random identification checks had eased slightly since Mark first arrived in Cameroon. Expatriates were usually allowed to pass through the control points now, though there was no guarantee.

Newcomers quickly learned where the posts were located and how, if possible, to avoid them. There were also a few rules that helped; making eye contact with a policeman or *gendarme,* for instance, was a sure way to get stopped. The checkpoints were a pale legacy of the curfews and ubiquitous—sometimes terrifying—roadblocks employed during the civil war in the 1960s and early 1970s.

Since then, the police and *gendarmes* had cleaned up their behavior, particularly towards expatriates, but getting stopped could still be an unpleasant experience. Even with all papers in order—residence permit, driver's license, insurance card, and registration, all with up-to-date stamps—it could take an hour or more, and sometimes, like at the end of the month when the gendarmes were broken and looking for a dash, a lot longer than that.

Mark's driver muttered to himself, then leaned out the window and yelled something at an African standing in the middle of the street, directing one of the *Brasserie du Cameroun* trucks that was backing slowly out of the brewery's loading area. The man yelled something back, then ignored the *Bassa,* who got even by leaning on his horn every five seconds or so.

Brasserie du Cameroun was Cameroun's oldest and largest brewery and its most profitable, but its 33 Export was lousy beer. Even ice cold, it was a headache waiting to happen.

Mark had thought that the first time he'd tasted the stuff, long before Deborah took off with the son of a bitch financial director.

The only local brew he drank was Gold Harp, the lager Guiness made out at its brewery in *Bassa,* beyond the airport. It wasn't Gala or St. Pauli's Girl, the favorite of prestige-minded Cameroonians, but it was good beer. All of Cameroon's breweries ran their operations 24 hours a day, seven days a week, and still had trouble keeping up with demand.

Cameroonians, of course, loved their beer. But the major reason for the crush was the presence of Nigeria and its 100 million people right next door. None of the breweries encouraged smuggling, of course, but neither did they ask too many questions of the large distributors that lined up in 10-ton trucks outside their loading areas every day.

The truth was that a lot of the trucks made a bee-line for the Cameroonian side of the *"creeks,"* the maze of mangrove swamps and estuaries whose western banks were in Nigeria.

It was a lucrative business, given the chronic beer shortage in Nigeria and the artificially elevated value of the *naira,* the Nigerian currency. That allowed the smugglers to double or even triple the price they paid for the beer in Cameroon and still find ready buyers across the border.

A lot of them worked it both ways, bringing back Nigerian goods that, legally imported into Cameroon, would have carried customs duties of 100 percent or more. There were risks, too, of course: both Cameroonian and Nigerian patrols in the creeks were heavily armed, and both had orders to fire on boats that refused to stop. The bigger operators hedged their bets by paying off officials on both sides, but that didn't always matter in the swamps at night.

By the time Mark's taxi driver forced his way into the merging traffic on *Avenue Douala Manga Bell,* the main thoroughfare of *Akwa*, rush hour had begun.

Traffic jams, like high-rise buildings and oil workers, were new to Douala and part of the growing affluence. It wasn't the chaos of Lagos yet, with its legendary *"go-slows,"* but traffic in Douala had worsened steadily during Mark's time there. There were now bottlenecks at key intersections not only morning and night but also coming and going at lunchtime since the three-hour siesta was an ironclad tradition in Douala.

At the *Carrefour de Deux Eglises,* named for its two Protestant churches whose exact denominations Mark had never been clear on, traffic came to a complete stop. Mark's driver instinctively pounded on his horn, though whether out of frustration or simply solidarity with the cars all around him wasn't clear. Mark was getting a headache from the noise and the exhaust fumes pouring into the open windows. It was still hot, so rolling the windows up was out of the question.

He pulled three 100 CFA pieces from his pocket and leaned forward.

"I'll walk from here," he said, forcing the startled Bassa to take the money. No one in Douala walked if it could be avoided.

"Et moi, chef?" The African shouted, excited now, waving a hand at the traffic.

"What do you want me to do about it?" Mark asked as he climbed out the back door. He slammed it closed, slung the bag onto his shoulder, and put his free hand casually over the envelope in his back pocket.

The *Bassa's* angry curses, which Mark couldn't understand anyway, faded then disappeared altogether into the cacophony of horns and angry shouts as he wound his way between and around the cars, going nowhere.

CHAPTER 10

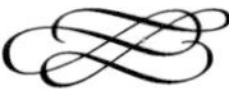

International Accounting gave Mark two weeks to find another place to live. Under the circumstances, that was pretty decent of them since Deborah had given them no notice at all. The local accountants Deborah had trained were good, so the office didn't fall apart, but the U.S. companies in Douala made it clear they wanted an American taking care of their accounts.

Phil McKenzie, the president, flew in from New York to calm them down. He ended up staying three weeks until Deborah's replacement could pack up his family and get a visa. Mark had lunch with him once at the Novotel's terrace restaurant near the pool. Phil had insisted on staying there, though the apartment, and everything in it but Mark's clothes, belonged to his company.

He and Mark drank too much wine and talked too much, like two Irishmen at a wake. Mark had trouble later remembering exactly what he'd said. In a way, Phil took Deborah's leaving harder than Mark did. The Cameroon office had been his idea, over the objections of most of the company's board. Its success had been his, a confirmation of his brilliance and, by extension, Deborah's.

She and Phil talked several times a week by phone or telex, and he came through Douala at least twice a year. They were friends and close collaborators more than boss and employee, bound by a common vision and enthusiasm and, of course, by shared success. Even in the early days, when Deborah was struggling just to get in to see companies, he never pressured her; to Phil, problems were never anyone's fault, just obstacles to be overcome.

He made a point of reading Mark's articles whenever he could, even going so far as to take a subscription to a newspaper that Mark wrote for regularly. Mark had never seen him patronize anyone, not even the *plantons* who made the coffee in the Douala office and whose names Phil always remembered.

But Mark couldn't help him. Phil, he knew, assumed it was the marriage and not the job she had run away from, and that was probably true. But he didn't really know. Mark had been away the day Deborah left, up in the Northwest, near Bamenda, doing an article on African art for a Chicago-based specialty magazine.

So, they didn't talk about it. Her brief note didn't give a reason; she just said she was leaving and wouldn't be back. It was only later that he learned, second-hand, that she had left with the Frenchman.

Mark punched the light switch for the stairway, but nothing happened.

"Shit," he muttered. The Douala bastard still hadn't fixed the damn thing. He climbed the stairs in semi-darkness, with only thin bars of light straying in the diagonal slits cut in the cement walls.

At least it was cooler than the street.

He opened the door on the fourth floor, took a step back, and waited a minute while the hot, stale air near the door escaped into the stairwell. Then he entered his apartment.

Phil just assumed Mark would leave Douala; Deborah

probably did, too, if she thought about it at all. That was part, though only part, of the reason he stayed.

"Oh, you're the other dependent husband," the woman said, smiling warmly, happy to have located him. She was very young, probably no more than 25, and Douala was her first posting after the State Department training. She had told her husband that he was not the only one to have followed his wife out, and now she could prove it.

"Uh, I'm not sure what you mean," Mark said, knowing exactly what she meant. Deborah was outraged when he told her about it; she made too much of it, really, and never liked the woman after that.

Mark opened the front windows. The noise from Akwa rushed in: the cars honking and people yelling, workmen pounding metal somewhere, and women talking and laughing, too loud, so they could be heard over the children crying. They were, by and large, the sounds of every African *quartier* of every city on the continent, and they rarely stopped entirely, not even late at night.

One of the first things that struck Mark about Africa was how little the people slept. Often in Diarrere, he woke in the blackness of his hut, from a nightmare or just to pee, and he could still hear voices coming from where the village men sat under the Baobab tree. The women, who rose hours before dawn to pound the millet, often sat talking together in their compounds until past midnight.

The cities were the same, just more voices, so that late at night, when there were no cars or motorcycles to distort the sound, the *quartiers* seemed to murmur in the darkness, or maybe to it, like lovers whispering the same secret over and over again.

The apartment felt like an oven. Mark shielded his eyes and looked out the windows, which faced West. The sun hadn't yet slid down behind two high-rise apartment towers going up near the river, which Mark counted on for late afternoon relief. He glanced over at the apartment's only air conditioner. It was a rusted, noisy monster that leaked about a liter of water an hour, so he had to keep remembering to empty the pan underneath it, or it overflowed all over the floor.

Mark considered turning it on, then decided not to. It didn't work that well anyway, and the damn thing cost a fortune to run.

He peeled off his sweat-soaked shirt and walked toward the back of the apartment. There was a small bedroom—four walls and a foam mattress with a mosquito net suspended from the ceiling—behind the living room. Mark threw the shirt in the direction of the bed, then pulled off his pants and heaved them into the room, too.

He walked down the hall past the tiny bathroom, with its squat latrine and a sink, and the separate shower closet, and entered the kitchen at the far end of the apartment.

He opened the half-sized refrigerator, prepared for disappointment. But he was wrong: he had left himself one Gold Harp. He pulled it out, delighted at how cold the green bottle felt against his hand. The can opener was where he'd left it in the sink. Mark pried the bottle cap off, took a long sip, and walked over to the dust-streaked louvered windows at the back of the kitchen.

The windows overlooked the compound behind a small *gendarmerie.* A handful of prisoners, mostly young men in filthy uniforms—rough cotton shorts and shirts that had once been white—were pulling up weeds as two gendarmes sat in the shade of the building.

One of the guards was reading the Cameroon Tribune, the government-owned daily newspaper; the other was asleep or close to it, with his head slumped forward almost to his knees. Any one of the prisoners could easily have left; he just worked his way to the edge of the compound and slipped off into the *quartier*. If he stayed calm, he could make it.

People in Akwa saw prisoners all the time, doing road work or cleaning the streets; besides, few Cameroonians went out of their way to help the *gendarmes*. Then it would just be a matter of getting to a friend or relative for a change of clothes and some money, and then back to the bush, to the home village or somewhere else where there were no phones and nobody wanted anything to do with the police.

But none of the prisoners would take the chance, Mark knew. He had watched them often from his window and seen others around the city, cutting weeds and sweeping the gutters. They all had the same look on their faces as if something had caught them by surprise, and it was all they could do to focus on the simple labor expected of them.

Mark walked back to the living room and sat down on the wicker couch he'd ordered from an Anglophone artisan out by the stadium. Two chairs made by the same artisan and the foam mattress constituted the rest of his furnishings.

He didn't even have a bed when he moved out of International Accounting's apartment to a smaller place near the Central Post Office. It was one of the newer high-rises, a styleless cement bunker owned by a *Bamileke* trader and thrown up in a hurry to cash in on the housing shortage.

Mark was one of its first tenants, but there were already cracks in most of the ceilings and walls, like rivers on a map, and they were spreading. The first time they filled the building's swimming pool, the adjacent parking lot flooded.

So, they drained the pool; it was still empty the last time Mark had passed by. Still, the building was centrally air-conditioned and on the good side of town, where there wasn't much traffic and no overcrowded *quartier* nearby, so it was quiet.

Mark drained the beer, then held it to his mouth, waiting for the suds at the bottom to slide up the bottle.

But he hadn't been able to afford the place, not after the bastard raised the rent. He sold his car, and that got him a few extra months. He should probably have moved then and saved some of the money, but he didn't. He kept hoping his regular "strings" would up their retainers. He even put together a resume of his costs and a short list of his better stories to each of them, but they all refused.

When he finally moved to the apartment in Akwa, he had barely enough money for the downpayment.

Mark sat up and felt instinctively for the envelope in his back pocket. He had a momentary stab of panic when he didn't feel the reassuring bulge but then realized he was in his underwear. He got up quickly and retrieved the envelope from his pants pocket. It felt heavy, in a nice way, and thick, too, like a medium-sized paperback.

God, another beer would have been nice. But he didn't have enough CFA left to buy one, and it was too late to exchange any of the dollars. That would have to wait until tomorrow. Even then, he'd have to be careful; technically, it was against the law to hold foreign currency in Cameroon for more than 24 hours —and you were supposed to say where it came from.

Mark took the money out of the envelope and counted it again, laying the $50 notes in two neat piles of $1,000 each. It had been a long time, a long fucking time since he'd seen that much cash—in any currency.

Yeah, he'd have to be damn careful.

CHAPTER 11

"Your balance?" Wanna asked and started to laugh, a deep staccato rumbling that accelerated on its own until the stutter he worked so hard to control overpowered him.

"You m-mean your im-im-imbalance," he managed, then laughed harder, out of control, his whole body bobbing up and down behind the desk.

Mark smiled to be polite. It wasn't that goddamn funny, not to him, anyway, but he knew better than to try to cut Wanna off when he got going.

Wanna N'Dele was the token Anglophone in Paribanque's Douala subsidiary. They hired him in the hope of luring away U.S. clients from Chase and Bank of Boston and also to satisfy government employment requirements, which insisted that regional and tribal diversity be taken into account.

Wanna didn't bring in any U.S. companies; they banked with Chase and Boston, of course, not only to speak English but to speak it with other Americans. But he did fulfill the bank's hiring obligation, at least as they saw it, and he was a competent banker.

Deborah and Mark had met him at a party shortly after they

arrived and liked him, so they opened their personal checking accounts at Paribanque.

(Despite Wanna's lobbying, Deborah kept the company's account at Chase because of a long relationship between the bank and International Accounting in New York.)

Like many of the educated Anglophones who hailed from the small slice of western Cameroon that was once British territory, Wanna had spent years in the US. First, at a college in Iowa that Mark had never heard of, and then at St. Louis University, where he earned an MBA.

He toyed with the idea of staying in the States, but then Cameroon hit oil, and Wanna decided there was more opportunity for an educated Anglophone at home.

"How's the taxi business?" Mark asked when Wanna calmed down.

"More headaches than profits," Wanna said, shaking his head. He never found his own money troubles as funny as Mark's.

Like everyone else in Cameroon with any money at all, Wanna was heavily leveraged, borrowing frantically to start up a business or buy land in areas of the city that showed promise. He owned a villa in Bonaberi, across the river, but rented it out for the income, while his family was packed into a dingy little house in the industrial zone in Bassa, out by the Guiness brewery.

He was also building a house in his village, up in the mountains north of Bamenda, but that was more or less required of village sons who had made good elsewhere. In addition to his job at the bank, Wanna had recently ventured into the taxi business, buying three beat-up Renault 12s—one from Mark—and *dashing* someone at the Transport Ministry for the required registrations.

He dragged three young cousins down from the village to drive for him. Wanna paid them next to nothing and made them drive 14 hours a day, but they ate and slept—albeit on mats on the floor—at his house, and it was understood that they were stealing from him.

Douala taxis didn't have meters, so it was only the driver's word on how much he took in on a given day. If revenues fell too much, Wanna threatened to send them back home—occasionally, he did it—and that kept the skimming to a manageable level.

Wanna reached into a drawer in his desk and pulled out a file. He opened it and started to laugh again, though this time under control.

"I'm going to cover it," Mark said quickly. "That's why I'm here."

When Deborah left, the French bastards at Paribanque pulled his overdraft privilege, but Wanna, when he could, looked the other way. They had been friends even when Deborah was around, but after she left, Mark saw a lot more of Wanna. He was married, with two small children, but as with most Cameroonian men, that didn't keep him home nights.

Mark couldn't afford to do it often, but when he had the money, he and Wanna sometimes spent a night crawling through Douala's bars and discos, which ranged from the chic, upscale clubs where champagne flowed freely at $150 a bottle, to squalid *"boites"* in the *quartiers* where the only thing to drink was cheap beer, and customers relieved themselves just outside the door.

"How much do you want to deposit?" Wanna asked.

Mark took out the envelope and slid it across the desk.

"Will that be a problem?" He asked. Wanna opened the envelope enough to see inside but did not remove the money.

"How much is it?"

"Two thousand dollars," Mark said quietly.

Wanna sat back in his chair a moment, thinking; then he

shook his head. "No, it's OK. Where'd you get them, Chad?" He asked.

Mark nodded, surprised. "How'd you know?"

"The northerners have been bringing in suitcases of them for a couple of weeks now," Wanna explained. He smiled. "We give them a better rate than the Nigerians."

"How many dollars have you handled?" Mark asked.

Wanna shrugged.

"I don't know, really. The northerners usually use the back stairway," he said, smiling.

That was the private entrance of Jacques le Richer, Paribanque's French managing director.

"They don't like to deal with lowly Anglophones," Wanna said, laughing. "But it's at least a hundred thousand."

"Dollars?" Mark hissed. Wanna nodded.

"Holy shit. How do you square that with the Central Bank?"

Wanna's laugh started again, gaining speed. "We g-give some to-to the g-governor," he said, his head bobbing up and down again. Mark laughed this time, too. And he had been worried about two thousand dollars.

Wanna filled out the deposit form, then went with Mark to the cashier to sign for a withdrawal of 20,000 CFA against the deposit.

They made plans to eat dinner that night at a fish restaurant in Akwa, and then Mark left.

His first stop was a *patisserie* that had recently opened next to the Akwa Palace, Douala's oldest decent hotel. It was owned by an Italian couple and was sparkling clean, even the sidewalk terrace. It served real croissants and steaming hot cafe au lait, with the milk whipped into a foam on top like in French cafes. There were also free copies of *Le Monde*, usually only two or three days old, scattered on the tables inside and on the terrace.

Mark ate breakfast at the *patisserie* whenever he could afford it, which meant he hadn't been in a while. It was still early, so he sat on the terrace, though far enough back from the street that the vendors couldn't reach him. The waiters were supposed to shoo them away, but they couldn't get them all; anyone sitting too close to the sidewalk was bound to get a lottery ticket or a package of biscuits shoved into his face before he was finished.

Mark grabbed a two-day-old *Le Monde* from the table next to his and scanned the headlines while he ate. There was a short AFP piece on Chad buried inside, but it was nothing new, just Alain churning out words to keep Paris off his back.

There wasn't a word about U.S. dollars.

No one named Antoine worked at Antoine's Travel Agency, nor was it owned by anyone of that name. If Mark had ever heard how the agency came by its name, he had long since forgotten. It wasn't the biggest or busiest travel agency in Douala, and it wasn't the best; some people, Deborah among them, after non-existent reservations, stranded Mark and her overnight in Rome, swore it was the worst.

But that didn't bother Victor Mawanga, Antoine's owner. Nor did the fact that the agency often had more staff—all of them Victor's relatives—than customers. In fact, Victor rarely showed his face there; when he did, it was only to pick up his own tickets or to scream at his nephews for their laziness and stupidity.

In his absence, his wife Rosalie ran the agency. She was, like Victor, a Bakwere from Buea, the old capital of British West Cameroon; like Victor, she had lived under British rule long enough to know that if it was British, it was better. Rosalie had never been attractive—she and Victor were well suited on that score—and she dressed accordingly.

Her elaborate dresses were dowdy enough for the Queen Mother, so much so that Mark suspected some tailor in Buea was making a fortune copying whatever the Royal women were wearing in the English magazines that still sold well in western Cameroon.

Rosalie had a superficial, practiced friendliness, which, Mark discovered quickly, hid a nasty, vindictive temper that was offset only by her incompetence and all but impenetrable thickness.

"Good morning, Mr. Reilly," she said, smiling, in the sing-song accent that he hated because it should have been a parody but wasn't. "We haven't seen you for some time."

"Hello, Rosalie," Mark said, hurrying for the stairs, talking as he moved. "I had to go up to Chad for a while."

"I hope your trip was an enjoyable one," she said. She wasn't kidding.

"Uh, thanks, it was lovely," Mark said. He was halfway up the stairs when she called out again.

"Mr. Reilly." Mark leaned over the banister.

"Yes, Rosalie?" He asked, pretending he didn't know what was coming.

Her smile was still there, with all the warmth of a stiletto.

"I am still wanting payment for last month's telex bills," she said, waving a folder at him. "I have many bills to pay, and the PTT will take away our machine if we are late."

That was a lie, of course. The PTT was always at least six to eight months behind on its billing. Not that it mattered; he didn't owe Rosalie a thing.

"Rosalie, if you recall, my clients pay directly into your account in London," Mark explained for the hundredth time.

"Yes, but I have heard nothing from them, Mr. Reilly," she complained. Gone now were the smile and the veneer of cordiality; they were replaced by the nasty stupidity that made any discussion with her pointless.

"Did you check your bank statement, Rosalie?" Mark asked, struggling to keep his tone polite.

"We have not received one for some time," she snapped. That was a lie, too. Victor was a careful man when it came to money, particularly his own, but it was a good bet he never showed the statements to Rosalie. She went on muttering about the consequences of not paying their bills, but she wasn't looking at Mark anymore, which meant they'd finished for the time being.

It usually ended like that; on the few occasions that it got out of hand—Rosalie had once threatened to cut off his access to the telex—Mark went to see Victor. For the next day, or maybe two, Rose left him alone, but within a week, she was nagging again, as if Victor's explanation was good for only a short time, and then things reverted to their natural order.

Victor, unlike his wife, was delighted with the arrangement with Mark.

For Victor, Antoine's was a plane ticket, or more correctly, lots of them. He was an Oxford-educated lawyer and the only Cameroonian partner in Nigeria's largest law firm. He had seen the unification of the two Cameroons coming and took the time and trouble to learn the French legal system. Within a few years of the union, Victor had made the law firm and himself a fortune representing Anglophone clients in Francophone courts.

The arrival of the U.S. companies was an unexpected windfall but one that Victor quickly exploited. He represented all of the American oil companies in Douala, and according to Deborah, who saw his billings to them, regularly charged exorbitant fees for even the simplest legal procedures.

Victor, of course, steered the Americans to Antoine's for their travel needs, and despite the agency's shortcomings, most of them remained loyal customers. But that was just a bonus; Antoine's real value to Victor was its travel privileges, specifically, cut rates and often free airline tickets. Victor traveled frequently, to Lagos, of course, for the law firm, but more often to London, where against all sorts of Cameroon laws, he held several pound sterling accounts and owned substantial rental properties in Brixton and other rundown areas of the city, which was why Victor was happy to accommodate Mark. Victor made money on a machine his small agency only rarely used—but had to have. He tacked on a hefty user fee, which Mark passed on to his clients, and most importantly, Mark's people paid their portion of the telex bill directly into Victor's London accounts.

That allowed him to get money out of the country without going through the very long Central Bank request procedure, which, in any case, always required *dashing* someone high up at the Bank.

At first, Mark had worried about what the authorities would do to him if they ever found out; Victor sure as hell wasn't declaring the pound income. But he had tried without success for 18 months to get the PTT to install a machine in his apartment, and as Douala had no public telex service, he had no choice.

So, Antoine's became his mailing and telex address.

In his box, he found a letter from his mother, another one from a college friend in New York, and a thick, expensive envelope from a law firm in Paris that he'd never heard of. Mark slipped them into the small leather case where he carried his residence permit and press card. He'd read them at home.

The telex messages were the usual: an urgent request for the weekly coffee and cocoa export figures that the Commodity Stabilization Board issued. He'd missed them while he was away. It was idiot work, but easy money.

"Thks yr offer for feature on CFA franc zone, but 'fraid will pass for now. Best rgds JJ" from the bastards at the New York Times Sunday Economic Section.

"Thks yrs on drop of Soviet influence in black Africa, but 'fraid not what we hearing exWashington. Frankly, cudst take piece saying just the opposite if you feel can handle. Rgds" from a Boston paper.

"Assholes," Mark muttered, crumbling the telex and tossing it into the cardboard box Antoine's used for garbage.

Then he took out his notebook, read quickly through his notes from Chad, and turned on the telex machine.

In the past, he had found it difficult to write up reporting trips, especially to Chad. As if making it up there and back was the real job, one that required so much effort that reducing it all to 500 or even 1,000 words seemed an impossible task.

But this time was different. He had a major story, and he was all alone on it.

Ndjamena, Chad, March 22—The Libyan government has begun paying Chadian soldiers with dollars, flooding the nearly bankrupt country with U.S. currency, according to Chadian and French sources.

As much as two million dollars has poured into this war-ravaged city in the past three months, according to…

Mark realized he didn't know Calvady's first name. He sat back and concentrated, trying to remember anyone addressing him as anything other than Monsieur Calvady. It was no use; he'd never heard it.

"Goddamn it," he muttered, staring at the words on the telex as if they could help him. He hesitated a second, then wrote, "...Jean-Claude Calvady, a French businessman, who has made a fortune buying the dollars at deep discounts, then exchanging them in Europe."

It didn't really matter, certainly not for a nobody like Calvady. Hell, maybe his name was Jean-Claude.

Mark glanced over at his notes, then began typing again. Besides, Calvady was the only one likely to call him on it, and the bastard would have other things than his name to worry about when he saw the article.

CHAPTER 12

Wanna picked him up in a new Peugeot 305.

"Where the hell did you get this?" Mark asked, climbing in. Wanna smiled.

"I bought it when I was in Paris for that training program last month," he said.

"How'd you get it so fast?" Mark asked.

Big ticket items like cars and machinery took a long time to clear customs; the paperwork was endless, and duties often ran more than the purchase price.

Wanna laughed. "The c-customs chief is my c-c-cousin," he said, having trouble getting the last word out.

Mark laughed, too. "So, he's a little richer, and the government's a little poorer."

"Better for the economy," Wanna said, laughing harder. "The government p-people only st-steal it anyway and p-put it in a b-bank account in Europe," he said. "At least, my c-cousin will k-keep it here."

"What if someone at the port found out?" Mark asked. Wanna's whole body was shaking now, so he had trouble spitting out his answer.

"Th-then I'd h-have to *d-dash* him, too," he said and didn't stop laughing until they were parked near the restaurant.

Marie's hadn't always been in Akwa. It had started out as a "chop house" in Bonalembe, a poorer *quartier* further west. The "restaurant" then consisted of a few benches and tables crammed under a corrugated metal roof behind a tiny, run-down wood frame shack.

The only way into the place was down an open sewer that ran alongside the property; diners had to straddle it carefully to keep their feet dry, then hop off, at a certain point, into the backyard.

That was where Mark first met Marie. Deborah had asked one of her local accountants to take them to a real Cameroonian restaurant, and even back then, Marie's reputation was spreading. She never cooked anything but fish, which she bought fresh every morning from the fishing villages at the mouth of the Wouri. She packed it in large styrofoam ice chests that she kept near the entrance. Customers selected the fish they wanted before they sat down.

Marie grilled the fish over an open fire built inside an old oil drum. She stood for hours, the sweat pouring down her soft brown face, fanning the flames and turning the fish often, each time basting it generously with a marinate made from oil and hot red peppers.

She served it like that, with a dollop of *pili-pili,* a fiery red pepper sauce, and some kind of starch, either baked plantains or a handful of manioc sticks, to cut the heat of the pili-pili. There were no knives or forks; clients ate with their hands. Marie's son, a quiet, polite boy in his late teens, was the only waiter. He brought the fish and took orders for drinks, which essentially meant beer. They stocked local and imported brands, and it was always ice cold.

Over the years, Mark had eaten there—and at her new place —at least a hundred times. He'd never heard of anyone, African or white, getting sick from the food, which was more than he could say for the overpriced French and Vietnamese restaurants in Douala.

Marie moved in 1979 to a corner lot in Akwa, where she claimed to have been born. During the rainy season that year, she tore down the shack on the lot and built a spacious, five-room cement house with a large covered terrace outside that could handle three times as many customers as the old place.

The new restaurant had real tables and chairs and no sewer, and Marie, who acted as kind of a hostess, had ceded her place at the fire to her son—though she kept a close eye on him. There were three waiters now, all relatives of Marie's.

Her clientele in Akwa was different, too. The Africans tended to be professionals, wealthy businessmen, or, like Wanna, management staff in large expatriate companies. White faces, which had been a rarity in the Bonalembe place, were common and some nights took up almost half the tables.

The only thing that hadn't changed was the food; it was still the best fish Mark had tasted anywhere.

"Salut jeune hornme," Marie said, reaching way up to peck Mark on both cheeks. *"Vous allez bien?"*

"Oui, merci, Marie, et vous?" Mark asked.

"Ca va," she said, smiling.

She was wearing a black cocktail dress that stretched dangerously across her ample hips and bosom. It looked out of place there in Akwa, but it was a sure sign things were going well for her. That kind of dress cost plenty in Douala, and it was a long way from the sarong and kerchief Marie wore, sweating over the fire at the old place.

"Oof et toi," she said, swiping a hand playfully at Wanna. "Where's your little girlfriend?"

Wanna tried to keep from laughing but could not.

"She was m-my c-c-cousin," he managed, and they both doubled over laughing.

Marie's son greeted them politely when they walked over to pick out their fish. They were late, and the ice chest had only a handful of fish left. The boy held up a hand to them and said something sharply in Douala to one of the waiters, who hurried into the house.

A moment later, he returned with another ice chest full of fish.

"Merci," Mark said to the son, who smiled and nodded, then went back to fanning and basting the fish. Mark and Wanna picked out a good-sized *barrh*, a thick, white meat fish with few bones, then went to find a table. The terrace was crowded, but a Cameroonian couple was just finishing, and the waiter who had brought out the ice chest motioned them over. They both ordered St. Pauli's Girl, which for whatever reason had recently supplanted Beck's as the status symbol among successful Cameroonians.

"How's Therese?" Mark asked.

"Fine, fine, thanks," Wanna said quickly. Wanna's wife was a bright, pleasant woman from Bamenda who had taught English in a French lycee for several years before their first son was born. She was attractively plump, the way Cameroonian men liked their women, with a tireless, natural smile that not even Wanna's infidelities seemed to erase. Of course, that sort of thing was common, almost expected really, of Cameroonian men of a certain age and position.

It had driven Deborah crazy, and even Mark had felt a pang or two of pity for Therese, but at least Wanna had the class to keep it discreet.

"Have you heard from Deborah?" Wanna asked. Cameroonians were direct about most things anyway, and Wanna was a good friend. Hell, he'd known Deborah as long as he had Mark.

Mark took a sip of beer and shook his head.

"Not really. I got a letter from a lawyer in Paris asking me to sign some divorce papers."

Wanna made a face. Divorce was rare in Africa, and the idea made most Africans uneasy. A bad marriage was preferable to none at all.

"Are you going to sign them?" Wanna asked.

Mark shook his head. "I threw them in the rubbish."

They sat for a moment, drinking, not saying anything. Wanna was the only one Mark had really been able to talk to after she left. Maybe that was because he never once felt that Wanna derived any pleasure or satisfaction from his misfortune—if indeed that's what it was.

They didn't do it often, usually only after Mark had had too much to drink. Later, he always wished he'd shut up, but who could say; maybe it helped. Not tonight, though. He just didn't feel like it.

"How was Chad?" Wanna asked. He was good that way, too; he knew when to let things drop.

"Pretty much the same," Mark said, "except that you get a feeling that Goukouni might be getting a little tired of the Libyans."

"He better not get too tired," Wanna said, starting to laugh. "Qadaffi will p-put him t-to sleep." Mark laughed.

"Yeah, maybe. But the Libyans there don't look too happy either," Mark said. "No electricity, no running water, lousy food, and most of them are living in tents."

"They should feel honored," Wanna laughed; "Q-Qadaffi says he prefers living in a tent."

Mark smiled. "Yeah, but Qadaffi's got his harem living with him," he said. "Apparently, even the Chadian whores don't want anything to do with the Libyans."

"Th-that's because Arabs are such l-lousy l-lovers," Wanna said, laughing harder.

"What makes them so lousy?" Mark asked, grinning.

"T-too much p-praying," Wanna said. His whole body was shaking now. "All t-that b-bowing and kn-kneeling c-c-cuts off circulation to their p-puds."

Mark laughed. Wanna always amazed him with his grasp of American slang. There were a few whites in Douala Mark still saw: a couple of Brits from Guiness and now and then a French couple with whom he and Deborah had been friendly.

But he saw more of Wanna than any of them, and that was by choice. It was just easier: no expectations to fulfill, or more likely, to disappoint, and no morning-after second thoughts about what he'd said or didn't say. He drained his beer, a little surprised that it was gone. He raised a hand until he caught the waiter's eye, then waved the empty bottle and stuck up two fingers.

He felt good, relaxed for a change, the way he always did after one beer so that his body seemed to melt into the chair. It was the money, too, of course; he'd been scraping by for months, and it was nice, damn nice, to have a little extra again.

Calvady and the Libyans could go fuck themselves; they couldn't touch him in Douala.

"You didn't tell me how you got the dollars," Wanna said after he'd calmed down.

"A small *dash,*" Mark said, smiling. Wanna grinned, thinking Mark was kidding.

"To d-do what?"

"Actually, it was to not write a story," Mark said. The waiter brought the second round of beers. Wanna was still smiling, but he was curious now, too.

"Hey, you *dash* the governor of the Central Bank not to report the dollars you're taking in, and your cousin at the port not to see the car you're driving away in, so why shouldn't I get paid not to write a story?" Mark asked.

Wanna still wasn't sure whether Mark was pulling his leg.

"In fact," Mark added, feeling the alcohol surge out from his stomach to his arms and legs, "$2,000 is about four times more than I ever got for writing anything. Maybe that's the new journalism: you know, I could be like the American farmers who get paid not to grow things."

Wanna laughed. "What story are you n-not g-going to write?" He asked.

"About the dollars," Mark said.

"Somebody paid you dollars not t-to write about them?" Mark nodded, smiling.

"But I wrote about them anyway," he said. Wanna's eyes widened a little; then he started laughing again.

"You're beginning t-to behave l-like a Cameroonian," he stammered.

"Or a Frenchman," Mark said, laughing now, too, thinking of Calvady across the table at the hotel.

"Y-yes, maybe l-like a Frenchman," Wanna agreed, wiping his eyes with the back of his hand.

The waiter brought their fish. Wanna broke off several pieces to speed the cooling, then fanned them with his hand. Mark knew that was mostly for his benefit. Like most Africans who grew up eating with their hands, Wanna had a high tolerance for hot food and could have handled the fish right off the grill.

He was about to tell Wanna the rest of the dollar story when he saw Koumba walk in from the street. It didn't really surprise him. She came there a lot; they'd even eaten there together a few times. A white man followed her in, and that wasn't a surprise either.

When they got a little closer, Mark saw it was Gilles. That wasn't really his name. He was a Greek with some unpronounceable name from mythology who had grown up in Douala and then gone off to school in Paris.

Most of his friends were French, and Gilles liked to pretend he was, too, so he called himself Gilles.

His family owned a thriving hardware store in Douala and a not-so-thriving coffee export business down by the port. Like a lot of the younger Greeks in Cameroon, Gilles had never lived in Greece. His father, along with most of the community's older generation, arrived in the late 1940s after Nasser expelled them from Egypt.

Like the Lebanese further up the West coast and the Indians in East Africa, the Greeks in Cameroon were an insular group. The older ones lived a modest, almost peasant-like existence and never flaunted their wealth, though the truth was they controlled much of the country's vital middle-level commerce.

And like the Lebanese and Indians, they were hated for it.

Mark had once interviewed Gilles' father for a feature on the Greek community. He was a stern, taciturn man and a tough interview, though he opened up a little when Mark got him talking about the early days in Douala before independence.

That was the first time Mark met Gilles. He was working in the family hardware store. He was just a clerk then, and that's the way his father treated him. He even made Gilles serve them coffee.

But Gilles had recently opened a "marina" on the Wouri, with a dozen slips and a small restaurant/bar, where his worthless friends kept their speed boats and got drunk. Deborah had once referred to Gilles and his friends as the "sleazebags"; it was a name that stuck so that after a while, she and Mark simply referred to them collectively as "the sleazebags" and almost never by name.

They were a group, mostly French but a few Greeks, all with plenty of money and no class.

Most of them worked in family businesses, then spent their nights crawling the nightclubs, usually the expensive ones like le Tunnel, but sometimes the raunchier spots like le Cafe des Sports down by the port.

They all drank too much and talked too loud, like high

school boys competing for attention. Many of them, like Gilles, were married; but they never brought their wives along, preferring the company of young African women, whores mostly, whom they treated with a mixture of possessive, pawing lust and machismo disdain.

Koumba wasn't exactly a whore, but she was close.

Mark watched her joke with Marie, flashing her beautiful teeth, laughing too hard, with one arm draped over Marie's shoulder as they walked toward the grill to pick out their fish.

Koumba was tall, like most Serrer women, and towered over Marie. She had on skin-tight designer jeans and three-inch heels, and a yellow tube top stretched so tightly across her enormous tits that it seemed only a matter of time before it snapped.

Gilles strutted in front of Marie and Koumba, a lit Gaulois smoking in one corner of his mouth. He nodded to some of the other whites on the terrace and shook a few hands. After a moment, he turned, his impatience too obvious, said something to Koumba, and then walked down the terrace without waiting for her.

He had on what Deborah called the uniform—black pants, tight in the crotch and loose in the leg, black shoes and a short-sleeved white shirt, unbuttoned most of the way down his stomach. As he approached, Mark could see that the shirt was already stained with sweat in several places and almost transparent where it clung to the flab that ringed Gilles' waist and jiggled when he walked.

Gilles saw Mark before Koumba did.

"Ca va?" He mumbled, eyebrows up, just to make certain that Mark understood he didn't give a shit how it was going. Gilles didn't smile, and he didn't even think about shaking hands.

"Bon soir," Mark said evenly, nodding once.

Wanna glanced up quickly at Gilles over his shoulder, then went back to eating. Mark dug into the fish, too, pulling off a large chunk and dipping it into the pile of pili-pili on the side of the platter.

He didn't really mind saying hello to her, but if she wanted to walk on by while he was eating, that would be even better. But she didn't. Out of the corner of his eye, Mark saw the blue-jeaned crotch stop and then bump against the table edge. He finished the bite of fish and leaned back in his chair.

"Bon soir," he said, smiling.

She stared at him, her lips pursed outward in a feigned pout, exaggerated like all her movements, mindful of the audience, even when there wasn't one. Koumba made a point of greeting Wanna first, holding out her hand to him until he noticed.

"Ah, hello Koumba, *ca va?"* Wanna asked politely, taking her hand, then letting go. He immediately went back to his fish. To Wanna, Koumba was a whore, and even then, nothing special. He liked his women wide and sturdy; Koumba's long legs and tight, round ass didn't do a thing for him.

She held her hand limply at Mark, still pouting. Mark shook hands.

"Bon soir, Koumba," he said. Out of the corner of his eye, he could see that Gilles had stopped and turned to wait for her. Maybe that would hurry her up.

"Na fio, bok?" She asked, truculently, like a small child, making it clear she didn't forgive him.

"Me, he men," he answered automatically. That was how they met, really; Koumba had never met a white man who spoke Serrer, and she'd been impressed, or at least curious.

"Ca va?" He asked, switching to French. He didn't mind speaking Serrer when they were alone; he even liked it sometimes. But he wasn't going to offend Wanna just to please her.

"When did you get back?" She demanded, ignoring his question.

"This afternoon," he lied. Wanna didn't even look up.

"Koumba, tu viens?" Gilles hissed from behind them, furious at being kept waiting—or more precisely, being seen kept waiting—by an African whore.

She had been with Gilles the night Mark met her, too. At the Cafe des Sports, the cheapest and roughest of downtown Douala's night spots. Sailors liked the Cafe des Sports because it was close to their ships and because the whores, though not much to look at, were affordable. It wasn't air-conditioned, so it smelled constantly of the river, sweat and old beer, and piss from the filthy bathrooms.

Mark went there a few times right after Deborah left. The beer was cheap, and for some reason, the noise helped, and he knew he wouldn't run into anyone he didn't feel like seeing just then.

Gilles and his friends were pretty drunk when they came in and, as always, too loud, making sure people knew they were there. Gilles staggered off to the bathroom at the back, and Mark found himself standing next to Koumba at the bar. She didn't look Cameroonian. She was too tall, for one thing. It was conceivable that she was from one of the northern tribes, but Mark didn't think so.

He was feeling good after several beers, so he asked.

Koumba looked over at him for a moment, then shook her head. She was from Senegal, she said, then went back to waiting for Gilles, making it clear she wasn't interested.

"Nanga def ?" Mark asked in Wolof.

She smiled but didn't look at him. Lots of whites knew a little Wolof. And she was a Serrer, she explained.

"Wo hey moussa apah, hado fia mene?" He asked, getting as close as he could in Serrer to 'what's a beautiful girl like you doing in a place like this?' He wanted to add: "with an asshole like that," but he didn't.

She turned then, unable to hide her curiosity.

Gilles was rude, bordering on ugly, when he saw Mark, but

by then, it was too late. Koumba was fascinated by a white man speaking her language, maybe even a little homesick after not hearing it for so long. Mark didn't know much about Gilles back then, just who he was and, second-hand, that he had once told the other "sleazebags" that he'd give a month's salary to be able to fuck Deborah.

So, he didn't mind annoying Gilles; he may even have wanted to provoke him that night to get just one solid punch in the prick's sneering face and maybe hit a few of the others, too, before they stopped him.

Mostly, though, it was Koumba. He had just lost his wife and didn't feel too good about it, but standing there with her at the crowded bar, their arms pressed against one another, and when she turned, her tits straining against her knit blouse only inches from his chest, Mark forgot all about Deborah.

Before Gilles dragged her out of the Cafe des Sports, Mark asked her in Serrer to have dinner with him the next night. She accepted.

"Bon appetit," she muttered, still pouting, and turned to rejoin Gilles. As she moved past him, Mark felt her long fingernails scrape gently across the back of his neck. It gave him goosebumps right down to his groin.

Wanna had ignored it all, but now looked up and smiled at Mark.

"You're p-paying with your ill-gotten g-gains, right?"

Mark smiled. "Right."

Wanna hailed the waiter as he hurried past with a tray of fish. He held up his empty St. Pauli Girl and then two fingers.

CHAPTER 13

The meal cost him 10,000 CFA, about $50, which was more than he'd ever spent at Marie's. She'd raised her goddamn prices again, but they'd also had four beers each, which accounted for almost three-quarters of the bill.

By the time he got to the top of the stairs, Mark was sweating freely, mostly from the climb, but also from the beers and the pili-pili.

Not that whites really needed an excuse to perspire in Douala. He pulled the key from his pocket, then groped in the dark for the keyhole.

The Douala bastard had been promising to fix the light for two months, but that was par for the course, too.

"It always disappoints, doesn't it?" Mary, a British friend of theirs, had said once, referring to the place and Africa in general. Well, she and Simon, her husband, had it worse than Mark. They'd lived out in the goddamn bush for five years.

He got the key in on the third try and unlocked the door. Even that late at night, a blast of hot, damp air rushed out at him and dissipated in the stairwell. Mark peeled off his shirt and draped it over one of the wicker chairs near the front windows. If there was any breeze at all during the night, it would dry.

He walked down the hallway to the kitchen. He'd gone shopping in the afternoon, after he finished the article, for fruit, mostly, which was all he ate at home, and beer and coffee. He opened the refrigerator and pulled out a Gold Harp.

St. Pauli's Girl was fine once in awhile, but more than that, and he'd be in trouble. As it was, most of the 20,000 CFA he'd withdrawn that morning was already gone. He'd have to be careful. $2,000 was nice money, more than he'd seen in a long time, but it could go fast in Douala. He still had to pay his rent, though not until the son of a bitch fixed that goddamn stair light.

Of course, the dollar piece would pay well if all three newspapers he sent it to use it; he might even get a longer news analysis out of it, but he'd wait until they asked.

Tomorrow, he'd go by the Cameroon Tribune office and check the issues he'd missed. There was usually something in it he could re-write and sell to someone. Mark opened the beer and then walked back toward the living room. He didn't turn on any lights; electricity was expensive in Cameroon, and besides, the dark was cooler.

He sat down on the couch. The wood felt cool against his back, but only for a minute. Then, the stale, damp air glued his skin to the wicker so that it made a ripping noise when he moved. The stupid bastard had built the place with all the windows facing west so that from noon until sundown, the apartments baked in direct sunlight. At night, the windows caught the breeze from the Wouri and, farther out, the Atlantic, but it was never enough to chase the heat entirely.

Only the rains brought any relief, and then everything—clothes and shoes and sheets and towels—stayed damp for months on end.

Mark took a sip of beer and then held the cold bottle to his face. The leather *gris-gris* he always wore was stuck to the sweat in the middle of his chest, so he pried it loose and flipped it over his shoulder. The villagers in Diarrere had given it to him as a parting gift the night before he left. It was a simple one—*gris-gris* were expensive, and it was a poor village—just a leather cord and a thick, leather medallion about the size of a big postage stamp hanging from it.

Kofaye Diouf, the village chief, tied it around Mark's neck, and Mark, in his farewell speech, promised never to take it off. That way, he said, he'd never forget them. It had bothered him at first, especially the medallion swinging under his shirt. Mark didn't like jewelry and, except for his miraculous medal days in grammar school, had never worn anything around his neck.

But he wore it, first out of conviction, then habit. Over the years, the leather blackened; the medallion, which was really several layers of leather pressed and stitched together, had become smooth and hard, like a stone, from the alternating wetness and drying.

If nothing else, it had proved a convenient ice-breaker with women the first time he slept with them. When he'd finally bedded Deborah, he told her it was from a witch doctor and gave him extraordinary sexual powers.

"Doesn't work too well," she said, still short of breath but wanting seconds and trying to coax him to life again only minutes after they'd finished. Deborah could be funny in bed, lewd even, which surprised Mark in the beginning, before he knew her well. She was so serious about other things, school and then work, and when he'd met her, she'd seemed so...correct.

"That's great; the country needs as many accountants as it can get," he said, smiling.

It was in a bar just across Broadway from Columbia. She'd come in with a group that included a friend of Mark's from the journalism school. The place was crowded, and Mark had a table to himself, so they sat down. Deborah, who took the chair next to his, smiled at first because she thought he was serious, but then her face flushed pink, and her mouth tightened.

"You rude butthole," she said, embarrassed but angry too. She looked at him for a second, then turned away and began talking to the friend on the other side of her. It was the prim, almost prudish modesty of the insult that attracted him. As if she couldn't say "fucking asshole" like everyone else.

He was kidding; he apologized and made several deprecating remarks about journalists to prove it. She didn't let him off the hook right away, listening more than she talked, and even then, only short, non-committal items like where she was from and how long she'd been in New York.

Later, when he pressed her on it, she said it was probably the Peace Corps thing that kept her from walking out that night. Anyone who'd done what Mark had couldn't be all bad.

He put the beer down on the floor next to the couch and got up. He switched on the overhead light and then fished a crumpled-up letter from the paper bag near the door that he used for garbage.

Mark sat down again and straightened the letter out. It was in French: "Monsieur Reilly," the lawyer began; divorce was an unfortunate and disagreeable development for all concerned. But a lot of the sadness and, yes, pain, he acknowledged, could be assuaged for both parties by simply putting it behind them. The lawyer was certain Mark wanted to avoid any unpleasantness; the easiest way was to sign and return the enclosed papers.

Mark crumbled the letter into a ball again and heaved it in the general direction of the paper bag. That was even easier.

He'd met the French SOB once at a *Brasserie du Cameroun* party Deborah dragged him to; they weren't clients, but she was marketing them hard. He was an inch or two shorter than

Deborah and solidly built, though it wouldn't have hurt him to lose five or ten pounds.

Mark's first impression was that he was a lot older than he and Deborah, but that was probably due to his position at the *Brasserie* and from hearing he had two teenage children. The bastard probably wasn't fifty.

He praised Deborah's *professionalisme* until she blushed, and he asked Mark if he ever played tennis. They'd have to have a game sometime. They didn't, of course, which was just as well. Mark's game was erratically mediocre, and the Frenchman, Deborah told him on the way home, was one of the top over-40 players at the Douala tennis club.

At the time, he hadn't wondered at all how she knew that.

Mark stared over at his mother's letter on the table and thought about re-reading it, but didn't. It was just family news that never changed much: about his brother, whose law practice was booming and whose two kids were getting big, and his father, who should stop working such crazy hours at the small women's apparel factory he owned, but never would.

And at the end, as always, a carefully worded query about when he was coming home for a visit, which was her euphemism for forever. He could probably get a job, not with any of the big papers, but with a local one somewhere, even if it was just on the copy desk. Or even with his father, like he'd done all those summers if he just wanted to make money. Mark had thought about it and still did, but like he'd thought about the priesthood as a boy in Catholic school, just because they talked about it so much.

Once, shortly after they'd arrived in Douala, Mark drove out to Victoria, the old British port city in Southwest Cameroon, to interview a tea expert at the Cameroon Development Company.

The CDC, formed by the British after World War I, reverted to the Cameroon government at independence, but its top four or five managers were still Brits. It was the oldest and largest plantation group in the country, with thousands of hectares of oil palm, rubber trees, and, to a lesser extent, tea under cultivation throughout the Southwest province.

CDC headquarters and the dozen or so colonial-era villas where senior management was housed were located just west of the city, on a sea-front estate. Manicured lawns ran right to the edge of the Atlantic, where the ocean, churned into an angry white foam by crosscurrents, pounded endlessly against the black volcanic rocks that made up Cameroon's western coastline.

The tea expert, whose youth was spent on a plantation in Kenya, had been with the CDC since before independence and was closing in on retirement.

He invited Mark—begged him, really—to lunch at his villa. Mark drank beer, but the old Brit polished off most of a bottle of Johnnie Walker. By dessert, he was slurring his words and rambling on about the early days. He and his wife had come out after their honeymoon, back when Victoria dwarfed Douala as Cameroon's busiest port, and the only blacks at CDC were the field hands and the houseboys.

Then came independence. "Bloody Africans running around like chickens with their heads cut off, pretending they knew what the hell they were doing," he muttered. "Buggers didn't have a bloody clue; still don't." He poured what was left of the whiskey bottle into his glass and threw it down his throat.

His wife, who was sick a lot in the beginning, caught a ship home at the start of their third rainy season to see a doctor. It turned out to be intestinal amoebas (which couldn't survive in England), and she got better. But she wasn't on the return ship in October; just a letter saying she wouldn't be coming back.

Back then, expatriate leave was once every five years, and the tea expert had two to go.

"I wrote her, begging her to give it another try, but she never even wrote back. At first, I thought I'd go out of my bloody mind. But you don't, you know. You just get on with it, and after awhile, you almost start enjoying the bloody misery."

Mark picked up the empty Gold Harp bottle and walked back to the kitchen. There was a deposit on the bottles, and it was damn expensive.

He was tempted to have one more. It had been a long time since he'd had a refrigerator full of them. But he didn't want to get drunk, and he was already pretty close.

He checked his watch; it was 10:35.

She probably wouldn't be late. Gilles' wife wasn't much to look at—a plain, dark-haired Greek girl with wide hips and more than a hint of a mustache—but her father and Gilles' had come out from Egypt together and were like brothers.

Mark had met the old man only once, but that was enough to know he'd never stand for his son, blatantly insulting his best friend's daughter. And Gilles, for all his swagger, was scared shitless of his father.

So, he'd feed Koumba, then fuck her at a friend's place if it was available or in the cheapest room at the Beau Sejour if it wasn't. And then he'd go home. And Koumba would come to Mark's place.

It hadn't started like that. At first, she stayed there only when they went out, which wasn't too often, as Mark couldn't afford it. But then she began showing up, often very late at night. That was all right with Mark. It was nice, flattering even, to have a beautiful woman interested in him, and it meant he got laid, if he wanted to, without having to spend any money.

When he figured out what was going on, he got angry and threw her out. But a week later, she was back, and he let her in.

It still bothered him a little having her like that after Gilles. But Mark didn't have the money to ask her to leave the bastard and might not even if he had it.

He heard the scrape of footsteps on the stairs outside. He waited until he was sure they were past the floor below him, then went and opened the door. He could hear her breathing in the black stairwell before he could see her. Koumba wasn't in great shape, at least not for that kind of exercise, and she hated the climb.

"Bon soir, Koumba," Mark said when she'd dragged herself up to the landing. She didn't say anything; she just stared at him as if he offended her by being there. She was still pouting about his not letting her stay at the apartment while he was in Chad. He wasn't sure what the Douala bastard could do to him if he found out, but mostly, he didn't want her getting too comfortable there.

So, he lied and said the landlord was going to do some work in the apartment while he was away. She didn't believe him and said so. Mark didn't give a damn what she thought and said so. That's the way they'd left it.

He walked back into the apartment, and she followed, reluctantly, like some freshman co-ed, not quite sure she wanted to go through with it.

"Alors, c'etait bien?" Mark asked his back to her. He turned when she didn't respond. She was still pouting, but now she was angry too.

"Le diner, c'etait bien?" He repeated, trying not to laugh.

Koumba ignored him and walked slowly around the living room.

"Il n'a rien fait," she said accusingly.

"He fixed the faucet," Mark lied. Koumba pushed her lips out and looked defiantly over at the wall. She still didn't believe him, and he still didn't care.

"Tu peut au moins m'offrir une biere," she said, looking at him finally.

"I don't have any," he said. "Didn't have time to go to the supermarket."

Koumba made a sound through her teeth.

"Tu n'as jamais rien" she said disgustedly.

"Fuck you, Koumba," he said in English, surprised at the blood rushing into his face. He even took a step toward her before he caught himself.

"Qu'est-ce que ca veut dire, fuck you?" Koumba asked warily. She didn't pronounce it right, and it came out closer to "fack yoo."

Mark exhaled and shook his head. What the hell was he doing? It was only Koumba, for Christ's sake.

"It means I'm very tired," he said. "Will you turn out the light when you come?" She made a face again but didn't say anything.

Mark's bedroom was the hottest room in the apartment. There were no windows, so the air that baked in the room all day had no place to escape at night. Once in awhile, on the hottest nights, he dragged the mattress out to the living room and slept in front of the windows. But the mosquito net was nailed to his bedroom ceiling and couldn't be moved. So, it was a trade-off, and he usually chose the heat.

The bedroom was darker, too, the way he liked it. He tugged off his pants and underwear and slipped quickly under the net to keep the mosquitoes from getting in with him. He lay on top of the sheet; sometime toward dawn, he'd climb underneath if the room had cooled off enough by then.

It was too dark to see Koumba come in, but he heard her getting undressed. First, the tube top going over her head and then the jeans scraping softly down her legs. Mark reached for her as soon as she was under the net, his breathing already short and hard. Koumba relaxed into him, her petulance gone now, as she stroked his chest with her long nails, then moved slowly down his stomach.

She was big and beautifully proportioned and, like so many African women, very strong, so that it wasn't always clear who was fucking whom. Even in the hot room, her body was cool and smooth as marble. She never sweat, not even on their most energetic nights, so that afterward, Mark always felt a vague self-disgust at the perspiration that covered him and matted his hair to his forehead.

She was his first African. There had been a young girl in Diarrere—her name was Koumba, too—that he'd wanted in the worst way. She might have wanted him, too; it was hard to say. But it wasn't possible, not in a place where everyone knew—and discussed—when he went to sleep or took a bucket shower behind his hut or even squatted over the latrine he'd built.

So, they sat on mats outside her hut and waited until everyone in her compound went to sleep. Then they kissed, and sometimes he slid his hand up inside her tunic. But that was it. Mark begged her to come to his hut, and she often said she would, but never did.

He slid out of Koumba and rolled off her, his sweat making a soft slurping sound as he pulled away. She got up immediately, as she always did. Mark heard the bathroom light click on and, a moment later, the toilet flush. He threw an arm across his eyes to block out the faint glow coming from the hallway.

He fell asleep before Koumba got back to bed.

CHAPTER 14

The Frenchman waited for Emil to serve the beers and leave.

"Vous ne croyez pas que vous exaggerez un peu?" He asked. It wasn't really a question.

Calvady took a sip of his beer. "That's easy for you to say, my friend," he scoffed. "It's not you risking his skin over there."

"It's not me with an illegal Swiss account, either," the Frenchman replied, feeling the blood spread into his cheeks.

He took the pipe out of his mouth. He was glad they'd chosen a table in a corner, away from the lights. He was working on his temper. It was the only thing holding him back, they said; but scum like Calvady brought out the worst in him.

The Frenchman tapped the pipe on his shoe, letting the ashes fall to the floor. He was calm again.

"Besides, I thought Chad was like home to you," he said, refilling the pipe.

Calvady stared across the table. "I am as French as you, my friend," he said, his voice up a notch. He sipped his beer, then spread his hands in front of him.

"Ecoutez," he said, calmer now. "If I stop now, what will the Libyans think? Halloud is not an idiot."

The Frenchman shrugged, not willing to concede that but not wanting to get sidetracked.

"You could tell them you are worried that French authorities are watching you, and you need to stop for awhile," he suggested.

"And how do I know that?" Calvady shot back. "Besides, they would only find someone else," he added, reasonable again. "Somebody will always change dollars for a price." Calvady shook his head. If he had to explain that, it was no wonder they had lost Chad.

"Et l'americain?" The Frenchman asked. "Will he do it?"

Calvady shrugged. "I think so," he said.

The Frenchman smiled. He sat forward a little and pulled a paper from his back pocket. He unfolded it and slid it across the table.

"Vous lisez l'anglais?" He asked. Calvady shook his head.

"Your partner sent that telex to three newspapers in the U.S. this morning," the Frenchman said. "It's a very detailed piece on your operation; it even quotes you," the Frenchman smiled," though he got your name wrong."

Calvady stared across at the Frenchman, who appeared to be enjoying himself.

"Fortunately, the director of the Douala PTT is French."

"What do you mean?" Calvady asked. He knew he was in trouble.

The Frenchman took his first sip of beer. "We were able to...take steps," he explained. "Apparently, *monsieur* Reilly has had a few problems with facts before, like your name," he smiled.

"So, we put out rumors in Washington that reports of Libyan dollars in Chad were part of a disinformation plot by our people."

"I see," Calvady said, not seeing at all. He didn't want to give the pink-faced bastard the satisfaction, but he couldn't help it.

"Wouldn't the story do exactly what you want?"

The Frenchman smiled. "Our friend Qadaffi does many things with his dollars that the Americans don't like," he explained. "Giving them to Chadian soldiers wouldn't even be near the top of the list."

"Besides," he said, "Americans are so much more..." he began puffing on the pipe, looking for a word ... "decisive when they discover things on their own."

Calvady didn't say anything, waiting for the verdict.

"So, you have another chance," the Frenchman said. "I think you've had your fair share of chances, no?"

The blood was rushing into his face again, but this time he didn't care. He took one more sip of beer and stood up.

"I will be interested to hear how you get on," he said, looking down at Calvady. He put the pipe back in his mouth, inclined his head an inch or so, then walked out.

The road back to the *militaires'* compound was awful, with potholes everywhere and the laterite "washboard" broken or worn away in many places. But the Frenchman didn't seem to notice, or if he did, didn't think slowing down was a viable alternative.

The Peugeot pitched and bumped violently, and he bit down harder on the pipe stem to keep it from flying out of his mouth. *Les salauds!* Calvady wasn't even the worst. How could they expect *canaille* like that to respect anything when there was no threat—a real one that instilled fear, which, after all, was the basis for respect—to hold over him? The Frenchman tightened his grip on the steering wheel as the car rattled over a particularly bad patch of road. And now they were sitting in Paris wringing their soft white hands and messing their *coulottes* over a filthy Arab who wouldn't last a half hour if anyone had the balls to make a decision.

At the compound gate, he leaned on the Peugeot's horn. The lazy bastard was probably asleep. An African suddenly appeared, shielding his eyes from the car lights, and swung the gate open quickly.

And what if the Socialists won in May? Even that wasn't impossible anymore. They'd probably ask Qadaffi if he wanted Gabon as well. The Peugeot fishtailed to a stop outside the main building, and the Frenchman got out. He needed something stronger than a beer.

CHAPTER 15

Mark had been to the marina only once, right after it opened and before he knew who owned it. Or at least who ran it. Gilles told everyone it was his place, but it was probably the old man who put up the money and whose name was on any documents.

The road into it was a rugged, bumpy dirt track that ran from Avenue Charles de Gaulle three kilometers through the swamps to an isolated spot on the Wouri. During the dry months, it was a slow, careful ride for anyone who cared about his axles and underbody; in the rainy season, it was impossible without four-wheel drive.

For a lot of expatriates, though, that heightened the marina's allure. There were a few rickety fisherman's shacks nearby, built precariously out over the river on the exposed mangrove roots; otherwise, nothing but swamp and the river so that it was easy to forget that Cameroon's largest metropolis was just beyond the trees.

The marina itself was nicely done, with a lot more taste than Mark would've thought Gilles capable of. (Which was another reason to suspect the father's hand in it.) It was a large, simple building with a peaked roof and a spacious covered veranda, built on pilings out over the river. They had used mostly hardwoods harvested in the rain forest near Kribi, in the south, and it fits well with the jungle-like setting.

It had only a dozen slips, but there weren't that many boats in Douala, mostly those owned by Gilles and the other sleazebags.

And it was definitely "their" place. They spent Saturdays and Sundays roaring around on their boats and drinking at the marina. During the week, a lot of them drove down for drinks after work and stayed until Gilles closed up around eight o'clock.

Koumba said they had used it occasionally for private parties, too, but after one of his friends got drunk and fell through a window, Gilles put a stop to it. Mark had made the mistake of going to one of their parties once. It was right after he met Koumba, and she begged him to take her, insisting it didn't matter that Gilles would be there. He was bringing someone else, too.

It was in Joss, at a Frenchman's villa; not the biggest or chicest the *quartier* had to offer, but a nice house. A few of the single sleazebags brought whores, but most of the women were white. It was a rare night out for the wives, and Gilles brought his—which was why Mark was invited.

Koumba was at her worst, laughing too loud, swiping playfully at the men who teased her, and grinding so hard against anyone she danced with that Mark moved over by the bar so he wouldn't have to watch. The sleazebags took turns pawing her on the dance floor, except Gilles, who danced dutifully with his homely wife. He didn't look like he was enjoying it much, though.

Neither did anybody else, for that matter, except maybe the whores, and Koumba, of course. The wives, especially, seemed ill at ease, standing in groups talking quietly among themselves and trying not to be obvious when they watched their husbands dancing with the whores.

Even the sleazebags were off their form; they were loud and, before long, drunk, but there was a manic kind of apathy underlying the frenzy as if they had to go through the motions, and that was the only way they knew. Around midnight, one of the single men, a blond-haired Frenchman named Jean-Jacques, who managed the rooftop restaurant at the Beau Sejour, began what Koumba later explained was a ritual at their parties.

He grabbed a bottle of vodka from the bar, took a long drink from it, and then began circling from group to group, forcing everyone else to do the same. A few of the women tried to refuse, but Jean-Jacques was drunk and insistent, and none of the sleazebags wanted his wife designated a poor sport. So, in the end, the women acquiesced, though most of them clearly weren't used to, and didn't enjoy, drinking straight vodka.

Koumba was dancing, but she laughed, leaned her head back, and let the son of a bitch pour the vodka into her open mouth. He poured until she gagged, and much of the liquor ended up down the front of her blouse.

At the bar, Jean-Jacques hesitated a second in front of Mark, then pushed the bottle up next to his lips.

"Alors, buvez, mon vieux," he yelled over the music.

"Merci," Mark said, politely pushing the bottle away.

"Buvez!" The Frenchman yelled, shaking Mark's hand off the bottle and bringing it back so it actually touched his lips.

Mark pushed it away hard this time and got up from the bar stool. Jean-Jacques tried not to but couldn't help staggering back a step.

"Mais qu-est-ce que t'as?" He bellowed, trying for mean mean but sounding shrill.

The host, a Frenchman named Gabriel, stepped between them, and it stopped there.

"Allez, Jean-Jacques," he said quietly, steering him toward the living room. Jean-Jacques pretended to resist, then walked away. *"Espece de con,"* he muttered over Gabriel's shoulder at Mark.

Gabriel shrugged at Mark. *"Desole, il est un peu sul,"* he said. *"Ca va,"* Mark said, nodding. Gabriel ran a small construction company, and Mark had interviewed him once for a story on public works in Douala.

Except for the company he kept, he was all right. Around two, the sleazebags started another ritual: smashing glasses on the tile floor while they danced. Jean-Jacques initiated that, too, but the others soon joined in so that before long, the music was regularly punctuated by the sound of breaking glass.

At that point, one of the uniformed Africans who had been working the bar went into the kitchen and returned with a small broom and dust pan. For the rest of the night, he discreetly moved among the dancers, cleaning up the broken glass so that no one cut themselves.

Mark let himself out. He thought about telling Koumba, then didn't. He didn't feel like arguing. Outside, he saw that it had rained. He couldn't recall hearing it. But the music was loud, and besides, it rained so often in Douala that he sometimes didn't notice.

It had been a good one, though, from the looks of it; one of the tropical storms that swept in off the ocean at that time of year, bringing near-hurricane force winds and heavy rain, then disappeared just as quickly. Puddles were everywhere and deep. Mark's shoes were soaked through before he reached Avenue Charles de Gaulle.

The streets were strewn with leaves and the fan-shaped branches from the palm trees. He was mildly surprised that the power hadn't gone out. He couldn't find a taxi at that hour, so he ended up walking home. It wasn't that far, though, and the rain had cooled the air some, so he didn't mind.

Koumba didn't show up at his apartment for a couple of days

after that; when she did, she informed Mark that he wasn't welcome at their parties anymore.

He laughed in her face.

Mark stopped the taxi he'd borrowed from Wanna at the gate. An enormously muscular African dressed in running shorts and nothing else eyed him from a cheap wooden chair, where he sat reading *Paris Match*. Mark waited a moment, then gestured through the windshield at the gate. The African stared for another second or two, then got to his feet slowly and strolled over to Mark's window, rolling his head on his thick neck.

"Monsieur?" He said, glancing down at Mark then away again, so Mark understood just how unimpressed he was with the beat-up taxi.

"Is the marina open?" Mark asked.

"Vous voulez voir quelqu'un?" The African asked, ignoring the question.

"Oui," Mark said.

The African waited, then glanced back down at Mark.

"Qui?"

"I didn't know this was a private club," Mark said.

"Ce n'est pas un club prive, monsieur," The African said, annoyed now.

Private clubs were illegal in Cameroon, but there were other ways to keep people, Africans mostly, out of places. It was a good bet the local fishermen didn't drink at the marina.

"Well, if it's not a private club, and it's open, I'd like to go in and have a beer," Mark said, staring back at the African.

The African whistled his contempt through his teeth, then sauntered too slowly over to the gate. He opened it only halfway, barely enough for a car to pass.

Mark slammed the car into gear and stomped on the gas pedal. The African, expecting Mark to inch the car through, scrambled away from the gate in case Mark hit it. When he didn't, the African yelled angrily after him, but Mark was too far away to hear what he said.

He parked the Renault close to the building, got out, and walked around to the veranda. Calvady was already there, sitting at a table near the back. He had a half-empty 33 Export in front of him. A group of Gilles' friends sat at a larger table that looked out on the boat slips. They had three African women with them, but Koumba wasn't one of them. They stopped talking and turned to watch Mark go by, but he didn't look over.

As he passed, one of the sleazebags mumbled something, and the others, including the whores, snickered. Calvady saw him coming, but he didn't get up, and they made no pretense about shaking hands.

Gilles appeared from the building and came over.

"Ca va?" He asked because it was his place and he had to say something.

"Bonjour," Mark said. *"Une biere, s'il vous plait."*

Gilles walked back toward the building. Mark's back was to him, but he heard one of the sleazebags say something; Gilles and the whole table laughed,

"It's very nice here," Calvady said,

"You think so?" Mark asked.

"You don't?" Calvady was genuinely surprised.

It was his kind of place, though lots of low-class Frenchmen and Africans in their place.

Mark shrugged. He didn't give a damn what Calvady thought of the marina. Gilles brought his beer and a glass but didn't pour it for him.

"It's not Gala, is it?" Calvady smiled.

Mark tilted the bottle of 33 Export, which was the only local beer Gilles carried, into his glass. *"Non,"* he said.

He hadn't been that surprised to see Calvady's note in his

box at Antoine's, but that was before he read the rest of his messages.

"Thks yr Chad-dlr piece, but we hearing exDC that tis French smokescreen to get US help in ousting Qadaffi. Yr French "businessman" probably part of game. 'Fraid can't use w/o lot more proof, but wud look favorably on piece saying Frogs trying to get U.S. to do their dirty work for 'em if you think can handle. Best rgds."

The other two messages were much the same. Smokescreen his ass! He'd seen the goddamn dollars. Mark fired off telexes arguing his case: the goddamn soldiers said they got them from the Libyans. How in the hell could the French manage that? They weren't even allowed to set foot in Chad.

None of the three papers even telexed back.

So, Calvady wasn't there for that.

"How'd you find me?"

Calvady spread his palms and smiled.

"Le celebre journaliste americain de Douala?" He asked.

Fuck you, pal.

"Tu as choisi ton negre?" He asked, serious again. Even in French, the word was ugly.

"I have a friend in mind," Mark lied, bearing down on "friend." Calvady thought that was funny.

"Oh, excuse-moi," he chuckled. "You're American; I forgot the Africans are your friends."

Mark put his beer down. It was time to go. He didn't have to listen to the asshole, and if he stayed, he might do something stupid. It had only been curiosity that brought him out in the first place.

Calvady could kiss his ass for the $2,000. Most of it was gone, anyway, and there wasn't a helluva lot coming in from anywhere else. He'd assumed the income from the dollar story would take care of expenses for awhile after Calvady's money ran out, so he hadn't chased the stories he normally did in leaner times. Well, the vacation was over.

Mark pushed his chair back from the table. Calvady's smile vanished.

"Where are you going?"

"Home."

"I thought we had a deal," Calvady said quickly. "I gave you $2,000."

"I don't remember," Mark said, smiling and shaking his head. He got to his feet.

"Wait," Calvady said, grim all of a sudden. He lowered his voice. "That was only to test your...good faith," he said. "Of course, if we can agree to a few details, there will be more. A lot more."

Mark was still leaving. He didn't want anything to do with the son of a bitch. He could cram his money up his ass. Calvady reached down and picked up his *portefeuille* from the ground next to his chair. He glanced over at the sleazebags, then pulled out an envelope and put it next to him on the table.

It was thicker than the last one, quite a bit thicker, like a very long paperback.

"$5,000," Calvady said, sparing Mark the calculation.

Mark glanced out toward the river. Two power boats were coming straight for the veranda, both going too fast. When they got closer, he saw that Jean-Jacques was driving one, and another sleazebag, whose name Mark didn't know, the other.

At the last second, both boats veered sharply away from the marina, sending their wakes slamming up against the pilings and spraying the tables nearest the edge. The group on the veranda jumped back too late; the whores squealed in protest, and the men swore vociferously but didn't really mean it. A couple of them jumped up and hung over the railing, laughing and flashing the international arm gesture at their friends in the boats.

Mark looked back at Calvady, who had been watching and clearly enjoyed the joke. Yeah, it was his kind of place. Mark didn't want anything to do with the bastard.

"Of course, that's only for expenses," Calvady said as if belaboring the obvious. "Your...salary will be paid once the...affair is completed."

"How much would my salary be, exactly?" Mark asked, more as a last question, a way to leave gracefully than any real interest in Calvady's scheme.

"Two hundred and fifty thousand dollars," Calvady said very quietly, staring up at Mark.

Mark tried to keep his lips from moving, but couldn't. The smile was too strong, and so was a short laugh that seemed to come from someone else.

"Won't you at least sit down to hear my proposition?" Calvady asked, gesturing politely at the seat Mark had vacated.

Mark hesitated a second, then lowered himself back into the chair. Calvady smiled the way he had that morning at the Tchadien.

"That's a lot of money," Mark said. Calvady nodded, still smiling. "Not to my friends," he said.

"Why don't you just set up your own company, Calvady, and keep the $250,000 for yourself?" Mark asked, pressing a little.

Calvady made a face and shook his head. "The Cameroonians don't approve of me," he said, proud of it.

"How'd you get in the country then?"

"Ouf, I can come in and out; they just don't want me doing business here," he explained.

"Forget to pay someone?" Mark asked.

"No, no, nothing like that," Calvady said quickly, obviously not wanting to go into it. "In any case, my friend, this company must be American."

"Why?" Mark demanded.

Calvady smiled and held up one hand. "In a minute. First, have you really found a partner?" He asked.

"Yes," Mark lied again. Hell, Wanna would be his partner, assuming there was money in it and no risk. And Mark was walking out of there as soon as Calvady started talking about breaking any local laws.

"Tres bien," Calvady said. He reached into his *portefeuille* and pulled out a folded sheet of paper. He opened it up and passed it across to Mark. Mark left it on the table in front of him to read. It was a business letter, in English, to a company in Houston that Mark had never heard of. Calvady reached over and pointed to a blank space in the form letter.

"Have you thought of a name for your company?" He asked.

"Uh, how about Rinky Dink Inc.?" Mark asked, pressing his lips together to keep from smiling.

"Qu-est-ce que ca veut dire?" Calvady asked, suspiciously.

"Rinky dink means someone who, uh, who you can count on," Mark explained. Calvady stared across the table at him a moment, then, apparently satisfied, pointed back at the letter.

"Bon, d'accord," he said. "You put in the company name there," he said, waving a finger at the blank space.

Mark picked it up now and read it through. It was an order for parts, lots of parts, that he didn't recognize, but assumed had something to do with oil drilling. The letter asked the company to bill him and then air freight the parts to a container shipping company in New York City. Mark recognized the shipping company's name; they had ships in the Douala port all the time.

It didn't make any sense. Calvady could have hired anyone, another Frenchman or even a Cameroonian, to do it and paid them a fraction of the fee he was talking about paying Mark.

"How am I supposed to pay for this?" He asked. "No U.S. company is going to ship this kind of order to an unknown importer on credit."

Calvady smiled and shook his head. "When they

acknowledge the order and send the bill, you are to telex the amount to this address," he said, pulling a business card from his shirt pocket and handing it to Mark.

It had Calvady's name on it and a telex and telephone number whose prefix Mark recognized as being in Paris. There was no company name on the card.

"As soon as the amount is received, a confirmed letter of credit will go out to them for the full amount," Calvady continued once he was sure Mark understood.

That answered one question: Mark wouldn't handle the money.

Calvady pulled another folded paper from his *portefeuille,* and handed it across to Mark. It was addressed to the shipping company in New York, and simply ordered the container and notified the company that the parts from Houston would be arriving by air freight.

Mark looked up when he'd read it through.

"Same procedure for them," Calvady explained. "When they've received payment, they will wire you with an estimated date of delivery. Is that clear?"

"Where am I supposed to put this stuff once it gets to Douala?" Mark asked.

Calvady looked at him for a second, then realized Mark didn't get it. He smiled down at the table, then up at Mark.

"You don't put them anywhere, my friend," he said, keeping his voice low. "You hire a truck, put the container on the back of it, and drive it to Kousseri."

Mark stared across the table. Holy shit, he was thick! Of course, it was going to Kousseri or N'djamena more precisely. And from there, into the belly of an Anotov. Mark picked up the letter from the company in Houston. Pump barrels. He had no idea what they were, but no doubt it was something the Libyans wouldn't be able to get any more if, as everyone expected, the new administration in Washington banned sales of oil equipment to Qadaffi.

The Libyans could switch to European suppliers for some of the spare parts, but not all of them. There were even reports that U.S. intelligence was watching cargoes of sensitive equipment bound for Europe and elsewhere to make sure they weren't re-routed to Tripoli.

But Cameroon was different. It was a western-leaning country several thousand miles from Libya, and all kinds of oil equipment was pouring into the place. Chances were good that no one would pay any attention to an American company, one of dozens doing business in Cameroon, ordering U.S. oil equipment.

Calvady saw that Mark understood. "Technically, you will be selling the equipment to me in Cameroon," he explained. "So, you have nothing to worry about."

Mark gave a short laugh.

The Frenchman slid the envelope across the table.

"Just before the... merchandise arrives, we will meet again," he said. "To make sure of the details and, of course, to cover any other expenses you may have."

Mark let the envelope sit where it was on the table. As if by not reaching for it, he preserved some choice, some power to decide what was or was not in his best interest. Calvady smiled and gestured at Mark's almost empty beer glass.

"Will you allow me to buy you another beer?"

Mark stared at him for a moment, then nodded, almost imperceptibly, as if his head had fought and lost a battle with the rest of his body.

CHAPTER 16

"Next stop's the bloody bush, Mark boy," Simon Perth-Hockney boomed, laughing as he stepped around Mark into the apartment.

Mark laughed, too, even though it hurt his head. Simon always made him laugh. Mark squinted at the glare coming in the front windows. It was later than it should have been.

"Want a beer, Simon?"

"You bloody degenerate; it's only nine o'clock," Simon laughed. He followed Mark down the hallway to the kitchen. Simon hated to sit down or even stand still. He only did either when he had no other choice.

"How'd you find me?" Mark asked. It had been a while since he'd seen Simon and Mary, and he forgot to let them know he'd moved.

"I saw Wanna at the bank," Simon said. "I went by the other place first, though. Some cheeky African started rabbitting on about you still owing him a month's rent."

Mark handed Simon a Gold Harp, and they walked back to the living room. He was glad Koumba had already left. Not that it mattered, really; it was just one less thing to have to explain.

"He's full of shit; I don't owe him a dime," Mark said, picking up his shirt from the floor and putting it back over one of the wicker chairs.

"The cheeky bugger asked me who I was," Simon said; "probably thought he could get some *bam* out of me." *Bam* was *pidgin* for money. Simon didn't really speak it, but living out in the bush for five years, he had picked up a lot of the words, and he loved to mix them in with his public school English. It drove Mary nuts.

"What'd you tell him?" Mark asked.

"That I was the British ambassador, and he could bloody well bugger off with his questions," Simon said.

They both laughed hard. It was nice to see Simon; he and Mary were the best, maybe the only white friends Mark had left in Cameroon. They'd had him out to visit quite a bit right after Deborah took off.

The Gold Harp tasted good, too; it was cold, and it washed away the awful taste he'd had in his mouth from too many St. Pauli's Girls the night before. He and Wanna had celebrated their partnership. It didn't help his headache much, though.

"What the bloody hell have you been up to?" Simon asked, smiling. "Wanna looked worse than Fritz after he's been at Maxie all night, and he said it was your fault."

Mark tried not to laugh because it made his head throb, but he couldn't help it. Fritz and Maxie were, respectively, male and female bush dogs on the palm oil plantation where Simon was the financial director.

"He led me astray, Simon," Mark smiled, sipping his beer.

"Worse than bloody bushmen, the two of you," he snorted. He took a small sip of his beer, but Simon wasn't a morning drinker.

He was a British aristocrat whose philandering father, unfortunately, had pissed away the family fortune, forcing Simon to become the first Perth-Hockney to actually have to work for a living. Somehow, he'd managed to get an accounting degree, then went to work for a European conglomerate. He was climbing the corporate ladder nicely, with a home in Sussex and a commuting schedule he set his watch by when they asked if he'd take on an emergency assignment in Cameroon.

Two years at the outside, just long enough to sort out the plantation group's disastrous finances at the Lobe and N'dian estates, over near the Nigerian border. Then back home, with a bonus and promotion, and they implied, the pick of posts in Europe.

The two estates were on a sound financial footing and turning a profit within two years, but Simon and Mary were still there after five years. Things were tight in Europe; the conglomerate was cutting back. They'd have to see what they could find for Simon.

Simon complained to Mark and Deborah when they were together and to Mary most of the time, but never to London. Just wasn't done.

And while he was sick to death of the job, he was damned good at it. Simon didn't consider anyone from north of the Thames to be 100 percent British, but somehow, he got along beautifully with Africans.

Once, Mark had waded, ankle-deep, through the mud at the *Kumba* marketplace with Simon, who thought his Cameroonian salesman wasn't trying hard enough to convince the market women of the quality of their palm oil. The women were shocked at first to see the small, balding man in a shirt and tie—Simon always wore a tie—striding through the mud, but he had them howling at his *pidgin*, and most of them decided to give his oil a try.

Mark had met Simon through Deborah when the plantation changed accounting firms, to the screams of the small British community, after Deborah showed him how to save a bundle on local taxes. He invited them out to Lobe for a weekend, and though Simon and Mary were ten years older than Mark and Deborah, they had all become fast friends.

"Mary said I'd be eating dry *cocoyams* if I didn't find you and haul you out for the weekend," Simon said, putting the almost full bottle of beer down on the table.

"Are you going back now?" Mark asked. Simon shook his head.

"I've got to see that bloody bandit, Victor Mawenga; some legal mumbo-jumbo that he said he'd have done a month ago," he said, shaking his head. "How about if I pick you up about one?"

Mark drained his beer and thought for a moment. There was no reason not to. Wanna had *dashed* someone at the Chamber of Commerce, and they'd have their documents in a week. The whole deal sounded almost too good to be true to Wanna, but when Mark dropped by the bank on Monday with $5,000, he believed it.

And $25,000 for doing next to nothing was too good to pass up. Wanna was too polite to ask what Mark was going to make, but after three beers, Mark told him $50,000 if all went right. That was a figure Wanna could understand.

"I'd love to come out, Simon," Mark said.

"Great," Simon said, heading for the door. "I'll see you at one."

Mark let him out, then walked the beer bottles back to the kitchen. He didn't really want any more beer. But even with money in the bank, he didn't like to waste it, so he got a glass and drank what was left of Simon's Gold Harp. When he'd finished it, he walked back down the hall, slipped off the shorts he'd put on when Simon knocked at the door and stepped into the shower.

The smell of sweat and old beer and Koumba from the night before made the hangover seem that much worse; a shower would help. The water sprayed out of the nozzle in a weak, uneven mist, even turned up all the way. It was enough to lather the soap and rinse it off, but that was about it.

Mark considered trying to find Koumba to let her know he'd be away, then decided to leave a note on the door. She hung out and occasionally worked at an illegal dress shop over behind Monoprix, but there was no guarantee she'd be there. It was a long walk, with a hangover, if she wasn't.

CHAPTER 17

Mark stepped out from the shade of the stairwell when Simon's Peugeot 504 pulled up. Joseph, Simon's regular driver, hopped out of the car and put Mark's bag and tennis racket in the trunk.

"How are you, Joseph?"

"Fine, suh," he said, smiling.

Mark caught a glimpse of boxes filled with canned food, cheese, and wine—all things they couldn't get in Lobe—before Joseph slammed the trunk shut. The air conditioning was on high, and the radical change made Mark shudder; even so, the cold air felt good.

"How now, Mark boy?" Simon boomed, laughing.

"Fine, suh," Mark said. Joseph chuckled as he put the car in gear and pulled away.

It was a good time of day to travel, so long as the car had air conditioning. The lunch hour crowds were gone, and even outside Douala, the roads would be clear. With any luck, they'd be in Lobe in three hours.

Simon pulled two plastic cups and a bottle of Johnnie Walker from under the front seat. He poured carefully because even

Douala's streets weren't great, then handed a half-full cup to Mark.

"*Bon weekend, mon vieux*," he said, holding his cup out so Mark could clink it with his.

"You too, Simon," Mark said. "Thanks for the invite."

"Mary told me not to come back without you," Simon said. "Bloody woman is driving me crazy."

Mark smiled. Simon and Mary disparaged each other in public and sometimes went at it damn hard, but they were still together after five years in the bush. Mary didn't take the easy way out, either, by spending four or five months a year back in England, where their two boys were in school.

"Listen, I've just got a few things to look over, Mark, if that's all right," Simon said apologetically. "Then I'll be clear for the weekend."

"No problem, Simon," Mark said, meaning it. "Just put the whiskey up here where I can grab it."

"Bloody degenerate," Simon laughed. He put the bottle between them on the seat, then picked up a file.

Mark sipped the Johnnie Walker and looked out the window.

On a map, Lobe was only 100 kilometers northwest of Douala. But Mount Cameroon lay in between, so by road, it was close to twice that distance.

They crossed the Wouri Bridge into Bonaberi. There was little traffic because of the lunch hour; even the police checkpoints were unmanned. Just west of Bonaberi, Joseph turned off the *route nationale* onto the paved road to Victoria. Five minutes later, they rattled across the Mungo River Bridge into the Southwest Province and Anglophone Cameroon.

Most of the rain forest from the Mungo on had been cut back and replaced with either cultivated palm or rubber trees. It was all Cameroon Development Company land.

Mark started to pour himself some more whiskey, but stopped when Joseph slowed down and turned off the paved road onto a narrow dirt track in the middle of one of the CDC palm estates.

"Where are we going?" He asked.

Simon glanced up from his papers.

"Oh, this is a shortcut Joseph discovered," he said. "It cuts through CDC and hits the Kumba road on the other side of Buea."

"Really?" Mark asked. "That's great."

The usual route was west almost to Victoria, then up the mountain road to Buea, where the road turned east again to go around the base of Mount Cameroon. The roundabout way was only part of the problem. Buea, the old British capital, was the seat of the provincial government, and police and gendarmes were everywhere. Even late at night, it was almost impossible to get through the city without being stopped—sometimes more than once.

"Joseph, could you slow down a second?" Mark asked.

"Yes, suh," Joseph said, downshifting smoothly until they were moving at a crawl. Mark filled the cup more than halfway, then screwed the bottle cap back on.

"OK, Joseph, thanks."

"Yes, suh," he said, and speeded up again.

"Category five driver, eh Joseph?" Simon said, looking up from what he was doing.

"Yes, suh," Joseph said, smiling, a bit embarrassed at the attention.

The government set strict job category grades that companies had to follow, with corresponding salary ranges. Five was pretty high for a driver.

"You got a promotion, Joseph?" Mark asked.

"Yes, suh," Joseph smiled into the rear-view mirror.

"That's wonderful; congratulations."

"Thank you, suh," he beamed, embarrassed again.

"When the women find out, they'll be lined up at his bloody door, eh Joseph?" Simon said. Joseph laughed.

"No suh," he said, smiling.

Joseph was a Banso from a village in the mountains up near Bamenda. He had a wife back in the village whom he saw once a year or so when he got leave, but, at least according to Simon, he had a sizeable harem among the estate girls. Joseph wasn't Lobe's only driver, but he was the best, and Simon always used him unless Joseph was driving the estate's managing director.

Mark sipped the whiskey slowly. His headache had gone, but he didn't need another one. Besides, he hadn't seen Mary in a while and didn't want to show up drunk. He concentrated on the road, trying to memorize the shortcut as Joseph switched tracks within the CDC plantation. It would be good to know for future trips.

The palm trees lining the dirt roads were planted close together so that the branches overlapped, creating a canopy that blocked most of the sunlight. It was a sudden, pleasant change from the glare of the blacktop. Mark felt himself relax in the back seat. He was half-asleep when the Peugeot bumped back onto the paved road that led to Kumba.

They shuddered through the pot-holed streets in Kumba, arguably the worst-maintained city in Cameroon, past the grimy open-air market near the Catholic mission. It was just after three o'clock, and the stalls were opening again after lunch, so it was slow going. Africans heading to market jammed the street, and two-way traffic, mostly taxis, competed for the narrow strip of pavement that was still relatively intact.

From years of neglect, the asphalt had chipped away progressively from both sides of the road. Torrential rains then wore away the exposed soil underneath, digging deeper and deeper crevices on either side of the asphalt that remained. After a while, the only way two cars could share the road was for each to put its inside tires on the asphalt and the outside wheels on the steeply sloping dirt sides.

That tilted the cars precariously, like planes banking sharply for a turn; passengers on the pavement side had to hang onto something to keep from sliding down to the other side of the car.

"Jesus, when are they going to do something about this road?" Mark yelled as some of the whiskey splashed out of the cup onto his pants.

Simon closed the folder and put it on the floor.

"Hey, Mark, put mimbo for face, you drink-um," he said. *Mimbo* was a pidgin catch-all for anything alcoholic.

Joseph, who was concentrating on the road, laughed in the front seat. So did Mark; he didn't mean it to sound as ill-tempered as it had come out.

"Sorry, Simon, I didn't get too much sleep last night," Mark said.

"Bloody degenerate," Simon said in his best public-school accent. He reached for his cup and the bottle of Johnnie Walker and, with some difficulty, poured himself a generous shot. Just past the Catholic mission, Joseph turned onto the dirt road that led to Lobe. They lost most of the traffic there, and it was the home stretch, but that was the only thing good about it.

In the best of times, meaning when it hadn't rained recently, the Kumba-Lobe trip took a bone-jarring hour, with the car either stuttering over the uneven laterite or pitching like a power boat in heavy seas over, around, and through the potholes that were sometimes so wide and deep that cars disappeared from sight.

The rainy season was worse. The week-long downpours turned the dirt road to mud and the craters into ponds. Palm oil tanker trucks regularly bogged down in the thigh-deep mud, sometimes skidding sideways and blocking the road in both directions.

Simon and Mary had set the record their first rainy season: 12 hours to do the 40 kilometers to Kumba. Mary said that halfway through the ordeal, they had agreed to a divorce, but couldn't get to Douala to finalize it. It was a joke between them now, but Mark was pretty sure it hadn't been at the time.

He and Simon sipped whiskey and talked while Joseph did the best he could on the road he knew so well. They talked about the usual things: the palm oil business, living in "the bloody bush," and the frustrations of working with Cameroonians.

"That bloody bandit, Victor, hadn't done piss-all on this thing I asked him about a month ago, then had the cheek to hand me a bill," Simon complained.

Mark laughed. "What'd you say?"

Simon flicked his hand sideways. "I flipped the bill right back at the bugger and told him to stop mucking about," he said. "No work, no *bam,* eh Joseph?"

Joseph laughed. "No, suh."

Simon didn't ask about Deborah. He'd leave that to Mary, who would ask, just once, to show they still cared; then they'd drop it. The four of them had been good friends, and Deborah's absence weighed a bit, even now; mentioning her name seemed to maintain the pretense of a foursome, as if she had been called away suddenly and would return soon.

Simon asked about his trip to Chad, and Mark sketched it briefly because he knew Simon wasn't that interested. He left out Calvady and the dollars. The Peugeot skidded through a soft spot on the road, but Joseph pulled it out quickly and then slowed down to cross a narrow river. The car clattered over the boards on the bridge, and Mark felt the wood sag under them.

The boards would give out one day, probably as a full tanker truck passed over the bridge. The driver would be killed, either crushed or drowned in the fast-moving water below, and the plantation would be cut off for as long as it took to build a replacement bridge. Someone might eventually pull the wreck out of the water if they could figure a way to get it back up the steep bank; more likely, though, it would stay where it fell, partly submerged, until it rusted a dull orange.

People from the village nearby would talk about the accident for years, point to the rusting carcass, and tell their children how it happened. And the men would argue about who had first heard the boards cracking, and who had actually seen it go down, and who was the first one on the scene. And they'd all claim to have known all along that the bridge would give out someday.

It was a village like all the others that lined the road: the same mud brick huts, with palm frond rooves that only lasted a rainy season; the same pigs and chickens wandering freely, and the emaciated, half-wild dogs whose ear tips had been sheared off to draw flies away from the villagers, barking and trying to bite the wheels of every vehicle that passed. The same filthy naked children who didn't seem to mind, or even notice, the dust cloud the car kicked up, and the old people who stared blankly from where they sat in the shade.

The young men and women were gone, to Kumba mostly or Douala, if they could scrape up taxi fare and knew someone who would let them sleep on their floor until they could find a job and a place of their own. Most said they went for the money, but even the lucky ones who found work cleaning floors or loading trucks had to pay for food, rent, and transportation and ended up worse off than if they'd stayed in the village.

The truth was that they went for the same reason young people have always been drawn to cities: the excitement and the freedom to do as they pleased, away from the straight jacket of village traditions and the boredom that made a traffic accident a major event.

Joseph turned off at the Lobe entrance, a winding dirt road in marginally better shape than the Kumba-Lobe track. The estate and its sister plantation at Ndian were established by the British in the early 20th Century and hadn't changed much since. Workers' huts, smaller or larger depending on the worker's job category, were laid out in rows close by the palm oil refinery, a turn-of-the-century environmental monster that spewed great black clouds of ash into the air 24 hours a day.

The sour, chemical smell of crushed palm kernels permeated the place, though the expatriates and top Cameroonian staff were spared the worst of it; the prevailing winds usually blew the smoke away from the management villas and their club.

Simon told Joseph to stop the car as they passed the club. They could see Mary on the tennis court, playing doubles with Kate Meredith, the wife of the research director, against two Cameroonian women. Mary smiled and waved quickly between points, then went back to the game. She was a good tennis player and competitive, a bit too much so for some of the "lifers," the career expats, for whom the estate was "home" and the tennis court was an extension of the well-mannered life they led there.

Tennis was more than that for Mary. She played whenever she could, in the blazing midday heat or long past sundown, when seeing the ball became difficult. She didn't care whether the person on the other side of the net was black or white, male or female, only that they could give her a good match.

She didn't like to lose, but took it reasonably well when she did. Being able to play tennis just about whenever she wanted was, she said, the only thing she liked about Lobe.

"It's therapy, you know?" She said once after they'd played at noon.

Mark was so flushed from the heat that he was seeing spots, but Mary asked if he fancied another set.

"I think I'd go out of my mind here if I couldn't wear myself out on the tennis court," she said when he declined and slumped into a chair near the pool.

"Either that, or I'd drink myself to death." She laughed when she said it, but only to cut the seriousness of the statement, not negate it.

The management villas were spread out on spacious lots west of the club. The houses were all white, and all were variations on the same one-story, L-shaped design. Every villa was within view of at least one other, but they were far enough apart that couples could discuss their neighbors without fear of being overheard.

Mark thought Simon and Mary got the pick of the lot, if only for the view. Though Lobe was essentially flat, their villa sat on a small promontory and looked out over thousands of hectares, all planted in the palm, except for a lonely mound in the middle distance, which the locals called Monkey Hill.

It was nice to sit on the terrace just as the last streak of light flickered out in the West, drinking too much and watching the trees change from green to black.

Joseph pulled up the winding driveway and stopped the car at the front steps. Mark didn't have to ask whether he and Simon were expected to join Mary at the club; they were, and they would.

Since Mark and Deborah's first stay at Lobe, a routine had evolved to their visits so that after a while, it became synonymous with the visit, and any variation, however slight, took something away from it. If they arrived before dark, they changed quickly and had a game of tennis at the club, then a leisurely drink at the bar until the sun went down.

Then, it was back to the house to shower and dress. More

drinks on the terrace, and if Moussa, their moody cook and chief houseboy, got it right, dinner was served at about 8:30.

After dinner—always pork from the Kumba pig farms—they'd drink some more and talk for a while, then head for their separate rooms, either to read or to fall asleep. At seven the next morning, Moussa would bring them tea in bed, and Mary would roust them all out for a set or two of tennis before it got too hot.

Moussa had breakfast ready at nine-thirty, then it was more tennis or sunbathing at the pool until lunch—always salads—and a siesta. At four, they started all over again.

"How are you, Moussa?" Mark asked as the houseboy came down the steps to get his bags.

"Fine, suh," he mumbled, not looking Mark in the eye, but managing a thin smile. Moussa didn't smile much, but he made an effort for Mark, who had always *dashed* him well at the end of their visits. Moussa disappeared back into the house, and Mark and Simon walked slowly up the steps after him.

"That bugger was at with cutlasses with one of the pickers," Simon said, keeping his voice down.

"What?!" Mark asked, incredulous. "You mean they were fighting with machetes?" Simon nodded.

"Came in the other morning, bleeding like a bloody stuck pig," he said.

"Good God," Mark said. The locals called machetes cutlasses, but that was just the vagaries of pidgin; he had never heard of anyone using one for anything other than hacking the bush.

"Mary couldn't get anything out of him, but I threatened to send him off if he didn't tell me what the hell he was up to," Simon explained as they walked into the house.

"What'd he say?" Mark asked.

"Some mumbo-jumbo about the picker paying a *ju-ju* man to put a spell on him," Simon said, shaking his head.

Mark laughed, shaking his head.

"You fancy a game of tennis, Mark?" Simon asked.

"Sounds great, Simon," Mark replied.

That was part of the routine, too, pretending the weekend wasn't already set, that they had a choice in the direction it took. Of course, Mark could have pleaded a headache or fatigue, and Mary would have insisted that he sit out the tennis, even offered to give up her game, without a hint of reproach or disappointment.

But the truth was that Mark looked forward to the routine, to the reassurance of knowing before he started what was to come, with nothing more required of him than his active participation.

"I'll just get changed then," Simon said, heading for the hallway on the other side of the living room. "You know where your room is; I'll see you in five minutes."

Mark's room was the one they'd always stayed in. It was just off the living room, the length of the house away from Simon and Mary's bedroom. It was a nice room, large and airy, with two windows facing east and an overhead fan that Moussa had already turned on. There was a small but adequate bathroom just off the room.

On their first visit, Mary had apologized too much for the single beds, but they had laughed and assured her it didn't matter. Pretty soon, it didn't. Mark had always slept well there, with the windows open and the fan quietly swirling the damp night air until it was cool enough to slip under the clean cotton sheet. That was all he used for a cover.

He threw his bag on "Deborah's bed," the one closest to the window that she had insisted was hers. She was like that, and in the beginning, at least, it intrigued Mark, probably because he didn't give a damn what bed he slept in. Or what cupboard they kept the toilet paper in, or how he folded his underwear, or even whether he folded his goddamn underwear.

He had felt something when she left, but as hard as he had tried to read his own feelings at the time, he wasn't certain what it was, whether pain, shock, or just a variation on the anger that had become like a third person, a kind of intermediary, in his relationship with her by the end.

Whatever the feeling was, though, it had passed. As Mark flung his clothes in no particular order onto "her bed," he was glad to have the room to himself.

CHAPTER 18

"You had some nice serves, Mark," Mary said as they sat sweating in the shade of the club's veranda after a ragged but energetic set of doubles.

Mary was being diplomatic. Mark had played poorly, and Simon and Mary beat him and Martin O'Kimbe, Simon's local assistant, 6-3. Mark had double-faulted for the set.

"And a lot of bloody awful ones, Mary," he said, smiling and wiping a saturated sleeve over his face.

"You just haven't been playing," she said; "too busy chasing after Libyans, I wager."

Mary always made a bit too much of the dangers he faced. Mark always steered the conversation back to tennis, complimenting her game, which was damn good.

Simon would listen or half-listen—it didn't require any more than that—and the three of them, once four, would drink and wait for the sun to drop behind the rows of cultivated palm that stretched out from the club to the western horizon.

Occasionally, one of the other British couples joined them for dinner, though Simon insisted on keeping that to the minimum politeness and plantation politics required.

"I've got to see the buggers all day; I don't want to have to chop with them too," he'd mutter whenever Mary informed him that someone was coming.

It was just the three of them that night, for which Mark was thankful. Even after a shower, he felt tired from the tennis and too little sleep the night before. Sitting on the terrace, looking out at the blackening trees, he didn't feel like making the effort that other people would require.

"How for *mimbo*, Mark?" Simon asked, walking out of the house, his hair still wet.

Mary was in the kitchen overseeing the dinner preparation and would join them in a minute.

"A beer sounds good, Simon, thanks."

Simon switched to whiskey and soda, as he always did, then sat down in the wicker chair next to Mark's. Mark understood why they wanted out of Lobe; it was a claustrophobic, probably at times frighteningly isolated existence. There were only three other British couples, all lifers, for the regular company and no distractions but the club, with its well-stocked bar and the dank odor of old wood and bygone colonialism.

"And the bloody disgusting curry lunches," which Simon was forever threatening to boycott: expatriate and African managers, with wives, all pretending to enjoy themselves once a month in the managing director's garden, with even the Cameroonians sweating in the stifling heat, extolling the wonders of an overly-elaborate curry that never varied, and which many of the Africans could barely get down.

Five years must have seemed like a lifetime there.

But Mark loved coming out and always had. Partly, it was just the break from Douala: from work, the noise, even the smell, the vaguely unhealthy stench that permeated most urban centers in Africa. It was the easy, agreeable routine, too, not having to worry about anything because it was already taken care of; all he had to do was show up.

Mostly, though, it was the company. Other than Wanna, Simon, and Mary were the only people in Cameroon that Mark considered friends, and they were the only ones with whom he felt entirely comfortable.

"That awful bushman has chopped the avocado pears into little pieces," Mary said bitterly as she emerged from the house. That would be Moussa, who was still learning his way around a British kitchen.

"How for *mimbo*, madam?" Simon asked, smiling and getting up to get her a drink.

"Oh, shut up, Simon," she snapped, "You've gone completely bush, and you give me no bloody help at all. None whatsoever."

Simon smiled and spread his arms, asking what he'd done to deserve this, but that just made her angrier.

"You leave me to deal with that bushman all by myself while you galavant all over the bloody country, flogging that godawful oil."

Mary was getting it out now, as she often did when something went wrong. But Mark had seen her worse. Simon held up a hand to slow her down. He had to do it just right, or Mary would blow up, crossing some unseen threshold from which it would take most of the evening to return.

Simon grabbed her gently by the shoulders and eased her back toward a chair. Mary resisted, but not overly.

"Sit-um for chair, madam," he said, mimicking an African. I dee bring you *mimbo.*"

"Bloody bushman," Mary muttered, still annoyed but enjoying Simon's attention. He poured her a Campari soda, which is what she always drank at night.

"He's gone completely bush, you know, Mark?" She said, sipping the drink, her exasperation more form than substance now.

"Another year out here, and I reckon he won't be able to go back," she persisted. "He'll go out to lunch with a client and start asking for *mimbo* and what's for chop, and that'll be the end of his career."

Simon and Mark laughed, and after a moment, Mary did too. She was all right again.

They had a cognac after dinner and then said good night. That was customary, too. Reading was about all there was to do at night, and it was more comfortable doing it in bed. But Mark turned off the light as soon as he had undressed. Between celebrating with Wanna and then pumping Koumba in a drunken frenzy, he'd had little sleep the night before, and he was beaten.

She paid him back, waking him at dawn and forcing him to do it again, with his head pounding so hard that it felt as if it had somehow separated from the rest of him.

Mark flung an arm across his eyes to block out the dim light filtering through the curtains and smiled in the darkness. No telling what she'd do to him for the note on the door. He stretched his legs out straight until his feet hung over the edge of the bed. It seemed smaller now and narrow; hard to believe they'd ever both fit, easily too or so it seemed at the time.

Deborah stopped slipping in with him sometime during their first year in Cameroon. The first time, Mark waited, rigid as a flagpole, his stomach quivering with anticipation, the way it always did when he thought he was going to have her. But then he heard her breathing, deep and regular, in the dark and realized she'd gone to sleep. That, too, soon became part of the routine.

They never discussed it and, looking back, may even have gone to lengths to avoid the issue. Not that it would have changed anything. There was a reason why she didn't come anymore, of course; there were reasons for everything. Just maybe not explanations.

Mark played better in the morning and edged Mary 6-4. But Simon, a streaky kind of player who could be either very good or "bloody dreadful," as Mary liked to say, was on his game and whipped Mark 6-2. It was already hot when they finished at nine-thirty, and the three of them had to use towels on the car seats to keep the sweat from soaking into the leather.

After breakfast, Mary asked Mark if he fancied a swim or another game of tennis. He could tell she wanted to play another set. Mary wasn't a sore loser by any means, but she had a competitive streak, and she wanted another shot at him.

"You'll fry your bloody brains out there now," Simon warned.

He was right, of course, but Mark agreed to play anyway. He could fall into the pool right afterward, and it was important to him that Mary not get down.

Simon brought some work and sat in the shade while Mark and Mary played in the oppressive heat. In spite of a strong desire just to finish and dive into the pool, Mark played well again and had Mary down 4-3 when Father Voorhees, a Dutch missionary, pulled up in the only Volkswagen Beetle Mark had seen in Cameroon.

Mary wouldn't stop a match for too many reasons, but she was, to Mark's initial surprise, a devout Catholic. When Voorhees walked through the club and out onto the veranda, she glanced apologetically at Mark and went over to greet the priest.

Father Voorhees was over 60, but at least from a distance, didn't look it. He was solidly-built, with a strong, weathered face and more hair than Mark had, though the priest's was snow-white. Up close, however, it was clear that 40 years in Africa had taken its toll. What from a distance appeared to be a ruddy complexion was, Mary explained once, the visible manifestation of high-blood pressure.

Walking over to shake hands, Mark could see that Voorhees was short of breath, just from the walk through the club. Simon hopped up when he saw the priest and offered him his chair.

Father Voorhees protested lightly, then sat down when Simon insisted. He pulled a large white handkerchief from the pocket of his khaki pants and dabbed the sweat from his face.

"Hello, Father," Mary said, shaking hands.

"Are you vinning, Mary?" The priest asked, still struggling for breath.

"He's too much for me, Father," she said, smiling.

Mark stepped forward and shook hands with the priest.

"Don't believe her, Father," he said; "she was just about to finish me off when you pulled up."

"Vhere is your vife?" He asked politely.

"She's in France right now, Father," Mark said.

"Not sick, I hope?"

"No, she's not sick, Father," Mark said.

The priest glanced up at Mark, expecting an explanation, then nodded when none was offered.

"She's just taking a break, Father," Mary said, not looking over at Mark.

"Ah, vomen need it more than men," Father Voorhees said, putting the handkerchief away.

Simon grinned and winked at Mark.

"You think women need it more than we do, Father?" He asked, biting his lip.

"Oh sure; men can go a long time vithout it," the priest insisted.

Mary shot Simon a withering look, but Simon, who in his own way was a pretty decent Catholic, didn't mind needling the priest. Voorhees glanced over and saw Simon smiling and, to his credit, grinned a little. "Been a vhile since I heard your confession, Simon," he said.

"Nothing to tell, Father," Simon said, laughing but a little embarrassed now.

"That's one lie right there," Mary said. "Give him a good stiff penance, Father; he needs to spend some time on his knees."

“A couple of rosaries at high noon, out here on the tennis court, ought to do the trick, don’t you think, Father?” Mark asked.

Father Voorhees nodded curtly but didn’t smile, and Mark realized he’d gone too far. Voorhees was of the old school; jokes about penance, if not actually blasphemous, were frivolous, and that was almost as bad. Mark didn’t care, except for Mary; it was the priest’s problem if he couldn’t take a goddamn joke.

Mark felt the irritation rising in him and checked it. It was the heat, mostly. He glanced over at the pool, dying to jump in and cool off. But there was no way he could excuse himself now without making it look like a snub. For Mary’s sake, he wouldn’t do that. The irritation returned, stronger now. He and Voorhees had gotten off to a bad start, and that was part of it: a disapproval Mark could feel each time he met the old man, even when they discussed nothing of consequence.

It was Mark and Deborah’s second or third visit to Lobe. Mary had gone back to the house to see about lunch, and Simon had to check on a shipment from N’dian, Lobe’s sister's estate further up the creeks. Mark sat reading a paperback by the pool while Deborah swam laps. It was her exercise of preference, and she did it religiously; even on work days, she hurried down to the apartment pool and swam until well after dark.

Father Voorhees seldom wore a collar, and at first, Mark thought the old man walking up from the club, mopping his brow with the big white handkerchief, was one of the old planters they had not met yet. They shook hands, and even before Father Voorhees introduced himself, Mark realized from the accent that he was the Dutch priest of whom Mary had spoken.

Mark gestured at Deborah’s chair, and Father Voorhees sat down. Sam, the bartender at the club, walked out with a beer, which Mark found out later was the priest’s only apparent vice. They went through the banalities: Mark’s job and Deborah’s, how long they'd been in Cameroon, and how they knew Simon and Mary.

After a few minutes, Mark realized the priest was staring at his chest, or more precisely, the *gris-gris* that hung around his neck.

"Do you mind if I ask you vhat is dat?" The priest asked, finally pointing to the leather medallion.

Mark told him and explained how he'd come by it. The priest sipped his beer, frowning.

"And do you believe in dat?" He asked, leaving no doubt what he believed.

Mark felt his face redden. "Uh, I believe they believed in it, Father," he said. That didn't mean anything, and it annoyed him to sound so defensive. Father Voorhees leaned forward in his chair, about to launch a protest, when Deborah swam over to the side of the pool.

"Hello," she said, smiling up at the priest. She was breathing hard from the laps.

Mark, glad of the reprieve, quickly introduced them. With a single, powerful push, Deborah vaulted out of the water and got her knees up on the pool's cement apron, almost at Father Voorhees' feet. Another push and she was on her feet, shaking water from her right hand, then extending it to the priest.

Deborah was a Unitarian who had never had much contact with religious orders. Though she meant no disrespect, she viewed Father Voorhees as a man, essentially no different from the dozens of others she met every week.

And she greeted him the same way, shaking hands warmly and saying how happy she was to meet him. She stood back a step further than normal so as not to drip water on him, which meant she had to lean over that much more. That put her cleavage, already dangerously exposed from her surge out of the pool, only a few inches from the priest's face.

Father Voorhees may have seen a bikini somewhere, in a

magazine maybe, or even for real on one of his rare home leaves. But it was probably a good bet he'd never been that close to one before. His head jerked backward as far as the chair would allow, and his face turned an unhealthy scarlet.

More than likely, the old priest was no longer subject to weaknesses of the flesh—if indeed he had ever been—but the encounter could not have done his blood pressure any good. He stayed only long enough to finish his beer fast, then retreated, forgetting entirely about the *gris-gris.*

At lunch, Simon laughed politely at Mark's recounting of the story. Mary smiled but was obviously concerned that the priest had been embarrassed, and Deborah, who blushed a deep red, was furious and called Mark an asshole when they were alone later in their room.

"Vhen is your vife due back?"

"I couldn't say, Father," Mark said, looking the priest in the eye.

"How about a beer, Father?" Simon cut in quickly.

"Oh, vell, if you're having vone," he said.

"Mark?" Simon asked, begging really.

"Sure, thanks, Simon," he said, calming down.

"Darling?"

"I'll share yours, Simon," Mary said.

"I'll get some chairs," Mark said, hurrying off to the closet by the pool where the club stored its aging patio furniture. It was mercifully cool and dark in the closet, and Mark took his time, breathing in deeply a couple of times and exhaling.

He set up chairs for the three of them, then took the one farthest from the priest. Simon brought the drinks over and then sat down next to Mark.

"How are you getting on with the Bais, Father?" Mary asked.

Father Voorhees frowned and shook his head. "Very evil people," he said; "very evil."

The Bais were a small tribe living deep in the bush west of

Lobe, near the magnificent Bai waterfalls. They had resisted all efforts to Christianize them, preferring their own rites, which were heavily steeped in superstition and the local brand of *ju-ju.*

"You don bring-um small *dash*?" Simon said, smiling.

Father Voorhees, who spoke fluent pidgin, smiled thinly at Simon's attempt.

"Don't pay any attention to him, Father," Mary said. "He's gone completely bush."

"Small *bam* for hand," Simon persisted, slapping two fingers into the palm of his other hand.

"Stop it, Simon," Mary snapped.

Mark took a sip of beer to keep from smiling. Simon was kidding, but buying souls wasn't unheard of in Africa.

"What religion are you today, Leo?"

Leo Diouf, Mark's best friend, and translator in the early days in Diarrere, smiled. It was a running joke.

"*Hiay, refum catholique,* Modou," he said, and they'd both laugh.

Sometime during Mark's second year there, the French priests in Dioine, a village just up the road, lost most of their flock when an evangelical group from Germany blew in and began offering three thousand CFA and a new home to anyone who would sign up. The Catholics denounced the practice, but when that didn't work, they countered with 50 kilo sacks of millet.

The bidding war lasted only a few weeks, and then both denominations, realizing it was futile and expensive, stopped. But not before, a lot of the villagers had profited nicely, some of them more than once. Even some of the Muslims, a minority in Diarrere, seeing what Christianity had done for the others, decided there was no harm in converting for a little while.

"Will you have lunch with us, Father?" Mary asked, already knowing the answer.

"Thank you, Mary, but I am invited by the Smythes," Father Voorhees replied.

Ian Smythe, MD of Lobe for the past ten years, and his wife were solid Church of England, but were both the same age as the priest and, like him, had spent more than 40 years in Cameroon.

Father Voorhees ate lunch with them most Saturdays.

"Mark, can we finish the set later?" Mary asked. "I must get back and see how Moussa is coming along."

"Absolutely, Mary," Mark said.

"I'll drive you back, darling," Simon said, getting to his feet. *"Alors, mon vieux?"* He asked Mark.

Mark hesitated. He wasn't dying to be alone with the priest, but he had looked forward to a swim and was loathe to give it up. Hell, the old man would have to leave soon for the Smythes; besides, once Mary left, Mark didn't plan on entertaining Father Voorhees.

"I think I'll jump in the pool first, Simon," he said. "I'll walk back to the house."

"You sure?" Simon asked. "I can swing back around."

"No, really, Simon, that's not necessary."

"See you tomorrow, Father," Mary said.

For a second, Mark thought unhappily that that meant the priest was coming to lunch; then he realized she was talking about Mass. Mark and the priest, now separated by the two empty chairs, watched as Simon's Peugeot sped down the club driveway. Mark drained the last of his beer and leaned forward to get up when Father Voorhees turned and looked at him.

"Do you still vear dat thing?"

For a second, Mark considered telling the priest he'd burned it right after their last talk.

"Yes, I do, Father," he replied.

The priest frowned and shook his head as if Mark's answer physically hurt him.

“So dey vere not Christians,” he said. It wasn’t a question.

“As a matter of fact, most of them were Catholic,” Mark said, not caring if the priest caught the satisfaction in his voice.

Father Voorhees hadn’t stopped shaking his head, and now the swings got wider and more emphatic.

“Not if they believed in dat,” he said, flicking a thick, bent finger in the direction of Mark’s chest.

Mark hissed air through his teeth to keep from screaming.

“It didn’t keep the priests from baptizing them or giving them communion,” he said, trying to keep his voice under control.

“Did they believe in God?” Father Voorhees asked.

“The priests or the villagers?”

The priest straightened slightly in his chair, and his eyes opened a fraction wider as if to get a closer look at Mark, but his voice was the same.

“The villagers,” he said.

Mark swore to himself. It was exactly what he’d wanted to avoid. He should have left with Simon and Mary; he could have come back for the swim.

“Their word for God was *‘Rogg’*” Mark said, pronouncing it the same as the English word ‘rogue’.

“He was the sunset, ‘Rogg-sen’; and when they wished for something, it was *‘a faylanga Rogg’*: if it pleases God.”

“But did they believe He was the almighty God?” Father Voorhees asked, impatient now as if Mark had not answered the question.

Mark looked over at the priest, angry at himself for letting it go on as long as he had. All those years in Catholic school, and he still didn’t know better.

“Rogg a waga war n’galem, n’dah wageran woundin n’dohan,” he said, a little surprised that it came out so effortlessly. He hadn’t thought of it in a long time.

Father Voorhees stared across the two chairs at him, waiting for a translation.

"God can kill a camel, but he can't make him sleep on his back, Father," Mark explained, smiling. "It was one of the first things they taught me."

The priest looked as though he'd been hit in the stomach.

"And vhat do you believe?" He asked, his voice weary all of a sudden, as if he feared the answer.

Mark shook his head. There was a limit, even for a priest.

"It's not something I think about much, Father," he said firmly, hoping the priest could take a hint.

"And you don't tink that's dangerous?"

Not as dangerous as running around with a weak heart in a climate like this, fishing for souls that, even when they were netted, had to have an asterisk next to them.

"I don't know, Father," he said. Mark got up from his chair. "Can I get you another beer?"

Father Voorhees shook his head, though whether at the offer of a beer or something else wasn't clear.

"I hope you'll excuse me, but I really wanted to get a swim in before lunch," Mark said. "It was nice to see you again."

He hesitated, but Father Voorhees made no move to shake hands or even look up at him, so Mark nodded once and walked toward the pool.

He peeled off his shirt, dove into the deep end in his tennis shorts, and did two full laps underwater.

When he surfaced, he hung his arms over the side of the pool nearest the veranda, breathing hard. The priest was gone.

Sometime during the night, the rain woke Mark. It started slowly, the drops tapping lightly on the metal roof, then accelerated quickly until the sound was a uniform, constant roar, like a high-speed train approaching through a tunnel.

There was something awful about African storms, the speed with which they arrived, and especially their force, however quickly it dissipated, that made it difficult, even after years in the place, to view them as merely natural results of the atmospheric cycle.

Once, on a flight back from Malabo, a small plane Mark had rented ran into a storm over the ocean. He saw it coming through the window of the plane: the huge black clouds, stretching up into the stratosphere so there was no chance for the plane to avoid it, rushing at them so fast that he had the impression the plane had somehow stopped in midair.

The French pilot yelled back for Mark to tighten his seat belt, and a second later, the plane plunged into the storm and began shuddering and pitching so violently that, at one point, it felt as though they would flip over completely.

The flight took only 20 minutes. But sitting there, gripping the seat in front of him, his breathing fast and short as he watched the pilot struggle for control of the plane, the notion of time—minutes, hours, even days—meant nothing to Mark. Except for the erratic gyrations of the plane, they might not even have been moving. The blackness, as dark as night but somehow different, was everywhere, and the rain pounding the fuselage drowned out the sound of the motor; so, there was no reference, nothing at all, to reassure Mark that they were still heading in the right direction.

When the plane emerged, just as suddenly, back into the sunlight, Mark saw they were already over land, with the Douala airport just ahead of them. On the ground, the pilot grinned and made a joke about the rough ride. They had a beer together in the airport bar, and when Mark asked, the Frenchman laughed and said no, they hadn't been in any danger.

But up close, Mark noticed that the man's shirt collar was soaked through with sweat, and his hand trembled a bit when he poured the beer.

The tennis court was wet and slippery the next morning, but

they played anyway. Simon, who was on his game again, beat both Mary and Mark easily. Afterward, Mary and Simon showered and dressed quickly, then left to make nine o'clock Mass. As usual, they invited Mark to come along, and as usual, he declined.

"Coffe, suh?" Moussa asked when Mark emerged from his room after his shower.

"Yes, thank you, Moussa," Mark said. "Can I have it on the terrace?"

"Yes, suh," Moussa mumbled and headed back for the kitchen.

They had started earlier and hadn't played as long as usual, and the rain had cooled things off, so the terrace was not too hot yet. Mark turned one of the chairs around to face the southeast. There were only a few days a year when the top of Mount Cameroon was visible from either side; thanks to the rain, which washed away its cloud cover, this was one of them.

It was a deceptive-looking mountain, at least from a distance. The extremely wide base and the flat summit made it appear less than its 13,000-plus feet. But up close, say from Buea, it looked at every inch of it, and every now and then, it erupted without warning, usually killing people in the nearby villages.

After breakfast, Mary said she had to go over to the small general store run by the estate. Simon had invited a palm oil buyer to lunch, and she needed a few things.

"Will you be all right, Mark?" She asked.

"Fine, Mary," he said. "Maybe I'll go for a swim."

"Fancy a ride to the port, Mark?" Simon asked, walking back into the living room from the hallway. He hadn't heard what Mark had said about a swim.

"Why do you have to go over there?" Mary demanded. "It's Sunday, for God's sake."

"The Rio's in from N'dian, and Ian's away," Simon said. The

Rio was the ancient riverboat that ran supplies and passengers up to the N'dian estate.

"Why can't someone else go; why is it always you, Simon?" She asked angrily.

Simon held up both hands, but it was too late.

"Why can't one of the Africans go, or bloody Peter Heathcliff?" She yelled. "Probably too hungover to crawl out of bed and his simpering little wife making excuses for him. 'Oh, my poor Peter has such a headache,' she said, mimicking Sally Heathcliff.

Simon knew better than to interrupt.

"And what if your African oil buyer shows up? What am I supposed to do with him?" She asked.

"Darling, I'll be back in half an hour," Simon said quietly.

"Hah! You'll start *palabering* with some African, and we'll be lucky to see you for dinner," she countered. "And what about our guest?" She demanded, making Mark Simon's responsibility.

"I'll go with him and keep an eye on him, Mary," Mark offered. "I'll hit him over the head if he starts *palabering* with anyone."

Mary glared over at Simon, out of gas for a moment.

"You're a bloody impossible man, Simon," she said, then turned and stormed into the kitchen.

The "port," really just a loading zone hacked out of the jungle along the eastern edge of the creeks, was over in N'Kondo-Titi, a village that, if possible, was less impressive and more "bush" than Lobe. It had a handful of huts clustered close to the road, a Catholic mission school in desperate need of paint and a new roof, and the *gendarmerie*, up near the port.

Simon stopped the car outside the estate's warehouse, a ramshackle, all-corrugated metal inferno, where they stored supplies bound for N'dian. Closer to the water was a rusting fuel tank with a faded BP logo on it, which, along with the warehouse, made up the port's "facilities."

The Rio, the company's only functioning river boat, sat moored at the narrow wooden quai. It was 40 years old, with open decks and a small, covered cabin for the captain and any managers who had to make the 10-hour trip between Lobe and N'dian. There were three bullet holes in the wall of the cabin, souvenirs of an attack by Nigerian pirates, who terrorized the creeks for a short time right after the Biafran War.

Simon walked over to the riverboat, on his way, shaking hands with a young gendarme who watched indifferently as the Rio's crew unloaded sacks from the ship's hold. Further, down the quai, Jonas Foncha was talking quietly to an older African whom Mark recognized as the Rio's captain.

Jonas was the technical manager at the Lobe refinery and also owned the Jungle Bay, N'Kondo-Titi's only nightclub. The four of them had gone one night as Jonas' guests and came out almost deaf from a non-stop assault by two of the largest speakers Mark had seen anywhere.

Simon greeted Jonas, then turned to the captain.

"How now, M'Bee?" He asked, smiling.

"Fine, suh," M'Bee replied, shaking hands.

John M'Bee had been the Rio's captain since it was commissioned. He was over 60 now, with a bit of a stomach and more white hair than black, but he didn't look ready to retire.

M'Bee was something of a legend in the company. He was said to know the creeks better than any man alive, and his decision years earlier to ram the pirates' boat rather than cede to their demands had earned him a place in the estate's folklore.

He called out in pidgin to one of his crew, who hurried into the cabin and emerged a moment later carrying a small bundle of letters. He brought them over to M'Bee, who handed the bundle to Simon.

"Has it rained much?" Simon asked, shuffling quickly through the letters.

M'Bee shook his head. "No, suh; it's very treacherous."

The creeks, especially upriver, became dangerously shallow at the end of the dry season. Occasionally, the Rio could not reach N'dian and had to unload supplies at a point several kilometers downriver. The estate workers then had to haul them the rest of the way on their backs.

M'Bee and Simon drifted over toward the boats. Jonas turned to go, but spotted Mark and came over.

He smiled, turning his head slightly to avert the side of his face that had been paralyzed by an accident at birth. He did it instinctively so that even when talking to someone in front of him, Jonas appeared to be looking at something in the distance.

"Welcome, Mark."

"Hello, Jonas; how are you?"

"Fine, fine," Jonas replied, embarrassed, as always, to be talking about himself.

He was a painfully shy man, perhaps because of his deformity, but over the years, he had gotten to know Mark and Deborah and seemed to enjoy talking to them.

Mark liked him and knew the feeling was reciprocated.

"How's business?" Mark asked, smiling, so Jonas knew he wasn't talking about Jungle Bay.

"Not too bad," Jonas said, laughing a little.

Smuggling in the creeks was never bad business unless you got caught, and Jonas was too smart for that.

"Is that your canoe?" Mark asked, pointing to a boat moored 100 meters downriver from the Rio.

"Canoe" was a misnomer, really, like so many pidgin adaptations. In fact, the boat had the general lines of a canoe, with a deep, V-shaped hull and wide gunwales, but that was where the resemblance ended.

It was easily 30 feet long, made of heavy steel plating, and could carry five tons of merchandise and a half dozen crew or passengers. Jonas' canoe had two 100 horsepower Evinrudes mounted in the stern.

"Uh huh," Jonas said quietly as if there were no reason to advertise the fact.

Simon was still talking to M'Bee, so Mark wandered over to the boat with Jonas.

It was the only one at the "port" just then, but Mark had seen as many as five at a time, some loading, others unloading, all within a stone's toss of the *gendarmerie* and in plain view of the *gendarmes* who were posted day and night at the quai.

Jonas, as an owner, didn't actually make the runs between N'Kondo-Titi and the Nigerian side; he had a driver and crew for that. But he had to arrange orders and deliveries on both sides, as well as the payoffs to a variety of customs and military officials whose cooperation was essential. Even then, it was a risky business. But the rewards were enormous, and Jonas and all the other owners moved only at night, which reduced the chances of being spotted.

Two of Jonas' men, both shiny with sweat, were loading cases of Gold Harp into his canoe. When they were alongside, Mark saw that the entire front half of the boat was packed with boxes of the Guiness lager. Jonas said something quietly in pidgin to one of the workers; he nodded without looking up, jumped off the boat onto the bank, and disappeared behind some bushes. A moment later, he was back and handed Jonas two Gold Harps. Jonas handed one to Mark, and both of them opened the bottles with their teeth.

"Bloody degenerates!" Simon boomed.

Mark, who hadn't seen him coming, tried to swallow fast, to beat the laugh, but didn't make it. Beer shot out his nose onto the quai.

"Goddamnit, Simon," he said when he'd stop coughing.

Simon laughed and wagged a finger at Mark.

"You know what your problem is? Too much bloody *mimbo,* that's what," he said.

"Or not enough," Mark said, smiling.

Jonas, who was used to Simon's sense of humor, laughed quietly. "A beer, Simon?" He asked.

Simon shook his head. "Thanks, Jonas, but I've got to get back, or Mary'll be feeding me dog chop for a week."

Bottles were expensive, and it was considered bad manners to leave with one, so Mark chugged the rest of his beer and handed the empty back to Jonas. They shook hands all around, and Mark and Simon promised to come by the Jungle Bay again sometime soon.

As they pulled away from the port, a white Mercedes drove up and stopped. Behind the wheel was a slight, youthful African who looked out of place driving the big German car.

Simon stopped the Peugeot and rolled down the window, and the African did likewise.

"Hello, Francis," Simon yelled, smiling. "What are you up to?"

"Hello, Simon," the African called; "Just checking on a few things with Jonas." His voice was quiet and calm and had none of the deference that so many Africans used for addressing whites.

"You bloody bandit," Simon yelled, laughing.

The African smiled slightly. "See you at lunch, Simon."

"Right," Simon said, rolling the window back up and stomping on the gas pedal.

"That guy is the richest bugger in Kumba," he told Mark once he was sure they were far enough away.

"Really?" Mark asked, genuinely surprised. "He looks like a kid."

Simon shook his head but kept his eyes on the road.

"He's older than he looks," he said. "He's a Nigerian, married to an Anglophone woman over here,"

"What's he do?" Mark asked.

"Transport. The bugger has horned in on the Bamilekes' oil distribution business, and they're hopping mad. Even offered me a *dash* to cut him off," Simon said.

Mark laughed. "They tried to *dash* you? How much?"

"50,000 CFA," Simon replied, shaking his head. "The buggers! I told them to get stuffed, so they thought I wanted more money. Next time I went to Baffoussam, they had me flipping back champagne like bloody water, and then they handed me a sack with a million CFA in it."

That was five thousand dollars; not a fortune for the Bamilekes, but a damn nice dash nonetheless.

"What'd you say?" Mark asked.

"I was on the bloody spot, I'll tell you," Simon said. "I couldn't offend them; those guys sell 80 percent of our oil."

"So, what'd you do?" Mark asked, intrigued now.

"I gave 'em some mumbo-jumbo about Francis being a good friend of the MD, and I'd have to see what I could do; then I high-tailed it out of there," Simon explained.

He laughed, still watching the road. "They're all bloody bandits, you know."

Francis arrived promptly at 12:30 for lunch. He was still in the white Mercedes, but he had a driver now, and his wife was with him.

She was not tall, but had at least two inches and 50 pounds on her husband. She wore a traditional blouse and long wrap-around skirt and, except for gold earrings and a necklace, could have passed for a market woman working one of the stalls in Kumba.

Mary was more nervous than usual, which was customary when she entertained Africans. But Francis brought her a bottle of wine — a damn good Bordeaux—which immediately set him apart from the estate managers, who always arrived empty-handed. His wife, Helen, in spite of her appearance, turned out to be a lawyer and had gone to university in England, and that also eased the strain.

Up close, Mark realized that Francis was older than he looked, perhaps even older than Mark. He was a naturally shy man who had obviously made an effort to overcome his handicap. He praised Mary's cooking, though not to the point of insincerity, and asked about her tennis game. He didn't play himself, but knew the rules and enjoyed watching.

He expressed an interest in Mark's work and listened closely to his analysis of the Chadian situation. Francis had never been, he explained, but was considering a move into the lucrative Douala to N'djamena transport market if things got back to normal in Chad.

Francis was less comfortable talking about himself, but did acknowledge, reluctantly, that he owned trucking businesses in both Cameroon and Nigeria and an urban bus line in Lagos, his home town. Mark asked how he ran things in Nigeria from Kumba. Despite the proximity of the two countries, communications between Cameroon and Nigeria were almost non-existent.

He had a brother who looked after things there, Francis said. "And I go over from time to time."

"That must get expensive," Mark said. Air fares between even neighboring countries in Africa were prohibitive.

"I generally drive," Francis said, catching Mark's inference, "so it's not too bad."

Mark looked up from his meal to see if Francis was kidding. He had never heard of anyone except the cross-African caravan people, Germans or Scandinavians mostly, driving between Nigeria and Cameroon. The few roads that linked the two countries were awful; neither Nigeria nor Cameroon had any interest in facilitating the flow of goods and people, or troops, in the worst-case scenario, across the border, and so kept the tracks in a constant state of deplorable disrepair.

The customs and immigration authorities in isolated posts like that could also be unpleasant or worse.

Francis wasn't kidding, though; in fact, Mark realized he probably didn't kid too often about anything.

"You don't have any trouble with the immigration or customs people?" Mark asked.

Francis smiled just a little. "I know most of them," he replied.

Mark nodded. Of course, he did. The question, though, which Mark held off from asking, was why, if Francis had the money to dash them all, he didn't just use it for a plane ticket and avoid what had to be a week's ride over some of the worst roads in the world.

"Because he takes whole caravans of Mercedes across the border and flogs them in Nigeria," Simon explained after Francis and Helen had left.

They had not lingered after lunch. Francis had to make a courtesy call on Ian Smythe, then would stop by again for Mark. He was going down to Douala on business and insisted on giving Mark a ride back.

"I don't know what kind of mark-up he gets, but knowing that bugger, it's plenty," Simon added.

Mark nodded, doing a fast calculation. Easily double, maybe triple what he paid for them in Cameroon.

The Nigerian government, in an austerity move, had recently banned imports of the German car. That only heightened their appeal in status-conscious Nigeria, where a Mercedes was the ultimate symbol of success.

"Then he buys Nigerian goods—cosmetics, motorcycles, clothes, you name it—brings them back here and sells them for three times what he paid for them over there," Simon said, smiling and shaking his head.

"So, he makes it coming and going," Mark said.

"That bugger is raking it in," Simon laughed.

Helen sat up front with the driver between Lobe and

Kumba, but unlike most African wives, she talked freely, asking Mark questions about his work, mostly, but also a few pointed ones about U.S. government policy in Africa. Francis listened more than he spoke, but Mark had a feeling that was the way he was most comfortable.

They dropped Helen in Kumba at a pleasant, but unremarkable villa in what looked to Mark to be an upper-level *functionaires' quartier* on the north side of town. The houses were old, probably left over from the British days, and all of them needed a coat of paint at least. But there was a faded, musty prestige about them, and the cars on the street were newer Peugeots or the larger Japanese models that, in recent years, had cut deeply into what had been a French monopoly.

Helen said she hoped Mark would come out and have lunch sometime. She meant it, but clearly wasn't going to die if it didn't happen. Mark said thanks, he'd love to and meant it too. Francis said something quietly to her in what Mark assumed was Bakossi. She replied, then turned and disappeared into the house.

Mark had worried in a minor way that with Helen gone, the ride down to Douala might settle into fitful conversation and long, uncomfortable silences. But without appearing to make an effort, Francis kept the conversation moving. He preferred listening to talking and was good at it, eliciting further details with questions that, while direct, never seemed to pry.

When he had to, though, Francis had no trouble expressing himself. He answered Mark's questions directly, if briefly; a few of them he avoided, and once, smiling, asked Mark if he was writing an article.

Mark laughed and let it drop.

By the time they crossed the Mungo River back into Francophone Cameroon, Mark had cautiously sketched his new business venture to Francis. He left out the Libyans and the dollars and referred to the imports only as equipment. Francis asked about the buyer in Chad and whether he was serious; he was impressed, maybe a little surprised, to hear that Calvady was covering the cost of customs, transport, and Mark's expenses upfront.

He asked if Mark had contracted with any transporter yet.

Mark shook his head. "I was going to start making the rounds as soon as I got back from Lobe," he replied.

The sun was an orange ball almost touching the Wouri when they crossed the bridge back into Douala. Traffic was light, as it always was on Sunday evening. Other than the restaurants, there was little open in the business section and nothing at all to draw visitors. Cameroonians either stayed in their *quartiers* on Sunday or, if they had access to a car, headed back to the village.

Francis' driver pulled up outside Mark's apartment building in Akwa, and Mark hopped out.

"Will he be able to find it again in the dark?" He asked, leaning down and looking back in at Francis.

Francis spoke quickly to the driver, who nodded.

"No problem," Francis said, smiling. "See you at eight o'clock, Mark."

Out of habit, Mark slapped at the stairway light switch, but nothing happened. He hissed in disgust, then walked up in the semi-darkness. It didn't matter; he'd be out of there before long.

On the landing outside his door, Mark's foot kicked a ball of paper. He bent down and picked it up; it was his note to Koumba. At least it hadn't blown away. The apartment was stifling, so he left the door open and pushed open the front windows.

It had been nice riding in the air-conditioned Mercedes, but it made his apartment seem that much hotter. His next place would be different, with central air, like their first apartment. Mark took a fast shower and found his least wrinkled pants and shirt. He was almost dressed when he heard footsteps on the stairs outside. He made a face; the last thing he needed right now was a fight with Koumba.

But it was only Wanna, on his way back home from checking on his property in Bonaberi. Did Mark want to have a quick beer?

Mark hesitated a second, then asked Wanna to join them for dinner at Marie's. They all went in Francis' car, with Mark sitting up front. He introduced Wanna as a friend and partner. Sunday was a slow night at Marie's, and they had no trouble getting a table on the terrace. Marie welcomed Francis warmly, who, to Mark's surprise, responded in French.

Nigerians, in general, didn't like the French for a lot of reasons and viewed the language as the most irritating reminder of Nigeria's inability to enforce what it regarded as its natural hegemony in the region. Nigerians and Anglophone Cameroonians didn't always get along either, which was why Mark had hesitated before inviting Wanna. Francis was also everything Wanna aspired to be and wasn't—and would never be. Not that Wanna lacked Francis' intelligence or drive; he was probably his equal in both.

Missing, though, was a confidence that sprang not from arrogance, but almost its opposite: an instinctive serenity whose origins Mark not only couldn't understand, but could not imagine.

Mark needn't have worried. Francis steered the conversation to Wanna's job and his studies in the States. By the second round of St. Pauli's Girl, he'd asked Wanna's advice on a letter of credit problem and promised to stop by the bank in the morning to talk about possible financing for two new palm oil tanker trucks.

They didn't get around to the oil equipment until after the fish had arrived. Francis suggested that Mark might want to get a few quotes from other transporters but that if they could agree on a price, it was a venture that interested him. Mark nodded and asked what his idea of a fair price was, more for form than any concern over money. Calvady, or the Libyans, were paying, and Mark had decided that the fewer people who knew of the shipment, the better.

It was more than that, though. He barely knew Francis but, for whatever reason, had faith in him; not only that he would hold up his end of any bargain, but that simply having him involved would somehow increase the chances of success.

They dickered slightly over price, then agreed to 500,000 CFA, or about $2,500, for the truck and driver; gasoline, food, and lodging for the driver, and any other expenses would be extra. They shook hands and had another round of St. Pauli's Girl to celebrate the agreement. They were all a little drunk when Francis' driver returned to pick them up.

CHAPTER 19

Jim Richards had never spent much time around blacks. It wasn't that he was prejudiced; hell, he even had a couple of 'em working in the plant. Older boys, though, knew the goddamn value of a job and what they had to do to keep it.

But growing up in Oklahoma City, they'd had their own school (a damn good one, too), and they'd stuck to their kind, and no one thought anything about it. There weren't any that he knew of in the Houston sub-division where he and Ema lived, but that was just economics.

Any of 'em could afford it; nobody, well, at least not Jim Richards, would try to stop 'em. But he'd never been anyplace where they actually ran the goddamn show; it was going to take some getting used to.

Jim Richards stood, sweating, in the taxi line outside the Douala airport. He'd worn a medium-weight suit; hell, it was still cool in Houston, and he'd damn near frozen his ass off making the connection in Paris. Now, though, the jacket was soaked through, probably ruined, from sitting in the goddamn police room.

No problem, they said when he called the State Department: Cameroon is a bilingual country, and English will do fine.

The goddamn incompetent sons of bitches. Not one of the fucking ill-mannered bastards spoke anything but French. Jabberin' away at him like that, and when he couldn't answer them, one of 'em started yelling at him. So, he yelled back, in English, until some fat old cop in a red beret and sunglasses, even though it was midnight, yanked him out of line and dragged him into an office.

They forced him to sit on an iron chair, then ignored him for an hour until a young cop who spoke a few words of English threw his passport at him and told him to go and show some respect the next time.

Appreciate any assistance can lend, he'd said in the telex. First time to Africa, hell, first time out of the U.S. But shit, no, they couldn't be bothered; too goddamn busy at the consulate to help a visiting businessman who only paid their goddamn salaries.

A yellow taxi screeched to a stop in front of him, and an African, young and fat and bored, quickly opened the trunk without a key and tossed Jim's good leather bags onto what looked like several spare tires.

"How much?" He said slowly, louder than was necessary.

"Ou allez-vous?" The driver asked.

"How much?" Jim repeated, louder and slower.

The driver turned in the seat to look at Jim.

"Where?" He asked.

Jim held the tourist agency's package at an angle to catch the light from the airport.

"Hotel Meridien," he said.

"Mille francs," the driver said automatically.

"What the hell's that mean?" Jim muttered. "Don't you speak any English?"

"One tousan'," the driver said, forming the words carefully.

"One thousand what? You take dollars?"

The driver shook a finger into the rear-view mirror.

"No dollars," he said emphatically.

"French francs?" Jim pleaded. He didn't have anything else, and he had to get out of there.

"Ca va," the driver said, trying not to smile. *"Cent francs*; one hunner".

Jim reached quickly in his pockets and pulled out a damp wad of bills. He flipped through the francs he had picked up at Charles de Gaulle airport until he found a 100 franc note. He reached over the seat and handed it to the driver.

"Let's get the hell outta here," he said, glad to be in charge again.

The Meridien helped. It was new, clean, and air-conditioned. His room was big and had a double bed and fresh towels that still had lots of fluff left in them. There was also a damn nice bar, with a piano and small intimate-style banquettes, that was still open when Jim checked in. The help looked all black, but they spoke, or at least understood English; and the manager, a Frenchman, greeted Jim at the desk and had his reservation and spoke damn near perfect English.

Jim went up to check out the room and see that his bags made it, then came down again. He needed a goddamn drink or two or three. The bar wasn't crowded at that hour; a few groups, mostly white but a few black, and all well-dressed, sat up front near the piano listening to an African play songs Jim didn't recognize. He sat down at one of the booths in the back. When an African waiter showed up, he ordered a scotch and soda.

"Johnnie Walker?" The African asked. It came out funny, more like "Johnnie Walkcare," but Jim didn't give a damn. He knew what the son of a bitch was saying, and that's all that mattered. It was damn nice to hear a name he recognized.

"You know how to make a double?" Jim demanded.

"Un double?" The waiter repeated in French, not certain.

"A double; you know how to make a double scotch?"

"Monsieur voudrait un double," the waiter said, pretty sure now, but hoping for a confirmation.

Jim exhaled sharply.

"Look," he said slowly, "if you know how to make a goddamn double, do it. Otherwise, just bring me a scotch and soda, and we'll go from there, OK?"

The waiter hesitated just a moment, then smiled.

"Oui, monsieur," he said, bowing slightly and leaving.

Jim ran one of his big hands down over his face. This whole thing might've been a mistake.

"Bon soir."

Jim had been looking down at the table and didn't see her slide into the seat on the other side of the booth. It was probably as close as he'd ever been to a black woman, certainly one that good-looking. Her tits, enormous things, strained against the fabric of her knit shirt, stopping less than a foot from his drinking hand.

"Hello," Jim said, a little embarrassed. He wasn't sure if she was a hostess or what; maybe it was like one of those Hawaiian hotels where a nice young thing gave out leis.

The waiter brought his drink; he'd got it right.

"Mademoiselle?" He asked, not smiling anymore.

"Une biere," she replied, not looking at him. The waiter walked away.

Jim smiled a bit uncomfortably, and she giggled, leaning forward so that her chest grazed the top of the table, inches from Jim's hand. He had never seen hair like that: braided in tight furrows on top and cord-like strips dangling in the back, with colored beads attached at the end, which rattled softly when she moved her head.

She was as black as night, blacker than any Jim had ever seen in the U.S. She was big, too; not fat, but strong-looking, like she could swallow him up and still be lookin' for more.

"You work here at the hotel?" He asked, speaking slowly and enunciating his words carefully.

She giggled again, this time flashing her teeth that looked startlingly white against the black face. She dropped one hand down to her lap; a second later, Jim felt her fingernail scrape slowly and deliberately along his thigh and then up his zipper.

"Hey!" He said, stiffening in the seat. He looked around, but the tables on either side were empty. The other customers were intent on the piano player or their own conversations.

She did it again, skipping right to the zipper this time, and giggled when she felt his undeniable response.

"Goddamn, lady!" He said, a little out of breath.

She stopped while the waiter, who looked unhappy about something, dropped off her beer. When he left, she sipped it with one hand and let the other one slide underneath the table again.

His zipper sounded deafening as it went down, but there was no one looking over at them. Jim felt her long fingernails grope through the opening in his boxer shorts, and then he was free, her hand working him softly up and back while her thumb kneaded the tip.

"Oh goddamn," he sighed. "Uh, why don't we go on up to my room?" She giggled again, but didn't stop.

He yanked his room key out of his pocket and gestured with it in the direction of the lobby.

"D'accord," she breathed, gave him a last long stroke, and brought her hand back to the table. Jim took another quick look around, then zipped his pants slowly to minimize the sound. He threw back the rest of the drink, and they both got up. Jim signed the bill at the bar and dropped some French francs on a tray for the waiter.

"My name's Jim; I'm from Texas," he said as they walked to

the elevator. She giggled again. "What's your name?" He asked, pointing at her. They both laughed as the elevator door opened.

Inside, he pushed the button for his floor, then tapped his chest. "Jim," he said very slowly. Then he tapped her lightly on the chest, letting his hand linger for just a second, which made her laugh.

"What is your name?" He asked again.

"Koumba," she said, pronouncing it slowly, as if for a child.

CHAPTER 20

Goddamn frogs. They'd lost every war they'd ever fought; hell, even the slopes whipped their asses; and they still acted like they knew how to handle things, and nobody else knew shit. Martin Feraldi sipped his beer in quick, short bursts as if that might minimize the risk of infection from the germs that he was sure found the Relais' glasses a perfect home.

Well, if the motherfucker wanted to talk, they'd do it in English. After five years in Saigon, he understood frog reasonably well. But he never spoke it. He knew it drove the bastards crazy, and anyway, making 'em think he didn't understand it might give him an edge.

That's what the job was all about creating an advantage and then exploiting it.

"Your friend didn't like to come?" The Frenchman asked politely.

"He's busy," Feraldi said, taking another sip and staring over the rim of the glass at the Frenchman.

The Frenchman nodded. It had been worth a try. But he wasn't surprised that one of them had stayed at the house. Feraldi put his beer back on the table. If the frogs thought they were going to get a look that easy, it was no wonder they lost the goddamn toilet bowl of a country to Qadaffi.

"I thought we should know each other," the Frenchman said.

Feraldi sneered. Yeah, sure, *ami*; keep talking. It was a goddamn disgrace they couldn't do any better than this little pink-faced prick. OK, sure, Chad didn't mean fuck all to the U.S., except for Qadaffi; but goddamn it, the French-owned the place, and they'd let some goddamn rag-heads throw 'em out.

He took another rapid series of sips. Well, that was their fucking problem.

"We are on zeh same side, no?" The Frenchman asked, smiling across the table.

Feraldi laughed, an unexpected, ugly gurgling.

"I'm just a consular officer, friend," he said.

The Frenchman nodded and smiled down at the table.

"Still, you feel interested in what goes on over there," he said, jerking his head in the direction of the river.

Feraldi shrugged. "Not as interested as you," he said.

The Frenchman felt the blood spread into his face, and he was glad he had chosen a table at the back, away from the light.

"Has Emil asked you to change dollars?" He asked.

Feraldi shook his head. "No, but I'm not a bank," he replied, happy to have thought that one up so fast.

"You must need to be," the Frenchman countered; "he has more than five thousand of them." He wasn't smiling anymore.

Feraldi laughed again. They didn't know when to give up.

"We've checked the dollar rumors, friend," he said, making it clear they were not. "It's bullshit."

He looked at his watch. He didn't have anywhere to go, and it was a toss-up whether he felt less comfortable with this frog or the "partner" Washington had sent him, but he wanted the prick to understand he was wasting his time. The Frenchman leaned over the side of the table and pulled up a briefcase from the floor. It was almost midnight, and they were alone in the restaurant, though he could hear Emil talking quietly with someone out at the bar.

He glanced quickly over at the curtain that separated the restaurant and bar; then, he spun the briefcase around so it faced the American and opened it. Feraldi tried not to react to the piles of $50 notes. But if he'd been that good, he wouldn't have been in a place like Kousseri.

The Frenchman smiled, and when he was sure Feraldi had had a moment to do a rough calculation, he shut the briefcase again and slid it under his seat.

Calvady had gotten ugly about it. It was only a loan, the Frenchman had explained, but the bastard wouldn't hear of it, didn't understand the need for it. So, the Frenchman had hit him, hard, twice, and Calvady had understood that.

"One of our uh...friends accumulated zat in two days," he explained, just in case Feraldi was as stupid as the Frenchman suspected.

Feraldi stared across at the Frenchman, who smiled.

"The Libyans are paying zeh Chadians soldiers with dollars," the Frenchman said when Feraldi didn't respond.

"Why dollars? Why not francs?" The American demanded. He wasn't buying it yet, not by a long shot, but it'd be his ass if the frog cocksucker was right.

"They tried to buy francs, but they were...blocked," the Frenchman explained. He took his pipe from his shirt pocket and went through the ritual of packing and lighting it to avoid grinning.

He had him now, and rubbing the bastard's nose in it might backfire.

"You don't have to take my word for it," he said, between pulls on the pipe to get it started. "Go into any commercant in Kousseri and offer to buy dollars at, say, 100 CFA each."

"Maybe I will, pal," Feraldi shot back.

The Frenchman felt the blood rush into his cheeks again. He

put the pipe on the table and quickly drained his beer. It was time to go before he said something he'd regret. He didn't like Americans in general and Feraldi in particular; arrogance and stupidity made an almost intolerable combination. But he needed the Americans to pay attention now, and there was no point distracting them. They had a hard enough time as it was.

He got up to go.

"Oh, by zeh way, the Libyan commander has moved; he's taken a villa near to the airport. It looks like he will be staying some time," he said, friendly again, happy to be of service to an ally. Feraldi stared up at him but said nothing.

The Frenchman stuck the pipe in a corner of his mouth and picked up the briefcase.

"I must go," he said. *"Au revoir, monsieur. A bientot, j'espere."* He almost extended his hand, then thought better of it. No sense overdoing it. He turned and walked out without waiting for Feraldi's reply, which was just as well since none was forthcoming.

CHAPTER 21

The children at the *ecole primaire* just across from the French consulate looked up as Mark ran past. Some of the boys ran with him inside the schoolyard, laughing and jeering, until the fence stopped them. Even the young ones thought anyone running in that heat was a little funny.

Mark was breathing hard, but his legs felt all right as he passed the Meridien and turned down the short slope to the *digue,* a narrow spit of land that formed the western extremity of the port. It was a longer run for him now than when he was doing it every night from their apartment in the *Tour de Wouri,* but he didn't have much choice. There just weren't a lot of places in Douala to run, the *digue,* or out by the airport, and that was about it.

Anyway, old habits died hard.

He circled the warehouses and office buildings at the foot of the hill, then turned left, out the *digue* road. When Mark had started running there four years earlier, the road was a dirt track that ran straight as a ribbon between a heavily wooded swamp and a small lagoon until it reached the Wouri. It was a two-lane blacktop now. The swamp had been cut back, and the lagoon filled in, and offices and warehouses, some still under construction, lined both sides of the road. All are part of a major port expansion.

Mark turned around at the gate to a military complex that was off-limits and headed back toward town. The sun was almost down, and near the river, there was a nice breeze; still, it was damn hot running. Even after a month, Mark's wind and legs weren't what he'd hoped they'd be. Too much bloody *mimbo.*

He slowed down to a trot to catch his breath. He felt better than he had in a long time, though. He was eating better, too, mostly fruit at the apartment because he was too lazy to cook. But he stopped at the *patisserie* most mornings and was eating out just about every night. Marie's usually, but sometimes, a chicken house in Daido, the *quartier* upriver near the Wouri Bridge, and even once at "Le Champagne," his first real restaurant since before Deborah left.

Mark had to open his mouth to make it up the hill toward the Meridien. The hotel hadn't been there either when he first started running. He'd watched it go up from the groundbreaking. At first, Mark thought it was folly to build a luxury hotel there. For one thing, the site was too small. The consulate and official French residences crowded in on one side, and the road down to the *digue* cut in slightly on the other, reducing the area available for a swimming pool or grounds.

What's more, the 350-room Novotel, located just across the *digue* road, had opened only four years earlier and was rarely full. It had plenty of parking, an Olympic-sized swimming pool, and a large terrace restaurant and bar.

But the Meridien had pulled it off. A clever design provided just enough parking and somehow made the pool and terrace seem intimate rather than just small, which they were. The hotel made no secret of the clientele it was after its room prices were several thousand CFA higher than those at the Novotel, and its restaurant and bar were among the most expensive in town.

That worked, too. Businessmen from the U.S. and Europe always asked to be booked into the Meridien first, and the wealthiest Cameroonians, especially the northern traders, made it a home away from home. Well, hell, maybe he'd stay there, too, while he looked for another apartment.

Mark had expected a reply, of course, but even so, he'd been surprised when it actually arrived. The company in Houston sounded delighted with the order and offered to request an export permit to save time, even before payment was received. They would ship the equipment as soon as Mark's confirmed letter of credit arrived.

Calvady, or whoever took care of that quickly; 10 days after he telexed the number in Paris, Mark received a second letter saying the goods were on their way. That morning, there was a telex waiting for him at *Antoine's*. It was from the shipping company, saying the container would arrive in Douala on Friday.

Mark wasn't sure where the shipping company had got the telex number at Antoine's, but it didn't matter. The whole thing, except for the money, of course, had seemed remote, almost unreal, as if nothing could be that easy and so would somehow fall apart, and he'd go back to the way he'd been before.

Mark passed the tennis club where they used to belong and turned right on Avenue Charles de Gaulle. There were no more hills, just a flat stretch through Bonapriso past the *Brasserie du Cameroun* and home to Akwa. He felt stronger now like he always did near the end.

It was going to work. He'd taken the risk, maybe not jumped at it, but he hadn't said no, and sometimes that was all that mattered. And now it was going to work out. Mark had gone so long without one that he'd stopped even daydreaming about getting a break, how it would come along, and what he'd do when it did. Once or twice, when he was very drunk, he'd even wondered if he was one of those pitiful souls whom misfortune, or whatever, marked at an early age, then clung to, like a life-long case of acne.

He didn't have to worry about that anymore. Mark didn't like Calvady or trust him, and he knew the bastard felt the same about him. But as long as that was upfront, it was all right; hell, you didn't have to love somebody to do business with him. Maybe they'd even do another load later, a bigger one. Mark would have to be careful not to get too greedy, but there was no reason why not.

When he reached Akwa, Mark stopped running. He was tired, and it was almost dark, anyway, which made running there dangerous. The *quartier* sidewalks had whole cement sections missing, exposing the open sewer that ran just underneath. At night, the holes were difficult to see.

Running in the street was out of the question. It was still rush hour, and the drivers, who had little enough regard for each other, had none whatever for pedestrians.

At the bottom of the stairs, Mark took a deep breath and started up, taking the steps two at a time, almost running. It was tough after the eight kilometers, but it was a nice way to finish up, and it felt good later. At the top landing, he stood for a minute, catching his breath. He hurt, but it was a nice pain and nothing like what he'd felt when he first started running again. He'd let himself go for too long.

He left the apartment door open and, still breathing hard, walked back to the bedroom and flipped off his sneakers. He peeled off his shirt, running shorts, and underwear and left them on the floor near the bathroom. Then he walked back to the kitchen to get a beer. He was still drinking, but he'd cut back: two beers when he got back from a run and no more than three with dinner.

Mark held the icy bottle of Gold Harp against his cheek as

he walked back to the living room. He pulled one of the wicker chairs up close to the windows to catch the faint breeze blowing in and sat down.

The money would be a little dicey, as Simon would say, but he'd manage. He'd pay Wanna, then take a short vacation. He could check the money at the Swissair counter just to get it out of the country. It was a direct flight, and Swissair was a good airline, so the chance of a lost bag was pretty slim. The only real risk was walking it through the "nothing to declare" aisle in Geneva.

Shit, even if they caught him, what's the worst they'd do him? Switzerland hadn't got its reputation by discouraging people from bringing money into the country. Besides, he wasn't going to get caught. If a sleazeball like Calvady could do it, Mark would manage. He'd have a few drinks on the plane and never look back.

Mark spread his legs and put the bottle against his balls. The sudden coldness made them ache, but it felt good nonetheless. The running and not drinking so much had helped with Koumba; it was more enjoyable and less of an effort. She seemed to like it better, too; she didn't always jump up right afterward and, once or twice, had to lay there under him, scraping her fingernails softly up and down his back.

Mark would have given a lot to see her walk in right then. He wouldn't move; just pull her to him, yank those tight jeans down, and make her straddle him right there in the chair. He'd bury his face between those sweet, enormous tits and give her the ride of her life.

He leaned his head back and took a deep breath. But she wasn't going to show up, not then, probably not even later. The wife of a friend of Gilles had been medivac-ed to Paris for something or other, and her husband went with her. Koumba was staying at the suddenly empty house most nights.

Or so she said. With Koumba, the truth was often whatever

she thought would go over with a given audience. When they first met, she told him her father had been a diplomat, assigned to Cameroon; when he died suddenly, there had been some kind of argument, and the embassy refused to pay for her flight home.

But one of the whores at the Cafe des Sports laughed when Mark recounted Koumba's story. She said she had been working in Yaounde years earlier when Koumba showed up with a Lebanese trader who was trying to break into the cocoa business. The government refused his request for a license, she said, and he left the next day without Koumba.

Mark finished the first Gold Harp and got up to get another one.

He'd almost told Koumba about the money, that he had enough now to do the things she liked, and she didn't have to ... depend on Gilles. The son of a bitch had to be in heaven. Koumba was there for him whenever he wanted; hell, maybe even a fast one before he went home for lunch or before he opened the marina after the siesta.

Mark slipped the empty into the cardboard case under the kitchen sink, then pulled another full one from the refrigerator and opened it. The next time she came by, he'd tell her his strings had agreed to raise his retainer, so he had a little more money to spend. Just to see what she'd say.

CHAPTER 22

Jim Richards leaned down to inspect the hamburger and French fries closely.

"This well-done?" He demanded of the Cameroonian who had delivered it.

"Oui, monsieur."

Jim picked up his fork and cut into the meat: it was gray-brown, not a hint of pink. At least they'd got that right.

The waiter started to leave.

"Wait a minute." Jim quickly scraped the tomato slices and lettuce garnish from the side of the plate onto his butter dish and handed it to the waiter.

"You can take that back," he said, flicking his hand in the general direction of the Meridien kitchen.

The African took the plate but hesitated.

"I don't want it," Jim said, looking straight at the African and mouthing each word carefully.

"*Oui, monsieur,*" the waiter said. He bowed slightly and left.

Jim cut into the hamburger with his fork again, on the other side this time, just to be sure. He might not be a goddamn globetrotter, but he sure as hell knew better than to eat salad in a place like Cameroon. He turned over a piece of the meat with his fork. Even cooked, who the hell knew where it really came from? And who made sure they washed their hands? The French manager couldn't be everywhere.

The hamburger looked all right, but he couldn't get the idea out of his mind that it might not be beef after all, so he started with the French fries. Potatoes were potatoes, at least.

Goddamn, it was hot. Jim had eaten breakfast on the terrace early, and it was nice; warm, even then, but not uncomfortably so. Now, though, he was sweating through his shirt, even in the shade. The double-knit pants he favored because they always felt so light and comfortable were sticking to his legs wherever they touched and kept riding up the crack in his butt, like some goddamn rubberized weight-loss outfit.

He should've waited for a table inside, but he was hungry, and the goddamn restaurant was full. Jim sipped his bottled water and used the napkin to wipe his face again.

It hadn't been too bad walking the three blocks to the U.S. consulate because he went first thing. But the bastards kept him waiting, and by the time the imbecile got through, explaining how little he knew, it was almost noon. Walking back to the hotel felt like someone had locked him in a fucking steam bath with his clothes on.

Goddamn bureaucrats. There wasn't a more worthless breed in the world. It was a racket, that's all, getting working people to pay 'em a living, and a damn nice one too, for doing fuck all.

Jim exhaled deeply. No use getting worked up; it just made him hotter, and there wasn't shit all he could do about it there. But his congressman was going to get a goddamn earful when he got back.

He looked around to make sure no one was watching him, then ran one hand quickly inside the waist of his pants and scratched himself softly. He'd spotted the rash when he took a piss before lunch. He'd had a moment of panic, then realized

VD didn't come on that fast. It's just prickly heat, probably from the spandex rubbing against the sweat.

Even so, he'd have to see about getting a shot of penicillin before he left. Had to be careful who you asked about that sort of thing, though; most of the oil company boys were OK, but some of them had gone a little God-crazy lately. There's no point offending anyone.

If nothing else, it was bad for business.

The closest Jim had ever been to fucking a black girl was at the oil service industry convention in New Orleans in 1977. But Bobby Ray Whittaker from Hughes had snapped up the one black whore before any of the rest of 'em had a chance.

But hell, she was nothing up against Koumba.

Jim took a drink of water. When she pulled off those tight jeans and that stretch thing she was wearing on top and just lay down on the bed, black everywhere, with her knees up and spread a little, inviting him in, well, goddamn, if he didn't think he'd died and gone to heaven.

And it cost him all of 2,000 CFA. What the hell was that--$10? Nobody'd believe him. Maybe she'd agree to have her picture taken, just like that, on the bed. Hell, he'd pay her. Jim thought about that for a moment, then laughed to himself.

Maybe that wasn't such a good idea after all. Ema was a damn good woman, a first-rate wife and mother, and she understood that men had to let off steam every now and then. But shit, if she ever heard about an African whore, spread-eagled on a bed...

No, probably better not to take any pictures.

Jim felt the stiffness against the front of his pants and took a deep breath. He'd be ready for her tonight; even wished he'd told her to come by at lunch. He'd been a little tired and not a hundred percent after the airport and all; she'd almost been a bit much for him. Not anything serious; he'd given her her money's worth and then some, goddammit. It was just that, for a moment or two—no more than that—Jim hadn't been certain which of them was calling the tune.

She was so goddamn big and strong! But he'd been tired, damn tired. He'd be all right tonight; he could feel it. He'd have her flopping like a goddamn flounder out of water.

"Un dessert, monsieur?"

Jim looked down at his empty plate. He couldn't remember eating the hamburger. Goddamn, a good thing he'd sent the salad back.

"Uh, no, I don't think so," he replied.

"Un cafe?" The waiter asked.

Jim nodded. "Yeah, but with milk, huh?"

The African looked puzzled.

"I don't want one of them dinky little cups," Jim said. "I want a real cup of coffee, eh?" He made a circle with his two hands. "A big one, with milk in it, OK?"

"Un cafe au lait?" The waiter asked hopefully.

"Yeah, *cafe au lait,*" Jim said, pointing a finger at the waiter. "But in a big cup; not one of those things." He gestured at a *demi-tasse* on a nearby table where two Frenchmen had just finished lunch.

"I don't want one of those, OK?"

"Oui, oui, monsieur," the waiter replied, smiling, finally getting it. He left.

Jim looked at his watch. It was five after two. Well, maybe he'd rest until three-thirty or so, then go see a few oil companies. It wouldn't hurt to do a little marketing, and he'd picked up some names before leaving Houston. He'd give the goddamn good-for-nothing consul, or vice-consul, or whatever the hell he was, a day to find AmeriCam Services Inc. If he didn't, Jim would find it himself.

And that'd be one more nail in the bastard's coffin when he got back to Houston.

Shit, for $10, an African whore humped him silly. God only

knew how much the four-eyed bastard was taking of taxpayers' hard-earned money for doing nothing at all. The son of a bitch didn't know where to find an American company that had ordered more pump barrels than Jim Richards had sold in a year. Never even heard of 'em! The worst part was he wasn't even embarrassed to admit it. That was as good a reason as any why the greatest goddamn nation in the history of the world was going to hell in a handbasket.

CHAPTER 23

Kyle Mason opened the back door of the Ford, but turned to his driver before he got out.

"Park it and wait for me, Emmanuel; I don't know how long I'll be," he said.

"Yes, suh."

The heat hit him like a club as he slid out of the air conditioning and closed the door behind him. Three o'clock was the worst time of day in Douala. By then, the city had baked long enough so that everything, even the buildings and streets, seemed to emanate the heat, and any kind of breeze was at least an hour away.

It was the end of the siesta, too; going back to work in that heat, fighting the traffic for a third time after a big lunch and a long nap, made everyone irritable. Anyone who'd been in Douala more than a couple of months knew better than to count on getting anything important done in the afternoon. If it wasn't finished by noon, chances were it wouldn't be by six.

Kyle hurried into the shade of the Benga building, then walked to the far end, where Antoine's Travel Agency occupied the ground floor space.

"Hello, Mrs, Mawanga."

Rose looked up and smiled the way the British had taught her, not showing any teeth.

"Good afternoon, Mr. Mason," she said. She and Victor were prominent Anglophones and, as such, were at or near the top of the U.S. Consulate's invitation list. Antoine's also handled, or mishandled, as the consul often grumbled, the travel arrangements for U.S. diplomats and their families based in Douala.

"What can I do for you?" She asked.

"I'm trying to find Mark Reilly," Kyle replied. "Does he still use your telex?"

Rose's smile all but disappeared. "Yes, and we are having many problems to get paid," she said, shaking her head.

Kyle nodded, making his sympathy clear. That sounded like Mark Reilly.

"Does he come in very often?" Kyle asked. "I'd go by his apartment, but I don't know where he lives."

"He usually stops in the afternoon for his mail and messages," Rose explained, obviously unhappy with the arrangement.

"Would you mind if I waited for him, Mrs. Mawanga?" Kyle asked.

"Please," Rose said, gesturing at a chair on the other side of her desk.

"Thanks very much," Kyle said, sitting down. "Now, don't let me disturb you; I brought some papers to look over, so I'll just sit here and work."

"You will not be disturbing me," Rose said. She went back to balancing the agency's accounts, a job that she was, in fact, totally incapable of and which Victor had to re-do once a month.

Kyle put his battered leather briefcase across his lap and pulled out a copy of the letter Jim Richards had shown him that morning. He took off his glasses, which were for distance, and re-read the letter.

Kyle had never seen Reilly's handwriting, so he couldn't tell just by looking at the signature. It was possible there was another Mark Reilly in Douala that Kyle didn't know about, but he doubted it. It was hard to imagine Reilly owning a business; gosh, he was barely surviving as a freelance journalist. But Kyle had promised he'd check, so he would.

He was, for the record, the vice-consul in Douala, and among other jobs, he was responsible for commercial affairs, which meant, for the most part, promoting U.S. companies in Cameroon. It wasn't his only responsibility, or even the primary one, but they taught him to play it straight—more credible that way—and anyway, Kyle took that sort of thing seriously.

In fact, Kyle was serious about most things: about God and his marriage, certainly, and about the prayer group he'd started for the Cameroonian employees at the consulate; about keeping visas for Cameroonians to a minimum, even below the strict State Department guidelines, because some of them never came back.

He was serious about the American School in Douala, where, until the article appeared, he'd been an active member of the board and where Sue, his wife, had been so happy teaching English and Bible studies. They'd met at a Bible study group while they were both at SMU and were married their senior year. They had no children of their own yet, but that was God's will, which they accepted and never discussed.

Kyle took his other work seriously, too, of course, but for the moment at least, with the Soviets only a token Aeroflot office that seemed to be closed more than it was open and things quiet on the Nigerian border, he had plenty of time for the commercial work.

He glanced at the letter again, shaking his head, then slid it back into his briefcase. It didn't make any sense. Kyle turned to look out at the street, but there was no sign of Reilly. Well, he'd wait.

Kyle opened the briefcase again and pulled out a legal pad, which was already covered with notes. It was for a speech he had to give to the American Wives' Club—which Sue had started—and Kyle wanted to make sure he covered all the essential points for the new arrivals.

Unlike a lot of expatriates, Kyle and Sue had loved Douala from the beginning. They arrived just as the influx of Americans hit its peak so that almost from the first day, they felt a tight bond of community and shared hardship that, in turn, developed the kind of friendships they'd never had at home.

Most of the newcomers were Texans, too, just like them. They found a devout group of Christians, led by Reverand Eugene Yelen, that grew steadily as the American community in Douala expanded. Kyle and Sue found themselves invited out most nights, or else they had people over to their place, a modest but pleasant villa in Bonapriso.

They both went out of their way to help other Americans, especially the new arrivals, who often found Douala and Africa really overwhelming at first, with the heat and the language and police checks everywhere and no medical care to speak of.

Sue printed up a guide to living in Douala, with lists of stores and restaurants and churches and the going rate for cooks and houseboys. She included a short section of "do's and don't's": how to deal with the help when they stole food, what to say to the *gendarmes* when stopped at a checkpoint, how to carry a purse to keep the urchins outside Monoprix from grabbing it, and other helpful tips.

As president of the American Wives', Sue had also become something of an unofficial "welcomer" to arriving American women. She made sure the new ones knew she was available to help out or just to talk. And she organized morning "coffees" once a week, which was really the best way, she'd found, to absorb the new women into the American community.

For the ones whose husbands were with the big, established firms, the Mobils and Gulfs and Pectens, or even one of the banks, it was easier. They no sooner arrived than they were swept up by the other wives, the director's spouse usually taking charge, and the alienation and loneliness that could be so destructive to marriages in a place like Douala were beaten back by a wave of chatter about familiar American things like children, and shopping and vacations.

For the other women, though, the wives of lone salesmen or company representatives, there was a need to get them into the community fast, to let them know they weren't alone, that others had experienced the same disorientation and, yes, even depression. Sue found that the "coffees" were the most natural way to do that. Once a month, Kyle gave a talk, and that helped too, reassuring the women that the U.S. government was close at hand, just in case.

Kyle's calm, reasoned explanation of Cameroonian history and politics also allayed some of the fear prompted by the police road checks and the frightening ordeals some newcomers underwent at the hands of the immigration and customs officials.

Kyle had driven to the airport more than once in the middle of the night to negotiate the release of Americans, often frightened families who had never been outside the U.S., whose visas lacked a stamp, or whose health cards didn't show an up-to-date vaccination.

It was a lot of work, certainly more than was required of either of them. But Kyle and Sue loved it. They were doing something worthwhile together, and, in the way Africa had, they felt a closeness to each other and especially the other Americans, that was more intense than anything they'd experienced before.

Many of the people they'd met there, they just knew, would be their friends for life, no matter what happened or where they ended up after Douala. The experience had taught Kyle and Sue something about love, the good kind, and sometimes they both felt so full of it that they had to talk about it, just so they could get to sleep at night.

Mark didn't see the back of Kyle's head until he had one foot in the door. He stopped and tried to back out again, but Kyle, feeling the hot air rush in, turned and smiled.

"Just the man I wanted to see," he said, getting up from the chair. Kyle laid the briefcase down and came toward Mark, hand extended. His smile was an earnest one, full of sincerity and Christian forgiveness; it was all right, he was saying. No hard feelings.

They shook hands mechanically, like old fraternity brothers who had always hated one another but pretended they hadn't.

"Hello, Kyle," Mark said, feeling, for just an instant, an almost irresistible urge to bring his knee up hard into Kyle's groin. Right there in front of Rose, then walk out without a word.

"Mr. Reilly," Rose said, in the same sing-song whine that, even on the rare occasion when she wasn't complaining about something, made it sound as though she was.

"Yes, Rose?"

"I would like to talk to you after you've finished with Mr. Mason," she said, her irritation obvious.

Better yet, drop ol' Kyle with a knee to the balls, then walk over and put Rose out of her misery. Just squeeze her fat neck for a minute or two. Victor's long-suffering nephews, whose sins of a lifetime had long since been purged by their two-year penance working under her, would break into applause.

Hell, Victor would probably buy him a drink.

"Have you got a minute?" Mark heard Kyle say.

Mark shook his head slightly, not at Kyle's question but just to get his mind back in gear. Wanna had tried to talk him out of a second bottle of wine at lunch, but Mark insisted. It was a mistake.

"Uh, I'm pretty busy, Kyle," Mark replied, a hand at his mouth to block the smell of alcohol. "What's up?"

Kyle quickly reached back for the letter in his briefcase, then scanned it, looking for something.

"I just had a question for you about a company called...AmeriCam Services Inc.," he said, looking up.

Mark stared at him for a second. Goddamn Wanna. He wasn't supposed to tell anyone.

"Uh, I don't know much about it," Mark said, "But, yeah, sure, let's have a quick beer at le Paradis."

Kyle tried to smile, but it was closer to a grimace.

"Oh, Christ Almighty, I'm an absent-minded cocksucker," Mark said, shaking his head. "I forgot you don't drink."

Kyle didn't swear, either. He did his best, but couldn't help blinking, as if the words had physically assaulted him.

"No problem, Mark," he managed.

Le Paradis, a couple of doors down from Antoine's, was empty. Lunch hour was over, and they wouldn't fill up again until after six when most businesses closed. The lights were off to conserve electricity, so it was dark, but the air conditioner over the door was still humming.

"*Messieurs, bonjour*," a young African woman, short and unattractive, drawled when Mark and Kyle sat down in one of the wooden booths.

"*Salut, Nadine. Ca va*?" Mark said, smiling.

"Ouf, ca va," she replied, making it clear that things weren't all right. Whores always had problems.

Nadine worked at le Paradis in the days, but she earned her real livelihood at the *Cafe des Sports* at night. That's where Mark had met her. She leaned a hefty thigh against their table and lifted her eyebrows, or at least where her eyebrows had been.

Like most of the other Douala whores, Nadine had shaved hers and penciled in a thin black arch over both heavily-massacred eyes.

Mark gestured at Kyle.

"Uh, un coca, s'il vous plait," he said, not looking at Nadine.

"Je prends un Gold Harp," Mark said.

"Un grand?" Nadine asked, smiling.

"S'il vous plait," he said, smiling back.

He didn't even need a small one, but it didn't matter. He was just going to check his mail and go home to bed. Nadine laughed, the practiced one she used at night, and went to get the drinks.

"It's been a goddamn dog's age, Kyle; how the fuck's it going?" Mark asked.

Kyle blinked again, his smile closer to a wince, but he didn't take offense.

"Fine, Mark, just fine. Thanks."

Deborah insisted Mark did that on purpose, which, of course, he did, though not the first time.

Kyle and Sue were just two faces at a dinner he was trying to get through. They were new to Douala then, and somehow, Mark ended up alone with them before the food was served. He'd had a few drinks, but wasn't drunk yet. They asked the usual questions, and he gave the same answers he'd used countless times before.

It was Sue's fault, really, for asking about the Peace Corps, what it was like to live with "them," what "they" were like. Probably because of the alcohol, Mark mistook her question for interest rather than horror, so he made more of an effort than usual to explain. And at some point, he was under the baobab tree, the village men grabbing themselves between the legs and howling as Mark repeated the words for prick and cunt and all the others.

Later, Mark couldn't remember Kyle's expression at all;

probably just the same slightly embarrassed smile that had nothing to do with humor. But he remembered Sue. The thin, bloodless lips pressed together, screaming disapproval, and her facial muscles locked in place as if she were experiencing a particularly difficult bowel movement. Rather than stopping him, though, her disapproval infuriated Mark so that by the time Deborah came over and, appalled, forced him to change the subject, he had given them a detailed description of the Serrer's sexual habits.

Deborah gave him hell on the ride home, but for once, Mark felt no remorse at all, not the morning after or even the next time they ran into Sue and Kyle. Someplace else, Mark probably could have avoided Kyle or ignored him and would never have developed more than a mild dislike for the son of a bitch.

But he would have despised his wife anywhere.

Everything about her bothered him: her small, thin body, with angles where most women had curves; her skim-milk white skin and the way her brown hair hung, lifeless and flat against her skull, so it seemed to imprison her narrow face. Deborah had called him a "rude pig" for even thinking it, but Mark once suggested that Sue had nothing to worry about if the natives ever went on a rampage.

(That was every expatriate's unspoken nightmare, especially since the Katanganese rebels in Zaire made the white women of Kolwezi dance naked in between raping them).

Mostly, though, Mark hated the look on her face: a pinched, unpleasant expression that suggested either extreme myopia or a foul odor that wouldn't go away. Whether all that had something or nothing to do with the article on the American School wasn't important, it was a good story, and that's all that counted.

The U.S. Embassy was footing most of the bill for operating the school, and the school was teaching religion. Not just a general notion of God or Christianity, but the heavy fundamentalist doctrines. Kyle and Sue Mason, Reverand Yellen, and some of the other maniacs taught the classes and had almost total control over the rest of the school's curriculum.

A newspaper in Boston loved the article; one of the wire services even picked it up. Within a week, the State Department ordered all diplomatic personnel (meaning Kyle) to sever relations with the school and suspended funding until religious instructions there ceased.

The article finished Mark with the American community. Not that he cared; he wasn't spending much time with any of them by then anyway. But it was rough on Deborah. Many of the wives who taught at the school refused to have anything to do with her, which made it harder to do business with their husbands.

For a time, there were rumors that some of the big American firms would pull their accounts from International Accounting, but that never happened. Still, Deborah, who didn't know about the article until the damage was done, was furious. She accused Mark of going out of his way to embarrass her, that he was jealous of her success, and couldn't stand that she paid for the apartment and the food, even his goddamn vacations, and the article was his way of getting back at her.

"So, you don't care what they teach at a school our taxes pay for?" Mark asked, trying but failing to keep his voice even.

"Oh, c'mon on, Mark! What you pay in taxes wouldn't buy crayons for the kindergarten," Deborah shot back. "That's not what this is about, and you know it."

He should have walked away then, or just gone into his office and locked the door, or taken a ride, or gone for a run, or done anything except stay there.

"What I know is that you'll do anything, agree with anybody, kiss up to the most horrendous asshole, just so long as they do business with you," Mark said, leaning towards her so she could see him spit out the last words.

Deborah telegraphed the slap, so Mark was able to block it, though it stung his wrist. When she raised a hand to try again, he shoved her hard, out of range. She hit her back against the angle of a doorframe and started to cry, more out of anger than pain. That was the end of it. They spent several days not talking much, but little by little that passed. If Deborah had any more trouble with clients because of the article, she didn't mention it.

Kyle and Sue wrote a long, thoughtful letter to the editor of the Boston paper, explaining that parents who wished could have their children excused from the school's Bible classes. And they pointed out that life in Africa was difficult, so rules that might be reasonable elsewhere weren't always applicable in a place like Douala.

Mark almost laughed out loud, remembering it.

Everyone from the State Department in Washington to the Ambassador in Yaounde fried Kyle's ass for that one: for writing it in the first place, without authorization, but also for identifying himself as a diplomat and then sounding like some racist Jesus freak.

Shortly after the article appeared, Mark ran into Sue and Kyle outside Monoprix. He was, to be honest, a little uncomfortable. It was always hard confronting someone he'd slaughtered in print, but Sue helped him get over that fast. The disapproval was there, only harder now, in the slight downturn of her mouth and the pathetic way she refused to acknowledge him, though her eyes, so angry that he almost laughed in her face, never left him.

Kyle insisted on discussing it there on Boulevard Ahmadou Ahidjo, with the urchins swirling around them, begging for money or a chance to carry the bags Sue and Kyle clutched tightly in front of them. He was disappointed, he said, not only in the article but the way Mark had gone about it. Mark shrugged. So, he'd lied. He'd said he wanted to do a story on expatriate life in Douala and needed some details about the school.

Kyle began a detailed refutation of the main points of the article, which Mark realized later was a nearly verbatim repetition of his and Sue's letter to the editor. Mark listened for a minute, or half-listened really, as he struggled to keep a sudden rage under control, not at Kyle, but at her, with her fury and condemnation screaming at him though she hadn't opened her mouth.

He laughed, just to release the tension, then glanced quickly at Sue and told Kyle to stick it in his ear. He left them like that, Kyle's mouth open in mid-sentence, and walked into Monoprix. That was over a year ago; he hadn't spoken to either of them since.

Nadine brought the beer and the Coke, then walked back to the bar.

"....your name was on it, so I thought I'd check," Kyle concluded.

Mark took a sip of the beer. He hadn't heard most of what Kyle had said, and anyway, he would have to be careful. Goddamn Wanna.

"I'm sorry, Kyle. My mind wandered a little there," Mark said. "What exactly are you checking?"

"Just whether you're the Mark Reilly who wrote to Petroleum Products Unlimited in Houston," Kyle replied.

Mark cleared his throat. "And uh, what exactly is your...interest in this, Kyle?" Mark asked. That was as polite as he could get with Kyle.

Kyle smiled down at his glass of Coke, which he hadn't touched.

"I'm not prying, Mark."

Bullshit, you're not, asshole. "I know that, Kyle."

"Jim Richards just asked if I knew how he could get in touch with AmeriCam Services Inc. I said I'd never heard of them, but that I'd try to find the company," Kyle said.

"Jim, who?"

"Jim Richards, the fellow I just told you about. He's the president of Petroleum Products," Kyle explained, obviously repeating something he'd said earlier.

"You mean he phoned you?" Mark asked.

Kyle shook his head. "No, he's here. He dropped in the office this morning, showed me a letter, and was pretty darn annoyed when I said I'd never heard of the company."

Mark nodded. So, it wasn't Wanna. Holy shit! What the hell was the son of a bitch doing in Douala?

"Do you?" He heard Kyle ask.

"Do I what, Kyle?" Mark replied, the annoyance showing.

"Do you know anything about AmeriCam Services Inc?" Kyle said quietly as if dealing with a difficult child.

Mark nodded and took another drink of beer to gain some time.

"It's uh, a new company some Cameroonians formed to try and uh get into the oil service business," he said. "They thought it'd be easier to deal with the U.S. oil companies if they had an American, you know, sign their letters and make it look like a real joint venture."

Kyle smiled and nodded, though his disapproval was evident.

"So, are you, uh, a ... partner?" Kyle asked.

Mark shook his head. "I advise them a little on how to deal with Americans, and I help out with their communications," he replied.

"It doesn't take much time, and the pay's pretty good," he added, smiling. "Nothing illegal about that, is there?"

"Uh, no, not that I know of," Kyle answered, a little too fast. "Well, uh, congratulations," he said because he didn't know what else to say.

Mark laughed. Up yours, asshole. "Thanks," he said.

Kyle Mason read Jim Richards' letter one more time. It just didn't add up.

Kyle knew something about oil. Growing up in Texas, it would have been hard not to pick up a few things, but he'd learned a lot more about the business in Cameroon; most of their friends were in Douala because of oil, whether to find it, produce it, or service the companies that did.

Oil, in a way, was also the main reason Kyle had been sent to Douala.

The Gulf of Guinea had the distinction of not being anywhere near the Middle East, and with production, all along the West African coast increasing every year, there were a lot of people in Washington who didn't think the Libyan involvement in Chad, which bordered both Nigeria and Cameroon and was a short MIG ride from Gabon and Congo, was a coincidence.

He slid the letter back into his briefcase. No, it didn't make sense, or at least, he didn't think it did.

"Emmanuel, can you swing by the Mobil building, please?"

"Yes, suh," the driver said, glancing in the rear-view mirror. He checked quickly for police, then swung the big Ford in a tight U-turn.

CHAPTER 24

"What, uh, brings you to Douala, Mr. Richards?"

"Call me Jim, please, Mark; you want something to drink?"

"Uh, sure, I'll have a beer," Mark replied.

Richards held up a hand, trying to get the Meridien waiter's attention.

He looked like half the Americans in Douala: a middle-aged Texan in polyester whose hair still looked wet, but wasn't, at six in the evening.

There was the same garrulous familiarity, though a bit self-conscious, as if he half-realized that that back-slapping, good ol'boy bullshit was as out of place in Africa as an armadillo in a swimming pool back home.

What in the hell was he doing in Douala?

"Two beers," Richards yelled, holding up two fingers. The waiter smiled and nodded.

The bar wasn't crowded yet, but it would be soon. It was after six, and a lot of expatriates stopped off at the Meridien before heading home.

"What am I doing here?" Richards repeated. "Well, I guess I

came to see you," he said, laughing heartily. Mark felt obliged to smile.

"Yours was one of the biggest goddamn orders we'd had in quite a while, so I figured I better get my ass over here and find out what was goin' on," he explained.

Richards laughed again. "I'll be honest; I had to look in a goddamn atlas to find out where the hell Cameroon was."

Mark forced a laugh. Holy shit.

The waiter brought two 33 Exports. The Meridien was French, after all, and no one stuck together like the French overseas.

"We've done a little business in Nigeria," Richards said, "but it was never enough to send anyone over. We're mostly a domestic supplier."

Right. Just simple, God-fearing goddamn American capitalists, which was no doubt why Calvady, or maybe the Libyans, picked them. A small, hick company was a lot more likely to jump at a big overseas deal and not ask too many questions.

Except that here was Jim Richards, doing a little all-American marketing. Shit.

"But listen, I don't wanna take up your evening," he was saying. "Just point me in the right direction, and I'll stop by your office tomorrow morning."

Mark almost laughed. The son of a bitch had flown 10,000 kilometers to see him, and now he was trying to get rid of him.

Richards glanced over Mark's shoulder toward the bar entrance, then back at Mark, smiling. Maybe he was expecting Kyle.

"Actually, we're just in the process of setting up offices, which is why I came by," Mark explained.

"Ok, well, let's have lunch tomorrow or dinner if that's better for you," Richards said. He drained his beer, then glanced over at the entrance again.

Mark had barely started his beer, but now felt obliged to drink it faster than he usually did.

"Bon soir," she said, standing just behind Mark and not recognizing him. She drew the words out in what she no doubt thought was a provocative voice.

"Oh, hey, hello," Richards said, feigning surprise. He got up awkwardly from the table to let her slide in next to him.

Mark wasn't that surprised, but Koumba looked as though someone had slapped her. She puffed her lips out in a pout as if it were all somehow his fault.

So, she'd finally made it official. That explained all the new clothes she was wearing the few times he'd seen her lately.

"This here's Koumba," Richards said, smiling over at Mark. His Texas drawl made her name sound ridiculous.

"Ravi de vous connaitre, madamoiselle," Mark said.

Koumba scowled but didn't say anything.

Richards appeared a bit nonplussed by her behavior. He leaned down to get her to look up from the table.

"You want a drink?" He smiled, tapping his empty beer bottle.

"Oui," she said, almost whispering.

Richards got the waiter's attention again and ordered a glass of champagne. He even knew that.

"Would you care to join us for dinner, Mark?" Richards asked. The politeness looked like it pained him.

Mark smiled and shook his head. It would have been fun to say yes.

"Thanks, but I've got plans."

Richards did his best not to look relieved. "Well, how about lunch tomorrow?" He asked.

"Fine," Mark replied, sliding out of the booth. "About one?"

Richards struggled out of the seat again to shake hands. "That'd be just fine, Mark; I'll see you then."

"Thanks for the beer...Jim," Mark said, managing not to smile.

"Oh, my pleasure," Richards said.

Mark reached back over the table and held out a hand to Koumba. She hesitated a second, then put hers limply in his, though she didn't look at him.

"Tres heureux d'avoir fait votre connaissance, madamoiselle," Mark said; "amusez-vous bien."

She looked at him then, an angry scowl, and yanked her hand away.

"Goddamn, I wish I knew how to talk that stuff," Richards laughed, sliding back into the seat next to Koumba.

"See you tomorrow," Mark said, turning to leave.

"You have a good night now, y'hear?" Jim called.

"You too," Mark said over his shoulder, probably too quietly for them to hear.

Richards moved closer to Koumba and slid a hand under the table onto her knee. She was still pouting, so he moved his hand most of the way up her thigh and squeezed.

Koumba tried not to, but after a moment, couldn't help giggling.

CHAPTER 25

Kyle Mason switched on his desk lamp. He didn't use it much and didn't like to waste electricity, which was so darn expensive in Cameroon. But it was getting dark, and he couldn't afford to make any mistakes with the code. He went over the message once more. He hesitated a moment, then scratched out a group of letters and wrote some others in their place. He re-read the communique again, twice, his lips moving silently.

They said to use his judgment, but when in doubt, it was better to report. Well, he had some doubts.

Kyle got up and walked across the hall to a small room that served as a kind of mail room/storage area. Inside a closet, as far as possible from any of the consulate's exterior walls, the security people from Washington had installed a steel vault, a big walk-in kind as they had in banks.

Kyle dialed the combination quickly, then hit the black handle, which clicked. He pulled hard on the handle, and the heavy door swung open. Inside, there was a door made of thick iron mesh; Kyle opened it with a key and entered. He locked the mesh door behind him.

The employees had all left for the day. Kyle told Emmanuel he would drive himself home.

He didn't even have to worry about the consul, who had been evacuated to Frankfurt when the staph infection she developed defied the antibiotics the embassy doctor prescribed.

The light inside the vault went on automatically when the door was opened. Kyle sat down and put the coded communique in front of the large two-way radio the consul used for all its confidential communications with the embassy in Yaounde. He set the radio's dial to a frequency slightly different from the one used for normal embassy business, then turned on the power.

The radio crackled to life; a moment later, a voice came over, loud and clear.

CHAPTER 26

Calvady had lost weight since Mark last saw him. Not enough that anyone would mistake him for thin, but his shirt, which used to strain under the shoulders and all the way around his waist, hung loosely on him now as though he'd bought a size too big by mistake.

The smirking self-assurance, the way he had of insinuating that Africa was really a game whose rules he knew better than anyone, was gone now, too. In its place was testy impatience, or perhaps just a preoccupation, as if he had more important things on his mind than the oil equipment.

Hell, maybe he was sick. Most people who had spent that much time in Africa came down with something sooner or later. Well, that was his problem.

"What happened to your face?" Mark asked.

Calvady instinctively flicked his tongue over the corner of his mouth, where a crooked reddish-black scab ran almost an inch down toward his chin. Surrounding it like a halo was a purplish-yellow puffiness that looked like it had been a long time healing.

"Un accident," Calvady said quickly, making it clear he didn't want to discuss it.

"Dommage," Mark said, smiling.

Calvady stared at him a moment, then shook his head.

"What do you want, my friend?"

Mark glanced over his shoulder down the length of the marina terrace. It was a weekday afternoon, hours before Gilles' friends got off work. The place was empty.

Except for Gilles, whom Mark could see through one of the terrace windows; he was inside, behind the bar, arranging bottles. The sleazy bastard had abandoned all pretenses, not even acknowledging Mark's greeting when he brought them their beers.

So Koumba had dumped him, too. Well, what the hell? She was a working girl now. Time was money. Maybe she lied to Gilles, too; maybe he thought it was Mark's fault. Even if not, Gilles was the type who needed someone to blame and an explanation that didn't come within miles of his manhood.

"I need more money," Mark said, lowering his voice anyway. "The container arrives on Friday."

Calvady made a face, but pulled his little money sack from under the table and withdrew an envelope. Mark was surprised; he'd expected an argument.

"Even if you fucked half the whores in Douala, you should have some of the $5,000 left," Calvady said.

"With that," he added, nodding at the envelope, "you'll have plenty to pay for the rest. Even if you haven't arranged something with customs."

He was a little shit, but he wasn't stupid. Mark had slightly more than $2,500 left, and Wanna had already talked to his cousin, the customs inspector, about "facilitating" the paperwork.

Mark picked up the envelope and began to count the money.

"C'est dix mille dollars," Calvady said, the impatience showing again.

Mark was a little disappointed. He'd hoped for more. But, again, Calvady was right; it was more than enough. Mark slid the money into his wallet.

"OK. Where exactly do I deliver the container, and more importantly, when do I get my money?" Mark asked.

"When do you leave?" Calvady asked.

"Monday morning, as early as I can."

Calvady nodded and opened his mouth, then turned sharply to look out at the river as if something there had caught his attention.

Mark looked over, too. Except for a fishing *pirogue* in the middle distance, there was nothing, just the flat brown water and the mangrove swamp on the far side. It was May, and though not exactly cloudy, the sky was a hot, dirty white, the way it often got in the run-up to the rainy season.

Calvady turned back to Mark and leaned forward in his chair.

"*Tu connais Waza*?" He asked.

"The Game Park, you mean?"

"Oui."

Mark nodded. "Sure, I know it."

"I'll meet you there a week from Monday," Calvady said.

Mark stared at the old Frenchman. "I thought you said we'd do it in Kousseri."

"Waza's better; it's out of the way, and there are no *gendarmes*," Calvady said, flashing some of the old arrogance. "Why do you care, anyway? It's closer for you."

Mark looked across the table. It wasn't so much the change in plans as the change in Calvady that bothered him. He liked it better when the bastard didn't sound so sure of himself.

"How are you going to do it in Waza?" He demanded.

"I'll have a truck there," Calvady replied.

"What if I get held up somewhere?" Mark asked. He could probably make Waza in a week, but it was a rough trip, and any number of things could go wrong.

"I will get there on Monday, which is the earliest you could make it," Calvady said. "I will stay until you arrive."

Mark thought for a moment. Waza was an easier trip than Kousseri. Not by much, but still, it was two hours he wouldn't have to drive, and at least one roadblock, maybe more, that he wouldn't have to cross.

"I don't unlock the container until I've seen the money. All of it," Mark said.

Calvady laughed a little and shook his head.

"Bien entendu, mon ami," he said.

Maybe that was uncalled for. Mark didn't like the bastard, but he'd played it straight so far. Hell, if anything happened, it was Calvady, not Mark, who was out $17,000.

"If this works, are you going to want to do another cargo?" Mark asked.

Calvady smiled the way he had breakfast in Chad.

"C'est possible, mon ami."

CHAPTER 27

Martin Feraldi re-read the message he'd just de-coded. It still didn't make a lot of sense, but he didn't know fuck all about oil. Even so, it sounded like bullshit; just Kyle Mason jerking off too much again.

Yaounde wanted an answer, though. The question was whether to tell them to just forget it or wake up his partner. He probably knew something about oil; shit, the bastard acted like he knew something about everything. The truth was, the guy gave Feraldi the creeps. The only time Martin relaxed was when the son of a bitch went to sleep.

Maybe it was just cabin fever; the two of them holed up like that for months, in a shithole like Kousseri, with nothing to do but eat and sleep and count Libyan planes coming in or going out over the river.

But the bastard didn't make things any easier. Hell, they'd go days without talking, just: "you want some more spaghetti", "no, thanks" or "I make that an Anatov", "me too." The rest of the time, he sat there in his Army-issue shorts and a goddamn sleeveless T-shirt doing crossword puzzles.

In Latin, no less. He got 'em from some defrocked monk

somewhere in Italy, and he spent hours every day with a dictionary, so old it looked like a goddamn relic, doing the fuckin' things.

He didn't drink, not even beer or smoke, but didn't give two shits if Feraldi did. Never complained about the cigarette smoke, or anything else, for that matter. Didn't even seem to notice it.

The son of a bitch gave Feraldi the creeps.

CHAPTER 28

Jim Richards sawed off a good-sized chunk of steak.

"The meat doesn't taste half-bad, but goddamn, it's chewy," he said, smiling briefly between bites.

"It's got to walk a ways to get here," Mark said politely.

He'd sworn off beef years ago. By the time the Fulani herdsmen walked the cattle the 600 kilometers or more down from the Adamaou Plateau in the north to the *abattoirs* in Douala, the meat that was left on them was as tough as an old tire.

The waiter brought Mark's shrimp and apologized for the delay. Cameroon had been named for shrimp—legend had the shrimp so plentiful that it crunched underfoot as the Portuguese explorers waded ashore—and other than Marie's fish, it was Mark's favorite dish.

"You married, Mark?" Richards asked, giving his jaws a rest from the steak.

"Separated," Mark said evenly. He'd barely met the bastard, and already they were in his private life.

"Sorry to hear it," Richards said, shaking his head, then renewing his assault on the meat. "I've been married to the same gal for 29 years. Met her at a neighbor's square dance, and the minute I set eyes on her, I said that one's for me."

He laughed, with his mouth full, and Mark felt compelled to smile. Except for Kyle, the day before, he hadn't been around Americans in months. He'd forgotten what he was missing.

"You must miss her when you travel," Mark said.

Richards' head came up too fast from the plate, and for just a second, Mark saw something other than the good ol' boy nonsense. But then it was gone.

"I surely do, Mark; I surely do," he said. He cut another piece of meat. "But like I told you, I'm not away much. Coupla days here and there, to Oklahoma or Louisiana, but that's about it."

"And now Cameroon," Mark said, deciding it was time to change the subject.

"Yep," Richards replied, nodding his wide head. "That's your goddamn fault."

Mark had a mouthful of shrimp, so he just smiled.

"Tell you the goddamn truth, I might not have come out here even with your order, but right after we got it, I found myself sittin' next to a Frenchman at an oil association lunch in Houston. Goddamn if the son of a bitch didn't start telling me that Cameroon was the next Mexico," Richards explained.

"Really?" Mark asked. That was the first time he'd heard that. He'd also never heard of a Frenchman, any Frenchman, trumpeting Cameroon's potential to Americans.

They finished a bottle of wine between them. They both passed on dessert, but ordered coffee. They had sparred a bit over lunch, Richards prying, politely, for the names of Mark's partners ("It's just a helluva load of pump barrels, even for a go-go market like Cameroon") and Mark fending him off.

When Richards got his goddamn *cafe au lait*, he tried again. All he wanted was to talk to them and see if there wasn't something else he could help them with. Hell, he'd been in and around the oil business his whole goddamn life. And he knew a lot of people.

Mark nodded and repeated his story. His partners were very wealthy, and this was in the way of a speculative and very small investment for them. They were busy men, he explained, who didn't want to call attention to what they were doing. He managed to imply without actually saying so that they were also well-connected in Yaounde.

"But all of Cameroon's production is offshore, and those pump barrels aren't worth spit out there," Richards said.

Mark nodded and took a sip of his coffee. That was the first time he'd heard that. Had Richards heard of the exploration going on near Edea? Jim Richards shook his head and said he'd never even heard of Edea. Mark quickly explained that it was an on-shore site outside the city, and though nothing was being given out about the results, he implied his partners had access to certain information.

"Essentially, they can afford to take the risk, and they're betting that whoever has supplies and equipment in the country when drilling takes off can make a killing," he explained.

There was also some promising seismic work being done up north near Garoua, Mark added. He thought about mentioning Chad, where oil companies had done seismic work on and off for years, but decided even a legitimate reference was needlessly risky.

Shit, the son of a bitch had his money, and if he didn't push too hard, he'd make more.

Richards had apparently come to the same conclusion. He tried once more ("How 'bout just for a drink somewhere?"), but it was more to tell himself he'd done his best than a belief Mark was going to change his mind.

"Maybe once we're better organized and things are rolling, I can put together a quiet little dinner," Mark suggested. "Might even do it in the U.S.; New York, or hell, even Houston."

“We’d roll out a goddamn Texas welcome for ‘em, I’ll tell you that, Mark,” Richards exclaimed, liking the idea.

Mark laughed. That’d be something, he and Wanna in 10-gallon hats, sitting in some Houston backyard with half a cow on the barbecue.

“Sounds good, Jim, real good,” he said. “But like I said, it’ll be a little while yet. We’re just getting started.”

“Sure, sure, Mark; I understand,” Richards said. “But, uh, what’re the chances y’all might be orderin’ again soon?”

“Damn good, Jim, damn good,” Mark said, leaning across the table. “Between you and me, that first one was just a trial run to see how it goes.”

Mark leaned back in his chair and smiled. “We’re already talking about another shipment. A lot bigger one.”

“Goddamn,” Richards sighed, shaking his head.

CHAPTER 29

"Un autre cafe au lait, monsieur?" The waiter asked, pointing at Jim Richards' empty cup.

Richards looked at his watch. It was almost three o'clock. He shook his head. "No, bring me a whiskey, and put some goddamn ice cubes in it this time."

"Un whiskey; avec soda?" The waiter asked.

"No, no soda," Jim replied, shaking his head. "Just ice." He made a small circle with his thumb and forefinger.

The waiter smiled. *"Ah oui, avec glacon,"* he said,

"Yeah, *glacon*," Jim repeated. He remembered the word from a previous struggle at the bar.

The waiter departed. Richards was the last one left in the Merdien's restaurant. Siesta was over, and the other diners had already headed back to work.

Richards had planned to make some calls, just to say howdy at Pecten and Gulf and maybe Mobil, but now he didn't feel like it. He could do it in the morning when it wouldn't be so goddamn hot. Besides, he needed to get some sleep. Maybe it was still jet lag; hell, it'd been a long goddamn flight, and those SOBs at the airport hadn't made it any easier.

It was the heat, too. Houston could be almost as bad, but there was something different about it over here. Just sort of drained him so that even thinking of doing something robbed him of the energy to get up and do it.

The waiter brought his drink and left. Richards sipped it. They'd finally put in enough ice cubes, and the combination of the cold and then the warm afterburn, spreading out from his chest, made him feel better.

He wasn't a day drinker; hell, he'd fired more than one son of a bitch for doing just that. But there were times when it did more good than harm. Richards finished the drink and sucked a while on the ice cubes. He thought about having another, but then signed the bill and got up. He needed sleep more than another drink. He sure as hell wasn't getting any at night.

Richards hit the elevator button, and the doors opened immediately. He'd never felt skin like that before, cool and smooth like a stone, really, that'd been washed forever in a stream. And Christ Almighty, was she strong! Maybe it'd been a mistake to order that steak so rare in a place like Douala, but he needed something.

It wasn't that he was having trouble, really. Hell, he hadn't humped like that in a good long time. It was just that...he didn't feel he was running the show all the time. Of course, he was, but still... sometimes it was almost as though she was doing it to him as much as he was to her.

Sometimes when she got going, well, shit, he felt like he was just hanging on for the ride. The night before, she'd been underneath, and goddamn if she didn't just flip him over onto his back, like he didn't weigh a goddamn ounce, and start pumping away so goddamn hard...hell, he was almost frightened.

Well, maybe not scared, but damn surprised. He'd tried to tell her later the way he liked it, but she just giggled in the dark.

Richards opened his door, walked across to the windows,

and closed the curtains. He fiddled with the air conditioning to get it on high, then stripped down to his boxer shorts and lay down on the bed. Just a few hours, and then he'd be fine. He got hard thinking about Koumba in the dark there. He'd show her who was fucking who tonight.

Tomorrow, he'd check in with some of the oil companies. Hell, that's why he'd come all that way, not to screw himself silly. But goddamn, he'd have some stories to tell! He laughed out loud. The bastards wouldn't believe him, not without a picture. Well, he didn't give a damn. He'd remember, and that was enough.

Richards took one of the pillows and put it across his eyes to block out the faint light sneaking in around the sides of the curtains. The lunch had been a waste of time. He'd been paid, so it didn't really matter, but the rest of it sounded like bullshit. Mysterious Africans stocking parts for wells that hadn't been drilled yet. Hell, hadn't even been found yet.

If they didn't do it right—and whoever heard of Africans doing anything right—the stuff would rust in no time in a climate like Douala's. And then it'd be useless. Richards removed the pillow and stared at the ceiling.

Of course, it was bullshit! He hadn't even considered it, but now it seemed obvious: Nigeria was right next door. One of the biggest oil-producing countries in the world. That's where the pump barrels were going. Smuggled in, no duties, and the Nigerians were notorious for running low on everything. It was the only thing that made sense.

Richards shook his head slightly in the dark. He had to give Reilly credit for some balls.

Even so, he didn't like the man. Richards didn't care for New Yorkers as a general rule, especially in the oil business. Just wasn't their place. With Reilly, though, it was more than that. He was a liar, of course, but Richards had told one or two himself in the interests of business. No, it was his attitude, like that crack about missing his wife. The boy was laughing at him and didn't think Richards knew.

Well, they'd see who the goddamn idiot was. Richards had the bastard's money in the bank, and he'd take as much more of it as Reilly and his "partners" could shovel his way. But he wouldn't be surprised, and he sure as hell wouldn't lose any sleep if the son of a bitch's little scheme blew up in his goddamn smirking face.

Richards reached over for his traveling clock and set the alarm for seven. Koumba was coming at 7:30. He put the pillow back over his face and went to sleep.

CHAPTER 30

Sue Mason's hands shook as she laid out the third-place setting for lunch.

God forgive her, but she hated Mark Reilly. Not disliked him intensely, or even despised him, but hated him so that when she thought about him, which she did too often, she seemed unable to get control of herself. This time was a little different, though, not so anguished, despairing that God would ever answer her prayers.

"God doesn't need your prayers to punish someone," Kyle had said, smiling the way he always did when he admonished her. "He'll do that in his own way and his own time."

Kyle was right, of course, as he almost always was. That's why Sue married him. He knew the Bible better than anyone she'd ever met, not just the words but what God was trying to say through them. He always knew exactly what to say to the other Americans when something happened: when one of the wives had her purse stolen by those awful little boys who preyed on the whites or when an arriving family, not knowing anyone and still exhausted from the trip and the heat, was strip-searched by the *gendarmes* at the airport.

Sue had to stop a moment to get the thought of one of those Africans touching her out of her head. Kyle had been right, too, about the fraternity boys at SMU who never left her alone, calling her those names and talking that filthy smut when they knew she could hear them.

God was testing her, Kyle had said, and he'd been right. Sue found that praying for them, even while they taunted her sometimes, brought her a tranquility she'd never experienced before, as if their filth could no longer reach her, even though she still heard it.

But she was not strong enough to pray for Mark Reilly. She wasn't even strong enough to ask for the strength to do it. God forgive her, but she was happy, ecstatic, really, when his wife left him. Sue didn't really like Deborah; didn't approve of wives working, unless they had to to keep a roof over their heads or food on the table. And it was a sin not to change her name. (Though Sue could forgive her that.)

As far as Sue had been able to determine, Deborah didn't go to any church, either. But for all that, she was polite and well-bred, and she must have suffered mightily with him. Her leaving was God's wrath, swift and sure, for that man's attack on their school. Sue even thought, stupidly, that it might shake Mark Reilly off his path to hell.

But it only made him worse. Without Deborah, he lost his last tenuous link to the American community, which might have been able to help him. She'd heard the stories they all had. Jack and Sarah Reynolds, against Sue and Kyle's advice, occasionally ate in African restaurants, and they saw him once with one of his black...women. He'd even had the nerve to say hello to them. They ignored him, of course, so when he was leaving, he leaned over their table and told them to kiss his...well, more of his filth. Sarah had to hold Jack to keep him from going after Reilly.

God forgive her, but Sue was sorry she did. Not that

violence was a solution, but weren't there times it served a purpose? Wasn't it a kind of violence what he did to them?

Sue had somehow managed not to cry until they had loaded the groceries and were inside the car, but then she couldn't stop them; bitter, raging tears, so that she was almost hyperventilating.

"Damn him!" She screamed between sobs.

"It's all right, Sue," Kyle said, calm as ever. But she saw his hand shake a little as he struggled to get the key in the ignition.

"Damn you!" She screamed louder, her face only inches from his ear so that he flinched.

But that was the end of it. They drove home, Seymour unloaded the car, and Sue cooked dinner. They didn't talk about it, ever, except the next morning, when he was leaving for work, Kyle asked her to try and understand that Reilly was his test. When she heard his car pull out of the drive, Sue got down on her knees and, sobbing, asked for forgiveness, Kyle's as well as God's. And she prayed for Him to make Reilly pay.

She didn't know how—Sue had never had much imagination—but God help her, she shook with desire, a need really, to see him punished.

Sue hesitated with the glasses. Would he want wine with lunch? They kept a few bottles just in case, but of course, she and Kyle never drank any. She could always wait and ask when he arrived, but that might embarrass him.

She'd have to phone Kyle at the consulate. He hadn't told her much. He wasn't allowed to, and Sue never pried. Only that there was someone coming to lunch who would probably like a home-cooked meal.

And that it had something to do with Mark Reilly.

"Is he in some kind of trouble?" She tried to sound only curious.

"I don't really know," Kyle said. Then he smiled, that

controlled, sincere smile, with his lips, pressed firmly together and no teeth showing that he used when he wanted her to know everything would be all right.

CHAPTER 31

Nadine wasn't much to look at, even by Cafe des Sports standards. She was short and squat, with a thick neck and a waist as wide as her hips.

When she walked, Nadine seemed to be dragging some heavy load behind her, and in a sense, she was. Even on busy nights at the Cafe, Nadine was often available, which was why she worked days at le Paradis.

Mark had always assumed the large, puckered scar on her cheek was from a burn, but up close, his nose almost touching it, he realized it was a birthmark.

She wasn't much from a professional standpoint either, just writhing on top of him in a jerky, circular motion that she had probably picked up watching bad French films at the Wouri, Douala's oldest cinema.

But she was willing and available, and after four beers at le Paradis, that was enough for Mark.

"C'est bien pour toi?" She moaned, her mouth close to his ear, her breathing heavier than it should have been.

Nadine had looked a bit surprised that he wanted to do it

right there, on the hard wicker couch, with the lights on, but she didn't say anything.

"Oui, c'est bien," Mark replied, grabbing her thick haunches and forcing her up and down to get it over with.

Wanna had begged off dinner at Marie's; other plans, he smiled. So Mark stayed for one more beer, and when Nadine brought it, he invited her home.

It was Friday night, the ship was in, and he wanted to celebrate.

The telex said the container would arrive that afternoon, but Mark took a taxi down to the port just to be sure. Then he went back to the bank and removed all but a few thousand CFA from his account.

Even if it was only African francs, it made an impressive pile.

Wanna had talked to his cousin. They'd see him first thing Monday morning; Mark would be on his way north by eight o'clock, nine at the latest.

It would take a week to get to Waza, maybe a little longer if there was any problem with the truck. But then they'd be rich, Wanna by Cameroon standards, Mark by just about anybody's.

He was nervous leaving the container like that over the weekend—the port was notorious for its thieves—but he had no choice. The customs office was closed on Saturday and Sunday.

Besides, Mark still had to arrange with Francis for the truck. Wanna had loaned him one of his taxis to drive out to Kumba in the morning.

Nadine had finally got the idea, and her wide behind was pumping up and down; she had her thick arms locked around Mark's neck, and her breathing, hitting him in the ear, sounded legitimately labored now.

She wasn't worth the 3,000 CFA Mark had agreed to on the way over, probably not even 2,000, but it didn't matter.

As he cupped her behind in his two hands for better

leverage, there was a knock on the door; not loud, maybe even a little tentative, but unmistakable.

Nadine froze.

"J'espere que ce n'est pas Koumba," she whispered, her eyes wide and her breathing taking on a new cadence.

Mark shook his head. It wasn't impossible, but he doubted it. "She works nights," he said.

He eased Nadine off of him and hurriedly slipped on the pants he'd dropped on the floor by the front windows. He walked to the door and opened it a foot, keeping his legs and the bulge in his pants behind it.

The sun had set a half hour earlier, and the landlord still hadn't fixed the stairway light, but even in the dark, there was no mistaking Kyle Mason.

"I'm really sorry to disturb you at home, Mark," Kyle said, the words coming so fast he almost stuttered. "But Mrs. Mawanga said you hadn't been by Antoine's in awhile, and then I ran into Wanna N'Dele, and he told me where you lived."

Goddamn Wanna.

"No problem, Kyle," Mark said. His side was starting to ache from standing like that. "Uh, what do you want?"

"Uh, this is Mr. Rieper from the Commerce Department in Washington," Kyle said, turning slightly to the darkness just behind him on the landing.

Mark hadn't seen the man at first. But now he stepped forward into the light from the apartment, a thin, extremely pale hand extended toward Mark.

Mark had to open the door a little more to shake hands.

"How do you do, Mr. Rieper?"

"Please call me Mort," the man said.

His hand felt dry and bony, but the grip, for a man that old, was surprisingly strong. He was tall, even an inch or two taller than Kyle, though his large bald head hung forward and down a little as though it were too heavy to hold upright.

Mark could hear Kyle breathing from the climb, or nerves, or both, but Rieper wasn't winded at all. It might have been the light, but even in a suit, the old guy didn't look like he was sweating, either.

"Mr. Rieper's uh, visiting some of the countries in the region and uh, especially wanted to meet Americans who are doing, who have joint ventures with uh, local businessmen," Kyle said, still talking too fast. He'd rehearsed that a few times.

Mark nodded, shifting his weight a little to ease the pain in his side.

Kyle looked awful. Probably worried that Mark would embarrass him in front of his boss, tell him to get lost, or worse.

Mark cleared his throat. "Uh, look, Kyle..."

"Alors, c'est qui, Mark?" Nadine called from behind him. Now that she was sure it wasn't Koumba, she wanted to finish. She had to get to work.

Nadine stepped away from the couch to peek around the door. Mark turned instinctively to wave her back, but in so doing, he opened the door further; not much, just a few inches, but enough to give the two men standing outside a brief, but full frontal view.

Kyle's head snapped back as if someone had hit him.

"Oh my God," he whispered.

"We seem to have caught you at a bad time," Rieper said quietly. It didn't appear to have bothered him at all.

"Actually, Mort, I was having a pretty good time," Mark grinned. That was for Kyle.

Rieper smiled. Or at least, that's what Mark assumed it was; the old man's lips retracted quickly into his sallow cheeks, exposing a sudden gash of yellowing teeth. It wasn't pretty.

"Perhaps we could have lunch tomorrow?" He asked.

"Uh, tomorrow I'm out of town," Mark replied.

"Sunday, then?"

What the hell? "Sure," Mark nodded. "Where?"

“I’m staying at the Novotel. Would that be all right?”

“Fine; I’ll see you then,” Mark said.

“Would 12:30 be all right with you?” Rieper asked.

“Yeah, that’s fine,” Mark said.

Rieper turned to go, but Kyle didn’t move for a second; he might have been a statue, some pedestrian sculptor’s idea of art.

“Night, Kyle,” Mark said, then couldn’t resist. “Give Sue my best.”

Kyle moved at last; he might have stared at Mark for a second before following Rieper, but in that light, it was hard to tell. It didn’t matter anyway.

Mark swung the door closed, so they had to walk down the five flights in the dark.

CHAPTER 32

Mark got to Kumba about 10:30 the next morning. Francis wasn't at home, but Helen said he was probably in the garage. Francis had pointed it out on the ride down to Douala, but Mark let Helen give him directions anyway. It was back the way Mark had come, on a hill overlooking the river that marked the entrance to Kumba from the south.

The river was crowded, as usual, with women washing clothes and what looked like most of the Kumba taxi fleet hubcap deep near the shore, their drivers soaping, then rinsing the cars off with buckets of river water.

Mark parked Wanna's taxi in a small area in front of the building, an all-corrugated metal structure with no windows, and went inside. The big barn-like doors were open wide, but even so, it was damn hot inside. Mark's shirt was sticking to his back within seconds of entering.

And it was only 10:30. By three o'clock, the walls and ceiling would be too hot to touch, and the air would be as heavy as a steam bath.

Mark spotted Francis at the far end of the garage, talking to two men who were working on a 10-ton *Berlier*. He was wearing the same kind of pyjama-like outfit as the last time, though this one was black and yellow paisley.

In addition to the truck, there were three Mercedes Benz cars, all different years and models, with their hoods up and sweating African mechanics leaning over their motors. The far corner of the garage was covered with tires. In the middle of the pile, a heavily muscled African, his skin glistening, was prying what looked like a truck tire off its rim.

Mark didn't want to interrupt Francis, so he stood near the door. After a moment, one of the workers spotted Mark; he turned and said something to Francis, who turned quickly and, smiling, walked over.

"Welcome, Mark."

"Hello, Francis; how are you?" Mark asked.

They shook hands.

"Fine. Are you on your way to Lobe?"

"Actually, I came to see you," Mark replied. "My shipment has arrived, and I wanted to arrange for the truck to transport it up north."

Francis nodded, reflecting for a moment.

"Let's talk outside," he said.

They walked around to the back of the garage, to an open space where Francis kept his cars and trucks when they weren't on the road or being serviced.

There were two palm oil tankers, streaked the distinctive orange from the raw oil; several more cars, all Mercedes; and one Mercedes truck, a flatbed designed to carry containers.

"You have a container, right?" Francis asked.

"Right," Mark answered.

"When do you want the truck?"

"I'll have it out of customs Monday morning," Mark said.

"And it's going to Kousseri?" Francis asked.

"Right. Uh, well, actually just to Waza," Mark said. Francis' eyes opened a little wider.

"The game park?" He asked.

Mark nodded, not feeling too comfortable.

"The uh buyer wanted to do it there," he said. "He'll have his own truck, and his people will do all the unloading."

Francis nodded, then didn't say anything for a moment.

"You'll have all the documents with you?" He asked finally.

"Absolutely," Mark nodded. "He's worried that his competitors will find out what he's up to if he does it in Kousseri," he added. "He's a little neurotic."

Francis hadn't asked for one, but Mark felt some sort of explanation was required.

Francis nodded again. "OK. Let's go back to the house and discuss it," he said.

It didn't take long. They had already settled on the price, and Mark didn't quibble about Waza being a slightly shorter trip than Kousseri.

Francis wanted to send the truck on Tuesday, but Mark made a face and explained that he was pressed for time. Finally, Francis agreed that the Mercedes truck Mark had seen behind the garage would be at the port Monday morning. In fact, it would be there Sunday morning; the truck was scheduled to pick up five tons of cocoa from a cooperative in Mamfe later that afternoon and deliver it to one of the big exporters' warehouses in Douala the next morning.

It was a rush order, and the exporter had paid Francis extra to guarantee delivery at dawn Sunday so the cocoa could be on a Norwegian ship leaving at noon.

Normally, the driver would then return to Kumba, but Francis agreed to have him sleep overnight at the port to be ready for Mark on Monday.

They drank some champagne to toast the deal, though only one bottle, not two or three as the Bamilekes did. Helen insisted Mark stay for lunch, and he accepted. She was a good cook. Her pork roast was as good as Mary's; the steamed plantains and corn fufu with the okra sauce and the Anglophones called gumbo were the best Mark had tasted in years, and he said so.

It was just the three of them, and they talked as easily as they had the first time about politics and Africa and places Mark had been. Helen and Mark did most of the talking, but that seemed normal now, too; Francis just preferred to listen.

Mark drank two beers with lunch. It wasn't enough to get him drunk, not even close, really, but when he climbed into the car to head back to Douala, he felt as good as he had in a long time.

CHAPTER 33

Back home, Jim Richards wouldn't have walked across the hall to kick a bureaucrat in the ass. They weren't worth the energy. He'd never met one that knew a goddamn thing. Shit, being an ignoramus was a prerequisite for the job. But he'd said OK. He wanted to give the son of a bitch from Washington his opinion of how they worked out there—didn't work was more like it—and he didn't give two shits if Kyle Mason squirmed a little.

Maybe do him some good; remember who the hell paid his goddamn salary.

That was most of it. But it might not be a bad idea to sit and talk with a couple of Americans, even if they were bureaucrats. Maybe that's all he needed: to get back with his own kind, get his bearings again. Hell, other than Reilly, he hadn't talked to anyone but waiters for a week, and Koumba, but you couldn't count her.

He kept meaning to get out and make some calls, but he was having trouble getting out of bed in the morning; hell, before he knew it, it was lunchtime. He'd started taking a nap after lunch just to catch up, but all it seemed to do was make him more tired.

It was the goddamn heat; fifteen minutes out in it, even in the morning by the pool, felt like hours anywhere else.

Richards checked with the desk at the Meridiem again, just to make sure the Novotel was the building across the street, then walked out the lobby door. The wet heat wrapped itself around him, like some invisible body suit with his name on it that was always there, waiting for him whenever he stepped free of the air conditioning.

Houston could be hotter 'n hell, and damn muggy too, unbearable at times, but this was a different kind of heat altogether. Not temperature-wise, but something else that just sapped the energy right out of him.

It was no more than a hundred yards or so between the two hotel lobbies, but by the time Richards reached the Novotel, his white polyester shirt was matted against his back, and the sweat from his brow was running down onto his sunglasses.

In the shade of the Novotel entrance, he wiped the glasses with a handkerchief and then put them back on. He yanked his underwear out from the crack in his behind one last time and went inside. The Novotel was only a few years older than the Meridien, but it was going to hell. The minute he was inside the door, Richards could smell the mildew from the carpeting; no amount of cleaning would ever remove that.

The brown uniforms worn by the African staff behind the desk looked faded and unpressed, not anything like the impeccable white jackets and pants of the Meridien workers.

The Novotel obviously had also given up trying to keep the whores out. They sat in the low-slung lobby chairs, blatant in their tight jeans and stretch tops or ridiculously short miniskirts, legs open and eyebrows penciled in, eyeing every man that entered.

Two of them smiled at Richards as he passed and whispered something in French that he didn't catch.

He ignored them. He didn't need any more of that. No sir.

The problem was that she just didn't understand what the hell American fucking was all about. Every time he tried to explain or even show her, she just giggled.

Richards wasn't even sure it was worth the trouble anymore. The night before, she practically took over, and he was just hanging on like it wasn't him who was paying anymore.

She wanted more money, too, and pouted when he gave her the 2,000 CFA. He gave her another two, but he wrapped them around his drilling rig and made her pull them off with her goddamn pouty lips.

That had helped, but only a little.

Richards stopped at the entrance to the restaurant and looked around. It was really a long terrace, open on the side that faced the pool, with a bar along the inside wall and a roof over it all.

It wasn't air-conditioned, but I felt comfortable after the walk across the parking lot. The restaurant was three-quarters full; waiters, all clad in dark brown pants and lighter, matching tie-dyed shirts, rushed between the tables and the kitchen, which looked to be off somewhere behind the bar.

The decor was more African than at the Meridien. The tables were of a rich-looking dark wood that was probably local, and behind the bar was a massive wooden frieze of African figures.

Most of the faces at the tables were white, though, and the food, at least what was on the tray that sped past Richards, looked more Hawaiian than African.

He didn't see Mason anywhere. He looked at his watch. It was 12:40, and the bastards weren't even there yet. If anyone pulled that shit in the private sector, their asses would be on the unemployment line faster than they could say free market capitalism.

But then he heard someone calling his name. He turned and squinted against the glare from the pool area; it was Kyle

Mason, half out of his chair, waving. Richards slipped his sunglasses back on as he moved from the shade of the terrace back out into the sunlight. The pool was pretty crowded, but except for Mason and the old guy with him, the dozen tables set out on the tile apron were empty.

"Hello, Mr. Richards," Kyle said; "thanks for coming." He stood up to greet Richards, but the old guy didn't move.

"This is Mr. Rieper from Washington."

"Mr. Rieper," Richards said, nodding curtly at the old bastard. He'd be damned if he was gonna shake hands with someone who didn't have enough manners to get up when a guest arrived.

"Please call me Mort," Rieper said. "Won't you sit down?"

Richards pulled out the chair facing back toward the restaurant and slid into it.

"Thanks very much for taking the time to talk to us," Rieper said.

That was a little better. Hell, maybe he had something wrong with him and couldn't stand up. But he shoulda said so.

"My pleasure...Mort," Richards replied, smiling like a salesman at Rieper.

The old boy didn't look too damn well, that was for sure. His skin was dry and just sort of hung across his bones, even on his face. Washington should have known better than to send a guy that old out to a place like Cameroon, but shit, that was par for the goddamn course.

The two of them didn't even know enough to get out of the heat.

"You boys like to fry?" Richards asked, raising his eyebrows at Mason, who, he was glad to see, was dripping sweat down on the tabletop.

"Oh, does the heat bother you, Mr. Richards?" Rieper asked. The bastard must have been sick; his face, hell, even his goddamn cue-ball of a head, were dry as a bone.

"I'm from Houston, Mort," Richards grinned. "This'd be a chilly day for us in August."

An African waiter walked out from the restaurant.

"Uh, what'll you have, Mr. Richards?" Kyle asked.

He wanted a goddamn whiskey, but that might not have looked too good, with Mason and Rieper both drinking mineral water, so he ordered a beer.

"You doin' a survey of U.S. businesses in Africa or something, Mort?" He asked when the waiter left.

"Actually, I'm looking at one particular business, Mr. Richards," Riper explained.

"You mean oil," Richards said, tired of it already. Somebody ought to drop a bomb on Washington and get it over with. Hell, nobody'd notice for a week, and then they'd probably vote to keep it that way.

"Oil equipment, really," Rieper said, sipping his water.

Mason cleared his throat as if he were planning to add something, but then didn't.

"I'm not sure I'm the man you want to talk to then, Mort," Richards said. "I've shipped all of one cargo of pump barrels and sucker rods over here."

"Yes, well, that's the equipment we're interested in," Rieper said, his voice no different, though he had put the water glass down on the table and was staring across at Richards now.

Richards let the waiter pour him half a glass of beer, but he didn't take his eyes off Rieper. Goddamn, it was hot. The sweat was rolling down his back and chest like someone had left a faucet running in his collar.

"I'm not sure I follow you, Mort," Richards said when the waiter left. His tone was still friendly, but it was an effort now.

"The equipment you sold to Mr. Reilly's company is for what kind of work, exactly?" Rieper asked.

"What do you mean, what kind of work?" Richards countered, his annoyance starting to show.

Rieper didn't seem to notice. "Well, for one thing, can they be used anywhere, under any conditions?"

Richards exhaled noisily and glanced over at the restaurant.

The incompetent bastards sent someone 6,000 miles at the cost of God knew how many taxpayers' dollars, and he didn't know the first fucking thing about what he was supposed to be studying.

"No, they can't be used anywhere, under any conditions," Richards said, looking back at Rieper and shaking his head. "But that's true of just about every goddamn piece of equipment in the oil business." He took a long sip of beer to avoid saying something else.

"I see," Rieper said, nodding. He didn't say anything for a moment, as though thinking something over, but he never took his eyes off Richards.

Well, two could play that game, too. Richards stared right back.

"Can they be used in off-shore oil work?" Riper asked finally.

"No, they can't," Richards replied, keeping his voice even.

"But that's where all of Cameroon's oil is, isn't it?" It wasn't really a question.

"They got something going out by uh...Edea, I understand," Richards shot back.

"That's a swamp," Rieper said; "would your equipment be of use in a swamp?"

"We don't recommend it," Richards said. "But if I were you, I'd ask Reilly what he's planning on doin' with them. All I do is sell 'em."

He could feel the sun burning the side of his face. The son of a bitch must've used one helluva sunscreen. His bald head was white as an aspirin tablet; it hadn't even started to go pink.

"Yes, well, we'll do that, Mr. Richards," Rieper said. "But we thought we'd check with you first."

Richards took a long drink of beer. It would have been nice

to put the cold glass up against the side of his face, even for just a second, but he couldn't do that.

"I hear they think there's oil somewhere up north," he offered. This was a waste of time like he thought it'd be; well, shit, he'd be polite and finish his beer at least.

"But isn't it unusual to be buying pump barrels before the seismic work is even completed?" Rieper asked. Again, it didn't sound like a question.

"Like I said, Mort, you ought to check with Reilly," Richards said. He was finished dicking around. He swallowed the last of the beer and pushed his chair back.

"Like I said, we will," Rieper replied. "But first, I think you'd better tell us what you know about where those pump barrels are going."

Richards stared across the table. Rieper's voice hadn't changed at all; it was the words that carried the threat.

"And I think you better go to hell, Rieper," Richards said, pushing himself out of the chair. His face felt hotter now, not just from the sun.

He was going, but he leaned down and tapped the table, hard, right in front of Rieper with a finger.

"And if you think you can start fucking around with Jim Richards, you and your goddamn good-for-nothing Commerce Department got another fucking thing...."

"I don't work for the Commerce Department, Mr. Richards." The voice was quiet, still, and under control, but the words came faster as if the old bastard was running out of patience, too.

"I don't give a good goddamn who you work for," Richards hissed, furious for a second until it hit him.

He spun abruptly to look at Kyle Mason, who didn't look too damn comfortable, but didn't look away.

"We just need to ask you a few questions, Mr. Richards," he pleaded.

Richards looked back at Rieper and caught what might have been irritation in the glance he flashed at Mason, but then it was gone. Well, at least that part was right: the old guy was running the show.

"Look, Rieper, if that's even your name," Richards said; "I don't really care, don't even wanna know who you work for. I sold one load of pump barrels and sucker rods to a company here in Douala. I got the export permits from the Commerce Department, all the paperwork was in order, and I got paid."

"Almost a million dollars," Rieper said quietly.

Richards was a little short of breath, so he stopped and drew a deep one.

"All I'm doin' over here is a little marketing, tryin' to drum up some business," he concluded.

"Do you know where the closest on-shore production to here is, Mr. Richards?" Rieper asked.

Richards, still standing, shrugged.

"Nigeria, I guess, but I don't really know."

Rieper shook his head once. "No, theirs is all off-shore, too, or in the Cross River swamps," he said. "Same with Gabon and the Congo; even Angola."

Richards shrugged again. So he'd been wrong. Well, OK, now he had nothing to tell them.

"No, the nearest producing fields that could reasonably use your pump barrels are in the Libyan desert," Rieper added, staring up at Richards.

"You're out of your mind," Richards replied. "Libya's a couple of thousand miles from here. Across the goddamn Sahara desert."

"But Chad is not," Rieper countered. "It's only 1,000 kilometers from here, and trucks make the trip all the time. It takes a week or ten days."

"So what?" Richards challenged him.

"So the Libyans have several thousand troops in Chad right now, as you no doubt are aware," Rieper explained.

Richards nodded curtly. He wasn't even sure where the hell Chad was, but he'd be damned if he was going to admit it to this old son of a bitch. And he couldn't care less where the goddamn Libyans sent their troops, so long as it wasn't the United States.

"Like I said, so what?"

"So they fly cargo planes in and out of Chad several times a day," Rieper explained. "Your equipment could be in Tripoli in ten days; two weeks from now, they'll be at work helping to keep Libya's only source of income flowing."

Richards stared down at Rieper, trying to decide if it made sense or if it was just one more of the bastard's games. It was so goddamn hot; he wanted to get out of the sun. But he couldn't leave it like that.

"We have no reason to believe you knew of all this, Mr. Richards," Rieper continued.

"Damn straight, I didn't," Richards shot back, angry and a little nervous now. "I still don't."

Rieper spread his hands. "It's always possible we've made a mistake," he said quietly. "But I'm certain you wouldn't mind helping us to make sure."

He extended a long, thin hand, the bones pushing against the skin as if they were trying to escape toward the chair Richards had vacated.

Richards pulled his handkerchief from his pocket and removed his sunglasses. He wiped the sweat from his burning face, then pressed the handkerchief against his eyes for a moment and sank slowly back into the chair.

CHAPTER 34

Mark took the shortcut through the CDC plantation, as much for the shade the palm trees offered as a desire to avoid the police in Buea.

He remembered most of the turns, though twice he went too far and had to backtrack. Even so, it cut almost a half-hour off the trip, and he was back in Douala by 2:30.

Mark stopped briefly at Antoine's. It was closed on Saturday afternoon, but he knew that one of Victor's nephews cleaned up then and would let him in. He had several angry telexes and a frantic one from the commodity service; they all wanted to know when he'd be back or whether he could find someone to at least send the routine weekly items.

The last one was from the paper in Boston. "FYI, we now hearing exDC. There may be something to yr dlrs in Chad piece. Know you offheading soon but grtfl if cudst update and refile soonest."

Mark hissed in disgust. For a second, he thought about replying—'grtfl you offfuck soonest'—but then tossed the telex in the garbage.

He also had one letter from Paris. The envelope had no

return address, and it was typed. But he knew only one person in Paris. Mark folded the envelope and slid it into his back pocket. He'd read it later. He thanked Victor's nephew and left.

The African at the Meridien reception said Richards was still at the hotel, but that he'd gone out, he thought to the Novotel. He didn't remember seeing anyone with him, but he couldn't say for sure. It was still damn hot, but Mark was tired of driving, so he left the taxi in the Meridien lot and walked across the street.

He didn't want to talk to Koumba in front of Richards, assuming she was even with him, but he didn't have a lot of time, so he might have to. The redneck bastard wouldn't be able to understand them anyway. It wouldn't take long; just tell her he was leaving for a while and give her a key to the apartment. Even a busy whore needed a place to sleep once in a while.

Richards, if that's who she was with, could think what he wanted.

In the Novotel lobby, Mark recognized a girl from the Cafe des Sports. She was sitting in one of the low-slung leather chairs, legs apart so that anyone passing through to the restaurant couldn't miss her black panties.

"*Salut, toi,*" she said to Mark, flipping a limp hand up for him to shake.

"*Ca va?*" He asked, looking around the lobby.

She made a sucking sound with her tongue on the roof of her mouth, then pushed her lips out in a pout that Koumba would have envied. Things were tough all over.

She shook her head slowly, still pouting, when Mark asked if she'd seen Koumba.

"*A toute a l'heure,*" he said, dropping her hand. She didn't answer him.

Mark walked quickly through the small air-conditioned bar at the back of the lobby, then out the other side onto the terrace near the outdoor bar.

They weren't there either.

The bartender walked over, and Mark ordered a small Gold Harp. There were other places he could check, the marina or the bars where the sleazebags hung out, but he was already late getting the car back to Wanna, and there was no guarantee she'd be at any of those places either.

The bartender brought the beer, and Mark told him to keep what was left of a 500 CFA note.

"*Merci, monsieur,*" the African said and walked back down the bar.

Mark swiveled halfway around on the stool so that he could take in the restaurant, the side of the lobby nearest the reception desk, and the pool. It was almost three o'clock, and the restaurant was empty. There were a few people milling around the lobby, but Koumba wasn't one of them.

There were no Africans at the pool, either, just a dozen or so whites trying to turn brown.

And one table of fools sitting in the direct sun.

Mark squinted behind his sunglasses into the bright light. It was Richards, facing back toward where Mark sat. It was hard to tell from that distance, but the Texan didn't look like he was enjoying himself. It took Mark a moment to realize that the other two men were Kyle Mason and his boss from Washington.

He hadn't felt the tingling in his stomach and bowels for a long time—maybe not since Chad—and it surprised him now. It wasn't that Richards was there; Mark knew he had met Kyle already, and the guy from D.C.—what the hell was his name?—was Kyle's boss.

Nor was there anything unusual about three Americans having a drink at the Novotel, except maybe that they were sitting in the sun and had been for a while, judging from the color of Richard's face. It was more the way Richards sat there, leaning forward slightly, his arms crossed in front of him. The redneck swagger was gone; he wasn't giving Kyle and his boss any of the hick camaraderie Mark had to swallow.

No, Richards didn't look like he was enjoying himself.

For one thing, he was listening more than he was talking, mostly to the old guy from Washington. Mark removed his sunglasses, and it helped a little. He had a clear view of Richards, though Kyle and the older guy had their backs to him.

Richards nodded tightly at the old guy, said something briefly, then glanced over at the bar—directly at Mark. At that distance, Mark wasn't sure Richards could see him, but he started to nod politely, just in case. He stopped when he saw the look on Richards' face.

The son of a bitch managed a smile and then a short wave, but it didn't matter by then. Mark was aware of the pounding in his chest now, and in his ears, and for just a second, he thought he might piss in his pants.

If he needed confirmation, Kyle gave it to him, spinning around and half out of his chair like he'd been stung, smiling too hard and waving as if Mark were going somewhere. The old guy handled it best, which, for some reason, now didn't surprise Mark. He just shifted casually in his seat to look over his shoulder; no hurry at all, just curious.

But for a moment, really just a split second as he turned, his head was in perfect profile to where Mark sat. A door opened in Kousseri, and Mark caught a glimpse of an identical profile; only for a second again, and then a pimp in a bathrobe was closing the door again.

"Son of a goddamn bitch," Mark muttered to no one.

It was his turn now, and he did it badly. He stared too long and saluted too late, but it was the best he could do. He swung around to the bar to give himself time to think.

He had barely touched the beer, and he knew he should finish it. But there was no way. He looked down the bar at the bartender, who was washing glasses at the other end. Mark thought he'd paid for the beer, but couldn't remember for sure now. He groped in his pocket and pulled out several bills, all 1,000 CFA notes. That was way too much, but it didn't matter. He put one under the Gold Harp bottle and stood up.

Mark forced himself to glance over at the table by the pool. None of the three was watching him anymore. Kyle and the bastard from Washington, or Kousseri, or wherever, had their backs to him again. Richards was listening to the old guy and looking down at the table.

Mark kept his walk under control back through the lobby and out the hotel's front door. He didn't start running until he was in the parking lot.

CHAPTER 35

Wanna's nephew didn't even bother to open the gate. He just took the keys from Mark, climbed into the car, and left.

Mark didn't blame him for being angry; he'd no doubt been waiting for hours.

Mark pushed open the metal gate and walked into the courtyard that was all but filled by Wanna's new Peugeot. The house wasn't much either, just a small, squarish villa with a rusting metal roof. The place had probably needed a coat of paint when the French pulled out, and it was still waiting.

It was out by the Guiness brewery, past the airport, in what the government had designated as Douala's principal industrial zone. Wanna's nearest neighbors were two warehouses and a bottling plant. But it was cheap, and that had allowed Wanna to build the rental property over in Bonaberi and the new place in the village.

Wanna walked out the front door as Mark approached the steps.

"I'm sorry I'm late, Wanna," he said.

Wanna shook his head and shrugged. "Saturday's pretty slow anyway; did you have some trouble?"

"Not with the car, no," Mark replied.

All the way out, he'd gone over it, even practicing out loud to see how it sounded. Twice, he decided to forget the whole thing, but by the time he got to Wanna's, he'd convinced himself there was a way, and it was worth a try.

"I need to talk to you, Wanna," he said.

Wanna stared at Mark for a second, then held the front door open.

Therese was breastfeeding Maichas, their second son, on the couch in the living room. Mark hadn't seen either of them in a while and was surprised at how big the boy was.

"Welcome, Mark," Therese said, smiling. She had been an English teacher in a lycee before she married Wanna and still spoke slowly, enunciating the words, as if her audience was forever made up of disinterested Francophone adolescents.

It was a helluva contrast to Wanna's machine-gun delivery.

"Hi, Therese; how are you?" Mark asked.

"Fine, thank you," she replied.

Wanna said something quietly to her in Banso; she went to get up, but the little boy squirmed away and toddled over to his father. Wanna picked him up and spoke to him in Banso, then handed him back to Therese. Maichas started to cry. Another time, Mark would have protested and insisted they could stay. He smiled at Therese, hoping she knew it was important.

"Can you stay for dinner, Mark?" She asked from the doorway that led back to a small kitchen.

Mark glanced over at Wanna, who had turned to look out the window toward the courtyard.

It was Saturday night, and he would have plans, no doubt, that didn't include staying home.

Mark smiled at Therese. Maybe she wasn't so blind after all, and maybe it did bother her.

"Thanks, Therese, but I've got to meet someone," he lied.

She nodded and smiled, a little embarrassed now.

Wanna said the same thing in Banso again, louder and harsher this time.

Therese's smile wavered a little; she turned and, jiggling Maichas gently to stop his crying, disappeared into the kitchen.

A moment later, a young boy of about 16, whom Mark hadn't seen before, brought two Gold Harps, gave them to Wanna, and disappeared back into the kitchen.

"What's up?" Wanna asked, handing Mark one of the beers.

"Thanks," Mark said, taking a quick sip of beer. "Something's come up, and uh, I was wondering if there was any way we could see your cousin today."

Wanna drank some of his beer and studied the floor.

"I need to get the container tomorrow," Mark added.

"Mmmm," Wanna said, still not looking up.

Mark knew he wasn't going to like it.

"The port's closed on Sunday," Wanna said.

"I know, but I thought a customs inspector might be able to, I don't know, arrange something," Mark countered.

Wanna shook his head an inch or two.

"It's just one container, Wanna; it shouldn't take more than an hour to do the paperwork and get it loaded," Mark said.

He was talking fast, pressing Wanna, and he knew it. But there was no other way, and it was all Wanna had to do for his $25,000. Just then, Mark would have changed places with him in a minute.

"I don't know if he's in Douala," Wanna said. "He goes back to the village a lot."

"Can we go by and see?"

It was a yes or no question, the kind Africans hated, particularly when they wanted to say no.

"Why do you n-need to g-get it tomorrow?" Wanna asked, "My c-cousin will w-want to know too."

Mark expected the question and had gone over it in the car, trying and rejecting several answers.

The truth was out of the question. The CIA had an almost mythical omnipotence for Africans; even someone like Wanna, who knew it was nonsense, probably wouldn't be willing to defy them.

"I just got a telex from the buyer," Mark explained. "He needs the equipment in Kousseri by next Saturday, or the deal's off."

Wanna was looking at him now.

"Even if I get it tomorrow, and we drive at night and don't have any trouble, it's going to be tight."

"Why d-does he n-need it by Saturday?" Wanna asked.

"He didn't say," Mark replied, impatience creeping into his voice. "Look, Wanna, I wouldn't ask if it wasn't urgent."

Wanna put his beer on the floor and stood up, but didn't look at Mark.

"I'll g-get my k-keys," he said.

The inspector was home, as Wanna probably knew all along.

He lived near the Central Post Office, just behind the Commodity Stabilization Board building, and no more than a long stone's throw from his office at the port. The house wasn't much; like Wanna's, it was a colonial-era villa that was neither large nor well-maintained. But the Port Authority owned it, and it came, rent-free, with the position.

In any case, Wanna explained, people in customs and immigration and the other big *dash* jobs generally showed poverty in the cities, where Ahidjo's dreaded secret police were concentrated.

If the inspector was surprised or annoyed to see them, he did a nice job of hiding it. He greeted Mark warmly in English, then wagged a finger at Wanna and lectured him playfully in Banso.

"This is a bad one, Mark," he said, laughing. "Don't let him lead you astray."

Wanna was clearly uneasy about being there, but he laughed and said something quickly in Banso that drew an explosive laugh from his cousin.

Mark smiled to be polite.

"He says I was the one that led him astray," the inspector translated, still laughing.

He ushered them into the living room and gestured at a worn, brown velour couch set back against one of the walls, which long ago had been painted a bright, sky blue.

Wanna's cousin sat down in a matching armchair that faced the couch. He was heavier than Wanna and at least ten years older, but there was, if not a family resemblance, at least a tribal one.

They both were on the short side but solidly built, with the same black pearl coloring and a head that sloped from the brow upward toward the back of the skull.

The inspector even spoke like Wanna, in short, quick bursts, as if he couldn't wait for one word to get out before he started the next. He called out something in Banso, and a moment later, two girls, about five and eight, Mark guessed, came timidly into the room.

They were dressed identically in bright green and yellow print tunics and long wrap-around skirts. Wanna spoke quietly to them in Banso; they both smiled and nodded but never took their eyes off the floor.

The father said something, and the girls shuffled over to Mark, curtsied, and held out their hands. Mark leaned down to try and make them look at him, but the girls locked their chins against their chests. Mark shook both their hands, and the girls hurried out of the room; a moment later, he heard them giggling somewhere in another room.

The inspector yelled again, and a young man, maybe 20, brought out three St. Pauli's Girls, with glasses, on a tray. He served Mark first, then Wanna, and handed the last beer to his patron.

Ice cold St. Pauli's Girl wasn't what poor public servants

usually drank, but then maybe he didn't feel like he had to pretend with his cousin.

Mark wasn't complaining. The beer tasted damn good; for the first time since he'd left the Novotel, he relaxed a little.

Wanna bantered with his cousin for a few minutes in their native language, then cleared his throat and switched to English. He explained why they'd come.

Mark decided to let Wanna do the talking—it was his cousin —unless the inspector asked him a direct question.

But the inspector surprised him. He nodded slowly as Wanna explained the situation, then glanced at Mark, drained most of a full glass of beer, and said quietly that they could probably work something out.

He had to go into the office for a short while in the morning, and there was always a crew to operate the loading crane, so there shouldn't be a problem.

Wanna, who had been leaning forward, sank back into the couch, and Mark heard him exhale. Mark smiled and said that was wonderful and that he really appreciated the help. Wanna's cousin smiled right back and said it was his pleasure.

There was an awkward silence as the three of them drank their beers.

Driving over, Wanna and Mark came as close to an argument as they ever had over the size of the *dash.* For the Monday pick-up, Wanna had suggested 500,000 CFA; now he said it would have to be a million.

That was $5,000. With the $2,500 Mark had already paid Francis for the truck, that would wipe out most of his cash before he left Douala.

Mark argued that 750,000 CFA was plenty; hell, it was only the difference of a day.

Wanna reluctantly agreed to start there.

His cousin's eyes widened slightly at the figure. He took another enormous swallow of beer and nodded slowly, not agreeing to anything, only acknowledging that that was a reasonable starting point. They were almost finished with their second beer when Mark caved to the inevitable and agreed to pay Wanna's cousin a million CFA. He'd been polite but adamant, reminding Mark that normal duties on the container would be at least double that and might take a week or longer to clear.

The 5,000 CFA note was the largest denomination the African franc zone put out, so the pile that Mark pulled from his portefeuille covered much of the top of the coffee table in front of them. Wanna's cousin offered them another beer, but they declined. Mark had a lot to do before morning.

The inspector walked them out to the gate. He shook hands with Mark and said he'd see him at seven o'clock at the port. He and Wanna shook hands and spoke briefly in Banso.

"He says I must bring you out to the village when his new house is finished," Wanna said, smiling.

"Why not? I'm paying for it," Mark replied.

"At l-least the g-gold faucets," Wanna managed before he started to laugh.

"Shit," Mark said, feigning more disgust than he felt.

It was more than he'd wanted to pay, and he'd really have to watch his money from now on, but it was done, and Wanna was all right again.

And it was going to work out. In a week, ten days at the outside, it'd be over, and all anyone would be able to prove was that he sold some oil equipment to a Frenchman in Cameroon. There was no law against that.

And Kyle Mason could go to hell.

CHAPTER 36

Mark got up from the bed and walked down the hallway to the kitchen.

He pulled a Gold Harp from the refrigerator, opened it, and walked back toward the darkened living room. He should have been asleep, or at least lying down; God only knew when he'd sleep in a bed again. But it was no use, so he sat on the wicker couch, drank the beer, and stared out the windows.

He glanced around for his watch, then remembered he'd left it near the bed. He'd look after he finished the beer. When he'd first gone to Diarrere, he hadn't taken a watch. Or a clock, or a radio, or even a calendar. He was afraid time would pass too slowly that way, and two years seemed long enough already.

There were days, sometimes weeks when he had no idea what date it was; unless one of the few villagers with a watch mentioned it, he never knew the precise hour. But before long, he could tell "village time" other ways: from the length of the shadow cast by his hut, or its absence, or from sounds (the thudding of the pestles as the women began pounding millet meant he could sleep some more, the first men's voices meant it was time to get up); or the position of the sun (when it reached the top of the giant Baobab tree west of his hut, it was time to walk to the well for a bucket of water that he used for his shower).

Later, it was other things too, like the older boys walking barefoot by his hut before dawn on their way to the fields to get what milk they could from the emaciated cows or the pigs, whose squeals sounded so much like babies crying, as they fought over the morning swill; even the wind, when it picked up, or when it died, and how hot the sun felt on his arms or face.

So that by his second year there, Mark didn't have to ask or even think about it; he knew what time it was, just as certainly as he knew when he was thirsty.

All he knew now was that it was late, and he couldn't sleep.

Mark glanced over at the front door. The leather traveling bag Deborah gave him was packed and sat on the floor where he couldn't miss it. His *portefeuille,* a lot thinner now, was on top of it; in addition to the money, it contained his resident's permit, driver's license, and passport because he'd need that now.

Mark had no idea what Kyle Mason and his friend's resources were in Francophone Africa. He didn't even know how much they knew. Hell, he hadn't told Richards anything.

But he couldn't take any chances. So he had to make sure they couldn't find him until it was finished. Then Kyle and the old man could think what they wanted, but they wouldn't be able to prove a thing.

Mark unclenched the fist he'd been unaware of making and shook his fingers to relax them. In a way, it was his own goddamn fault. It was kind of a game among expatriates in a place like Douala to guess who it was, but Mark never suspected Kyle, not even after he came around asking questions. It was the Jesus stuff that threw him off; shit, was that just a cover? If so, it was a damn good one. Even his tight-assed wife was in on it.

Mark sucked the suds from the neck of the bottle, then set it down on the floor next to the two other empties.

He'd wavered a couple of times after he left Wanna: once eating alone at a chicken house in Daido (Marie's was too well known in the American community), then again walking home from the movie theatre, where he sat through two French films, not watching really, just staying away from his apartment until it was late.

Mark knew he could drop the whole thing. Sell the equipment to one of the African *bricoleurs* who bought anything if the price was right, and that would be the end of it. He had almost $5,000 dollars, more than he'd had at one time in years, and Calvady couldn't touch him.

But the money would go fast. He'd already gone through almost that much, and then what?

He picked up the empties and took them back to the kitchen. He thought about having one more, decided against it, and then grabbed one out of the refrigerator just as he was about to turn out the light. One more would be all right.

He walked back down the hall, then turned suddenly into the bedroom. He'd forgotten about the letter. He dug it out of the back pocket of the pants he'd flung in a corner, picked up his watch from the floor near the bed, and walked back to the living room.

Mark flicked on the light and sat down again. It was five to three. He'd have to leave in another three hours. He laid the envelope across his legs until he had finished half the beer; then, he opened and read it.

Dear Mark,

I told the lawyers it was no use; that you wouldn't sign the divorce papers. This letter is probably a waste of time, too, but I thought it was worth a try.

I guess I hoped that, even if it was just for old times' sake, you might do something based on something other than anger.

I know you're angry at what I did, and I suppose you have a right to be. But we both know it started a long time before that, Mark. The sad part is I can't remember exactly when and certainly not why. I guess it doesn't really matter.

I don't hate you, Mark, but I want to get on with my life.

The lawyers here say that because Cameroon uses the French legal system, they can sue for divorce in Douala. It would cost a lot of money because we'd have to hire a lawyer down there—but so would you, if you wanted to contest it.

I don't want to have to do that, Mark, but I will if you leave me no choice. Won't you please, please just sign the papers and be done with it?

I hope you're well.

Deborah

Mark picked the Gold Harp bottle up from the floor and drank while he re-read the letter quickly. Then he crunched it into a tight ball and tossed it in the general direction of the garbage bag.

CHAPTER 37

Sue Mason had never had much use for sex. Not that she was frigid; she knew Kyle had needs, and she took care of them. Nor did she loathe the actual experience.

It was more indifference, really, though there were some aspects of it, the mess afterward and the smell, like tuna fish left out too long, that she didn't like. Mostly, she didn't understand what the big deal was, and other than the nights when Kyle was restless, she rarely gave it a thought.

Occasionally, the younger women at the coffees, usually the less educated ones whose husbands worked out on the rigs, brought it up, even joked about it, but Sue always steered the conversation back onto a more suitable topic.

So, at first, she didn't understand the pleasant tightening in her stomach as she sat at dinner; when she felt the wetness between her legs, she was surprised but not disgusted, which, in a way, surprised her more than the wetness itself.

It wasn't anything Kyle said. Even if he had wanted to tell her, Rieper was there, so it was out of the question. No, it was more the way he smiled at her, and particularly the way he spoke and acted toward Rieper now; still respectful, differential even (as Kyle always was to his elders and superiors). But there was a change.

Kyle seemed more at ease as if some great uncertainty had been erased, and now he and Rieper could relate, if not as equals, then at least as real colleagues, both with something to offer.

God forgive her, but Sue said a small prayer: Rieper wouldn't have coffee or want to sit and talk after dinner. And it was answered: he thanked her for the meal and asked that they excuse him for heading straight back to the hotel, but he was still tired from the trip.

For the first time in her life, Sue Mason wore no panties under her nightgown. As she slid under the sheets, the insides of her thighs were wet almost down to her knees, and her heart was thudding so heavily in her narrow chest that it seemed impossible Kyle couldn't hear it.

He finished in the bathroom, turned out the lights, and climbed into bed. He knew she wanted to ask but wouldn't, so he leaned over so she could see him smile in the dark and said Mark Reilly had a lot of explaining to do.

It was the first time in ten years of marriage she had initiated anything, but when she reached for Kyle, her hand trembling violently at the opening in his boxer shorts, he was ready for her.

Sue felt his stomach muscles shiver involuntarily as she struggled to push his shorts down.

Her mouth was dry, so that she had to open it wide just to get enough air. Her narrow, bony hips seemed to be working independently of the rest of her, jerking spasmodically at first, then thrusting rhythmically up into Kyle with such force that even with him on her, and Kyle was a big man, Sue was arching her back effortlessly.

And still, it wasn't enough.

From somewhere else came a noise that could not have been part of her, and Sue tried to cut it off. But it was impossible to close her mouth and still get enough air, so out it came, long and low and guttural, not her voice at all, more like some wounded beast she couldn't recognize or even imagine.

CHAPTER 38

Jim Richards sat in the chair and stared across at the bed. The shades were drawn, so he couldn't really see Koumba, just a vague form, really, a shade blacker than the night, lying on top of the covers to catch the air-conditioned coolness.

He'd tried to explain it was only the pressure. Goddamn, he could have been in one helluva lot of trouble; there was no guarantee he still wasn't. The son of a bitch wouldn't promise him anything.

But she'd just smiled and shrugged and kept saying "sonny pa grav" or some such bullshit. But she sure as hell didn't forget what she was doing there.

When he'd tried for the third time and then pushed her head down to see if that'd work, and it didn't, she'd rubbed her fingers together and said "argent," and Richards knew what the hell that meant. He flung the wallet at her so hard it slapped against one of her big, beautiful tits, then fell on the bed. She looked at him a moment, then picked it up, extracted four 1,000 CFA notes, and handed the wallet back to him.

He wouldn't take it, so she laid it on the night table next to the bed.

It rose in his throat so suddenly, like some great force pushing its way out, that Richards at first thought he had to vomit. Before he could even turn toward the bathroom, he was crying, the sobs pouring out of him so fast that it was hard to breathe.

Koumba sat staring at him, not saying anything, until he staggered into the bathroom and closed the door. It took only a couple of minutes to get himself back under control. Hell, it was only frustration and the pressure and maybe not sleeping too goddamn much; but she was asleep when he came out again.

Richards rubbed his forehead gently with the tips of his fingers and thumb. He was all right; he just needed to get the hell outta there and get back to a normal routine again. He'd only been there a week, but it seemed longer, a helluva lot longer, so that the things he knew, Houston and his business, even Ema, weren't as clear in his mind as they should've been, but more like memories from a long-ago vacation.

Richards used both hands to massage his temples. The blood was still pounding too goddamn fast, but shit, after the day he'd had...

He'd be fine. He just needed to get home.

CHAPTER 39

Wanna's cousin had said seven, probably to minimize the risk of running into any other port officials. But that was fine with Mark; he wanted as big a head start as he could get. Kyle and his "boss" wouldn't do anything until Mark didn't show up for lunch. Even then, on a Sunday, they might not find out he and the container were gone for quite a while. If he was lucky, he might have 24 hours.

Mark had to wait a good ten minutes before a taxi stopped, but he'd expected that and left enough time. When he climbed in with his bag and *portefeuille,* and told the driver the port, it was not quite 6:30.

He was undecided almost until it was time to go, then slipped a key into an envelope, wrote her name on it, and taped it to the front door of his apartment. That was dangerous in a place like Akwa, but chances were good Koumba would find it before any of the *quartier's* thieves did.

Mark had considered writing a short note but decided that Kyle and the old guy might stop by, and then they'd know and start looking sooner. It was doubtful they could find Koumba—not fast, anyway—and even if they did, she couldn't tell them a thing. He was glad, damn glad, he'd held off telling her what he was doing.

The taxi passed a few pedestrians, child vendors walking God knew where with a few sacks of biscuits, and women heading to market with enamel bowls on their heads, but it was early yet, and the streets were largely deserted.

The only question now was whether the truck would be there. Francis had said it would wait there after making the dawn cocoa delivery, but there was no guarantee. The driver wasn't expecting Mark for another 24 hours and could have decided to visit a girlfriend or a relative in one of the Anglophone quartiers.

But he worked for Francis, so the Mercedes was there, in the truck lot near the port, when Mark pulled up in the taxi. There were two other trucks in the overnight lot; the three drivers sat on a mat together, eating, when Mark walked up and stopped next to Francis' truck.

One of the three men rose quickly and came over.

"Are you Rudolph?" Mark asked.

"Yes, suh."

Mark stuck out a hand, and the African, a little startled, took it. He was several inches shorter than Mark but very muscular; his hand was heavily calloused and felt as hard as a piece of wood.

"I'm Mark Reilly. I think you're supposed to help me pick up a container, right?"

"Yes, suh, tomorrow," Rudolph said, eyeing Mark's bag.

"There's been a slight change in plans, Rudolph," Mark said.

"Uhhh," Rudolph said, unsure.

Mark explained quickly that he'd managed to get authorization to pick up the container that morning and that he was sure it was all right with Francis.

"Is that a problem?" He asked.

Rudolph thought a moment, then shook his head.

"No, suh."

Mark didn't think it would be. Rudolph might have been surprised by the change in plans but probably wasn't unhappy about it.

Douala wasn't as dangerous as Lagos, but the port had its share of thieves and assorted rough trade; an Anglophone bushman like Rudolph couldn't have been looking forward to spending another night there in a parked truck.

If it was possible to earn a million CFA in less than an hour, Wanna's cousin did. He had the papers all ready for Mark to sign when he walked into the office.

He gave Rudolph directions in *pidgin* to the container and explained that the crane operator was waiting for him. The container was loaded, and Rudolph was back with the truck, waiting as Mark was sliding the packet of documents into his *portefeuille*.

The inspector shook hands and insisted that Mark come to visit his new house in the village once it was finished. Mark said he'd look forward to it. They both knew it would never happen.

Mark and Rudolph rolled back out the port gate, past a lone guard, whose head was slumped forward onto his chest, just before eight o'clock.

Excluding the bush tracks that wound through the surrounding mangrove swamps, there were only two roads out of Douala: one started out beyond the airport and headed southeast about 100 kilometers to Edea, a steamy industrial city on the Sanaga River, in the heart of Bassaland.

The Sanaga dam, the source of most of the country's electricity, and Alucam's sprawling aluminum processing plant were in Edea; the road was built to service them.

But that's where it stopped. From Edea, there were dirt roads heading east to Yaounde and south to the port of Kribi, but both were difficult in the best of times and all but impassable in the rainy season.

The other way out of Douala started at the Wouri Bridge, crossed over to Bonaberi, and then turned north through Nkongsamba, the coffee-growing capital, to Bafoussam, the Bamileke stronghold. There, the road split. The western fork went on to Bamenda, where it ran out.

The other fork, however, headed northeast to the ancient walled city of Foumban, the southernmost limit of Islamic penetration in Cameroon and, for millennia, home of the Sultans of Foumban, once the most powerful tribal rulers in that part of Africa.

The paved portion of the *route nationale* ran out in Foumban and didn't resume again until N'gaoundere, some 600 kilometers northeast, on the great Adamaoua Plateau. From there, the road was good, paved and straight as ribbon, almost all the way to Kousseri: 750 kilometers up the tapered neck of Cameroon.

The problem, however, was getting to N'gaoundere. From Foumban, the road was a badly maintained dirt track that could take several days, or as long as a week, to negotiate. But it was the only land link between North and South in Cameroon and the main supply route for goods destined for Chad.

It was the road Mark had planned to take.

Just past Bonaberi, Mark ordered Rudolph to take the Victoria-Buea turnoff.

"Excuse me, suh?" Rudolph's English was only so-so, and he no doubt thought he misunderstood.

"We have to go to Kumba first, Rudolph; I need to see Francis," Mark explained.

"Yes, suh," Rudolph said. He swung the truck left onto the turnoff but didn't look as though he liked the idea.

Twenty minutes later, at the CDC estate, Mark ordered him to turn into the palm plantation.

"Suh?"

"It's all right, Rudolph; I know a shortcut," Mark said.

"Uhhhh," Rudolph wheezed. He didn't like this at all.

He eased the truck very slowly under the canopy created by the overhanging palm leaves. The combination of the sudden twilight and the proximity of the tightly clustered trees produced claustrophobia that Mark hadn't felt in a car.

He had seen trucks in there before, so he knew they'd fit, but Rudolph cringed every time one of the fronds scraped along the roof.

"It's no good, suh."

"It's only leaves, Rudolph," Mark assured him. "Trucks go through here all the time."

Rudolph downshifted and slowed the truck to a crawl; they still hit the branches, but the noise wasn't so bad. The African shook his head and muttered in a language Mark didn't recognize, but he kept going, which was all Mark cared about.

It was Sunday morning and still early, so it was possible the police checkpoints at the Buea Circle weren't manned yet. But he couldn't take the chance.

Mark had no idea who Kyle's contacts were or even if he worked like that, but if no one saw the truck, no one could tell the son of a bitch anything. The shortcut saved them nothing at all because Rudolph refused to budge out of second gear, but back on the paved road, they made good time. There was little traffic, and even the roadside villages seemed less crowded than usual.

They reached Kumba just after 10 o'clock. At the outskirts of town, two gendarmes had raised their hands to stop the truck, then, apparently recognizing it, smiled and saluted to Rudolph.

Francis had friends everywhere.

Rudolph said he'd be at the garage, even though it was Sunday, and he was. Francis emerged from the building as Rudolph carefully bumped the truck over the dirt road.

Francis was wearing an all-white outfit that, even up close, looked remarkably spotless.

"Welcome, Mark," he said, smiling.

Mark took the proffered hand and shook it.

"Hello, Francis," he replied. "Sorry about the change in plans, but something's come up."

"Problems?"

"Sort of."

Francis thought a second, then nodded. He spoke quietly in Bakossi to Rudolph, who nodded and disappeared into the garage. A moment later, Francis' chauffeur emerged. He hurried behind the building, and a moment later, a Mercedes Mark hadn't seen before pulled around to the front door.

"Let's go back to the house and talk," Francis said, holding the back door for Mark.

Helen didn't appear surprised to see Mark either.

"Welcome, Mark," she smiled, shaking hands.

"Hello, Helen. Sorry to drop in unexpectedly," Mark said.

"Don't be silly," she said, waving a hand at him.

Francis said something to her in Bakossi. She nodded and went into the kitchen.

Francis led Mark into the living room and gestured at the couch. "Please sit down, Mark." Francis pulled one of the matching armchairs a little closer and sat down.

"Will you have some coffee or a beer?" He asked.

"Uh, coffee, if it's no trouble," Mark said, wanting a beer badly.

"So, what's up?" Francis asked. For a second, even his accent sounded American.

Mark had gone over in his head what he planned to say most of the way out from Douala but still was uneasy. Francis wasn't stupid, and Mark sure as hell needed his help, so lying was risky.

But the truth, all of it, anyway, might be worse.

"I need to go north by a different route, Francis."

Francis, who knew the geography as well as Mark, nodded slightly, raising his eyebrows.

"Which way were you thinking of going?" He asked.

"Through Nigeria," Mark said.

Helen came in with the coffee and cups on a tray. She smiled briefly at Mark but said nothing and didn't stay. Francis took his time fixing Mark a cup—he remembered how he liked it—then poured some for himself and sat back.

Francis' expression hadn't changed, but Mark knew what he'd said, and maybe what he hadn't said weighed on the African.

"The problem is that there are some people, Americans, not Cameroonians, who would like to see me fail," Mark explained. He was talking faster now, feeling he had to fill the silence.

"And they would probably go to a lot of trouble to make sure I did."

"Why?" Francis asked.

"Because they think the oil equipment in the container might end up in Libya," Mark said quietly.

"Will it?"

Mark shrugged, shifting his regard from Francis to the coffee cup. "I made a deal to deliver it to a Frenchman up north," he said. "I didn't ask him what he planned to do with it."

Francis sipped his coffee and nodded slowly.

"And how will going through Nigeria help you?"

Mark exhaled heavily. They were over the worst part.

"They don't know I'm gone yet," he explained. "If I'm lucky, they won't for another 24 hours or so. By then, they'll be in a panic trying to find me along the *route nationale*. I doubt they'll even think about Nigeria. They probably don't even know it's possible."

"It's not," Francis said, putting his cup down and looking directly at Mark.

The tingling started in Mark's stomach and spread quickly downward.

"You take cars across all the time," he pleaded, trying but failing to avoid raising his voice.

Francis nodded. "Cars, yes, but not a loaded truck, Mark," he said, almost apologetically. "We always go in the caravan, so if one of the cars gets stuck, and they always do, everyone gets out and pushes."

Francis shook his head. "Even then, it can be very difficult; with a loaded truck, even if you took 10 or 12 men, it would be impossible, especially now that the rains have started."

Mark sat staring at the coffee cup, which suddenly felt awkward out in front of him. He should have taken a sip or put it down at least, but somehow, he couldn't make his arms do it.

With a lot of Africans, "impossible" simply meant a bigger *dash* was required, or they didn't feel like doing it. Francis was different, though; he always meant exactly what he said.

"Mark," Francis said, leaning forward. "If they don't know you've gone yet, you might be able to make it if you hurry."

Mark nodded because arguing was pointless now, but he made no move to leave.

"Are you sure they'll find out tomorrow?"

Mark heard the question, but it took him a moment before he nodded again. Tomorrow at the latest; even then, it'd be a cinch to locate him before he got to Waza. Hell, probably long before that.

He looked over at Francis, who was staring back, clearly worried.

"There's no law against selling oil equipment to a Frenchman, is there?" He asked, trying to help now.

Mark shook his head. "These guys aren't lawyers, Francis," he said.

Francis looked down at the floor for a moment, then back up at Mark.

"May I see the customs documents for the container?" He asked.

Mark mechanically unzipped his *portefeuille* and pulled out the thick packet of papers. He handed them to Francis. Francis sat back in the armchair and slowly scanned the documents. Mark watched him for a moment, then hung his head, looking at nothing.

The worst part was that he thought he could pull it off. Hell, most days, he couldn't write a simple news article without fucking it up. Mark took a deep breath, exhaled, and leaned his neck against the back of the couch. There was a ceiling fan directly over where they sat, but it wasn't turned on. Maybe it didn't work.

He'd have to kiss some ass with his strings. He'd left them high and dry for a couple of weeks and hadn't even answered most of their telexes.

He'd try the oil companies first, but if that didn't work, he'd sell the equipment to anyone who'd take it off his hands. Fast.

At least he still had $5,000, or almost.

Francis said something, but Mark didn't catch it.

"I'm sorry, Francis?"

"Is this all it weighs?" Francis repeated.

"Is what all it weighs?" Mark asked, finding it hard to concentrate.

Francis smiled and tapped a page of the documents.

"The oil equipment, net of the container, only weighs 1,800 kilos?"

Mark shrugged. "If that's what it says," he replied. Then, afraid he had offended Francis, added: "I know it isn't much; the whole thing took up only about a third of the container. They, sorry, we rented the whole thing just to make shipment easier."

Francis was leaning forward again, flipping the pages of documents faster now.

"You have the key?" He asked.

"Sure," Mark nodded.

Francis put the papers on the table and poured himself some more coffee.

"There might be a way, Mark, but it will cost you more," he said. "Do you have much cash with you?"

Mark leaned forward, trying not to look anxious.

"Some," he shrugged, already bargaining.

CHAPTER 40

The proximity of the hotel pool didn't help at all; it was even a kind of torture.

Kyle Mason had tried to steer them to a table on the terrace, but Rieper wasn't looking and headed straight for where they'd grilled Jim Richards the day before. Kyle's shirt was soaked through with sweat, but Rieper didn't seem to notice the heat; his massive bald head had hardly a bead of sweat on it. Even after hours in the sun the day before, his skin was as white as bleached bones.

Kyle thought about asking what kind of sunscreen he used, then decided they didn't know each other well enough yet.

"He's pretty late," he said instead to break the silence. They were both on their second mineral waters, and there was no sign of Mark Reilly.

Rieper nodded without looking at Kyle.

"Reilly's not the most reliable fellow in the world," Kyle explained. "Things like being on time just aren't important to him." Kyle wanted to be fair, not let his own prejudices influence Rieper's judgment, but darnnit, Reilly didn't make it any easier.

"He's not coming, Kyle," Rieper said. It was the first time he'd spoken since they sat down.

Kyle looked at his watch, though he'd done so only a minute earlier. It was after one o'clock.

"I don't know, Mort," he replied. He'd switched from Mr. Rieper the night before at dinner.

"He could just be late. You see, Reilly doesn't care about .... punctuality or things like that."

He'd wanted to say "anything" but thought that might sound unprofessional.

Rieper shook his head an inch or so to either side.

"He's not coming. I should have known," he said to himself more than Kyle. "I did know; I just wasn't paying attention."

"To what, Mort?" Kyle asked, then regretted it when Rieper looked up at him from across the table.

"Do you think Richard's warned him?" He asked, looking over at the entrance to get away from Rieper's stare.

They, Rieper, really made it clear to the Texan what would happen if he said anything about their conversation.

Rieper shook his head again. "No, it was when he saw us, me really, here yesterday."

Kyle still had the uncomfortable feeling he wasn't part of the conversation.

"But he doesn't know who you are," Kyle protested. "And we were just having a drink with an American businessman."

Rieper shrugged and shook his head, slowly, in a wider arc this time.

"Perhaps Mr. Reilly is more perceptive than we gave him credit for," he said.

Kyle couldn't tell if that was a reprimand or not; Rieper might have leaned a little on the "we," but Kyle was hypersensitive about criticism, hearing it when it wasn't intended, so he couldn't be sure.

Kyle looked at his watch again so he didn't have to meet Rieper's gaze.

He should have felt some sense of triumph, or vindication at least; he'd been right, after all. Even Rieper had to admit that. It wasn't his fault Reilly didn't show up; he'd done everything the man asked.

"What should we do now?" Kyle asked, to be polite, though hearing himself, he was afraid it sounded stupid.

"Find him, Kyle," Rieper said, getting to his feet.

PART III

WAZA

CHAPTER 41

Mark saw the car from a long way off, the swirling brown cloud of dust trailing it like some out-of-control parachute unable to slow it down. But all the Lobe management cars were white Peugeots, so he couldn't be sure until they were almost upon it.

Simon never took his eyes off the road but did raise his left hand up against the windshield in the briefest of greetings, then rattled on by. For a second, Mark had the urge to lean across Francis and yell out Rudolph's open window to get Simon to stop. Just to talk, not about where Mark was headed, but anything else: Mary's tennis, or the price of palm oil, or what kind of trouble Moussa was causing.

But Simon probably wouldn't have heard him anyway. He had the air conditioning on and the windows up; if any noise at all reached him, he would simply have assumed it was one of Francis' drivers shouting a greeting.

They stopped at Jungle Bay first and got lucky. Jonas was there, counting cases of beer that apparently had just been delivered. Mark had been in the club only once, at night; now, in the light, it seemed pathetically small, just a square room with no windows and walls stained reddish-brown in places where the roof must have leaked.

Francis shook hands and said something quietly in Bakossi. Jonas nodded, smiled, and said something back. The tone was familiar and friendly.

Jonas instinctively turned the good side of his face to Mark when he shifted to greet him.

"Welcome, Mark."

"Hello, Jonas," Mark said, taking the extended hand. "How are you?"

"Fine, fine," Jonas said, nodding quickly.

Francis said something else in Bakossi, and Jonas smiled; then Francis' tone changed, and Jonas wasn't smiling anymore. He listened, his face set as if he might be slightly hard of hearing, and didn't interrupt except to moan softly now and then to let Francis know he was listening and understood.

At one point, Jonas looked quickly at Mark, and the moan rose slightly in inflection—a question or maybe a mild protest. Mark expected him not to like the idea. Running beer into Nigeria was one thing; what Mark was asking was quite another.

Francis finished talking and turned to Mark.

"I've explained what you want. I'll wait outside."

Mark nodded. Francis had warned him that he'd have to do his own negotiating. Francis was willing to help with some things but had already gone way out of his way, and it wasn't finished, but he did a lot of business with Jonas and so would not get involved in the price.

It was already afternoon, and the Jungle Bay was breathlessly hot, even with the door open. The low metal ceiling trapped the heat like an oven; even Jonas was perspiring, though part of that might have been nerves.

Mark's shirt was plastered to his back and chest, and he was suddenly aware of the streams of sweat rolling down from his scalp onto his neck. He didn't feel too comfortable, either.

"So, Mark," Jonas said, smiling tightly and looking at Mark finally from the good side of his face.

"I'm sorry to bother you, Jonas," Mark began, meaning it, "but I need your help."

Jonas nodded a little, but he looked miserable.

"Is your boat here, Jonas?"

Jonas looked as though he wanted to say no, to end it, but then nodded.

"I'd like 'to...rent it," Mark said, not sure that was the word.

Jonas sighed. He was damn unhappy. "Would you like a beer, Mark?" He asked, brightening a little as if glad to be back on familiar ground.

"I'd love one, Jonas, thanks," Mark said.

The N'Kondo-Titi *gendarmerie* was not right at the port, but about 200 meters back toward the village, so anyone heading for the port had to go by it. Mark waited uncomfortably in the truck with Rudolph. The land all around the *gendarmerie* had been cleared, probably to give them a clear view of the port and the road, so Rudolph had had no choice but to park in the sun.

It was just after two o'clock, and even with both windows open, the truck cab was stifling.

Rudolph had dozed off shortly after Francis went into the *gendarmerie*; his chin was resting on his chest, and his breathing was noisy and even.

Mark closed his eyes for a couple of minutes, his head against the seat back, but it was no use. He was nervous, scared, really, but even without that, he would have found sleeping impassible. On an impulse, he'd insisted on buying Jonas another beer when they'd settled on a price for the canoe.

Mark hadn't eaten since the night before; his head ached dully from the beer, and his mouth felt dry and tasted vaguely of something foul. He could smell the beer in the sweat that poured out of him now, and it made him nauseous. Westerners often complained that Africans "smelled," but the truth was, adrift from their air conditioners and daily showers for a few days, whites reeked far worse.

They had a peculiar odor, too, not like an honest sweat after strenuous exercise, but something stronger, though in some ways easier to get used to: like the sweet, fetid smell of rotting fruit. Mark rarely noticed it anymore, but sitting there in the sweltering truck, not even started yet, the idea of going a week or more without bathing sickened him so that he wanted to climb down, just to get some air.

But Francis had made a point of telling him to stay in the truck until he called him, so he did. Mark's faith in Francis was by now unquestioning, rooted in something well beyond the awareness that there was no alternative. It had been 20 minutes since Francis went in, but Mark had no idea whether or not that was long for this kind of thing.

They were both aware that it was the most precarious aspect of the plan. Francis knew the *commandant*, of course, and no doubt paid him plenty.

But *gendarmes* were an unpredictable lot, better paid and more intelligent than either the army or the idiot police, but arrogant too, and sometimes brutal.

"If he says no, that's it," Francis stressed on the ride over from the Jungle Bay. "Don't argue or offer more money; just leave, OK?"

Mark nodded. But they both knew if the *commandant* refused, he might not be allowed to "just leave."

Francis stepped out of a door on the side of the grimy, whitewashed building and walked down the steps toward the truck. He motioned for Mark to come. Mark's stomach tightened, and the awful tingling spread out and down so fast that when he opened the door, his legs, though they did what he wanted, felt as though the muscles had been removed.

It took what seemed like a long time to reach Francis, who waited for him near the steps.

"What'd he say?" Mark asked when he got close.

Francis shrugged. "He wants to see you."

It was the first time since Mark had met him that Francis appeared uncertain. It wasn't fear or even apprehension, only an admission that there were some things he couldn't control. There was no reason to expect anything else; they'd even discussed it on the ride over. But Mark couldn't stop the disappointment or the panic that quickly overtook it.

He was afraid his knees wouldn't obey him this time, but he made it up the four steps to the *commandant's* door. It was an effort, though, pathetically so, and his mouth, so dry that it felt as though he might choke on his tongue, hung open, sucking for air that wouldn't come fast enough.

A young *gendarme* who sat outside the door got up to open it for them. Francis entered first, and Mark followed. He nodded his thanks to the young officer and got a cold, hard stare for his trouble.

Mark had never been there before, but he'd seen that office dozens of times, all over West Africa. It was small and dark, with the louvered shutters closed against the heat, which was, nevertheless, oppressive by that time in the afternoon.

A ceiling fan that wasn't moving hung over the green metal desk where the *commandant* sat. There was also a single light bulb on a wire hanging halfway between the peaked metal ceiling and the floor. It wasn't turned on, either.

The *commandant* did not rise or even look up when they entered the office. He was writing something in a file on his desk and continued to work for a good two minutes before he glanced up at them.

"Asseyez-vous," he said, jabbing his pen hand at two metal chairs that faced him from the other side of the desk. It was not an invitation.

Mark and Francis sat down, and the commandant went back to his *dossier*. He was very black, with a smallish, slender head and almost delicate features. A northerner, no doubt about it, though Mark couldn't place him any more precisely than that.

Well, that made sense. Ahidjo was an expert at deploying *gendarmes* and soldiers to areas outside their native regions, which, for several reasons, minimized the risk of local uprisings.

He especially liked his own people in strategic posts, like along the Nigerian border.

The *commandant* ignored them for another five minutes, then put down his pen and closed the *dossier*. He sat back in his chair—a cheap, swivel kind the French made—and raised his eyebrows at Francis.

"Captain, this is Mr. Reilly, who I was telling you about." Francis' voice was the same, quiet and respectful, with no hint of fear.

"Hello," Mark said stupidly.

"*Votre passport*," the commandant ordered, looking at Mark for the first time.

Mark fumbled among the documents in his *portefeuille* until he found his passport. He handed it across the desk.

So they were going to speak French. The *commandant* was definitely a Francophone, but he had to speak English, probably pretty well, to work in that part of Cameroon.

From Francis' introduction, it was clear they spoke English when they were alone.

But he wasn't going to do it with an American.

The *commandant* took his time leafing through the pages of Mark's passport.

"*Vous voyagez beaucoup*," he said finally. It wasn't a question.

"*Oui, mon commandant*," Mark replied.

The African frowned, then flipped through the pages again,

faster this time. He was looking for something and wasn't too happy at not finding it.

"Vous travaillez pour une compagnie petroliere?" He asked, finally, falling back on what Francis had told him.

U.S. passports, almost unique in the world, did not list the carrier's occupation.

"J'en ai travaille pour une," Mark replied, correcting the tense as politely as he could. "I was fired a week ago."

"Les documents du cargaison," he ordered, holding out a hand.

Mark pulled the packet of customs papers out of his *portefeuille* and handed them over.

The *commandant* studied them for a long time, slowly turning the pages. Whether he was looking for something out of order or even knew what he was reading wasn't clear.

Finally, he put them down on his desk. He stared at Mark hard, not moving, for too long.

"La cle, s'il vous plait."

Mark had the key to the container in his shirt pocket and passed it over quickly. The *commandant* called out, and a second later, the young *gendarme* who had held the door entered and stood stiffly in front of the desk.

The *commandant* gave him the key and told him to inspect the contents of the container.

"Oui, mon capitaine," the young one said, saluting. He turned and left.

Francis had said that was likely; accepting a *dash* to turn a blind eye to some equipment was one thing. But anything else, guns, for example, which were always a hot commodity in Nigeria, would almost certainly be confiscated and the smugglers arrested.

The *commandant* tapped Mark's passport against the edge of his desk.

Why had Mark been fired, he asked after a moment.

"Une affaire personelle, mon comandant," Mark replied, knowing what Francis had said already.

But the gendarme wanted to hear it again from Mark.

Mark kept it as brief as he could. His boss, *un francais,* had taken an interest in one of the secretaries. She was a Cameroonian, whom Mark had helped get the job because he was a friend of her husband.

Mark tried to concentrate on Wanna and Therese while he spoke.

She told the Frenchman "no" repeatedly, but he wouldn't leave her alone, even implying she might lose her job unless she... agreed, Mark continued. She was afraid of what her husband might do, so she came to Mark in tears.

"I was furious, *mon commandant,* but I went and tried discreetly to convince the man to leave her alone," Mark explained. "He told me it was none of my business and to go to hell."

Mark looked across the desk. The African was staring at him, but it was impossible to read anything from his expression.

"I got angry and told the bastard I'd break his neck if he ever went near her again," Mark concluded. "He fired me the next day."

The commandant absorbed the story for at least a minute.

"Et le cargaison?" He asked.

Mark took a deep breath.

"C'est mon billet de retour, mon commandant; c'est tout," Mark said.

He had a return ticket guaranteed in his contract, but the Frenchman refused to give it to him. He'd even locked him out of his company apartment and had the houseboy toss his clothes out the window.

That might have been overdoing it, but he'd said it now; he couldn't take it back.

The *commandant* stared silently again.

"So you stole the container?"

Mark inclined his head; that didn't sound too good.

"It's not even worth half what he owes me," he said.

Pourquoi le vendre au Nigeria?" The African demanded.

"Because the company won't be able to trace it there," Mark said quickly. This part was easier.

The *commandant* began tapping the passport on the edge of the desk again.

"*Vous countez revenir au Cameroun*?" He wanted to know.

"Non, mon commandant," Mark assured him. *"Je partirai directement du Nigeria."*

That was important. There was no way the corrupt son of a bitch would do it if he thought Mark might get caught and talk about it later.

The *commandant* pursed his lips, still tapping the passport. Mark wished he'd stop.

"Attendez-nous en dehors," he said, finally, motioning slightly with his head toward the door.

Mark hadn't expected that and hesitated a moment.

"Wait outside," Francis said, a little urgently, thinking Mark hadn't understood.

Mark nodded and got to his feet. *"Merci, mon commandant,"* he said, bowing a little. The African stared but said nothing.

Outside, Mark blinked hard against the sudden light and fumbled to get his sunglasses out of his shirt pocket. When he had them on, he squinted in the direction of the truck. Rudolph was standing near the back now with another *gendarme*, not the young one who had taken the key. Both doors of the container were wide open.

The young one was no doubt inside. Well, that was OK; there was nothing to hide in there, and if they went ahead, they'd have to take it all out of the truck anyway. Mark didn't envy the assignment, though. The container had been closed up, in the sun most of the day. It had to be like an oven inside.

Mark walked the length of the narrow cement veranda that ringed the building. At one point, he could hear Francis and the *commandant* conversing but wasn't able to pick up the words.

At the end of the building facing the port, Mark stopped just inside the meager shade offered by the roof's overhang. Even there, he could feel the heat, like some malevolent presence waiting, with infinite patience.

The port was visible from that end of the *gendarmerie*; Mark could even smell the swampy dampness of the river. The *quai* was empty; the workers and the gendarme on duty no doubt slumped in the shade on the far side of the small warehouse or under a tree somewhere, sleeping or playing cards and waiting for the first faint breeze of the afternoon to summon them back to work.

Mark turned to walk back the other way, toward the *commandant's* office but stopped when he saw the young *gendarme* coming back from the truck. He had his red beret crumbled in one fist and swung his arms in front of him as if he needed a little extra effort to walk the 100 meters. When he got closer, Mark saw that his brown shirt was uniformly darker now, as if he'd taken a shower without bothering to undress.

Mark spun around back toward the port when the *gendarme* got to the bottom of the stairs. He heard him knock on the *commandant's* door and then enter. He was in the office less than a minute, then re-emerged and resumed his place on the chair near the door.

Mark turned partway around so his back wasn't to the *gendarme*, but he didn't look over. He watched Rudolph swing the big doors of the container closed again.

There was a muffled scrape of chairs behind the *commandant*'s door, and a moment later, Francis came out. He glanced at Mark and nodded toward the truck.

"What's the verdict?" He asked when they were too far from the building to be overheard.

"A hundred thousand," Francis said, looking straight ahead. "It would have been more, but he appreciated your gallantry."

He smiled for a second but kept his eyes on the truck. "He doesn't like the French."

That's what they'd counted on, but goddamn, 100,000 CFA was a lot of money just for someone to look the other way. Mark was going through the $5,000 fast, and he hadn't even started yet. $1,500 to Jonas, another $500 to the gendarme, and $300 he'd agreed to pay Francis for his help, and added costs in Nigeria.

That was a bargain, though.

"Does he want it now?"

Francis shook his head. "You can give it to me, and I'll see that he gets it." The quick smile again. "He comes to dinner at my house about once a month."

Mark laughed; not loud, just enough so Francis saw he understood, but it felt good. He hadn't had much to laugh about in a while.

It took Jonas' three workers about an hour to transfer the crates of equipment to the canoe. When they were almost finished, an older man appeared, and he and Jonas walked down the river bank and stood talking for 15 minutes.

When they came back, the old African nodded curtly to Francis, then climbed into the boat and began minutely checking the twin Evinrudes. He didn't even look at Mark. Francis walked back to the truck and had a few words with Rudolph. He would stash the container in Kumba until Mark got back to Douala; if anyone asked, Rudolph was to say someone dropped it off, empty, and contracted with Francis to take it back to Douala in two weeks.

Past that, he knew nothing and had never heard of Mark Reilly.

The old man started one of the giant outboard motors. It coughed once, then caught and built to a steady roar. Two of the three workmen hopped out, and the other moved to the bow of the canoe.

Jonas held out a hand to Mark. "Good luck, Mark," he yelled, the big smile back in place now.

"Thanks for everything, Jonas," Mark shouted, shaking hands.

Francis rejoined them and leaned close to Jonas to say something. Jonas smiled and nodded, then turned to one of the workmen on the bank and said something quickly.

The worker nodded and hurried up to the bank.

Francis and Mark climbed carefully into the canoe and sat down on the metal seat that ran the width of the boat up toward the bow. There was enough room for both of them, but they had to rest their feet on equipment crates.

Jonas' worker re-appeared from over the river bank carrying a case of Gold Harp. He handed it quickly to the African still in the canoe, who wedged it between two crates just in front of where Francis sat.

"It's a long trip," Francis smiled, leaning close to Mark's ear so he didn't have to shout over the motor's roar.

The worker who was going with them cast off the bow line and, with the help of the two others on the bank, shoved the canoe out into the river's channel.

Mark smiled tightly at Jonas and waved once; Jonas did the same. And then he was gone, disappearing with his two workers over the bank.

It was past 4:30 when the canoe slid by the main N'Kondo-Titi *quai*. Jonas' driver had the Evinrude at less than half-throttle, though there were no other boats on the river.

A palm oil barge, no doubt down from Ndian, was docked just downriver from the warehouse. Two muscular Africans, dressed only in grease-stained shorts, struggled to attach a thick rubber hose to the barge's reservoir in order to pump the oil to a tanker truck parked on the *quai.*

"Is that one of yours?" Mark asked, raising his voice because of the motor. Francis smiled and shook his head.

"One of the Gang of Four," he replied.

Mark grinned. That's what Simon had dubbed the four Bamileke distributors who, until Francis came along, had controlled the palm oil market for years.

The two Africans glanced over at the sound of the motor, perhaps staring for a moment longer than usual because of Mark. Then they went back to wrestling with the hose. Whites from Lobe made regular trips up to Ndian, of course, but they either took the Rio or the managing director's speedboat.

No one ever went by smuggler's canoe.

Two *gendarmes* lounging in the shade of a tree straightened and stared as the boat sped by, but it, too, was curiosity and surprise more than any inclination to act. They had no time for that anyway. Jonas' driver was already increasing the throttle, slowly but steadily, as they reached the limit of the port; once clear of it, he pushed it quickly all the way open.

Even loaded with the equipment and four men, the canoe surged through the muddy green water.

Mark leaned over toward Francis. "Does he ever run it with both motors?" He asked.

"Only if he has to," Francis said, smiling.

Mark stared at him for a second, then grinned, shaking his head. He hadn't thought about that. Even for a Nigerian patrol boat, twin Evinrude 100s had to be a tough catch. He turned quickly to look back at the port, but it was already gone, lost behind a curve in the river.

Suddenly, there was nothing but the river, no sounds but the hum of the Evinrude, no activity but the boat knifing up the middle of the mangrove swamp. The mud-green water reflected nothing, not the boat or even the raffia palms, whose leaves, heavy with humidity, hung over the water and sometimes into it.

Mangrove trees, their tangle of ungainly roots protruding above the water, seemed to be fighting each other for space along the river's edge, with the loser, or maybe the winner, moving out further into the channel. The smell was stronger now, too, without the distractions: a stench of sulfurous dampness and decay that Mark found almost intoxicating once he grew accustomed to it.

He closed his eyes and took a deep breath. The wind created by their speed felt wonderful against his sweat-soaked shirt; the sun was still hot, but the breeze and the constant canopy of shade in the swamp made it bearable.

And it was nice, damn nice, to be moving again.

Francis tapped Mark lightly on the arm, startling him. Mark smiled, a little embarrassed.

Francis had opened two beers; he handed one to Mark.

"Thanks," Mark shouted, clinking Francis' bottle lightly with his own and taking a long, grateful sip.

Given a choice, Mark always opted for a cold beer over a warm one, but there were times in Africa when drinking it warm seemed to fit so well with what he was doing that he could almost convince himself he preferred it that way.

With each successive swallow, the beer rinsed away more of the tension Mark had lived with since the Novotel. Was it only 24 hours ago?

Well, Africa did funny things to time. Stretched out the days, with its endless, debilitating heat, so that even a single merciful night seemed impossibly remote; then bunched months, even years together so quickly that half a lifetime in the place blurred into insignificance.

"Another?" Francis asked, bending toward him.

Mark glanced at his beer. He hadn't realized it was empty. He nodded, smiling. He was getting tired of shouting. Francis reached in for another beer. In the bow, the spotter was crouched low, peering straight ahead of them, eyes trained somewhere in the middle distance.

The tides washed all sorts of debris up into the creeks, and the heavy rains and fierce electrical storms often toppled whole trees into the river. Most of the trip would be in daylight, which made spotting hazards easier, but the last leg, into Nigerian waters, would be at night.

Francis handed Mark another Gold Harp. Mark smiled his thanks. Francis smiled back but then leaned closer, looking serious.

"You know, you can never go back to Lobe," he said, his voice just loud enough to be heard over the motor.

Mark took a sip of beer and nodded. He'd thought of that.

"Even Douala," Francis added uncertainly. "He took down your visa number."

Mark looked over sharply at Francis. He hadn't thought about that. The bastard might have done it just to look competent in front of Francis; he sure as hell wasn't going to report the incident to Yaounde.

But there were other than official ways to check on things in Cameroon, especially for a northerner.

Mark looked back at his beer and nodded. He'd have to think about it. He'd concentrated so hard on just getting to that point, to moving, even if it was on a boat, in the right direction, that he hadn't given much thought to what would happen afterward.

He took a long drink of warm beer. It didn't matter just now, anyway. Mark felt as relaxed as he had in days, maybe longer, though that sort of thing was hard to recall. He'd worry about it later.

Maybe it was time to leave Africa; maybe that was an omen. He'd have to fly back to Douala, or at least through it, but maybe he'd just keep going. To Europe, perhaps; he'd always liked it when they'd vacationed there.

Wouldn't that blow her mind? If he showed up in Paris and took an apartment. Maybe even started a small business. Hell, he'd have enough money.

Then it wouldn't matter anymore. He'd go by and sign the goddamn papers. Maybe they could even be friends again. Probably not, but it was hard to tell with that sort of thing.

Mark didn't hear the other boat until Litumbe, the driver, slowed the throttle on the Evinrude. The spotter rose up slightly in the bow, and Mark felt Francis stiffen on the seat next to him.

They slowed to less than half speed, and Litumbe veered the canoe as far in toward the bank as he dared. As they rounded a bend in the river, a Zodiak-style dingy, still moving fast in the opposite direction, passed within several feet of them. The driver, a young African who sat back near the motor with one arm draped nonchalantly over the control arm, obviously hadn't heard them coming.

Though it was no longer necessary, he jerked the small boat over to the far side of the channel and slowed its speed. Father Vorhees, who sat alone in the bow of the Zodiak on a small wooden seat stretched between the rubber pontoons, straightened when he spotted Mark.

It was the same look of startled disapproval he'd shown at the sudden immediacy of Deborah's cleavage. He no doubt knew the boat and its use.

"Vhere are you going?" He shouted urgently as the two boats crossed.

Mark turned in his seat. He cupped one hand over his ear and shook his head.

The old priest, looking anguished, yelled again, but Mark really didn't catch it this time. He shook his head, smiling, and pointed upriver. The Zodiak disappeared around the river bend. Mark heard the diminishing whine of its motor for a moment; then, it too was gone as Litumbe eased the Evinrude's throttle back up.

Mark glanced over at Francis, who smiled. He wasn't worried. There probably was no reason to be. Vorhees might tell Simon and Mary but would have no reason to say anything to anyone else.

As far as Mark knew, Kyle had never met Simon or Mary, so he wouldn't go looking for him in Lobe. Even if he got that far, Simon would probably tell him to sod off. Simon didn't like diplomats much. "Jumped up bloody twits," he called them.

Shortly before sunset, the river suddenly opened into a wider body of water, at least a kilometer wide and twice that long.

"Big Belly," Francis yelled over, smiling.

Mark looked over to see if he was kidding.

"Is that what it's called?"

"Probably not on any map, but that's what the people call it," Francis explained.

Litumbe cut at a diagonal northwest across what Mark realized was the confluence of several rivers. Near the far side of Big Belly, they turned north into another river slightly wider than the N'Kondo-Titi.

"The Ndian River," Francis said, leaning close to Mark's ear.

Mark nodded. He'd guessed that. He'd once planned to do a story on the creeks and spent time studying maps of the area. Though the swamps were sparsely populated and entirely undeveloped, they had brought Cameroon several times to the brink of war with Nigeria.

Neither country accepted the other's delimitation of the border in the creeks, with the result that armed patrols from both sides sometimes crossed paths in what each considered its territorial waters. The "incidents" had left a dozen or so men killed over the years and, on both sides, a residue of bitterness and hostility.

Mark had never done the story; he couldn't recall why not.

The sun was an orange glow behind the tangle of mangrove

trees that made up the western bank of the river when they came upon the first human they'd seen since passing the priest's boat.

In the twilight, Mark at first mistook the man for part of a tree, broken off at some unlikely angle, that was floating slowly down to the sea.

Litumbe cut the motor to not much more than an idle, and drifting closer, Mark realized it was a lone man, fishing from the crudest *piroque* he'd ever seen.

It was no more than six feet long, maybe less, and a foot across. Unlike the extensively excavated dugouts used by the coastal tribes or the *piroquiers* on the Chari up north, it was little more than a lightly scooped-out plank, whose gunwales, if they even deserved the name, hovered an inch or two above the water.

It seemed a pathetically precarious perch in a swamp known for its crocodiles and snakes, but the fisherman, seated near the rear with his thin legs extended in front of him so they rested on either edge of the boat, seemed not just at ease, but as if he and the canoe were parts of the same thing.

He was repeatedly casting out a small net, flinging it across his body in a graceful circular motion so it hit the water off to the side of the boat, then dragging it slowly back toward him. The river channel was narrow at that point, so Litumbe had to bring them close to the African's *piroque* to slip by. He cut their speed further still to avoid frightening the fish.

Other than the legitimate pygmies living near Kribi, in the south, he was the smallest African Mark had ever seen. Not just short, but so slightly built that he and the tiny boat seemed hardly to displace any water at all, like a raindrop on a leaf floating in a puddle.

The African glanced over at them as they passed, not with anything like interest or curiosity or even annoyance, but more just a reaction to the sound. Mark at first thought the man was smiling, but that was only the genetic set of his face, with the corners of the mouth turned permanently up and the tiny brow knit tightly, forming evenly spaced furrows on his forehead. Because of his size, he looked like a young boy, but up close, Mark could see lines under the man's eyes and a few swirls of white in the matted, wild hair.

Francis turned and said something to Litumbe, who grunted.

"There's a village just ahead; we can get out and stretch our legs," he said, turning to Mark.

Mark's eyes widened. "Really?" He asked.

Of course, the fisherman had to come from somewhere, but it seemed impossible there was a village anywhere around there. There was no land, for one thing, just the muddy water, turning black now in the gathering darkness, and the trees that grew straight out of the river, up from the dense web of exposed roots.

But it was there, just around a curve in the river: the most primitive, inhospitable habitat Mark had seen anywhere in Africa. "Village" wasn't the right word. There were only two huts, somehow built across the mangrove roots, in an area that couldn't have been 10 meters across. The swamp leaned in from all sides as if biding its time until it could reclaim the tiny clearing.

Litumbe cut the motor and let the canoe drift in until it bumped against the roots closest to the village. The spotter hopped from the bow and quickly tied the line securely to the nearest tree.

Holding onto the tree with one hand, he then helped Francis and Mark out of the canoe with the other. Mark hadn't been mistaken: they were standing on roots no more than six inches above the waterline. In some places, there was a kind of spotty, crude mudpack that gave the roots the semblance, though not the feel, of more solid ground.

It might have been the "villagers" who did the packing, or

maybe they just chose the site because, by some caprice of nature, the silt from the river settled there. The spotter was barefoot and moved easily over the roots, but Francis and Mark stepped cautiously, testing each root before committing themselves. The roots were damp and very slippery, and God only knew what was underneath them.

The mud, a sickening grayish-black goo, stank of swamp gas and rotting wood, and to Mark at least, appeared to be a perfect home for snakes. At one point, Mark balanced on two roots and turned carefully to look back at the river. Litumbe hadn't followed them. He sat unmoving in the stern of the boat, like a statue silhouetted against the darkening river.

There couldn't have been much danger to the boat there, but Litumbe worked for Jonas, and like Francis, Jonas only hired careful men. The spotter, going ahead of Francis and Mark, said something in the direction of the huts. A moment later, a young boy emerged from one. Like the fisherman, he was dressed only in what looked to Mark like a little boy's underpants.

A woman, holding an infant, appeared from the small opening in the other hut. Except for the breasts drooping flat and lifeless almost down to her waist, she was an almost perfect replica of the fisherman: the same birdlike smallness, same childlike features, betrayed by the age lines and graying hair.

If she recognized the spotter or Francis, she made no sign. She stared, like the fisherman (her husband?), not with distrust or curiosity, but the opposite; more like an instinctive indifference, as if noting the presence of another, common species doing what it always did.

The spotter said something to her. The woman turned to the boy, who darted back into his hut. The two structures were close together, with the entrances facing one another. They were as bush as anything Mark had seen anywhere, just a jumble of twigs and branches, no doubt pulled from the river, with palm fronds woven together for the rooves. Both huts had gaping holes in walls and rooves and couldn't have provided much shelter at any time, let alone when the heavy rains came.

The boy reappeared and handed something to the spotter. He, in turn, pulled two beers from inside his shirt and gave them to the woman. The woman and boy turned without a word and ducked back into their respective huts. The spotter handed Francis whatever the boy had given him, then led the way back to the canoe. Seated again, Francis handed Mark something. He held it up close to his face and saw it was an English tea biscuit.

"Sorry, it's all they had," Francis said, raising his voice as Litumbe started the motor and slowly pulled away from the roots.

Mark shook his head. "Don't be silly, Francis. This is great."

Normally, Mark hated them, but after almost 24 hours without eating, they tasted fine.

"Where do they get them?" He shouted. Litumbe increased the canoe's speed, but because of the darkness, he couldn't push the throttle all the way up now.

Francis leaned over toward Mark to make it easier to talk. "They trade for them with boats coming the other way," he explained.

Mark nodded. He'd seen the biscuits in markets in Nigeria. "What do they have to trade?" He asked, jerking a finger over his shoulder back toward the village.

Francis shrugged. "Mostly fish. Sometimes snake or monkey."

"Do they eat these things?" Mark asked, waving the biscuit in the darkness.

"I don't think so," Francis said, shaking his head. "I think they just use them to trade for beer with boats going to Nigeria."

"They like beer?" Mark asked, a little skeptical.

"Almost as much as you," Francis said, laughing hard for the first time since Mark had met him.

Mark smiled, then couldn't help laughing himself. From anyone else, that might have been an insult. Francis, still laughing, pulled half the biscuits from the package and handed most of those to Mark. He turned halfway in his seat and held the pack open for Litumbe, who, without taking his eyes off the river, pried several biscuits out.

Francis turned back toward the bow. He called to the spotter and carefully tossed him the rest of the package.

"Another beer, Mark?"

It was too dark to see Francis' face, but Mark knew he was grinning.

"Why not?" Mark shouted, smiling back in the darkness.

CHAPTER 42

"Damn."

Rieper didn't raise his voice, but it was the first time Kyle had seen him exhibit any kind of emotion since he'd arrived.

Not that Kyle blamed him; they'd been looking for three days and still didn't have a clue.

But Kyle wasn't sure if he was supposed to respond, and it made him uneasy.

"He's got to be hiding somewhere, Mort," he said finally. Rieper looked over from the map that was tacked to the wall of the consulate's vault room.

"Where do you think that might be, Kyle?"

Kyle glanced at the map to avoid Rieper's gaze. It was an extremely detailed one of Cameroon, but it hadn't helped, either. Kyle shrugged. He had managed to confirm that Reilly picked up the container on Sunday morning and crossed over the Wouri Bridge, but that was all.

None of his contacts in the police or *gendarmes* had seen it along the *route nationale* or anywhere else.

Kyle hadn't liked just entering Reilly's apartment with the

key they'd found in the envelope taped to the door, but Rieper was right; they had to check everything.

They'd found out nothing, though, except that Reilly lived like an animal, which Kyle considered more a confirmation than a revelation. The apartment smelled more like an African's place than an American's.

They went to see Wanna N'dele at the bank, but he denied knowing where Reilly was. He was lying; Kyle could always tell with Africans. But he couldn't prove it.

"He might be in trouble, Wanna; a lot of trouble," Kyle said, with what he thought was the right mix of ambivalence and menace.

"Then, I h-hope you f-find him," Wanna replied and walked away.

The ... woman at le Paradis either didn't recognize them or felt no shame if she did, but she hadn't seen Reilly either.

"Demandez a Koumba," she suggested.

"Where can we find her?" Rieper asked. He'd left the questioning until then to Kyle, but he was interested in Koumba. That was the name on the envelope.

The woman shrugged. "Try *le Cafe des Sports.*"

They did, two nights in a row, sipping mineral water for hours, trying not to take a deep breath amid the stench of urine and sweating Africans—and a few Frenchmen and Greeks who might as well have been, from the way they carried on.

Everyone seemed to know Koumba, but no one had seen her in weeks. One Greek, an oily, swaggering type with his shirt wide open and an African girl hanging around his neck, got belligerent when Kyle asked politely if he knew her.

His friends restrained the man, but not before he shouted something Kyle, thank God, didn't hear over the disco music and spat a yellowish wad in his direction.

Rieper turned back toward the map, shaking his head. Kyle

relaxed a little. He found it easier to deal with the man when he wasn't facing him.

"His friend N'dele is from around here, right?" Rieper asked, tapping the map at Bamenda.

"Yes, he is, Mort," Kyle replied.

"Do you know where, exactly?" He turned when Kyle didn't answer right away.

"No, I'm sorry; I don't," Kyle admitted. Good grief, how was he supposed to know every African's home village? "I can probably find out, though."

Rieper turned back toward the map without answering.

It was a waste of time, but Kyle would do it. Emmanuel, his driver, was from up there somewhere, and they all knew one another; he'd know N'dele's home village or know someone who did.

But it didn't matter. Kyle had checked and re-checked with the police and *gendarmes* all the way up to Bafoussam. On the chance they'd missed him, Rieper had Yaounde rent a plane and fly from Foumban to N'Gaoundere, though there was no way Reilly could have made it that far so soon.

No one had seen the container or Reilly anywhere.

Rieper traced a finger along the Victoria road, all the way up to Buea and around to Kumba.

"You're certain he would have had to pass through Buea if he went this way?"

Kyle nodded. They were repeating themselves now. "It's the only road, Mort, and the police were there from seven o'clock in the morning on Sunday."

Not only that, but the road didn't go anywhere near Chad. It ran out in Kumba, though there were a few dirt tracks up the Western mountains to Dschang and Mamfe.

Kyle, who was sitting at the radio desk, suddenly stood up and walked to the map.

"I don't think he went anywhere, Mort," he said, trying to

sound natural, though excitement always added timbre to his voice.

Rieper's eyebrows rose halfway up his forehead.

"I think he'd hiding right here," Kyle said, smacking the map at Bonaberi with two fingers. "On one of the side streets, or even at a villa of one of his African friends. Waiting for us to give up."

Kyle turned and stared at Rieper and couldn't keep himself entirely in check now.

"Wanna N'dele owns a villa in Bonaberi, Mort."

Rieper stared back for a moment.

"Maybe, Kyle," he said. "Why don't you go check?"

Kyle didn't understand for a second. "You mean right now?"

"Yes."

Kyle cleared his throat and stumbled back a step.

"Uh, all right, Mort," he said. "Uh..." he wanted to ask what Rieper planned to do but then didn't. Heck, maybe the old guy just wanted to rest. They'd been going pretty much nonstop for three days and nights.

"I'll come by the hotel if I find out anything," Kyle offered.

"Fine, Kyle," Rieper said, staring until Kyle had no choice but to go.

Rieper closed the vault door behind Kyle and then walked back to the map. He studied it for a moment longer, then walked to the desk and picked up the phone.

Reilly wasn't in Bonaberi or anywhere near it. He was on his way to Chad. Rieper didn't know how Reilly had managed it or even how he himself could be so sure, but he was. He just knew.

Like he knew Kyle Mason was a fool whose only hope of redemption was that he suspected the truth.

Imagine, though, thinking God could save him from it!

He knew it like he knew Kyle's wife, who suspected nothing, would sooner or later jump the track—sooner was his guess—and never find it again.

Like he knew, Reilly saw it all that afternoon at the hotel. That was a mistake, and Rieper didn't make many. He'd been concentrating on Richards, confirming what he already knew, and that was foolish. Still, Reilly surprised him. He'd thought he had time, though, at least another day, but that was overconfidence, pride really, and Rieper had had trouble with that in the past.

Under other circumstances, he would have been interested to hear how Reilly vanished with an entire truck. But no one paid Rieper for explanations. Even thorough ones exposed only part of the truth, anyway, and in the end, they made no difference at all.

Rieper dialed an overseas number that few people knew. No one would answer—it was the middle of the night on the East Coast—but he would leave a message. That was a formality, anyway; they always did what he suggested. That's why they paid him and sent him over: to tell them what to do.

Rieper kept the message brief, then hung up, sat down at the radio, and flipped on the power switch. He didn't need to look in the book; he knew the frequency by heart.

CHAPTER 43

The Frenchman swatted futilely at the flies around his face and exposed arms. There were swarms of them now, thanks to the gathering humidity.

The worst part was that they were no guarantee of rain. For some years, the mugginess built until it hung like an invisible weight that everyone carried, day and night.

It could last for months until clothes and sheets—and humans—stank from the mildew and sweat that never dried. And still no rain fell.

Then, suddenly, it was the dry season again.

The thin gray clouds did nothing to ease the heat, either; in some ways, they seemed even to amplify it.

The Frenchman walked down the line of *pirogues* and climbed into one that was pulled up far enough onto the river bank that he wouldn't get his shoes wet. There was no one in it, but after a moment, an African sitting up the bank with several other *piroguiers* stood up and walked slowly down to the canoe.

The Frenchman lit his pipe as he watched the African approach.

"Alors, on y va aujourd'hui, chef?" He asked impatiently. Did

they ever move fast for anything?

The Chadian studied him from the bank without getting in the canoe.

"Cent cinquante," he said.

"C'est cent francs, le prix," the Frenchman said, shaking his head angrily, the pipe clamped between his teeth.

He didn't give a damn about 50 CFA; it was only one French franc. But you had to draw the line, or there'd be no end to their exploitation.

"Cent cinquante," the Chadian repeated, louder this time.

"You're a thief," the Frenchman said, furious.

The African didn't move. *"Allons-y,"* the Frenchman hissed, turning from the piroguier and looking out at the river.

The *piroguier* spat onto the sand, then pushed the boat off the bank and jumped in.

"Salaud," the Frenchman muttered, glancing back at the Chadian.

The *piroguier,* who might or might not have heard him, stared back impassively but said nothing.

Twenty-five years earlier, a Frenchman would have set the price, any price, and the African would have been glad to get it. But that's what happens when a country loses its nerve. The Frenchman held a hand up to shield his face. He'd been too damn angry when he left and forgot his hat. It was only nine o'clock in the morning, but already the sun was searing the soft skin on his cheeks and arms.

It was the one thing he admired about the Americans: they weren't afraid to use force, and they didn't give a damn what anyone else thought about it.

The Frenchman took the pipe out of his mouth to give his jaw a rest. The Americans, of course, did it more out of stupidity than resolve. They were almost savage in their ignorance, not much better than the Africans on that score.

A bloodthirsty bunch, too. Not that he minded a show of

muscle from time to time—that's what the handwringing *pedes* in Paris didn't understand—but he derived no particular pleasure from the actual violence.

For the Americans, it was almost a need.

"Where is he?"

"Qui ca?" The Frenchman asked. He'd have to give them Calvady, but he'd be damned if he was going to do it in English.

"You know damned well who I mean," Feraldi snarled. "Your Libyan dollar changer."

The Frenchman smiled and waited until Emil served the beers and left before answering. Even with a table between them, the American smelled of whiskey and Marlboros.

"Aucune idee, cher allie," The Frenchman said. "Since you showed no interest the last time..."

"Look, I don't have time for your bullshit," Feraldi cut in. He leaned across the table slightly.

"I know you've been told to give me what I want, so stop jerking me off, or I'll take that pipe of yours and shove it up your ass."

The Frenchman smiled to hide the blood rushing into his face. He pulled harder than usual on the pipe.

"Pourquoi le voulez-vous?" He asked, happy at the control in his voice. As he spoke, smoke puffed out of his mouth and drifted across the table.

"You know damn well why we want him." Feraldi's lips moved, but his teeth were clamped shut.

"Ah, bon?" The Frenchman asked, eyes wide as if that were news to him.

"Fuck you, " Feraldi hissed, leaning further over the table toward the Frenchman. "I'll give you until tomorrow night; then, I file a formal protest with Paris."

The American bumped the table when he threw his chair back, hard enough that the Frenchman had to lunge to keep his Gala bottle from toppling over.

The *quai* on the Chad side was busy. The *pirogues* were lined several deep against the bank. A small army of men and boys, most dressed only in filthy shorts, hurried to unload sacks of millet and flour and the foul-smelling dried fish *onto pousses-pousses* that still other men and boys struggled to push up the sandy slope.

When the pirogue had squeezed between two others, the Frenchman stood quickly and stepped out. He dug into his pocket for the two coins and tossed them back toward the *piroguier*, who was walking forward, hand outstretched.

The Chadian caught the fifty CFA piece, but the other coin dropped into the shallow brown puddle of water at the bottom of the canoe.

The Frenchman shrugged. *"Desole, chef,"* he said, making it clear whose fault that was. The Chadian yelled something after him, but the Frenchman was halfway up the slope by then and not listening anyway.

It had taken less than 24 hours to find Calvady. The AFP correspondent confirmed he crossed over from Chad three days earlier, and there were few places a man like that could go in Cameroon.

A discreet inquiry in the French communities of Maroua and Garoua, and they had him.

The Frenchman wouldn't lose any sleep over it. Calvady's kind was, aside from the communists, the worst France had to offer; half-African, almost.

Even after they'd looked the other way, let him keep his filthy "profits," he couldn't give it up.

God knows, the Frenchman had tried to knock some sense into him, but with some people, even that didn't do any good.

Still, Calvady was French by birth, if nothing else, and that grated a little.

At the top of the hill, taxi drivers assailed him, but he ignored them and walked over to the car waiting for him. The driver hopped out when he spotted the Frenchman and held open the back door of the aging black Citroen DS.

"Bonjour, monsieur."

"Ca va, chef?" The Frenchman asked, smiling as he climbed in the back seat.

"Ca va, monsieur." He didn't return the smile, but then Chadians didn't smile much anyway. Certainly not at Frenchmen.

The driver closed the door and got back behind the wheel. When he started the car, the Citroen's air conditioning was already on; the Frenchman felt a welcome rush of cool air and settled back into the soft seats. The hydraulic suspension Citroen had pioneered lifted the body of the car as they pulled out.

It was a short ride, but the Frenchman enjoyed it anyway. The DS was the best damn thing France ever produced; it was a privilege to ride in one, even for a kilometer or two.

He was there just to talk, as he had been the week before. Nothing was settled. Yet. The Chadians were still angry, and besides, there was no hurry now. In the end, there'd be some meaningless concessions, arms probably, and development aid, but those were just the details.

The Libyans were already finished; it was really just a question of how and when they left.

The Frenchman relit his pipe.

In some ways, the Americans and Libyans had a lot in common. Both had more money than brains, and neither understood why nobody else could stand them. The Frenchman laughed suddenly, loud enough that the driver glanced in the rearview mirror.

Yes, yes. Just like the Libyans. Maybe he and Feraldi could discuss it the next time they got together. He laughed again, biting down on the pipe to keep from dropping it.

CHAPTER 44

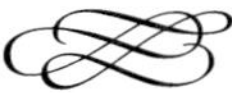

Through a coincidence of geology and colonial accident, Cameroon and Nigeria enjoyed, for most of their 1,500-kilometer common border, an almost unbroken line of natural barriers as well. The swamps in the extreme southwest gave way to the all but impenetrable rain forest; then came successive mountain ranges up through the highlands of Cameroon's West and Northwest provinces, followed by the massive Adamaoua Plateau that marked the beginning of the Muslim North.

From Garoua, the capital of the Northern province, the Mandara Mountains, an inhospitable, arid range of steep, jagged peaks, guarded Cameroon's western flank for another 150 kilometers. But the Mandaras ran out near Mora, 75 kilometers past Maroua, Cameroon's northernmost city.

The terrain leveled out quickly after that, and with one exception, the last 200 kilometers to the Chadian border were as flat as the surface of Lake Chad, which, thousands of years ago, extended that far south. The one exception was Waza, a tiny village 60 kilometers north of Mora, where an isolated pile of overlapping boulders provided the last elevation of any consequence in Cameroon.

Compared to the Mandaras, or even the towering dykes that had made the village of Roumsiki such a tourist attraction—and its children relentless beggars—Waza was unremarkable. The boulders rose no more than a hundred feet and, from a distance at least, looked like so many blocks left behind by whoever built the mountains farther south. But the rocks at Waza, thanks to their isolation, commanded an unimpeded, even impressive view of the surrounding flatlands.

And it was upon those rocks that Cameroon chose to build the *campement* for the Waza Game Park.

Like the park itself, the *campement* was modest by the standards of more famous game preserves in East Africa. Owing to the limited space on the boulders, there were only a dozen huts, plus a large, open-air restaurant.

The huts, built to resemble those of the nearby villages, were neat, one-room structures with cylindrical bases and peaked rooves of layered savannah grass, which sat like straw hats on top of the bricks.

The Waza huts, of course, were better built than the local ones: the bricks were made from cement rather than mud, and the grass rooves were overlaid onto cut lumber and attached with baling wire rather than the acacia branches and twined strips of bark the villagers used. The *campement* huts were also painted a dazzling white for aesthetic reasons and to keep them cooler.

They had cement floors, not dirt, and all had toilets and cold-water showers. But beyond that, there were few luxuries.

Services like hot water and electricity were extremely expensive and unreliable that far north. And Maroua, arguably Cameroon's prettiest and most agreeable city, was an easy hour's drive south. It had two four-star hotels, so tourists not interested in roughing it could still see Waza by day and eat and sleep in comfort in Maroua at night.

Over the years, however, an increasing number of people,

both Europeans on vacation and expatriates from Douala and Yaounde, preferred to stay at Waza, the hardships notwithstanding. Many of them found "commuting" to the game park tiresome and artificial, and there was a sense of satisfaction, exhilaration even, in living like Africans for a few days.

In fact, reservations at the *campement* during the peak season, from November through April, had to be made months in advance; there was always more demand than space.

The chances of seeing the park's wildlife—hippos, giraffes, a wide variety of antelopes, wild boar, and several prides of lion—increased as the dry season wore on and forced the animals to fewer and fewer watering holes. The best time of day to see them was early morning. For that reason, most visitors woke early, before dawn, and had a simple breakfast of Nescafe and *tartines* before heading off into the park.

For many, the mornings in Waza remained the trip's most potent memory: sipping coffee at the restaurant, a long, narrow terrace on the northeast edge of the rocks, from where the view was the most impressive, as the first yellow-white rays of sun crept over the horizon and spilled westward, eventually hitting the base of the boulders and climbing to the terrace.

The park's landscape was not, at least in any classical sense, beautiful. By the middle of the dry season, the savannah grass died off, leaving only the stunted acacias or knarled, shadeless thorn trees to break the monotony of the dusty plain.

But looking out from the terrace at dawn, before the sun made looking at anything for long painful before the horizon blurred into the shimmering heat, the vastness, even its monotony and what that implied, made the most cynical of diplomats glad he had come, not just to Waza, or Cameroon, but to Africa.

Jean-Phillipe Calvady didn't give a shit about the view, even that early in the morning, except that elevated as the terrace was, he could see a kilometer or more of the *route nationale* in each direction.

He sat alone at the table closest to the edge of the rocks, where he had a clear view of the dirt road that linked the *campement* to the highway. Calvady needlessly checked his watch. He knew what time it was, and he knew the date. Ten days since Reilly should have left Douala, four since he'd arrived in Waza. Even with trouble *en route*, Reilly was due.

If the bastard was still coming.

Calvady would give him one more day, then forget it. The money would be nice, but he didn't need it, and sitting there day after day was making him nervous.

An African, carrying a tray of coffee and bread, walked over from the small building that housed the kitchen.

"Ou est ton patron?" Calvady demanded.

"Il devait aller a Maroua, monsieur," the waiter replied.

"Il rentre aujourd'hui?"

"Je ne sais pas, monsieur." The African hesitated a moment, but when Calvady said nothing more, he left.

Calvady poured himself some coffee. The *campement* manager, Debache, was an *ancien,* and like Calvady, a Corsican, they'd gotten along. It was out of season, and the place was empty, so Debache had had time to sit and talk, mostly about the old days when a Frenchman could go where he pleased in Africa without worrying about a visa.

It had passed the time for both of them.

Calvady ripped off an enormous piece of *tartine* with his back teeth. It was going to be a long day if Reilly didn't show up. Debache hadn't mentioned he was going to Maroua the night before, and they'd talked and drank until midnight; well, Calvady hadn't said what he was doing there either.

He drank some of the ink-black coffee and sat up straighter in the chair. What the hell was the matter with him anyway?

In the early days, he'd spent weeks at a time alone on the

N'djamena-Abeche run when he didn't see a soul, not even an African; sometimes holed up in his truck for a day or more, the windows shut so tightly he could hardly breathe while a sandstorm raged outside.

He could make it one more day in Waza, but whether Reilly showed or not, it was his last. Calvady had plenty of money. If the bastards let him keep it. But they would; he'd done everything they wanted, and if he decided to talk, say to journalists in Paris, well, he had plenty to tell.

Still, the Libyans would pay a fortune for the spare parts. If he pulled it off, he'd never have to worry about money again.

Reilly might fight it, probably would, but what could he do about it? The Libyans had changed their minds; they wouldn't pay until it was delivered to N'djamena. Calvady had tried, but they were adamant. Reilly could accompany him, or he could eat the pump barrels there in Cameroon. He'd come, of course.

Haloud could do what he wanted with the American, and Calvady would fly out through Tripoli one more time. It had come to him that day in the marina, just like that. The plan seemed flawless; all the risks were the Americans'.

He hadn't counted on the wait there, on the rocks at Waza. He had never liked Cameroon, never felt at home there like he did in Chad. One more day, and if Reilly didn't show, then the hell with him.

"Vous permettez?"

"Uh?" Calvady almost shouted, turning around in his seat. He'd been watching the highway and the entry road and hadn't heard the old man approach.

"Oh, excuse-moi," the man exclaimed, clearly embarrassed.

"De rien, de rien," Calvady assured him, fighting to keep the annoyance out of his voice. *"Asseyez-vous, je vous en prie, monsieur."*

He'd forgotten the diplomat—some kind of UN nonsense—and his father, who'd arrived late the night before. Debache had invited them to have a drink. That was more than Calvady would have done, but Debache had responsibilities, and there were no other guests at the *campement.*

The father and son, English by their accents, had declined, and he and Debache were both grateful for that. Calvady didn't like foreigners and generally had nothing to do with them. In the end, they all wanted something, and It was better to steer clear of them.

The old man sat down across from him and smiled, obviously still a little uncomfortable.

"Where is your son?" Calvady asked, not caring in the least.

"Uh, he's taking a shower," the Englishman said carefully as if reciting it from a phrase book.

The waiter appeared, and in the same hesitant but correct French, the old man ordered coffee and bread for two. When the waiter had gone, the Englishman smiled again and waved a hand out toward the horizon. *"C'est joli."*

"Oui, oui," Calvady agreed, not bothering to look. He was stuck, at least for breakfast.

"Is this your first visit to Africa, *monsieur...?"*

"Rieper, but please, call me Mort," the old man replied.

Calvady smiled, then couldn't help laughing. The old guy's French wasn't too bad, but he didn't get the joke.

"Bon, d'accord, Mort," he said, bearing down a little on the name and laughing again. *"C'est votre premiere fois en Afrique?"*

The old man started to reply when the son showed up, his hair still wet from the shower. He was tall like the father but otherwise didn't look much like him.

Calvady shook hands without getting up. The son spoke better French than the father, though he too had the slow, self-conscious cadence of a language school student. The old man poured his son some coffee and smiled across the table at him. The younger one thanked him automatically but didn't look up from the table.

It was the old man who did most of the talking. It was his first trip to Africa, his first time out of Canada.

So they were Canadian.

He hadn't seen his son, who'd traveled all over the world with the UN, in years, and being an avid photographer, he decided to come over when the son suggested a trip to Waza.

Calvady half-listened, nodding and smiling occasionally. Anywhere else, he would have gulped down his coffee and excused himself. But he'd spent four- days alone, and he was tired of it. They had a rental van from the Novotel in Maroua and were heading out to the northeast corner of the park after breakfast. Some friends of his son, embassy people in Yaounde, had seen a pride of lion there in mid-April.

"*C'est vrai?*" Calvady asked the son, not caring.

The young man looked up, startled, then across at the father, who said something quietly in English.

"*Ah oui, c'est vrai,*" the son confirmed.

"Would you like to join us?" Rieper asked, but Calvady waved a hand and shook his head.

"*No, merci*. I'm expecting someone," the Frenchman said.

Rieper nodded but, after a bite of tartine, repeated the invitation. They were only going for a few hours and would be back before lunch. At his age, he smiled; he could only stand the heat for a few hours. Even that was going to be rough, given the man's complexion. It was a kind of deathly white, like powder, almost. The son was darker, so he'd be all right, but the old man, even if he stayed in the car, would have to be damn careful.

It was none of Calvady's business, though, so he said nothing.

"You could leave a message with the African, and we'll be back before lunch," the old man suggested.

"Best time of year to see lions," the son said, hurrying his French so that he almost stuttered.

Calvady smiled. They were nervous, maybe even a little

frightened, going off on their own; Africa did that to people. He'd seen it before.

"D'accord, Mort," he said, laughing again at the name. *"Je viens."*

As long it was only a few hours, it wouldn't matter; he'd instruct the waiter to tell Reilly to wait. Calvady had a feeling that if the American showed at all, he'd come at night, but if not, he could wait a few hours.

Calvady had waited four days, and he was tired of it. He walked over to the kitchen and gave the African the message and 500 CFA to make sure he remembered it.

"Have you ever seen a lion?" The old guy asked as the three of them descended the stone steps to the parking *area* at the base of the campement.

"Never, Mort," Calvady smiled. He loved that name. Forty years in Africa, and the wildest thing he'd ever seen was a camel. He'd never given a shit about animals; he still didn't.

The son climbed into the driver's side of the van. The old man insisted Calvady take the front passenger seat to see better. It would be easier to take photographs from the back seat, near the sliding door, anyway, he said.

The son gunned the engine, then turned the van around and headed it down the dirt road toward the highway. They crossed over the *route nationale,* found a set of worn tire tracks that headed northeast, and followed them.

The old man, clearly excited, sat directly behind Calvady but leaned forward constantly to point out something or to catch what Calvady was saying.

Calvady glanced back out the rear window once, but the *campement* was already gone, hidden by the brown cloud of dust kicked up by the van. He smiled at the old man, who smiled back; then he turned back around and watched for animals.

CHAPTER 45

Mark couldn't remember the name of the village, but it didn't matter. It was the closest one to Waza, probably no more than five kilometers north. More importantly, though it was only a hundred meters from Cameroon's *route nationale,* the village was in Nigeria.

Not that the border meant much that far north. There was nothing, natural or otherwise, marking it, and no one on either side paid much attention to it. The northernmost part of Cameroon was only 50 kilometers across at its widest; for much of its last 100 kilometers, the national highway ran almost on top of the Nigerian border.

Mark had no illusions that an unmarked line in the sand gave him much protection, certainly not from the people trying to find him. But Cameroonian authorities took pains to avoid giving the Nigerians any reason at all to bring up the question of the border, so at least he was safe from the prying eyes of gendarmes.

It probably wasn't much, but there was no way of telling whom Kyle and his "friend" had working for them.

Mark sat up halfway and shielded his eyes with a hand. The

sun, hidden behind a thin, white cloud, was still hot, but the worst was over. It was already halfway down in the western sky.

It would be getting dark in another two hours. He'd wait until then to leave for Waza.

He wasn't looking forward to the walk; he was tired and hungry, and he'd had diarrhea for the past two days. The bad kind, what they'd called "explosive diarrhea" in the Peace Corps, when even a small sip of water provoked cramps and then a sudden, uncontrollable need to squat, anywhere, to let the mustard-colored liquid, with the solidity of piss, shoot and sputter out of his ass.

The Lomotil that he'd brought with him, which usually worked wonders on even bad diarrhea, hadn't done anything so far.

Mark lay back down on the straw mat. Even in the shade under the truck, it was too hot to sleep. But at least they weren't moving anymore. He rolled his head sideways and glanced over at Tunji, Francis' driver, who lay on his back on another mat, up toward the front of the truck.

Tunji's short, thick arms were folded tightly across his chest, and his eyes, wide open, stared resentfully up into the truck's underbody. He hadn't moved in hours. That was fine with Mark. The Ibo son of a bitch could turn to stone under there for all he cared.

Things had started out well. They made it into Nigeria without running into any river patrols. Sometime around three o'clock in the morning, in total darkness, Litumbe cut the motor and let the canoe drift into an isolated spot on the western bank of the Akpa Yafe River.

The spotter hopped out from the bow to secure the boat. Almost immediately, two Africans, both dressed only in shorts, appeared from somewhere on the other side of the bank and began unloading the oil equipment.

Litumbe never moved from the back of the boat, and the

spotter stood ready to cast off at any sign of trouble. Mark followed Francis ashore. From the river, the bank had looked like a solid black wall of vegetation, but just past a line of bamboo, there was a small clearing.

Another African was waiting there. Francis conferred quietly with him for several minutes in a language Mark couldn't identify. The man said little but nodded so often while Francis spoke that Mark thought for a moment he was suffering from a nervous disorder.

All the while, the other two Africans hurried by with the equipment crates, disappearing into the blackness beyond the clearing and then returning a moment later.

"Mark, this is Tunji, your driver," Francis said, his voice very low.

"Hello, Tunji," Mark whispered.

"Hello, suh." He had a deep, rough voice that suited him well.

"That's about all the English he knows," Francis said. "He can understand a little if you speak slowly, but he doesn't speak it."

"No problem," Mark lied.

Tunji led the way back in the direction the porters had disappeared. There was a short path through dense foliage that brushed against Mark's face and arms, then another, larger clearing.

Halfway across it, Mark could make out the black outline of a truck. As they got closer, he saw that the back doors were open, and the two porters were loading the equipment onto it.

Tunji and Francis walked around to the front of the truck, talking, and Mark followed. From the other side of the clearing, the jungle surrounding them appeared impenetrable, but as he got closer, Mark could see a narrow opening between the trees closest to the truck.

In the dark, it didn't look wide enough for a small car to pass through.

Francis, apparently finished with Tunji, walked over.

"Does he mind going that far?" Mark asked.

"More money for him; he's happy," Francis replied.

Mark laughed quietly. It was a stupid question. If the man worked for Francis, he'd go where he was told. One of the porters leaped down from the back of the truck and said something quietly to Francis. Tunji, who had walked back to supervise the loading, quickly closed and bolted the truck doors.

"Ready to go, Mark," Francis said.

Mark felt the wrench at the bottom of his stomach and took a deep breath. His fingers shook, but not too badly, as he unzipped the portefeuille.

"That was sixty thousand, right Francis?" He asked.

Francis said something softly to Tunji, who nodded and disappeared into the darkness near the front of the truck. Mark heard the driver's door open long enough for him to climb in, then shut quietly.

"Pay me when you get back, Mark," Francis said.

Mark had to wait a second before he could speak.

"I've got it, Francis. It's no problem to pay you now."

"You may need it. I can wait."

"Are you sure?" It was a stupid question. Francis could wait forever for $300.

"I'm sure." Francis might have been smiling; Mark sensed that he was, but in the dark, even that close, it was impossible to tell.

"Thanks, Francis," Mark said, holding his trembling hand in front of him.

Francis found Mark's hand without groping. His grip was the same as always: firm and dry and cool.

"Good luck, Mark."

"Thanks," Mark said.

He wanted to say more; that was all that came out. And then Francis was moving back toward the river.

"I'll get the money to you as soon as I get back," Mark called louder than was safe. Francis, who knew better, said nothing and kept walking until Mark lost sight of him in the blackness on the far side of the clearing.

From the start, Mark counted on two things, without which his plan was inconceivable.

The first was Nigeria's roads. They were the best in West Africa, maybe in all of black Africa. Traveling on paved highways, even if it meant going 600 kilometers out of the way, would take no more time, maybe even less, than the more direct Cameroon route.

The second was Nigeria's switch from military rule to democracy a year earlier.

The dreaded and ubiquitous roadblocks were gone, and the soldiers had returned to the barracks. There were still police checks, but Tunji had proper documentation for himself and the truck and a standard set of forged papers for the cargo.

Mark had any number of legal Nigerian immigration stamps in his passport from previous visits, and most of the entry dates were illegible.

So they'd only be in trouble if someone looked closely at what they were carrying since the cargo did not match the papers Tunji carried.

But no one looked, closely or otherwise.

From the clearing, Tunji took bush roads to Calabar, where they stopped just before dawn to convert half of Mark's CFA into naira in the ancient city's black market.

A better but still unpaved road took them to Aba, just north of Port Harcourt, the center of Nigeria's oil industry. There, they picked up one of the country's major highways and headed north to Enugu, the capital of Iboland, and, Tunji explained, mostly with hand signs, his hometown.

From there, they climbed the south side of the massive Jos

Plateau, where the road turned northeast, 600 kilometers to Maiduguri, the last Nigerian city before the Chadian border.

Most of the major cities had police checks on one side or the other, but none posed any problem. Tunji's papers looked in order, and given the enormous expatriate population living and working all over Nigeria, Mark's presence in the truck wasn't unusual. The police, deprived of their army backing, seemed not only polite but a little uncertain of their authority, which no doubt was just fine with the average Nigerian.

Tunji was a good driver, confident and economical but careful, too. He rarely took his eyes off the road, even on the long, flat stretches where the pavement was good. And he treated the truck, a well-traveled Volvo ten-tonner, with a respect that bordered on reverence.

Tunji checked the oil, water, belts, and battery fluid every morning before getting underway; at night, he inspected the tires for gashes or heat cracks. If they stopped after dark, he did it with a flashlight.

Like Litumbe and the boat, Tunji never let the truck out of his sight. Crime, especially robbery, was a big problem in Nigeria, even in the smaller towns. A loaded Volvo truck was a tempting target.

Often, they simply ate while they drove, bread or fruit if they could find it, or British biscuits as a last resort. Tunji slept on a straw mat under the truck, a cheap wool blanket over him, and the truck's enormous lug wrench right next to him. Mark slept in the cab, stretched across the two seats, or when that became unbearable, sitting up, his head slumped against the window, with the overnight bag as a pillow.

Tunji's lack of English spared them both the need to talk, which suited Mark fine. When they had to communicate, they managed either through hand signs or a combination of slow English and rudimentary pidgin.

Once, near Enugu, Tunji had tapped his chest and said,

"Soldier," smiling. Mark assumed he meant he had been in the Nigerian Army, but Tunji frowned and shook his head emphatically. "Biafra," he said, almost shouting.

Nigerians, at least around Lagos, didn't talk about the war much anymore, but they were mostly Yorubas and Hausas, and they'd won. During their first year in Douala, Mark and Deborah got friendly with a British woman whose husband worked at the Guiness brewery. She had been raised in northern Nigeria, where her father was some kind of missionary.

She was only a little girl when the war broke out, so all she remembered, she said, was driving in their car and seeing the bodies of the massacred Ibos, stacked like cordwood, in neat piles along the side of the road.

Mark had been right about the roads. They reached Bukuru, on the Jos Plateau, in only four days. They made Bauchi, on the north side of the Plateau, by day five; from there, it was a straight shot, 500 kilometers across the savannah to Maiduguri. It would take a day, at least, from Maiduguri to Waza; the roads beyond Maiduguri weren't paved, and close to the border, they'd have to find their way on the bush tracks.

Even so, with a little luck, they could do it in three days. That would put him in Waza on the same day as Calvady. He might even have to wait for the bastard. But plans, like promises in Africa, were easier to make than to keep. Crossing the Gongola River on the second day out of Bukuru, the truck began to overheat. Tunji pulled it off the road in the shade of a small acacia tree.

A hissing cloud of steam exploded out of the radiator when Tunji, muttering to himself in what Mark assumed was Ibo, removed the cap. Mark sat under the tree while Tunji stood on the front bumper and leaned under the hood. Finally, Tunji, looking worried, came and sat next to him and made it clear that they had to let it cool down.

An hour later, Tunji filled the radiator with water from a ten-gallon jerry can that was hooked to the side of the truck near the driver's door. Tunji pulled out slowly and kept the speed down for about 20 minutes, long enough for Mark to be certain that water was all it had needed; then the motor began to overheat again.

For the next four hours, Tunji stripped down to his shorts, sweated over the hot engine, looking for the problem. Mark knew almost nothing about motors but leaned in under the hood as long as he could stand it on the off chance he could help.

After an hour of the midday sun on his back and the engine heat in his face, he climbed down, dizzy and slightly nauseous and sweating so heavily that his pants legs were soaked through. He grabbed a straw mat from the cab, crawled under the truck, and fell asleep.

There was a breeze blowing when Tunji shook him gently awake, waving an engine part in his other hand. Mark understood nothing but "thermostat," but that was enough. Like most African truckers, Tunji carried a number of spare parts, but a thermostat wasn't one of them.

An hour later, Tunji managed to flag down a bush taxi headed south back to Bauchi. Mark watched the taxi until it was a speck on the horizon, then pulled the mat from under the truck and put it near the front tire, on the side of the truck, away from the road.

He sat with his back against the giant tire and stared out at the flat, arid expanse where nothing moved but the shadows of the shadeless thorn trees as the sun slipped toward darkness on the other side of the truck. There were no villages in sight or animals, not even any birds; no sounds either, except the hot wind and, once in a while, a taxi going by too fast.

Mark had no food, not even biscuits, but there was plenty of water in the jerry can. It was warm, hot really, after all day in the sun, but that was all right. Everything in Africa was hot: the food, the beer, the days. It was just a question of getting used to it.

Tunji had tried to tell him something before he left, but Mark didn't catch any of it. He may have been guessing how long he'd be gone or just trying to reassure a white man left alone in the middle of nowhere. It didn't matter. Tunji worked for Francis, so he'd be back as quickly as he could.

And being alone was a lot like drinking warm beer: something Mark had become so accustomed to that, at times, it could seem preferable.

Just before sunset, he retrieved his portefeuille from the truck. He pulled out what was left of his money and counted it, putting CFA in one pile and naira in another.

It was going faster than he'd planned, but thanks to the money he hadn't paid Francis, he'd be all right, even if Tunji had to spend everything Mark gave him. The piles were small enough that he could stuff them in his pockets, so he did, the CFA in one and the naira in the other. It was safer there, anyway.

Mark was asleep when Tunji got back, but the car door slamming woke him. He sat up and watched the taillights, flickering like hot coals in the darkness, disappear in the direction of Maiduguri.

He looked at his watch, but it was too dark to see the time. It was late, though.

Tunji did not open the cab, probably not wanting to wake Mark. Mark heard him pick up the mat Mark had left outside and crawl under the truck. Mark reached for the blanket Tunji kept behind the seat. He pulled it out and climbed down from the cab.

"Tunji?"

"Yes, suh?"

"Here's your blanket," Mark said, swinging it in the dark

until it hit him. Tunji said something in Ibo that Mark took to be "thank you."

"Did you get the part?"

"Uh?"

"The thermostat," Mark said very slowly.

"OK, OK," Tunji said quickly, using up the rest of his English.

Mark climbed back in the truck and went to sleep.

It took Tunji most of the morning to install the "new" thermostat, which, in fact, wasn't new or even a standard Volvo part. It was from an older Mercedes model that a repair shop in Bauchi had cannibalized for parts.

At least, that was Mark's understanding of what Tunji said.

The "new" thermostat worked, but only after twice overheating, necessitating long stops to allow the engine to cool and Tunji to tinker with the ill-fitting part. After the second stop, Tunji kept the truck under 30 miles per hour, and they had no more trouble.

But it took three days just to make Maiduguri. And they still had to find their way to the border. It was almost dark when they reached the outskirts of the city, which was probably why Tunji didn't see the soldiers until they stepped into the truck's headlights.

He hissed angrily and stomped hard on the brakes so that the truck shuddered, then skidded slightly in the sand as he pulled it off the road. Tunji was muttering to himself when one of the soldiers, a young, slightly built Hausa, walked quickly around to the driver's side window. He had a rifle slung over his shoulder.

Another soldier, older and bigger, stood watching from in front of the truck. It was the first time they'd even seen the army, maybe because of the Libyan presence just across the border.

Just then, it didn't matter.

The young soldier said something sharply in what Mark knew was Hausa.

Tunji made a face but reached slowly over to the glove compartment for the truck's papers. While he was pulling them out, the soldier hopped up on the truck's running board so that his face was at the open window.

"Your passport," he shouted, pointing at Mark.

Maybe he didn't like the way Tunji drove or the face he made, or maybe it had just been a long day. It didn't look good, though. Mark's fingers shook a little as he opened the *portefeuille* and pulled out his passport. He handed it across. Tunji handed the truck papers over, too, then folded his arms and stared straight ahead. The soldier said something sharply to Tunji, but Tunji neither responded nor looked over.

The soldier stared hard at him for a moment, then got down and walked around to the front of the truck, where he gave the documents to the older man. He held them up to the lights of the truck, one by one, to read them.

Mark watched the older soldier closely, looking for any sign of trouble. At some point, he realized that Tunji was still muttering to himself. Annoyed, Mark glanced over quickly, but Tunji was still staring straight ahead, his face tight and angry. Mark went back to watching the soldier.

He had finished reading the passport and the truck papers and was going through them again when Tunji suddenly leaned forward and turned the lights off.

"Goddamnit, Tunji!" Mark said, trying to keep from shouting. "Turn the lights back on."

But it was too late. The young soldier was already on the running board again, and the older one was behind him, in the road, with the rifle off his shoulder.

The young one was furious, screaming, his face only inches from Tunji, who nevertheless refused even to look at him. When the young Hausa stopped for breath, Tunji shook his head and said something in Ibo. Mark caught the word "battery".

But the young soldier was past listening; he shouted the same short, emphatic Hausa phrase over and over.

"Tunji, please, turn the lights on," Mark pleaded, trying to sound calm but knowing he wasn't even close.

Tunji didn't look over or show in any way that he understood. The older soldier swung the rifle toward the truck, then jerked it down toward the ground and said something in Hausa. Mark didn't understand the words, but it didn't matter. He wanted them out of the truck.

Mark opened his door, his knees suddenly weak. But before he could move, the younger soldier leaned in the window and said something to Tunji's face. The tone was contemptuous and insulting; all Mark caught was "Ibo-mon."

Tunji looked at the soldier for the first time and, hissing, held up one hand an inch from the Hausa's face. His fingers were spread wide and slightly curved, almost as if he were palming an imaginary basketball.

Mark had seen it before, in Lagos mostly, where taxi drivers exchanged it all the time. It was an insult.

The Hausa knew what it meant, too. He flung open the door and surged into the cab to pull Tunji out. But Tunji surprised him by lunging out on top of the Hausa, one arm tightening around the soldier's throat as they tumbled, hard, out of the truck onto the road.

Tunji was older but heavier and stronger than the soldier; alone, he would easily have subdued him, maybe even killed him.

For several seconds, he was on top of the young soldier, working both hands around the man's neck.

But then the older soldier was on him, his rifle, like a cop's billy club, pulled across Tunji's neck so that he had no choice but to get off the prostrate soldier or choke to death.

Tunji staggered up, but the older Hausa kept the rifle pulled tightly across his neck and one knee in his back so that Tunji had to almost bend over backward to get enough air. Mark watched it all from the truck, like an unpleasant movie he couldn't walk out on. Though the whole episode hadn't taken a minute, he had the odd sensation of having been there like that for hours.

Mark forced his legs to move. He slid across to Tunji's seat and climbed down to the road. The older soldier still had Tunji in a chokehold and occasionally yanked it tighter, forcing a sickening gurgling sound from the Ibo's throat. The younger one was still on the ground, though he was sitting up now as if catching his breath.

The older soldier glanced over at Mark, then maneuvered Tunji around so he could watch him. The big Hausa said something urgently to his colleague, who did not respond. He probably had the wind knocked out of him, though it was possible that Tunji had hurt him seriously.

Mark held up his two hands, then slowly lowered one into his pants pocket and pulled out all the naira he had left. He took a step toward the soldier to make it easier for him to see the money in the darkness.

"I'm very sorry," he said slowly. "He's a little crazy." He pointed at Tunji and tapped his own forehead twice. Northern Nigerians were not famous for their English, so it was possible that "passport" was all they knew.

But they knew what naira looked like.

The older soldier shook his head angrily and said something sharply again in Hausa.

For a second, Mark thought it was directed at him but then felt the tip of a rifle pressed against the side of his head. It was the young one who had gotten to his feet while Mark was concentrating on Tunji's captor. He had to hold the gun higher than normal because of Mark's height, and the barrel bumped against his temple a couple of times until the soldier was comfortable.

There were expatriates all over Africa who swore that police and soldiers had no bullets in their weapons and that governments, mindful of the origin of most coups d'état on the continent, issued bullets only in emergencies. But standing there on the road, looking out the corner of an eye down the barrel of the rifle, Mark wouldn't have bet the filthy pair of pants he was wearing and trying not to pee in that the gun was empty.

For what seemed like hours but could not have been more than ten seconds, the four of them stood there, not moving at all except for their breathing. Finally, Mark raised his empty hand slightly toward the older soldier, then dropped it slowly toward his pants. The younger one shoved the barrel of the gun hard into his temple so that Mark instinctively flinched.

"I have more money in here," Mark said very slowly, tapping the outside of his pocket.

The older one, still holding the gun tightly across Tunji's neck, stared hard for a few seconds, then jerked his head up once. Mark pulled the wad of CFA slowly from his other pocket and held it out as far as he dared to give the older one a better look.

The young one said something angrily in Hausa, but the older soldier said nothing. He stared at the money for several seconds, then half-pushed, half-dragged Tunji over to the side of the truck.

There, he finally removed the rifle from the Ibo's neck but used it to shove Tunji hard so his face was pressed up against the truck. The soldier leaned forward and said something to Tunji in Hausa, then stepped back just far enough to give him room to jam the rifle butt into the back of one of the Ibo's legs behind the knee.

Tunji dropped to the pavement like he'd been shot.

Through it all, Tunji didn't make a sound.

The big soldier stepped over in front of Mark, very close, and stared into his face. He was maybe a little older than Mark and almost as tall. Mark could see thin ribbons of sweat running down one side of the Nigerian's black face. His breathing, not back to normal yet, hit Mark in the face as tiny puffs of wind.

Finally, the soldier held out a hand, though he didn't take his eyes off Mark. Mark gave him the naira first, then the CFA. The younger one, still with the gun to Mark's head, said something angrily in Hausa. The older one ignored him and walked off a few steps to count the money.

There was a faint light still visible in the West, but it was dark enough that the big Hausa had to hold the notes close to his face to see the denominations. The young soldier started to say something again, but this time, the older one cut him off harshly with an angry burst of Hausa. The young one shut up.

When the big one finished counting, he slid the money into the pocket of his shirt; without looking at Mark or Tunji, who was still in a heap on the ground, he walked back down the road toward Maiduguri.

He said something briefly to the younger one. It was unmistakably an order. The young Hausa hesitated a moment, then shoved Mark's head once with the barrel of the rifle. He turned and followed his superior.

Mark didn't move except to turn his head slowly to watch the two soldiers as they walked down the road. At a certain point, he couldn't see them anymore, though he could still hear them talking.

When they stopped, he expected them to come back. But after a minute or so, there was a distant click, followed by the sound of a small motorcycle engine catching.

The motor idled for a moment, then rose quickly to a whiny crescendo until the driver shifted into second gear somewhere down the road toward the city. Out there on the empty road at night, Mark heard the engine's whine for what seemed a very long time, but finally, it was gone.

A young girl walked by the truck on her way to the village well. She snuck a glance at the truck, but when Mark smiled at her, she dipped her head, fighting to suppress a grin, and hurried away. It was hot, so she wore only a wrap-around skirt. She was no more than 17, and judging from her firm, round tits, not married, or at least not a mother yet.

Mark felt a sharp, almost painful twitch between his legs. Shit, it was no time to be thinking about that.

He crawled out from under the truck and walked around to the other side. The sun, balanced on the horizon, would be all the way down in a half-hour. He'd leave then so he could make it to the road before it was dark.

He turned to walk back around the truck and caught a glimpse of himself in the side mirror. He'd been filthy before in Africa, certainly before they dug the first well in Diarrere, but this might have been the worst.

His face and arms were brownish-red, the same color as the dust coating the truck, and his clothes, all of them, had darkened from the dust and the overlapping stains of sweat. Well, Calvady could keep some of the money if he let Mark use his shower. That and a meal. Something simple, an omelette and frites; and a beer, a Gala if they had it, ice cold.

He'd shit it all out within a half hour probably, but even that, on a real toilet seat, would be a nice change. Then, he might even feel human enough to bring Tunji back something to eat.

Mark glanced under the truck, but the bastard still hadn't moved. He hadn't spoken, either, since that night. It was possible his vocal cords had been damaged, but Mark didn't think so.

But he didn't care, either.

Mark found his passport and the truck papers scattered on

the road where the soldiers had stood. When he got back, Tunji had managed to stand up by himself, but Mark had to help him back into the truck. Mark made it clear they had to get off the road right there, in the dark, without going into Maiduguri.

There was no guarantee they wouldn't run into more soldiers, and they couldn't afford that.

So they drove aimlessly, the headlights illuminating nothing but sand and an occasional thorn bush until they were out of sight of the road. The next morning, they headed west, hoping for a road, a village, or even a stray herdsman, but there was nothing. Several times, the truck almost got stuck in the deep, soft sand, but Tunji, using reverse, managed to keep them out of it.

But without even a horsecart track to follow, Tunji didn't get out of second gear; by late that afternoon, Mark figured they'd gone no more than fifty kilometers. And aside from heading west, he had no idea where they were. From time to time, Tunji seemed to be having trouble breathing, but he said nothing and never even glanced at Mark. Mark got across the directions he wanted any way he could but otherwise ignored the Ibo.

Except that he had never driven a ten-ton truck, he would gladly have left him on the road outside Maiduguri. Just before sunset, Mark caught the glint of sunlight on metal in the distance and ordered Tunji in that direction.

As they got closer, Mark saw that it was an oil tanker truck hidden in a thicket of thorn bushes. At first, he thought it was a wreck, simply abandoned where it broke down, but when they pulled alongside the thicket, there was an African asleep under the tanker.

The trucker crawled out quickly when he spotted the Volvo. He was a short, very fat African of about 40, wearing an elaborate and expensive *grand boubou.*

He greeted Tunji warily, especially when Mark approached behind him, but that was understandable. As it turned out, he was a Cameroonian "businessman" on his way back from Maiduguri with a full tank of Nigerian gasoline that he planned to sell in Maroua for about three times what he paid for it.

Once he realized Mark and Tunji posed no threat to him, he cheered up and said he'd be glad to show them the way to the border. His name was Omar, and he was a Fulbe from Garoua, like President Ahidjo. They were distant cousins, he explained. Mark smiled and feigned surprise. Everyone he'd ever met from Garoua was related to Ahidjo.

Omar didn't understand a word Tunji said, but his French was adequate, so he gave Mark directions and then drew a map in the sand with his finger for Tunji.

He was only waiting for dark to cross the border, he explained. He wasn't going as far as they were; he planned to cross further north and then follow a bush road to Maroua. But he knew the village Mark wanted. They could follow him as far as he went; the rest of the way would be easy with his directions.

The eastern sky was a pale gray when Omar honked once and waved out the window, then turned off the track they had followed for hours and sped off across a flat stretch of barren savannah that at some point became Cameroon.

Mark and Tunji got to the village just past eight in the morning. From high up in the cab, Mark could see the highway over the rooves of the huts. They'd made it.

Three men from the village came out to greet them: a thin, emaciated elder with white hair and lips that quivered even when he wasn't speaking, and two others, younger, with the lean, muscled torsos and thin legs so common to the Sahelian people,

One of them spoke rudimentary French and translated what the old man said: they could stay a night, but they were to leave the women alone and not use the well. It was the end of the dry season, the chief explained, and there was barely enough water for the village.

Mark said he understood and thanked them. They had enough water left in the jerry can to make it another day. He was half expecting some demand for money and was damn glad when it didn't come.

Maybe other times, they charged smugglers coming through to use the well, or maybe they made a few CFA selling them food. But there wouldn't be much food left, either. It was the start of the bad time in the Sahel, when the food supplies dwindled, and the back-breaking, all-day toil in the fields began. It was when the weak ones died: the very old, and the infants who caught a cold, or more likely malaria from the mosquitoes the humidity brought, and never recovered.

When malnutrition and exhaustion wore down the strong ones and weighed like grief on people's faces, even their wondrous skin color lost its luster.

So Mark and Tunji lay on the mats under the truck for most of the day. A few of the bolder village children had wandered close to get a look at Mark, but he ignored them, and eventually, they went away. He and Tunji had driven for more than 24 hours straight, but Mark found he couldn't sleep. He just wanted to get it over with, to find Calvady and do it, and get paid and fly back to Douala.

Calvady said he'd have a truck. So they could do the transfer right there, in the village, rather than Waza. It was almost the same thing and would be safer.

Tunji's truck had been running with the gas gauge on empty for hours; it probably wouldn't make the five kilometers to the *campement,* and Mark wasn't willing to take the chance.

Even with enough gas, he would probably do it the same way. A lone figure walking into the *campement* at night was more discreet than a ten-ton Volvo churning up the road.

Mark walked over to where Tunji lay.

"I'm going now, Tunji," he said, bending down so he could see the Ibo's face. Tunji didn't move.

Mark knelt and leaned under the truck.

"You stupid Ibo son of a bitch," he said, starting quietly but unable to keep his voice under control. "You think I give a shit whether you talk to me or not?"

Tunji's eyes were wide open, but they stared straight up into the bottom of the truck. For a second, Mark thought he might grab the African by the throat and finish what the Hausa soldier had started, but the feeling passed.

"You can turn to fucking stone under here for all I care, Tunji," he hissed, bending so close that any villager watching might have thought he was kissing the Ibo's cheek.

"But if you do anything stupid or move this truck an inch while I'm gone, I'll break your goddamn neck."

Tunji made no sign that he understood or even heard. Mark ducked his head back out from under the truck and stood up. He brushed the sand off his knees. He'd never spoken to an African like that, not even close. He started walking toward the highway.

Well, now he had.

The village children followed him a ways; a couple of the older ones even darted in and touched his arm, but he ignored them all, and they drifted back when he passed the last millet stalk fence.

It took only a few minutes to cross the stretch of deep sand in front of the village. Even so, it was almost dark when Mark reached the road and headed south toward Waza.

CHAPTER 46

The hut's cement floor was hard, and where it was uneven, dug into Kyle's knees. Both feet had long since lost all feeling. But Kyle didn't mind; he almost liked it, in fact. It kept his mind on the words as he lipped them silently.

Kyle always prayed on his knees. "A lazy prayer is an unreliable soldier in the Army of God" was how the pastor at Good Shepard of Jesus back in Texas put it. The Waza hut was a fine place to pray, too. Just the single bed and a plain, wooden dresser, nothing else to distract him.

Kyle was praying not for forgiveness but for strength. God knows he hadn't expected the call and certainly hadn't asked for it. But Rieper, or more precisely, God through Rieper, had given it to him; he asked only for the courage to do it right.

Near the end, the Frenchman seemed nervous; he wasn't joking anymore with Rieper, and there was a breathless, almost frenzied manner to the way he glanced around him and asked repeatedly how much farther they had to go. It might have been a premonition or even some latent sense that all creatures had, but kneeling there, bearing witness before his God, Kyle had to admit, with a wave of guilt and shame that made his eyes water, that it was most likely his fault.

He talked too much at the end; he couldn't seem to stop, not even when he saw Rieper staring at him in the mirror. His hand shook, too, whenever he had to shift gears, and he was perspiring heavily, even with the van's air conditioning turned up all the way.

And when he knew they were getting close, he couldn't stop himself from looking at Rieper in the mirror. The old man, though, handled it well. He never wavered or changed his manner; just the same measured tone, the same struggling French, now and then leaning forward to ask a question or point something out.

And the last time, pointing to a wild boar scurrying away from the noise of the van and looping the strap of his camera around Calvady's neck.

Even that seemed unhurried, almost natural. The Frenchman was arching backward and out of his seat before he seemed to realize what was happening.

Kyle stopped the van as Rieper had instructed. Once, Calvady, whose face was a ghastly crimson color, twisted toward Kyle, his eyes so wide they seemed to be straining in their sockets.

But that was just for an instant, and then the wretched man thrashed the other way, one hand clawing desperately at the strap around his neck and the other groping for the door handle.

Rieper, whose strength seemed extraordinary for someone his age, kept the strap twisted and tight for what, to Kyle, seemed a long time after the Frenchman had stopped moving.

At some point, the stench of human feces and urine filled the van so suddenly and completely that Kyle thought he, too, might suffocate. But then Rieper released the strap, quickly stepped out of the van, and opened the front door. He half-lifted, half-rolled Calvady's body out onto the ground. Then he climbed back into the van next to Kyle. He wasn't even sweating, Kyle noticed.

Kyle didn't move.

"Let's go, Kyle," Rieper said quietly.

"Shouldn't we bury him, Mort?" It was his voice, but Kyle had an odd sense that someone else was using it.

Rieper shook his bald head slightly. "We have no shovel, Kyle, and the ground is as hard as cement."

Kyle still didn't start the engine.

"Kyle," Rieper added, almost kindly, "if the lions don't find him, the vultures will. In a week, he'll just be another set of bones in the park."

They didn't speak at all on the ride back to the *campement*. It was noon when they arrived, and Rieper, normally a light eater, ordered a big meal of *cervelle de veau and steak tartare*, things that Kyle didn't eat even when he was hungry.

He ordered a salad and an omelet, just so Rieper would not think him squeamish, but he barely touched either dish. It wasn't the act that he had prepared himself for and, in the end, found less remarkable than he expected, but the smell afterward that was difficult to forget.

When the waiter brought the food, Rieper mentioned quickly that *monsieur* Calvady had fallen ill, and they'd dropped him at the airport in Maroua, where he caught a flight to Yaounde.

They had an address where Monsieur Debache, the *campement* manager, could send his things.

"Oui, monsieur," the African said. He probably would never have given it a thought, but Rieper was a thorough man. The waiter started to leave, but Rieper called him back. Had anyone come by looking for Monsieur Calvady?

The African shook his head. *"Personne, monsieur."*

Kyle and Rieper sat at the same table they'd shared with

Calvady at breakfast, the one with the best view of the highway and the dirt road leading up to the campement.

Shortly after the waiter brought them coffee, a car turned off the highway from the north onto the dirt road.

Rieper put his *demi-tasse* down and squinted against the bright sunlight.

"Should we...?" Kyle began but stopped when Rieper raised a hand like a traffic cop.

"It's Feraldi," Rieper said several seconds before Kyle recognized the Ford station wagon. He watched as the big car fish-tailed slightly as it rounded the turn leading to the *campement's* parking area, just below the restaurant.

The Ford was not even a year old—Kyle had cleared it from customs in Douala—but already looked worn and used up. It was filthy for one thing, more brown than white, and even from up there on the terrace, Kyle could hear the screech of brake pads when Feraldi stopped.

Feraldi was alone. He climbed out of the car and, shielding his eyes with one hand, scanned the *campement* rocks until he made eye contact with Kyle and Rieper. Then he walked quickly over to the steps leading up to the huts and restaurant.

Kyle looked over at Rieper. He'd gone back to sipping his coffee and gazing out at the highway. He didn't appear surprised at Feraldi's visit, but Rieper didn't show that sort of thing anyway. Kyle doubted he was expecting Feraldi.

He didn't mention it on the plane ride up from Douala when he'd explained everything else; besides, the Kousseri house was never supposed to be left unmanned.

Feraldi was breathing hard and dripping with sweat when he reached the restaurant. His short-sleeve knit shirt had large stains arced under both arms and smaller ones dotting the chest and stomach. Kyle had met him once at Douala airport when Feraldi arrived from the U.S. on his way to Kousseri. Like the Ford, he seemed to have aged too, and not gracefully.

His black hair was too long and dirty and looked as though he hadn't combed it in some time. He was pale as if just getting over an illness; when he got closer, Kyle could smell the cigarettes and whiskey mixed with sweat.

"I gotta talk to you," he said to Rieper. He ignored Kyle, not even a nod.

Rieper brought his gaze from the highway to Feraldi and raised his eyebrows just a notch.

Feraldi jerked his chin at Kyle. "It's classified."

"What is it, Martin?" Rieper asked. The voice was as quiet as always, but to Kyle, at least, there was a hint of annoyance.

Feraldi stared back at Rieper for a moment. Kyle squirmed slightly in his seat.

"The frogs say the Africans want assurances from us, too," Feraldi said. "Yaounde talked to Washington; they want you to handle it," he added, putting a little too much emphasis on the "you."

Rieper ignored Feraldi's sarcasm and gazed back out at the highway. After a moment, he turned his chair to face Kyle's and sat like that, staring, long enough for Kyle to be aware of the sweat dribbling down his back. They weren't friends yet, but Kyle liked the old man and felt almost like his protege or disciple, but he still hated when Rieper stared like that.

"I'll be right down," Rieper said, finally, to Feraldi, though he didn't look at him.

Feraldi sneered, like some bully trying to retain a measure of esteem after getting beaten up, then turned and walked back toward the steps.

Kyle said one more prayer, thanking God for the darkness.

It was a clear night—through the hut's only window, Kyle could see the Southern Cross, which dominated the Cameroon sky at that time of year—but there was no moon, and that would make it easier.

He got up stiffly and sat on the bed, rubbing his legs until the feeling came back.

Rieper's clothes fit him reasonably well, though the long-sleeve turtleneck, black like the pants and socks and even the soft-soled shoes, was a little tight. It was hot, too, and Kyle was sweating freely underneath it.

That might have been nerves, though.

Kyle sat for a moment, looking down at his black hands. He'd smeared the paste Rieper gave him on his face and neck, too, hours ago, but he couldn't get used to it.

He'd had to force himself to stop looking in the small mirror over the dresser.

There was no guarantee, of course, that Reilly would show up that night or any other. He might have turned back or had an accident or maybe arranged a signal that he wouldn't see now and so did not come.

When Rieper had taken Kyle to his hut before leaving and given him the clothes, the paste, and the knife, Kyle had felt almost giddy with the hope that Reilly wouldn't come.

But Rieper shook his head. "He'll come; I thought he'd be here by now," the old man said, looking, Kyle thought, worried for the first time since he'd met him.

Kyle stood up and patted the knife in his pocket. It was the same kind they'd used in training: a stiletto with a long, slender blade that tapered to a fine point for easier "entry and exit," as the instructor had called it.

Make sure the African waiter is in the kitchen, Rieper explained; if Reilly comes late, it won't be a problem. Drive the body well into the park for at least an hour and leave it.

Bring everything with you. Change clothes in the park, and make sure you get the paint off your face and hands. Then, drive straight to the airport in Maroua, no matter what the hour. There'll be a plane standing by.

The Novotel will be notified to pick up its van there.

Kyle got up and, avoiding the mirror, grabbed his small suitcase off the dresser and brought it over to the bed. He checked again to make sure he had everything.

Don't waste any time; do it as soon as you see him. Try for the back, with the other hand over his mouth, and make sure to bring it up in an arc for more force. Rieper had seemed uncertain near the end, reluctant to leave, even when Feraldi honked the horn once. Kyle liked him all the more for that.

They hadn't talked much, but they'd been through a lot over a short period, and that kind of thing could build a bond.

Kyle smiled to himself. The old guy had looked surprised, shocked, really, when Kyle grabbed his hand and shook it. Rieper was just one of those fellows who had a hard time showing how he felt.

Kyle looked at his watch. It was just after nine. Rieper had said he might have to stay awake all night, but that was all right; he could do it. He'd just have to stay away from the bed and keep his mind on other things. He tapped his other pocket to make sure he had the van keys, then walked over to a spot close to the open door. The steps up from the parking area, the only way into the campement, were visible from there.

Kyle turned out the light and knelt down on the hard cement floor again.

CHAPTER 47

Waza was a longer walk than Mark anticipated. He'd estimated five kilometers, but that was only a guess. It was probably closer to eight.

When he finally turned off the highway onto the dirt road, he was exhausted.

Mark held his watch up close to his face. With the lights from the campement, he could just make out the time now: twenty to ten.

It had taken him over three hours, a lot longer than he planned. Out on the black road, without landmarks, and only the momentary blaze of a taxi's headlights to break the darkness, it had seemed longer still.

He hadn't made good time, either. Several times, he had to stop because of cramps brought on by whatever was ailing him.

Twice, he'd had to squat in the dirt on the side of the road to relieve himself, the poisonous odor wafting up at him while he tried desperately to keep his feet wide enough and his pants out of the line of fire.

Mark hadn't eaten in days; he hadn't even taken any water since his last bout that morning, so he had no idea what was coming out of him. After each attack, he felt weaker and a little more drained; both times, he was dizzy for a time when he stood up again.

At some point, he remembered where he was and became concerned about the park's lions. They generally stayed far from the *campement*, but Mark had heard that in the hot season, they sometimes wandered out to sleep on the blacktop at night because it was cooler than the sand.

In the dark, it was easy to imagine one or more of the cats stalking him, unseen, on either side of the road; even, God forbid, pouncing on him while he shit.

It was an idea Mark found hard to shake: what it would feel like to have teeth tear into his flesh and massive claws shredding his entrails.

But with an effort, he forced himself to concentrate on the details of what still had to be done: how to convince, or force, Calvady to make the switch in the village; how to get enough gas for Tunji to reach a town on his way home (it was Francis' truck after all); how Mark would get to Maroua after it was all over; and where best to hide the money on the off-chance the gendarmes at the airport decided to look in his bags.

Being ripped apart by wild beasts was the least of his worries.

Halfway up the Waza road, Mark stopped to catch his breath. It wasn't much of a hill, but he felt suddenly spent, as if the worry and sickness and lack of food and sleep had somehow combined into a tangible burden he was having trouble carrying.

He could see the outline of the rocks now, illuminated by the weak, flickering lights the *campement* employed to keep guests from breaking their necks on the steps up from the parking area. There was something, a form, near the steps, but it didn't look right.

Mark took a deep breath and moved on. A hundred meters

from the *campement,* he stopped again. It was a van. There was nothing else in the parking area.

"Goddamn you, son of a bitch," he said, not loud but so angrily that his eyes stung; he had trouble getting his teeth far enough apart to take a deep breath.

He stood there for a long while, staring at the van, unable to move, like an oft-spurned writer who suddenly finds it impossible to walk to the mailbox for fear of what it might hold. But then it hit him: Calvady was almost certainly in the country illegally, and he knew he might have to wait several days, or even a week, for Mark to show up.

There was no way he'd leave a ten-ton truck sitting for that long, there in plain view of the road. Hell, the *campement* might not even let him.

Mark started moving again, faster now. Besides, where would the driver sleep for that long? Calvady wouldn't pay for a hut for him, not in a thousand years. Mark bent down close to the back bumper of the van; it was a rental from the Novotel in Maroua.

That's where the bastard was keeping it: no one would pay any attention to one more truck in Maroua. There were dozens of them passing through every week on their way to or from Chad. That meant Calvady would have to drive into Maroua; it was an hour's ride, two with the return. Mark checked his watch. Not even ten. If there were no problems, they could still have the equipment transferred long before dawn.

Calvady could head straight for the border with the truck. Mark would return the van to the Novotel and have plenty of time to catch the first flight in the morning back to Douala.

He'd be home for lunch.

Mark walked quickly up the stone steps. At the top, he stopped and looked around. There was a light on over near the terrace restaurant, but otherwise, the upper level was dark. There was no one in sight, but that wasn't surprising. It was almost ten o'clock and out of season. From the looks of the parking lot, Calvady might have been the only guest.

Mark knew the *campement* well. It had become something of a rest stop for journalists covering the war in Chad, and he'd had more than a few beers there on his way to Kousseri or heading back to Maroua.

The African who doubled as cook and waiter in the off-season slept on the floor of the kitchen, which was just on the other side of the restaurant. Once, Mark and two French hacks en route to Maroua had pulled in at midnight and dashed him 1,000 CFA to get up and serve them Galas and ham sandwiches.

Mark glanced over at the manager's hut. It was the same as the others, except for a small light outside. The light wasn't on, but that didn't mean anything. He would know which hut Calvady was in, but with no other guests, the African might too. Mark decided that if he had to show himself to someone, the African was a better risk.

The old Frenchman would ask too many questions.

Mark took a step toward the kitchen. It might have been the faintest of sounds, or caution, or simply chance, or even a sense like animals sometimes exhibit, that he was not alone that made Mark turn at that instant to look back at the steps.

As it was, he had only time to open his mouth before the black form was on him, so close Mark could smell the sweat. He never saw the knife, only a vague movement of black and then a sharp, tearing pain that spread outward from the middle of his chest.

Mark's body tried to lurch backward, away from the agony, but there was a hand clawing for the back of his neck, pulling him into it. The black man seemed to be all around him; his face pressed so close that Mark could feel the hot, quick breaths hitting his cheek.

Mark's arms hung uselessly, pinned by the man's embrace,

but his right knee, on its own, came up hard into the middle of the black shape.

The arm behind Mark's neck slipped just a little.

Mark brought the knee up again, fast and hard, and he felt it dig into the soft groin, smashing the balls into the pelvic bone above them. The hand came off the back of his neck, and the black face, so close a second ago, fell away; at the same time, a low, wounded noise replaced the frenzied breathing.

The figure still held onto the knife, which was stuck.

The *gris-gris* had not stopped it completely; the initial thrust drove the point and a half-inch of the blade through the tightly packed leather and into the flesh just to the right of Mark's chest bone. But it slowed the knife down enough that the thicker part of the blade got caught.

With both hands, Mark ripped at the black hand hanging onto the knife but could not pry it off. He brought his mouth to the knife handle and bit down hard. The blood tasted warm and slightly metallic as it hit the back of his throat; Mark swallowed to keep from choking on it.

There was a strangled kind of noise from somewhere down near his waist, and then the fingers opened. Mark released the hand from his mouth; with both hands trembling violently, he yanked the knife out of the *gris-gris.*

The black figure raised his head slightly, though he couldn't come close to straightening up. His eyes were wide so that Mark could see some white on his face, and his breathing sounded rushed and unhealthy.

"Please, no, Reilly," he wheezed as Mark lunged, crouching a little for better leverage, then bringing the knife up, underhand, as fast and hard as he could drive it.

Mark recognized the voice at the instant he felt the blade enter, just under the rib cage, and slide up and deep until his fist slammed into bone. Whether it was the force of the blow, or shock, or some last, confused synapse, Kyle's body jerked upright, stiff and erect, and his hands, instead of groping for the wound, went straight out from his sides, as if he were preparing to embrace someone.

His mouth opened, and a strange, suppressed noise, like radio static, dribbled out, though it was impossible to say whether he was trying to speak or was simply overcome by the pain. Mark stood, with his hand still holding the knife, staring at Kyle's face for what could not have been more than a few seconds, though both then and later, it seemed much longer.

Finally, he jerked his hand away. He looked around him frantically. Nothing had changed; the huts, dazzling white by day but a pale gray in the poor light, hadn't moved. The manager's light was still off.

Beyond, low in the sky and directly behind Kyle, the Southern Cross, which Mark had used as a kind of guide on the walk from the village, still dominated the sky.

But here was Kyle Mason, with a knife sticking out of his belly.

"Kyle."

Kyle didn't answer. His arms fell as if they'd become too heavy, and his chin dropped forward onto his chest, hard enough that his teeth clicked as his mouth slammed shut.

An instant later, Kyle's knees buckled. Mark jumped forward, but he wasn't fast enough; Kyle's head hit the rock with a dull, sickening crack that is unique to flesh and bone.

"Oh dear God," Mark moaned to no one at all.

Mark wasn't sure how long he stood there, not moving, not thinking anything at all, just staring down at Kyle Mason's body. When he did look up, an African was standing watching him from over on the far side of the restaurant. Mark couldn't see him clearly — he was too far away in a bad light—but it had to be the waiter/cook.

They stood like that, watching each other and not moving for what seemed to Mark an unnaturally long time. He glanced over at the manager's hut. It was a lot- closer to him than the kitchen, but there was no one, and the door was still closed.

Mark looked back at the African, who had not moved. How had he heard the struggle but not his patron? And why didn't he call out now and wake the Frenchman?

Maybe it was too dark, and the African couldn't see for sure what had happened. But that wasn't it: the African could see fine. He didn't call out because the manager wasn't there.

Of course, he wasn't there.

They were alone, he and the African, and the poor bastard had seen everything, or enough, anyway, to be scared shitless that he was next. Mark shook his head gently. He had to think. He looked over to make sure the African hadn't moved, then knelt down over Kyle's body and quickly pulled out both pockets of his pants.

He turned toward the lights on the steps and held up the keys just to be sure. They were unmistakably to a Volkswagen, which was the only kind of van the Novotel owned.

"Thank God," Mark muttered.

He took a deep breath, then hauled Kyle's body into a sitting position. Mark put his shoulder into Kyle's stomach, then staggered to his feet with the body slung half over his back.

Mark's face contorted from the strain so that the right side of his upper lip curled up, quivering, exposing the teeth on that side of his face.

He tried to force his lips closed, but the muscles wouldn't obey. From under the body, Mark took a last look at the African, who hadn't budged. The poor bastard would be there until Judgement Day.

For a second, he considered saying something—his friend was sick or drunk, and he had to take him to Maroua—on the off chance the African hadn't seen it all.

But that was unlikely. Besides, there was a better-than-even chance he hadn't recognized Mark from that distance at night;

no sense giving him another chance. Mark turned slowly with the body and staggered toward the steps, feeling careful with his feet for the irregularities in the rock.

The steps were flat and lighted, so getting down to the van was easier. The side door was unlocked. Mark opened it and dumped Kyle onto the floor of the back seat. He climbed quickly behind the wheel and started the engine. There was only a little more than a quarter tank of gas, but that was all right. It would be enough. Mark backed the van up and turned it around, back toward the highway.

He struggled to keep from putting his foot on the floor. He had to hurry now, but the last thing he needed was an accident. He glanced down at his shirt; it was ripped where the knife went in, and below that, the front was covered with blood, already half-dry. In the dim glow of the dashboard lights, it looked more black than crimson.

He'd have to clean that somewhere.

Mark slipped a finger through the knife hole and lightly felt the wound. It ached like hell, but at least the bleeding had stopped. Mark downshifted as he approached the highway. He had a lot more questions than answers just then, but most of them could wait.

The one thing that wasn't in doubt was how Kyle had found him.

Maybe they'd threatened the little bastard; more likely, they'd paid him. At least as much as the Libyans were offering. That would've done it. Calvady didn't care where his money came from and not at all what happened to Mark.

But there was no way Rieper, if he was running things, and Mark was certain he was, would pay a man like Calvady before the job was finished. Too much chance the fucker was lying.

Mark edged the van up close to the highway and looked both ways. It was ink-black in both directions. He crossed the blacktop and bumped carefully down the sandbank on the other side.

Calvady would be in Kousseri or across the river. It didn't matter; Mark would find him. The bastard would come to pick up the equipment with Mark's money up front, or Mark would deal directly with the Libyans. Even if Haloud hated his guts, they could work something out with a truckload of the things sitting only an hour from the border.

Mark would throw in the details of Calvady's deal with the Americans for free. And when he was sure they couldn't prove a thing, he'd let the U.S. "consulate" in Kousseri know he was still breathing.

That way, Calvady would have friends on both sides of the Chari.

But first, Mark had to get rid of Kyle. He drove slowly, swerving the van from time to time so the headlights played across a wide arc of the sand in front of them. Finally, the lights picked up a dirt track, and Mark swung the van onto it. The tires rolled easily on the packed sand, and Mark pressed gradually harder on the accelerator until he could ease the van into third gear.

That was as fast as he dared go in the dark; now wasn't the time to get careless.

CHAPTER 48

It was almost midnight, and the *gendarme* on duty at the entrance to Kousseri was asleep. Mark didn't wake him. He drove the van to an isolated spot at the very back of the central market and parked it. He locked the van, then walked quickly through the market in the direction of the river.

The market, so busy during the day, was dark and empty now, except for a few stall owners asleep on mats in front of their "shops." If Calvady turned out to be in N'djamena, Mark might have to sleep in the van until dawn, when he could cross over.

But he hoped that wouldn't be necessary. No one had seen him in the van, and he wanted to keep it that way. The Novotel would probably track it down eventually, and there'd be an outcry about all the blood, but that wasn't his problem, either. He hadn't rented it.

Mark could feel a breeze coming from the river, and it felt good against his wet shirt. He'd stopped at a marsh, a residue left by the receding Lake Chad, and washed it as well as he could in the muddy water.

The wound in his chest still hurt, but it was more a dull

throb now, not the stabbing pain it had been. Maybe Emil had some alcohol. The last thing he needed was an infection.

The *Relais* parking lot was empty except for a single car parked back under the trees near the road. Mark was counting on it not being crowded; he sure as hell didn't want to run into any other reporters.

He took a deep breath and walked in.

The bar was empty except for two Cameroonians who looked like low-level *functionaires,* sitting at one of the two wooden tables.

"Mark, bonjour," Emil said, thrusting a hand across the bar.

"Salue, Emil," Mark said, shaking the hand.

Emil glanced quickly at Mark's shirt, but only for a second; then, he was smiling again.

In the decent light, Mark saw that all he'd managed to do at the marsh was cover the blood stains with a muddy, black residue. He looked like shit.

"You want a room, Mark?"

"C'est possible, Emil," Mark replied;" *mais d'abord, il faut que je trouve monsieur Calvady."*

"Qui?"

"Calvady," Mark repeated. "He's an old Frenchman; short, fat, always wearing khaki shorts."

"Ah, Lui," Emil exclaimed, smiling and nodding his head.

"Is he here?" Mark asked, trying not to change his voice.

Emil shook his head. *"Non, mais demande a monsieur qui est derriere-la,"* he said, pointing back toward the restaurant. "They drink together sometimes."

The curtain hid the *monsieur* Emil referred to, but Mark remembered where he'd seen the Peugeot parked in the lot before.

"Merci, Emil," he said, already walking, his voice not much louder than a whisper.

"Un Gala, Mark?" Emil called after him.

Mark nodded automatically without turning around.

The Frenchman sat at a table near the back; he had a glass and a nearly empty Gala bottle in front of him. His eyebrows went up just a little when Mark parted the curtain and walked toward him, but that was only for a second; then he was smiling.

"Tiens," he said, too loud; "I was waiting for one American friend, and here's another." He smiled so hard his eyes almost closed.

"Je peux?" Mark asked, a hand toward the chair across from the Frenchman.

"Oui, oui, mon ami; asseyez-vous," he said as if he'd momentarily forgotten his manners.

For a wild second, Mark wanted to hit him in his pink, smiling mouth, but it passed, and he sat down.

"Je cherche monsieur Calvady," Mark said quietly.

"Qui?"

"Calvady," Mark repeated. The son of a bitch was getting even, but Mark didn't care. He could have all the fun he wanted so long as he told him where Calvady was.

"Ah, le Chadien," the Frenchman smiled, knowing Mark got the joke. *"Il n'est pas la."*

"Is he over there?" Mark asked, tilting his head in the direction of the river.

The Frenchman pulled his pipe and tobacco pouch from his shirt pocket and began filling it. He took his time, pulling hard on the pipe several times until he was sure it was lit.

"Je crois que non," he said without removing the pipe from his mouth. He was enjoying himself.

Mark took a deep breath and exhaled. "Do you know where I might find him?"

The Frenchman sat back and thought about that one a moment before shaking his head, smiling. *"Non, desole."*

Emil brought Mark the beer.

"Monsieur?" He asked, pointing to the Frenchman's bottle.

The Frenchman shook his head but didn't take his eyes off Mark.

"Did you have an accident, my friend?" He asked when Emil had left, pointing at Mark's shirt.

"Nothing serious," Mark replied. He didn't bother with the glass but took a long sip from the bottle of Gala. It was very cold and tasted as good as anything Mark could remember. But the beer made him dizzy so that he had to close his eyes for a moment.

It would have been nice to press the icy bottle against his chest, where it ached, but that would have to wait. He looked back at the Frenchman, who was still staring as if he couldn't quite believe Mark was sitting there.

"Do you think you might be seeing him anytime soon?" Mark asked.

"*Qui, Calvady?*"

"Yes," Mark said. The beer might have hurried it, but he suddenly felt like he couldn't take much more.

The Frenchman removed the pipe and sat back again.

"No," he said, finally, shaking his head. "But then, I didn't expect to see you, either, so who knows?" He put the pipe back in his mouth and laughed, not loud, but a kind of chuckle, so his chest bounced up and down.

"You fucking asshole," Mark said quietly in English.

The Frenchman kept laughing, but his face, even in the meager light at the back of Emil's, flushed pink, then a darker, uglier shade.

Mark was surprised, then vaguely disgusted, by the satisfaction he derived from that.

The Frenchman stood up suddenly. For an instant, Mark thought the bastard might swing at him, and there was no way he could get out of the way.

It was the beer, probably, and no food and all the blood, and God only knew how long without sleep, but his arms felt too heavy to lift off the table. He didn't think he could stand up if his life depended on it.

"Adieu, pauvre con," the Frenchman said, leaning down toward Mark just a little as he walked by on his way out.

Mark watched the Frenchman sweep the curtain out of his way and disappear out the open front door. Then he folded his arms on the table in front of him and lowered his head until it rested on top of them.

The bastard was probably lying to protect Calvady. The French in Africa always stuck together. Hell, maybe he was in on it; he and Rieper doing some kind of deal.

It didn't matter. Mark would cross over in the morning and find Calvady, or else the Libyan; what the hell was his name? Haloud.

They could work something out.

He needed to rest for a little while first, though.

The Frenchman stood for a moment on the *Relais* steps and took a deep breath, then exhaled. He tapped the tobacco out of his pipe, checked to make sure it was empty, and then slid it back into his shirt pocket.

He pulled the keys from his pocket and walked toward his car. No wonder the other one didn't show up; they couldn't even do that right.

And Paris was willing to let them run the show. *Bon Dieu!*

The Frenchman didn't see the other car until he was halfway across the lot. It was parked back under the trees near the road, where it was darkest. He hesitated for a second, then kept walking and climbed into the Peugeot.

He started the motor but glanced over at the other car before he pulled out.

The figure leaning forward slightly behind the wheel of the Ford was in darkness, but the Frenchman didn't need to see his face.

The massive skull swung around toward the Peugeot; for a

second, the Frenchman considered getting out and walking over. They were the ones who had asked for the meeting in the first place.

The head swung around, in profile again, facing the entrance of the *Relais.*

The Frenchman slammed the Peugeot in gear and pulled away, fishtailing slightly as he swung the car around toward the exit.

The old man hadn't come for him, not tonight, and that was fine.

He drove faster than was safe on the rough, laterite road, but it was late, and driving fast was a French prerogative—about the only one left.

And he had an urge to be away from there, to drink a cognac, maybe two, and complain about the Socialists to anyone who was still awake at the compound.

"Une autre biere, Mark?"

Mark jerked his head up from the table. The bottle of Gala in front of him was almost full. He ran a hand quickly over his face.

Behind Emil, he could see the bar area was dark. Two of the three lights in the "restaurant" were out; only the one nearest Mark's table was still on.

"Uh, non, merci, Emil," he said, shaking his head.

Mark looked at his watch. It was almost two o'clock. He'd slept for two hours, but it felt as though he'd been there for much longer.

Mark smiled at Emil. The poor bastard wanted to close up, but he was too polite to just kick Mark out.

"Tu veut une chambre, Mark?"

Mark started to nod, then remembered he had no money, not even to pay for the beer.

"Emil, I don't have any money, not a centime," he said.

That was the third time Mark saw Emil's smile falter, but he wasn't sure whether it was the bad news or the way his voice cracked near the end that caused it. It was only for a second, though, and then the smile was back in place, and Emil was shaking his head.

"Ce n'est pas grave, Mark," he said, patting him lightly on the shoulder. "You can pay me tomorrow."

Mark nodded without looking at Emil. *"Merci,"* he managed, and even that was difficult.

Emil, happy that it was over with, grinned and touched Mark on the shoulder again.

"De rien, mon ami." he said. *"Je te fait confiance."*

He walked back through the curtain. A moment later, Mark could hear him cleaning up the bar.

There was no hurry; Mark could finish his beer. Emil would never throw him out or even ask him to leave; he wouldn't turn the last light out until Mark was ready to go.

Mark took a sip of the Gala, but it was warm now and tasteless. He pushed his chair back and stood up. He felt, if not great, better than he had in a long time. Even the cramps had subsided. Maybe the Lomotil was finally working.

He walked through the curtain to the darkened bar.

Emil wasn't there anymore; Mark couldn't hear him back in the kitchen, either. Maybe he'd gone to his room.

It didn't matter. Mark could thank him tomorrow and maybe borrow 100 CFA for a *piroque* to get across the river. He'd pay him back once he got his money.

He groped with a hand until he found the light switches by the door. Then he turned off the last light himself and walked out into the darkness.

Manufactured by Amazon.ca
Acheson, AB